3

O-Tara

THE CALLER

ALSO BY JULIET MARILLIER

Shadowfell
Raven Flight
Wildwood Dancing
Cybele's Secret

THE CALLER

A SHADOWFELL NOVEL

JULIET MARILLIER

ALFRED A. KNOPF 🐎 NEW YORK

THIS IS A BORZOI BOOK PUBLISHED BY ALFRED A. KNOPF

All rights reserved. Published in the United States by Alfred A. Knopf, an imprint of Random House Children's Books, a division of Random House LLC, a Penguin Random House Company, New York.

Knopf, Borzoi Books, and the colophon are registered trademarks of Random House LLC.

Visit us on the Web! randomhouse.com/teens

Educators and librarians, for a variety of teaching tools, visit us at RHTeachersLibrarians.com

Library of Congress Cataloging-in-Publication Data
Marillier, Juliet.
The caller : a Shadowfell novel / Juliet Marillier.—First edition.
p. cm.
Summary: In the final book of the Shadowfell trilogy, Neryn, the rebels, and the Good Folk must work together to survive their final confrontation with King Keldec.
ISBN 978-0-375-86956-3 (trade) — ISBN 978-0-375-96956-0 (lib. bdg.) — ISBN 978-0-375-98368-9 (ebook)
[1. Fantasy. 2. Magic—Fiction.
3. Insurgency—Fiction. 4. Orphans—Fiction.] I. Title.
PZ7.M33856Cal 2014
[Fic]—dc23
2013031963

The text of this book is set in 12-point Hoefler Text.

Printed in the United States of America
September 2014
10 9 8 7 6 5 4 3 2 1
First Edition

Random House Children's Books supports the First Amendment and celebrates the right to read.

For my family

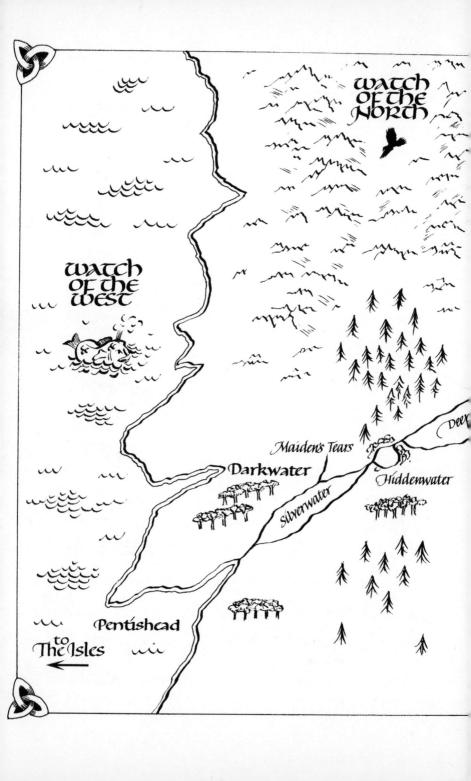

PROLOGUE

DONE. HE WAS DONE. NO MORE LIES; NO MORE acts of blind savagery; no longer any need to pretend that he was Keldec's loyal retainer. His precarious double life as Enforcer and rebel spy was over. He had turned his back on it, and he was going home.

Crossing country under moonlight, he pondered what his sudden decision would mean. He would be at Shadowfell, the rebel headquarters, over the winter. He would see Neryn again: a precious gift, though there would be little time alone together in that place of cramped communal living. His arrival there would bring a double blow for the rebels, for he carried not only the news of their leader's death, but also an alarming rumor, passed on to him by the king himself. Another Caller had been found; Neryn was not the only one. If true, these ill tidings set the rebels' plan to challenge Keldec at next midsummer Gathering on its head. An expert Caller should be able to unite the fighting forces of humankind and Good Folk into one mighty army. He shuddered to think

1

what might happen if two Callers opposed each other. He must take the news to Shadowfell as fast as he could. That, and his other burden.

He could not ride all night. He'd traveled far enough to be well away from Wedderburn land, and the horse was tiring. He stopped on the edge of woodland, unsaddled her, set the bag she carried carefully down among the stones, and shook out the feed he had brought for her. Tomorrow he'd need to do better. He did not make fire, but simply rolled up in his blanket under the moon. He allowed himself to think of Neryn; imagined her lying in his arms with her hair like honey-colored silk, whisper-soft against his skin. Felt something unaccustomed stealing over his heart, letting him dare to dream of new beginnings. Less than a day had passed since he'd chosen to walk away from his double life. Less than a day since he had found Regan's head nailed up over the gates of Wedderburn fortress, and had known he could be a spy no more. And yet, even with the pitiful remnant of his friend in that bag over there, and the knowledge that the rebellion had lost the finest leader it could ever have had, he felt a kind of peace.

He slept, and woke to something prodding urgently at his arm. Long practice had him on his feet, weapon at the ready, in the space of two breaths.

"Shield your iron, warrior!" snapped the little woman in the green cloak. "Dinna raise your knife to me."

It was Sage, Neryn's onetime companion and helper on the road: a fey being not much higher than his knee, with pointed ears, a wild fuzz of gray-green curls, and beady, penetrating eyes. Poking at him with her staff. Sage was one of the Good Folk, Alban's uncanny inhabitants, whose help would be so vital to the rebellion. His heartbeat slowed. He slipped his knife back into its sheath, then squatted down to be closer to her level.

"You could have got yourself killed," he said.

"So could you. Listen now." Sage's voice was hushed, as if they might be surrounded by listening ears out here in the midnight woods. "I heard you left Wedderburn in a hurry, on your own, without any of your Enforcer trappings. And before you ask, the news came to me from one of ours. A bird-friend spotted you. I cannot imagine that king of yours would be sending you out on a mission, on your own, at this time of the year. So you're turning your back on the part you play at court. That's not what Regan would be wanting, or indeed Neryn."

He bit back a *None of your business*. Now that the Good Folk were part of the rebellion, it was Sage's business. She was a friend; Neryn trusted her. "Regan's dead," he said.

"Aye," said Sage. "That sad news is known to me already. No need for you to bear it to Shadowfell; there's quicker ways to pass on bad tidings than a man on a horse. They'll know this by now, Neryn and the others."

Neryn had spoken of messengers with wings; beings that were birdlike, but not birds. Bird-friends, she'd called them. "I'm carrying him home for burial," he told the wee woman, glancing over at the bag he'd stowed among the rocks. "I could not leave him there for the flies and the crows. I regret nothing; only that I did not know where the rest of him had been laid."

"He would not want this," Sage said. "He would not want

you to quit your post. How are the rebels to learn the king's mind, with you gone from court? How can the challenge to Keldec succeed without the inside knowledge you provide? Unless I'm mistaken, and you are indeed on some kind of mission for the king here."

"I can't," he found himself saying. There was something about Sage that made it impossible to lie. "I can't do it anymore, I can't be that man. Besides, there's other news, something Neryn needs to know urgently. I must—"

A twig snapped somewhere in the woods behind him, and in an instant Sage was gone—not vanished, exactly, but somehow blended back into the light and shade of the forest fringe. With one hand on his knife hilt, he turned.

"Owen! By all that's holy, you led us a long chase."

His belly tightened as two riders emerged from the shadows. A fair-haired man with broad, amiable features: his second-in-command, Rohan Death-Blade. A taller, darker man: another from Stag Troop, Tallis Pathfinder. His mind shrank from what this might mean. These were the two he had increasingly suspected might know something of what he truly was, though neither of them had ever spoken openly on that most perilous of topics. And now here they were, and his choice stood stark before him: fight them to the death, both together, or step back into the prison of his old life.

"Rohan, Tallis. I did not expect to see you." *Stall for time. Don't draw attention to the bag, for if they find that, it's all up.*

"I won't ask what you're doing," Rohan said, getting down from his horse. He was in his black Enforcer garb, as was Tallis, but neither wore the half mask the king's warriors used to conceal their identity. Two men, three horses; the one on the leading rein was Lightning. Was this official business, a party sent to convey him unceremoniously back to court to face the penalty for insubordination? Or was it something else? "I'll only point out that our orders would have us halfway back to Summerfort by now. You seem to be headed in the wrong direction."

Not official, then.

"If we make an early start tomorrow, we can still achieve it in time," put in Tallis, his tone neutral.

"What about the others who came to Wedderburn with us?" There was no sign of anyone else.

"I sent them ahead by a different track," Rohan said. "Told them there was a covert mission involving just the three of us. Any reason we shouldn't make a fire? We haven't eaten since we left Wedderburn, and it's cold enough out here to turn a man's bollocks to stone."

"No reason." He forced his breath to slow; made his tight body relax. Saw how it would be, the return to court, the sideways glances from his fellow Enforcers, the hard questions, the demonstrations of loyalty Keldec would require of him, as the king did every time a subject strayed from his orders in the smallest particular. He felt like a bird that had escaped its cage and had just begun the first cautious spreading of its wings, only to find itself thrust back in and the door slammed shut. "You took a risk, coming after me," he said.

Tallis was gathering wood. The moonlight gleamed on the silver stag brooch that fastened his cloak, emblem of a king's man. Rohan began unsaddling his horse; Flint moved to tend to Lightning, whom he had left behind with some reluctance. When a man was traveling across country and wanting to stay unobtrusive, a jet-black, purebred horse was hardly an asset.

"If we head straight back to Summerfort in the morning, not so much of a risk," Rohan said, glancing sideways as if to assess his commander's state of mind. "That's my considered opinion anyway. You're troop leader; the decision is yours."

For one crazy moment he thought his second-in-command was suggesting all three of them defect to the rebels. Then common sense prevailed. There was no decision to be made. There was no real choice. He glanced over toward Tallis, who was not quite within earshot. "Sure?" he murmured.

"Nothing's ever sure," said Rohan.

Such a statement, made at court or before the rest of Stag Troop, would be sufficient to earn a man accusations of treachery. An Enforcer's code of existence required him to believe in the king with body, mind, and spirit; to remain unswervingly loyal no matter what he was required to do. So one thing was forever sure: the king's authority, which came above all. To question that was to invite a swift demise.

"We head off in the morning, then," he said. Last night he had felt a weight lift from his shoulders. He had believed himself free at last; free from the vile duplicity of his existence as Regan's spy at court. Some freedom that had been, short-lived as a March fly. Of course, an Enforcer should think nothing of inviting his two companions to sleep by the campfire, then knifing them in the dark and heading off on his own business. He had done worse in his time.

But not now. Not after he had drawn those first tentative breaths as a different kind of man. "Did you bring any supplies?"

Rohan and Tallis shared their food with him. He kept watch while they slept; he wondered if he was being given a chance to get away, or whether it was a remarkable demonstration of trust. At one point in the night, he got up to check the bag he had brought from Wedderburn, with its stinking, precious cargo, and found that it had vanished. For a heart-stopping moment he wondered if he had missed Rohan or Tallis opening it, finding him out, stowing it away to show the king. Then it came to him that Sage had taken it. *That's not what Regan would be wanting.*

In that, the fey woman was correct. For Regan, the cause had always come first; he had expected the same commitment from all the rebels. If Regan were still alive to be asked, of course he would want Flint to go back to court, to be an Enforcer, to do what had to be done in order to retain the king's trust. It had taken years for him to work his way into his position as Stag Troop leader and Keldec's close confidant. Despite his breaches of discipline in recent times, it seemed Keldec still viewed him as a trusted friend, or the king would never have told him about the second Caller.

He could almost hear Regan's voice. *For whatever reason, your comrades are getting you out of trouble here. You can still be at court within the six days Keldec gave you. You can accompany him to Winterfort and see this Caller for yourself. Assess the threat and get a message to Shadowfell. The cause comes before your personal inclinations, Flint. I shouldn't need to tell you that.*

Later, Rohan woke and took the watch while Flint snatched fitful sleep, his dreams fragmented and full of violence. At dawn the three men packed up and rode away, heading back to Summerfort and the king. They spoke barely a word.

Chapter One

With winter closing its fists tight on the mountains, the ground was too hard for even the strongest man to get a spade in. So we laid Regan's head to rest in stone, and sealed it there by magic.

The whole community of rebels was present, along with the clan of Good Folk who lived below us at Shadowfell in their own network of chambers and tunnels. The area called the Folds was deeply uncanny, a place that changed its form as it chose. So it was on the day we bade our beloved leader farewell.

Woodrush, the wise woman of the Northies, spoke a prayer and a charm, and a hollow opened up in the mountainside, just the right size for the head in its sealed oakwood box to fit snugly within. Tali and her brother, Fingal, placed the box; Milla held the lantern. Dusk seemed the right time to lay our leader down to his well-earned rest.

Tali spoke words of farewell and blessing. Her speech was brief; she was struggling to hold herself together. The flickering lamplight gave the ravens tattooed around her neck a curious life, as if they were really flying their straight, true course. Then Woodrush moved her hands over the stone again, and the hollow closed up as if it had never been.

We shivered in our thick cloaks. Snow lay on the mountaintops, and the wind whistled a song of winter. When we had made our goodbyes, we retreated indoors to the warmth of Shadowfell's dining chamber. The whole place was belowground, apart from the practice area. That was where Andra drilled Shadowfell's warriors while Tali, now leader of the rebel movement, prepared her strategy for the final challenge to King Keldec's rule.

We had less than a year to achieve it. The support of the powerful northern chieftain, Lannan Long-Arm, was dependent on our mounting the challenge at the next midsummer Gathering. Before that time came, we had to create a fighting force made up of humankind and Good Folk, a force sufficiently strong and united to stand up against the power of the king and his Enforcers. It was a near-impossible task. The Good Folk did not trust humans. They did not even trust each other. Why would they set themselves at such risk when they could simply go to ground and wait for the bad times to pass?

The answer, remarkably enough, was me. It had taken me a long time to accept that I was indeed a Caller, a person with the unusual gift of being able to see, hear, and summon the Good Folk no matter where they were; a person who could call forth uncanny beings and persuade them to work with humankind for the greater good. Call them to fight. I'd struggled with this. I still did. Summoning folk into possible harm, even death, felt deeply wrong to me. In Regan's eyes, all that had mattered was the cause. If the rebellion were to succeed, he'd said, we must set aside such concerns. We must be prepared to do whatever was needed to ensure the tyrant's downfall. It was a lesson every rebel at Shadowfell had taken to heart.

When I'd first made my way here, a scant year ago, my talent had been raw. I had been completely untrained, and the power of what I could do had frightened me, for I had seen what damage it could cause if not used wisely. So I had embarked upon a journey to find the four Guardians of Alban, the ancient, wise presences of the land, and to seek their aid in learning the proper use of my canny gift. Between spring and autumn I had made my way first to the Hag of the Isles, who had taught me how the call might be strengthened by the magic of water, and then to the Lord of the North, whom I had helped wake from a long enchanted sleep. In return, he had trained me in the magic of earth. Now I was back at Shadowfell, with the sorrow of Regan's loss still fresh, and the news about Flint filling my dreams with troubling visions of the man I loved. When Daw, the bird-man of the Westies, had brought Regan's head back home, he had told us an unsettling tale.

Sage's clan of Good Folk had seen a party of Enforcers ride into the stronghold of Wedderburn's chieftain, Keenan, the man who had ordered Regan's death. Later, they had seen Flint come out alone by night; they had watched him climb up above the fortress gates to cut down Regan's head, which had been nailed there in a ghastly display of authority. They had watched as Flint, dressed not in his Enforcer uniform but in ordinary clothes and riding an ordinary horse, had slipped

11

into the woods and traveled swiftly away. Not heading back to Summerfort and his duties at court, but up the Rush valley toward Shadowfell. He'd had Regan's head in a bag tied behind his saddle.

Sage had confronted him when he stopped to rest, and found her fears realized: he was giving up his hard-won position of trust at court, turning his back on the king, and bringing Regan home. He'd barely begun to explain why when two Enforcers had appeared and Sage had been forced to go to ground. That was what Daw had told us; and that the next morning Flint had headed off toward Summerfort with his comrades.

It was disturbing news. Flint had long been the rebels' powerful secret weapon, Regan's eyes at court, a source of vital inside information about Keldec's strategic plans. He'd been there for several years, since he'd completed his training in the ancient craft of mind-mending and gone to offer his expert services to Keldec. He had risen high; to do so, he had been required to demonstrate flawless loyalty to the king. I knew how much it had cost him, for under Keldec's rule a mind-mender must act as an Enthraller, using his craft to turn rebellious folk to the king's will. When I'd seen Flint last spring in the isles, he'd been strung tight; he loathed what he was required to do. But I had not for a moment expected him to walk away before our battle was won.

After the burial, we sat awhile before our hearth fire, drinking mulled ale and enjoying the warmth. We tried to remember Regan the way we should, with tales of our lost leader's courage and vision, and shared memories of the good times. But the shadow of Flint's action hung over us all.

I knew how momentous the decision would have been for him—he would not have taken such a step unless he'd been close to his breaking point. Selfishly, I wished he had indeed come on up the valley, leaving that old life behind, for here at Shadowfell he would have been safe, at least for now. I could have spent time with him. The others debated what it all meant and whether we could progress with our plans unchanged. Winter was closing in, and any movements out from the safe base here on the mountain would be limited. My own difficult decision was looming.

Tali was restless. Regan's death had not only made her our leader—it had unleashed in her a furious drive to get things done, preferably as fast as possible. She let us have a night to rest and grieve. Then she called us to a council.

It was an inner circle that met: Tali, her brother, Fingal, myself, Andra, Brasal, Gort, and Big Don. That was the human contingent. But councils had changed at Shadowfell since we'd won the wary support of the Folk Below, the clan of fey beings who lived in the chambers underneath our stronghold in the mountain. So we were joined by their elders Woodrush and Hawkbit, and the warrior Bearberry, who looked something like a short-statured man and something like a badger. In addition there was Whisper, the owl-like being who had accompanied Tali and me when we returned in haste from the north. If not for Whisper's magic, it would have taken us at least a turning of the moon to travel home; he had brought us back in a single night. Daw, the bird-friend and messenger from Sage's clan, had already flown out from Shadowfell, back to the forests of the west.

With Good Folk in attendance at our council, all iron weaponry and implements within our dwelling were shielded and set away. I had hoped my training with the Guardians would teach me how to protect our fey allies from the destructive influence of cold iron, for this was likely to prove a great obstacle when we stood up together in battle, but neither the Hag of the Isles nor the Lord of the North had possessed the secret. Some of the Good Folk had a resistance to iron and some did not; that was all I had learned so far. I'd been told the secret might lie with the most unreliable of the Guardians, the Master of Shadows.

We gathered in a small chamber with the doors closed. Tali welcomed us, her manner brisk.

"Thank you for being here. This has been a sad time for all of us, and I'm sorry there's the need to talk strategy so soon. But Regan would have wanted us to get on with things, and that's what I plan to do. As you know, Neryn and I witnessed the last midsummer Gathering. We saw Keldec's rule in action, saw it in acts of twisted violence that should have sickened the most hardened person in all Alban. We saw a crowd of ordinary folk stand by and let it happen without a word of protest, because every one of them knew speaking out against the king's authority is not only a death sentence for the person brave enough to do it, but can also bring down disaster on that person's entire family. It was thanks to Flint that we got away from Summerfort; him and another of the Enforcers. We don't know if that man is Flint's ally, or whether he's just somewhat less brutal than most of the king's men. All in all, the Gathering was a vile experience." She glanced at me.

"It was sickening," I said. The cruel events of the Gathering were burned on my memory; such monstrous acts must not be allowed to happen again. "If neither of us has talked much about it, it's because we couldn't bear to. You all know what Keldec's capable of. This was a display of his authority at its very worst."

"And Flint, as you know, was the prize performance of the day, singled out for particular attention," said Tali. "But we don't believe he's been exposed as one of us. If that were his crime, he'd have faced a far worse punishment than being required to carry out a public enthrallment. The fact that I was chosen as the victim must have been coincidence."

"If the king had known he was a rebel spy, he'd have made sure Flint didn't survive that day. We saw two Enforcers compelled to fight to the death."

"I'm certain Flint didn't know I'd been taken prisoner until they dragged me out for the enthrallment," Tali said. "He was shocked. Though, as you'd expect, he concealed it well."

"It surprises me that you were taken prisoner at all," said Brasal. "I'd have thought you capable of tackling a whole troop of Enforcers."

Tali grimaced. "I wouldn't be such a fool as to attempt that unless the alternative was certain death."

"Tali let the Enforcers capture her because putting up a fight might have drawn their attention to my presence as her companion on the road," I said. "It's fortunate that Flint was the one chosen to carry out her punishment, and that the two of them had the presence of mind to fake an enthrallment." A shiver ran through me as I remembered it, the pretense that

15

the enthrallment had gone terribly wrong, with Tali so convincing that even I had believed her a damaged, witless remnant of her true self. Afterward, the queen had demanded that she be disposed of, and Flint and his companion had taken us up into the woods, where they'd simply let us go.

"We were lucky," Tali said soberly. "Unfortunately, I was seen by the entire crowd that day. The king and queen and their court; every single troop of Enforcers; a large number of ordinary people who traveled to Summerfort for the so-called games. And because my appearance is a little out of the ordinary"—she glanced down at the elaborate tattoos that circled her arms, spirals and swirls and flying birds to match the ones around her neck—"those people would all recognize me again. That means I won't be able to leave Shadowfell until it's time for the final confrontation." She looked over at Fingal. "The same goes for you." Her brother's body markings were almost identical to hers.

"What about Neryn?" asked Andra. "She'll have to travel."

"I was in the crowd," I said. "People did see me, but not with Tali, apart from when they were dragging her out of the open area and I elbowed my way through to follow them. We did meet some folk when we were traveling toward Summerfort, of course. But I don't stand out as Tali does. Besides, as you say, I have to go; I'm only halfway through my training. I still have the White Lady and the Master of Shadows to visit."

"This fellow with Flint, the other Enforcer," said Fingal. "He must have got a good look at you."

"He did." I remembered the open-faced, fair-haired warrior who had checked whether I had supplies for the way, and had asked not a single awkward question. I had seen him in dreams too, for my dreams of Flint were especially vivid, thanks to his ability as a mind-mender. "I believe he's a friend. If he weren't, he'd have expected to make an end of both Tali and me in the woods that day. I'm sure that's what the king and queen intended to happen."

"Let's hope you're right, Neryn, because if you're not, Flint's in even more trouble than we thought," Tali said. "As it is, there's the account Daw brought of his meeting with Sage. I'm still finding that hard to accept. When we met Flint in the isles, he gave us no reason to think he'd suddenly walk away from his position at court, especially at a time when his services are so vital to the cause."

"It costs him dearly to do what he does," I said. "Of us all, he has the hardest part to play."

"The story was that he rode back to court with the En-forcers who came to fetch him," Big Don said. "What we don't know is whether he was in their custody, a prisoner, or whether he managed to give them some plausible excuse for heading off on his own like that. Flint's pretty good at lying; he's had a lot of practice over the years, and from what he's told us in the past, the king's often inclined to believe him where others wouldn't. Maybe he can talk himself out of this."

"Either way, it's disturbing." Tali's jaw was set grimly. "If there's any chance Flint's lost the king's trust, our source of information from court is gone. He won't be sending word out and we won't be sending messengers in. That will make it much harder to have everything in place for midsummer." She had many elements to coordinate: not only the fighting force of Shadowfell itself, but groups of rebels in various other locations, along with the personal armies of three of Alban's chieftains. And that was only the human part of the rebellion. Provided I completed my training in time, I would be calling in a substantial number of Good Folk to fight alongside Tali's human warriors.

"We'd offer our own kind tae bear messages," Woodrush said, "if it werena for the cold iron in those places. Your man will be travelin' tae Winterfort wi' the king and his court for the cold season, aye?"

"Correct," said Tali. "They'll be there until early summer. A long way, even for bird-friends. Your folk have been an asset to the cause; we wouldn't be where we are if you hadn't spread the word across Alban for us. But as you say, both the king's residences will be full of Enforcers armed with iron weaponry. If Flint's in some kind of custody, we can't help him. He's on his own."

"I'm hoping that before midsummer I'll learn how to protect your folk against cold iron," I said to Woodrush and her companions. "I've been told the Master of Shadows may know the secret. I'll visit him after I've traveled east to find the White Lady."

"It doesna add up." Hawkbit had been unusually silent. Now the wee man fixed his eyes on me in grim question. "Ye were gone frae first shootin' until last leaf-fall, seekin' oot the Hag and the Lord and learnin' what ye had tae learn. There's twa more Guardians tae visit, and ye've only till midsummer tae get it done. And one o' them's the Master o' Shadows. Ye canna—"

"We don't say *cannot* here at Shadowfell," Tali put in

firmly, silencing him. "And we don't say *impossible*. Neryn and I were caught up in the crowd heading for the Gathering; that slowed us. And before that, I made an error of judgment that took us out of our way."

There was a silence, in which I suspected everyone was thinking the same thing: *And that can happen again, or something very like it.*

"But yes," Tali added, "time is indeed short. Even if Neryn's gone from here as soon as the paths are open again after winter, she barely has time to do what must be done."

Whisper ruffled his snowy feathers. "Winter is close," he said. "But no' yet here in its full force. Why must you wait until next spring tae travel east? Go now, and you can be awa' frae the highlands before the snow lies ower the paths."

"Neryn might get through," said Brasal. "But at this time of year she's just as likely to get caught in a blizzard and perish from cold on the mountainside. We've seen that happen; we don't want it again."

Whisper was still looking at me, waiting for me to speak.

"But you could get me there much more quickly," I said, meeting his gaze. "Is that what you are suggesting? Overnight, as you did when you brought Tali and me home?" The prospect of heading out from the warmth and safety of Shadowfell again so soon made me feel sick.

"It would be possible." There was a *but* in Whisper's tone. "I havena attempted a journey tae the Watch o' the East before. It wouldna be easy. The White Lady is a private creature, and so are the folk o' her Watch. Or so I've heard. Taking you there so quickly would be a considerable test o' strength."

"But you could do it," Tali said, her eyes bright with enthusiasm. There was no doubt this would offer us a great advantage. "How soon?"

"As soon as Neryn can be ready," Whisper said, but there was a wariness in his voice. "I dinna promise I can find the White Lady, mind. But I can take Neryn tae the spot where I believe she is most likely tae be found, and I can stay wi' her while she undertakes her training."

"You wouldn't need to stay," said Tali, her mind clearly racing ahead. "You could return to the north until it was time for Neryn to move on again."

Whisper turned his great owl-eyes on her. "You would leave your Caller wi' nae guard?"

"We'll provide the guard. Gort has already volunteered to do that job; when they travel by human paths, they'll make a convincing husband and wife."

"Ah," said Whisper on a sigh. "This is a mair taxing journey, as I told you. I havena the strength tae take mair than one."

There was a silence, and then Tali said, "Couldn't you take Gort first, then come back for Neryn?"

"It isna like carrying folk across a ford or balancing on a bridge," Whisper said. "It sucks awa' strength. I can take only one. Neryn needs nae guard but me. I can keep her safe."

Tali opened her mouth, plainly about to tell him that what he was suggesting ran contrary to the plan decided on when I'd first reached Shadowfell, a plan made by Regan and herself with the agreement of the entire rebel community. The entire *human* rebel community, that was. It was only later that we had won the support of the Good Folk. There was a set of priorities, and one of the top priorities was my safety. Regan had not been prepared to let me leave the protection of Shadowfell without the best guard he could give me. On my previous journey, that guard had been Tali. Now Regan was dead and Tali could not come with me. But it was quite clear from the look on her face that she doubted Whisper's ability to keep me safe.

"Can you tell us where the place is?" Big Don spoke before Tali could. "If we have allies in the area, one of your bird-friends could take a message to them, and they could provide additional protection for Neryn."

"I'm not having messages flying around that could reveal Neryn's whereabouts," Tali said. "A bird-friend can fall into the wrong hands. Ideally, Neryn would have two human protectors, one to stay with her, the other to prepare the way for when she needs to head on. We have allies in the south; they can be useful to her. The word's gone out that we'll be wearing the thistle as our token, discreetly of course."

Whisper and the other Good Folk had gone rather quiet. "Don't forget why I'm traveling to the east," I put in, concerned that we might be causing them offense. "The person I'm seeking out is a Guardian, ancient, powerful, and fey. An entity who, if the rumors are correct, has retreated from the world to wait out the dark time of Keldec's reign. The White Lady may not be prepared to speak to me if I'm surrounded by human protectors, however well intentioned they are. She may even take exception to Whisper, since he's a Northie. But at least he is one of her own kind."

"The lassie speaks wisely," said Woodrush. "The word is, the White Lady's never been ower-fond o' company, save that of her ain wee circle. I dinna think she'll mak' the task easy." After a pause she added, "Her place o' refuge—I've heard tell it's a spot forbidden tae men."

"Another thing," I said. "When I do find the White Lady, I'll need to stay with her for training. That might take a while, and whoever comes with me may have to spend a lot of time just . . . waiting." I glanced at Tali. She had found waiting tedious in the isles, but she'd used her time fruitfully in the north. There, she had befriended the Lord of the North's captains and helped them reorganize their fighting forces. Between us, she and I had won the support of that army for the rebellion. "Whisper could use the time to talk to the Good Folk of the east," I suggested. "He could start winning them over. We have support from west and north now, but the other Watches . . . It seems those folk are not so approachable."

"Easties, they're odd folk," said Hawkbit, the wee man who was a leader of the Folk Below. "Flighty. Quick. Touchy. A body canna get a grip on them."

"Will-o'-the-wisps," put in Bearberry.

"Hoppity-moons," said Woodrush. "A glint, a flash, a flutter and they're gone."

"What about the south?" asked Fingal. "Is that going to prove equally difficult? Even if Neryn does go now, there's little time left."

"We canna tell ye aboot the Watch o' the South," said Hawkbit. "Save that we wouldna be venturin' there in a hurry."

I glanced at Whisper. If he was taking me to the east, he'd likely be the one going on to the south too. There would be no coming home to Shadowfell in between, with the entire mission needing to be completed well before midsummer. The more I thought about it, the harder it was to believe I could do it in time.

"If it werena for this matter o' cold iron," Whisper said, "I'd be suggesting you dinna trouble yoursel' wi' the Master o' Shadows. Dinna you think he's as likely tae teach you the wrong thing as the right? For now, I'd say we gae ane step at a time. I can take you tae the east. You'll save a season if you travel wi' me."

Tali folded her arms, her brows crooked in a frown. She looked at me. "You're the Caller, Neryn. In the end, this has to be your decision."

"You're the leader. I'll abide by your decision, whichever way it goes."

She managed a smile. "I'm not qualified to make the judgment. Whisper's offer seems to render it possible for you to get everything done before midsummer, which is essential. But it is risky. If you have doubts, then wait and travel in spring, taking Gort as well as Whisper. It's vital that you stay safe. We need you at the end; we can't win this without you."

Tali and I had not long ago returned from our travels to face the terrible news of Regan's death. The thought of heading off again so soon was a leaden weight on my shoulders. The vile things I had seen on my journey still haunted my dreams. But there was no defeating evil unless people had hope. There was no going forward unless folk held on to their belief that the future could be bright, that a lamp of goodness could still shine in this realm of darkness and despair. And, although it would be far easier to curl up and hide, as many

23

of the Good Folk had done, there would never be change unless people were prepared to take risks, to step forward and fight for a better world. I knew this well; I had known it a long time.

"I'll go with Whisper," I made myself say, and saw Tali's glance of recognition, the acknowledgment that goes from one warrior to another: *We're in this together.* "And we'll do it the way he suggests. Our first mission is to find the White Lady. Until that is done, there's not much point troubling ourselves with the Master of Shadows. Besides, when I met him before, I hadn't sought him out. He came to me."

"Aye," said Hawkbit in dour tones, "so ye told us. If that didna mak' ye suspicious, mebbe nothing will." After a moment he added, "But good luck to ye, lassie. May the wind blow ye fair and true on your path."

CHAPTER TWO

SAYING GOODBYE TO TALI WAS HARD. IT WAS made harder
by the knowledge that I'd likely not have time to return to
Shadowfell before midsummer and the challenge to Keldec.
Our army, such as it was, would not be marching openly to
the Gathering. Instead, we would travel there as ordinary
folk of Alban, taking to the road along with the crowds of
others headed in the same direction. The king had twisted
the once-popular midsummer celebration into a foul travesty,
but folk still flocked there in their hundreds. Attendance,
complete with enthusiastic shouting, was viewed as a sign of
loyalty; nonattendance by chieftains and their households
was likely to result in hard questions at the very least. We
would make our way to Summerfort not as an army but in
ones and twos, dressed like any other traveler and approach-
ing from various directions. Our uncanny allies were masters
of concealment, and would manifest when we needed them.

When everyone was present within the walls of Summerfort's practice area, we would reveal our true purpose. We'd

do it on the first day of the Gathering, straight after the king had made his introductory speech. Tali would stand up in the crowd and denounce Keldec. When the king's men rushed to apprehend her, as they surely would, the rebels would reveal themselves and do battle with the Enforcers. The chieftains who were supporting us would stand alongside us with their fighting forces; those whom we had not won over to our cause would no doubt fight on the king's side. Once battle was drawn, I would call in our most potent weapon, the Good Folk, who could use magic to fight. None of us doubted that it would be a bloody encounter, in which many would die. The Enforcers would not go down easily, and we had the support of only three of Alban's six remaining chieftains, though one was the powerful Lannan Long-Arm. Getting the timing right would be crucial.

"Make sure you stick to the plan," Tali said as we stood at Shadowfell's entry, waiting for Whisper. "Going off with only Whisper may be all right for the winter, when the Enforcers are less active. But you may still be in training when spring comes. Whisper can't travel with you openly, especially when there are crowds on the roads. I don't want you stranded somewhere, unable to get to us by midsummer."

"Whisper can transport me to anywhere in Alban overnight. Even to the Gathering, I imagine, though I haven't asked him and I hope I don't need to."

"I'll ask Bearberry to find me the most reliable bird-friend they have," Tali said, demonstrating how far her trust in the Good Folk had advanced. "We must be able to get messages to you, Neryn, and to receive yours. Then, once the tracks are passable again, I'll send Gort to meet you, and probably one of the others too. That way you'll have proper protection when you make your way back toward Summerfort. After what happened to us on the road before, I want to be as sure as I can be that you'll get there safely."

"Don't send Gort too early, or he'll be waiting around, as you were, while I finish the training. I have no idea how long it will take."

"Once you are sure, you must send me word. So much hangs on this, Neryn. You realize, don't you, that if you're not present at the Gathering, any attempt to use the Good Folk in battle is going to end in disaster." Her expression was grave. "I don't want to have second thoughts about sending you with Whisper. But I'm having them."

"Too late," I said as Whisper emerged from the entry. "It's time for us to go. Tali, I will take care, I promise. I know what I need to do. I know time's short. We must trust in the Good Folk to carry our messages, and in ourselves to stay strong and brave no matter what happens."

"Ready?" inquired Whisper.

"I'll miss you," I said, setting down my staff and giving Tali a hug. "I wish you could come with me. But your true work is here. I know you'll lead the rebel forces well and bravely. I can hardly believe that the next time we see each other might be at the Gathering, at that moment . . ."

Tali stepped back from my embrace, her hands on my shoulders. "We can do it," she said. "Never doubt it, Neryn. Go on, then, better be on your way." After a moment she added, "Sooner you than me."

Whisper's way of transporting folk quickly over long distances was challenging. Traveling on his own, he would fly like the owl he resembled. To bring Tali and me from the north back to Shadowfell, he had required us to stand in complete silence with our eyes shut for what had apparently been an entire night. It had not been an easy way to travel, but at least I'd had Tali with me. This time, there was no human companion whose hands I could hold for reassurance during the blind vigil.

"Ready?" Whisper said again.

"I'm ready."

"Shut your eyes, then."

I shut them, and the long darkness began.

My training in the west and the north served me well at such times, for I had been taught endurance and self-control. I had learned to stand still with my eyes closed for inordinately long periods of time without fainting or otherwise losing my discipline. The Hag of the Isles had taught me various modes of breathing that were useful during such trances; the Lord of the North had toughened my will.

I shut my eyes at Shadowfell in morning light, and opened them again hours later, at Whisper's command, to find that he and I were in a place of gently rolling grassy hills. We stood on a rise under a single, massive oak. Below us, in a flat-bottomed hollow, stood a group of rounded cairns, like inverted bowls, each the size of a tiny cottage. Elder trees, leafless in the cold, ringed the area like graceful, stooping women. Their shadows made a delicate tracery across the ancient stones of the cairns. The sun was low; it was late afternoon. I judged that we had traveled a long distance to the southeast.

Nobody in sight; the place looked deserted. But there was a deep magic here. I felt the familiar tingling sensation in my body and an awareness of presences unseen. Around us in the grass small birds darted about, foraging. Soon dusk would send them to roost in the great guardian oak. And we must find somewhere to shelter. Standing still all day had left my body full of aches and pains, and I longed for rest.

"Is this where we'll find her?" I murmured to Whisper. "It seems more a place of earth and stone than of air, but I can feel something close."

"I canna gae farther that way," Whisper said. "Doon there's a women's place. We'd best camp up here, between the rocks, and wait for morning. I canna tell you if she's there, only that it's a place folk come tae, your kind o' folk, tae seek her wisdom."

"But—" I began.

"Shh!" Whisper hissed, ducking down behind a convenient rock. I did the same, following his gaze. A woman had walked out from between the elder trees, heading into the place of the cairns. More followed, a procession of them, each cloaked and hooded. The leader was carrying a small basket; the second in line held a bowl of water. The third had a lighted candle, and the fourth a branch of greenery. They were not Good Folk, but human women. The practice of the old rituals was forbidden in Keldec's Alban. To be seen enacting a rite of this kind was to invite death at the hands of the king's men.

I glanced sideways at Whisper, but he had his gaze firmly fixed in the opposite direction. "I canna look," he murmured.

The rite unfolded with the solemn casting of a circle,

greetings, and prayers. I could hear little of what the women were saying, but I was drawn by the grace of their movements and the serenity of their expressions. The eldest was a crone, white-haired and stooped; the youngest was a girl of perhaps twelve or thirteen. At a certain point they took hands in their circle and chanted, all together, and the power of it rang from trees and stones. The light was fading now, and it seemed to me that around the heads of the women tiny, bright insects danced, so each wore a firefly crown. As the ritual came to its end, the women set an offering beside the biggest cairn, which had a low doorway to the interior. This, it seemed, was less heap of stones than beehive-shaped hut.

The dusk deepened. The cloaked women formed their procession once more and walked away on quiet feet. The shining insects flew upward, making a trail between the branches of the elders, then dispersing on the breeze. The place was empty again.

"They're gone," I said to Whisper, who was still resolutely not looking. "There must be a settlement close by or they wouldn't be able to get home before dark. So we'd best not make a fire."

After a frugal meal, I found a flat area between the roots of the oak and settled down to sleep. Whisper perched in the branches above me, where, he said, he could keep one eye out for danger.

My sleep was fitful. I was accustomed to living wild, fending for myself, staying out of sight as I crossed country. I'd had years of sleeping rough, running before the Enforcers, surviving on what I could gather or catch for myself. What kept me awake was the possibility that the White Lady might not be here, or that if she was, she might choose not to reveal herself to me. We might wander about all over the east and still not find her. We might run out of time.

When at last I fell asleep more deeply, I dreamed of Flint. He was in a stable, alone, brushing down a long-legged black horse. The look in his eyes told me he was blind to the horse, the stall, the stable walls: he was seeing something far different, something that saddened and sickened him. The brush stilled; he laid his brow against the horse's shoulder, closing his eyes. The animal turned its head toward him as if in comfort. I felt the despair in Flint's heart, the bone-weariness that engulfed him. It seemed to me that what was in his mind was, *I can't go on. I can't do this anymore.*

Then a door opened and other men came into the stable. Flint straightened. The brush resumed its steady movement. If his face had revealed, briefly, the burdens that weighed him down, now it changed. He still looked tired. But he managed a smile for his comrades, a word or two, and when all had finished tending to their horses, he joined the others as they went out in a companionable group. His horse lowered its muzzle to the feed trough.

I woke with this in my mind, and a longing in my heart to be able to reach him, if only with a word or two of reassurance. I feared for him. At the Gathering, I had seen how the king punished those he believed had betrayed his trust. Keldec's trust in Flint had been deep and long-lived. Let Flint not give up now, so close to the end of our great fight; let him not be destroyed before he could enjoy the time of peace.

A flurry of wings, and Whisper came down to join me.

"Awake?" he queried. "There's a wee stream no' sae far

awa'. I'll gae wi' you so you can wash safely. And then I hae a plan tae put tae you."

"What plan?"

"Wash first, set yoursel' tae rights, hae a bittie breakfast, then we'll talk aboot it."

The stream ran between more elder trees. I retreated behind a clump of ferns to relieve myself, then splashed my face and hands while Whisper kept watch. Was I imagining things, or did he make himself smaller when he went up to roost?

He made me eat breakfast before he would tell me the plan. It was bitterly cold; another reason for haste. If this search followed the pattern of the last two, once I found the White Lady and persuaded her to teach me, I could be reasonably sure of a warm, secure place for Whisper and me to stay until my training was complete. The Good Folk of the east would most likely supply what we needed for survival over the winter.

"Very well, I've washed, I've plaited my hair, I've eaten. And I'm wondering why you waited to tell me your plan."

"Ah," said Whisper, and something in his voice told me bad news was coming. "You slept sound, aye?"

"I'm used to lying on hard ground. Apart from a troubling dream or two, I slept well enough." When he made no comment, I said, "Did I miss something?"

"There was a commotion," Whisper said. "No' sae near, but no' sae far awa' neither. I didna care for what I heard. But I wouldna fly ower tae see what it was, no' while you were sleeping like a babe."

My heart sank. "What kind of commotion?"

"Shouting. Screaming. Horses."

Enforcers. Close by. What else could it be? "We can't stay here, then."

"As to that," Whisper said, "I think you'll be safe in that spot doon there." He managed to indicate the cairns without quite looking at them. "For a woman like yoursel', and a Caller besides, there'd be nae harm in creeping in through that wee door in the beehive hut if you're afeart. I canna see king's men marching intae such a place wi' their big boots and wreaking havoc. There's a powerful magic here; you feel it too, aye?"

"Yes, I feel it. But the king's men have no respect for the old ways. I doubt the presence of magic would keep them out if they were ordered to search a place."

"Even they wouldna dare interfere wi' a deep spot such as this, Neryn. There's a protection on it, same as the Lord o' the North has on his hall. It willna admit those who come in anger. Gae doon, stay in the circle o' cairns, and you'll be safe."

"But what about you?"

"I'll be flying ower the place where the screaming came frae, and seeing what's what. If we canna find the Lady here, or some o' her folk, we'll need tae move on. I willna lead you ane way or the other until I make sure it's safe. Or as safe as it can be."

He was brave, no doubt of that. What if a whole troop of Enforcers lay in wait just over the next rise?

"It seems a sound plan," I said, imagining crawling into the beehive hut and perhaps offending the White Lady so deeply she would not even want to speak to me, should I happen to find her in such an unlikely abode. "How long will you be gone?"

"I canna tell. I dinna ken what I may find. Dinna come back up here until you see me waiting."

"All right. Be safe, Whisper."

"Aye, and you, lassie."

He waited on the rise until I had walked down and stepped within the rough circle formed by the cairns. Then he flew away over the treetops and out of sight to the east.

I drew a deep breath and squared my shoulders. There was a job to do. I must be mindful of the right way to approach the Good Folk. The Folk Below had provided covert support to the rebel community ever since Regan first came to Shadowfell, for no other reason than that they had seen him observing the old ritual days with appropriate prayers. And when the Hag of the Isles had tested me almost to breaking point out on a wave-swept skerry last spring, a ritual had won me release. A desperate sort of ritual it had been, scratched together from memories of my grandmother's seasonal observances and my own knowledge of the power of water, but it had been what the Hag wanted from me.

Here in the Watch of the East, the element of air was foremost. I had imagined the White Lady standing on a windswept hilltop or drifting on a summer breeze, but I had learned to expect nothing obvious from the Guardians. The Master of Shadows had been three people in one: blind old man, mercurial youth, and noble mage. The Hag of the Isles had been no toothless crone but a strong island woman possessed of wry humor and, beneath her formidable exterior, a tough sort of kindness. The Lord of the North, at first locked away in his enchanted sleep, had proved on waking to be readiest of all to help, since he'd viewed me as a kind of savior. The White Lady would probably be as full of surprises as the rest of them.

In the old forbidden song, her line was: *White Lady, shield me with your fire.* I'd wondered about that, since fire was the element of the south, domain of the Master of Shadows. Perhaps the song referred to a different kind of fire—the fire of inspiration, or of courage. I thought of the ritual those women had enacted here not so long ago, how beautifully it had flowed, the sense of peace and power it had conveyed to me. I could not emulate that; I must offer what I could, and hope it was enough to satisfy the ancient inhabitants of this place, whether or not the Lady was among them. There were Good Folk somewhere close, I could feel them, but it seemed my presence alone was not enough to bring them out.

In the center of the circle, with the cairns all around me like watchful old crones under their stone shawls, I spread my cloak on the ground and sat on it cross-legged. Even in my layers of woolen clothing, I was cold. I closed my eyes, breathed in a slow pattern, and considered the many forms of air. A gentle breeze, a biting wind, a gale, a wild storm. A voice, whispering, speaking, chanting the words of a ritual as those women had. A voice shouting. Screaming. I hoped Whisper had not found anything bad.

Air supported the wings of birds and insects, helping them fly. Air made bubbles on the surface of a pond and whipped the sea to whitecaps. Air made candles flicker and fanned the flames of bonfires. In the isles of the west, I had seen trees beaten to prostrate surrender by the force of the wind. I had watched in terror as a violent storm drove the waves against the skerry where Tali and I were marooned. Air could whip like a scourge; it could destroy. But air was life, from the first gulping breath of a newborn babe to my grandmother's last rattling exhalation as the merciful kiss of death ended her suffering.

I opened my eyes, drew my own deep breath, and lifted my voice in the song of truth, the anthem Keldec had long forbidden. I could think of no better way to let the White Lady know why I was here.

> I am a child of Alban's earth,
> Her ancient bones brought me to birth,
> Her crags and islands built me strong,
> My heart beats to her deep, wild song.
>
> I am the wife with bairn on knee,
> I am the fisherman at sea,
> I am the piper on the strand,
> I am the warrior, sword in hand.

Something was here with me. A tiny presence, many presences, buzzing and whining around my head, making me want to swat them away. . . . I kept my hands still. No midges these, but something Other; each was a little light, a manifestation of the magic I had felt the moment Whisper and I first approached the place of the cairns.

> White Lady, shield me with your fire;
> Lord of the North, my heart inspire;

Hag of the Isles, my secrets keep;
Master of Shadows, guard my sleep.

The buzzing changed as I sang, tuning itself to the melody, wreathing me in a soft, high music. The tiny creatures moved so swiftly I could not see exactly what they were, but I sensed a shimmer of wings, flashes of shining color, a glow from each as if they bore light within their bodies.

I am the mountain, I am the sky,
I am the song that will not die,
I am the heather, I am the sea,
My spirit is forever free.

The song was done. The presences danced around my head a few more times, then settled on my shoulders, in my hair, on my knees. Their humming music died down.

Not insects. Not tiny birds. Good Folk, in shape not unlike graceful Silver of the Westies, but small, so very small—the largest of them was no bigger than a dragonfly. Their garments seemed fashioned of feathers and cobweb, gossamer and dewdrops, and each had delicate wings. Their small presences glowed with light. I hardly dared move for fear they might break.

"The song—" I said, then fell silent as the whole swarm of them flew up at once, as if startled. Yet my singing had not seemed to trouble them. I lowered my voice to a murmur, and they settled once more. "The song is my gift to you, offered with respect. I seek the Good Folk of the east and, in particular, the White Lady." That was, perhaps, a little blunt; but I must take the quickest path.

One of the tiny beings spoke, or perhaps sang; its voice was so high I could hear nothing but squeaking, and my heart sank. Among the Folk Below at Shadowfell had been five very small creatures whose voices were incomprehensible to human folk; one of the bigger Good Folk had translated for them. I had no interpreter now.

The wee being was trying again. It stood on the palm of my hand, waving its arms as if that might help it convey its message. Its hair was long and wild. Its features had a human complement of eyes, nose, and mouth, but their placement suggested an insect of some kind. Its garments appeared to be woven from strands of cobweb.

"I'm s—" I had forgotten to keep my voice down, and as one they shrank away. "I'm sorry," I whispered. "I can't understand what you're saying. I am Neryn. A Caller. I've come here from the north. Perhaps some word of our venture has reached you. Are there some bigger folk of your kind close by?"

The little ones broke into a mournful, squeaking chorus.

"Gone?" I guessed. "What of the White Lady?"

The being on my hand performed a dumb show, first shivering violently and wrapping its cloak around it. Then it pointed to me, and to the cairns, tilting its head as if asking a question.

"Cold, yes, I'm cold, and going to be colder, since we're on the threshold of winter. Are you suggesting I shelter inside that beehive hut? This is a place of deep ritual, isn't it? I don't wish to offend anyone."

The being gave a decidedly human-like shrug. It repeated the shivering, then keeled over sideways and lay on my palm as still as death. My heart skipped a beat—had touching me somehow killed it?

The others rose in a cloud, making a shrill sound that seemed akin to laughter. The cobweb-cloaked one bounced back to its feet, spreading its hands wide as if expecting applause. It pointed to me, then repeated the whole performance.

"Shelter in the hut or die of cold, I understand. If I face that choice, I will do as you suggest. I do need news of the White Lady, if you or others of your clan are willing to provide it. Is she close by? Can I reach her?"

In response, they swarmed into the air again and flew in a shining ribbon to the low entrance of the beehive hut. Almost before I could draw breath, they had disappeared inside.

I glanced back up the hill. Whisper's absence made me edgy and I wanted to watch out for his return. But perhaps this would not take long. I picked up my belongings—staff and traveling pack—and approached the hut. The entry would have been just the right size for my fey friends Sage and Red Cap. Pushing the staff and bag ahead of me, I crawled along the short tunnel on my hands and knees.

The space inside reflected the beehive design—it was circular in shape, with a domed roof. The whole construction was of drystone, meticulously laid. The floor was bare earth. Here and there in the walls were small recesses that might be used for candles or offerings at ritual time. It was not dark, for the tiny beings had placed themselves on the stones all around, filling the little chamber with glowing light. Apart from them and me, the place was empty. Empty, but full of magic.

I settled myself on the ground, waiting for what might come.

"Ye brocht a witawoo," someone said in tones of reproach. "Intae my place, among my wee folk, ye brocht a rendin', tearin' witawoo. Didna it occur tae ye that such creatures feed on the small ones o' the meadow, wee fluttery things such as these here? Didna ye spare a thocht for that, afore ye came trampin' in?"

Nobody here; only me and the tiny beings. The place was barely two strides across.

I cleared my throat. "A wita— You mean my companion, Whisper? He's not an owl; he's one of the Northies."

A tinkling sound arose from the tiny beings. I interpreted it as a gasp of shock. "It's true," I went on. "Whisper comes from the household of the Lord of the North. He's one of your own kind. True, he does resemble an owl. But he will not eat any of you, I give my word. He will not enter this area, or even fly over it, since it is a place of women's ritual."

"I dinna see this Whisper noo. Whaur did he gang? Just waitin' tae swoop, aye?"

The voice rang through the little chamber, wry, suspicious, and definitely female. Could this be the White Lady herself? "Whisper heard some disturbing sounds during the night. He flew off to investigate. He waited until I was safely within the protection of the cairns before leaving."

"Sounds? What sounds?"

"Screaming, shouting. Sounds of distress. Forgive me, I do not know who you are, or where you are, or even what you are." She sounded like one of the Good Folk. But a being who chose to remain invisible? That set doubt in me. When the Master of Shadows had tested me, I had seen the Guardians in a vision. The White Lady had been . . . In my mind, she had been a tall, slender human-like figure clad in flowing white robes, very similar to the serene Lady Siona, wife of the Lord of the North. But now that I recalled that vision, I realized I had never actually seen her. It was my own imagination that had conjured up her image. In the vision I had seen only myself, clad in a blue gown, with flowers in my hair and bright spring light all around me. I had heard the Lady's voice, bidding me see with the clarity of air. She had spoken like a noblewoman, her tone confident, mellow, and sweet. If anything was certain, it was that the voice I heard now was not the same.

"I don't wish to be discourteous," I ventured. "I am seeking the White Lady, Guardian of the East. I heard—we heard—that perhaps she might be found here. I need to speak with her on a matter of urgency."

"Oh, aye? And what matter would that be?"

Even though the Good Folk knew by instinct that I was a Caller, that did not mean they always welcomed me. Past experience with Silver and her clan had proved that—they had taken a long time to believe my mission was worthwhile, and their help, when they'd finally offered it, had been a two-edged sword. It must be uncomfortable to be stirred up by a Caller; worse to know that if I chose, I could compel them to act in ways they might not wish to.

I hesitated before I spoke. "Has any word come to your folk from the other Watches, about a . . . a venture that is planned?"

"What venture might that be?"

That could mean they had heard nothing of the rebellion. It might equally well mean they knew all about it but were treating me with caution until they felt I was trustworthy. I could hardly blame them for that, since I was doing exactly the same. "Before I tell you more, may I ask . . . are you a representative of the White Lady? One of her people?"

The invisible presence snorted in derision. "Ye're in the Watch o' the East, are ye no'? What were ye thinkin', that ye'd run intae a clan o' folk loyal tae the Master o' Shadows?"

A shrill chorus from the tiny beings suggested they concurred with this assessment of my stupidity.

"As it happens," I said, keeping my tone courteous, "when I met the Master of Shadows in person, it was not in his own Watch, but in the north. That made me wonder if perhaps he and his people may be found anywhere. I think it's possible they are no respecters of borders."

"Southies dinna ken the meanin' o' respect."

There was a pause; a silence that had an expectant quality. I did not speak, and after some time the voice came again. "Ye plannin' on tellin' us, then? Isna that why ye've come tae these pairts?"

"I had hoped some of your own kind, from the north and the west, might have traveled here before me and spread the word about this undertaking. That was the plan. They have done so in their own Watches. The news is widely known among the Good Folk there."

Another silence. Then, "Spread the word, ye say? Would that be a flock o' witawoos hootin' the message for any ear tae hear? Or hawks perhaps, flyin' doon tae gie the news tae a bunch o' oor wee folk and snappin' up ane or twa for supper just by the by?"

I suppressed a sigh. "Messengers. Good Folk who can fly."

"We might hae caught a wee whisper o' that sort. Somethin' aboot a battle, and cauld iron. Nae guid news. There's enough death and hurtin' in Alban already. Why would we be wantin' mair?"

"The news that came to you may not have mentioned a Caller. That is what I am. I'm seeking the White Lady in the hope of receiving some wisdom. I'm hoping she will teach me the better use of my gift." I could hardly make it plainer than that.

The invisible presence said nothing; instead, a rippling sound came from the tiny beings. I interpreted it as mocking laughter.

"I watched a group of women conducting a ritual here at dusk yesterday, and I saw some of you flying around them. I know most of your kind do not like dealing with human folk, but your presence there suggested you might be prepared to talk to me."

"Aye." The voice had a tinge of sorrow in it now. "The wise women dinna see the wee folk the way ye do, but they feel the presence. This here, the Beehives, 'tis the last place, ye ken?"

"The last place?" That had a particularly forlorn sound.

"The last place in a' this Watch where human folk conduct the auld rituals in the open. Could be the last place in a' Alban. There's a house o' wise women close by; they come tae the Beehives. If no' for that, I'd be a' gone awa'."

So my suspicions had been right. This was the White

43

Lady herself. How had she shrunk to this? "But the others"—
the protest burst out despite my attempt to stay calm—"the
Hag, the Lord of the North, they are still standing strong despite everything!"

"That's no' what I heard," the invisible presence said.
"Wasna the Lord sunk in a sleep sae deep his ain folk couldna
wake him? Three hundred years and mair, that was the word
came tae me."

"The Lord is awake now and restored to his old self.
When I went to his hall seeking learning, his household
asked me if I could wake him. I called his wife back from far
away, and she broke the spell he had set on himself. Broke it
with a kiss."

Utter silence.

"And the Hag of the Isles is a strong presence in the west,
known to the human folk of that place, if not always seen by
them. Three hundred years is a long time. The Lord of the
North did not withdraw from the world because of Keldec
and the woeful state of Alban. He did so out of grief for his
lost daughter. Sorrow sent him hiding away within himself.
Love brought him back."

"Ye callit his lady, ye say." The tone was flat with disbelief.

"I did. My gift is not yet fully developed, and it was challenging to do that, but it seemed the right way to bring him
back."

"Oh, aye? Why didna ye ca' the Lord himself? Wouldna
that hae been quicker?"

The voice had changed again; I heard a lively intelligence
there, a genuine wish to hear the truth. Perhaps we were
no longer playing games. And if I had correctly understood

what this being had hinted at before, my response was all-important. "I have never been told that a Caller must not summon a Guardian," I said. "But I think attempting that would be unwise. I feel . . . I feel in my bones that such a call should be made only in the very last extreme."

"If ye were facin' death, ye mean?"

"I've faced death before and saved myself, and others, by calling one of the Good Folk to help me. But a Guardian? Not if all that's in the balance is the life of one human woman. That's what I am, Caller or not. If the long story of Alban were a river, I'd be only one drop of it. And if I'm killed along the way, in time another Caller will step up to take my place." It hurt to say those words, for I'd been told it could be several hundred years before that might happen—while canny gifts were not uncommon among the populace of Alban, mine was a rare one. "But I plan to stay alive at least until next midsummer," I added. "And I have faith that our challenge to Keldec will succeed, and that Alban will be re-made as the peaceful and just realm it once was. I have a part to play in that, and I need your help to do it."

"Ye canna mend a pot that's smashed in a thousand pieces," murmured the unseen presence, sounding old and tired now. "Ye canna sew up a butterfly's wing when it's torn and shredded. Ye canna make hope frae despair. Alban's far gone."

"When I first set out to find the Guardians," I said, choosing my words carefully, "I was told they had all gone away, gone deep, and would wait out the time of Alban's darkness. I know that to such ancient and magical folk, human lives seem very short and human affairs slight. But the way Keldec has changed Alban is not slight. He might reign for another twenty years, thirty even. He plans to change the law so his son can succeed him as king, and he'll likely mold his child in his own image. For us human folk, that is a long time to wait. Too long. Alban might then be like that smashed pot, beyond mending. We need to act while we still have strength to do so; while we still have hope. You spoke of despair. But you are still here."

"A' the bittie pieces o' me, aye."

I looked again at the tiny, bright beings clinging to the walls of the cairn or perched in its niches. Each seemed as fragile as a butterfly. Might not each little light be snuffed out as easily as a candle flame? If that were to happen, would the White Lady herself be gone forever? I must tread delicately here. "While those women come and perform their ritual, you still remain," I said. "If the rebellion succeeds and Keldec is overthrown, Alban will become a place where such practices are allowed again. Ordinary folk won't be afraid to observe the old ways. People like me won't be called smirched anymore; our canny gifts will be accepted. And . . . the bittie pieces of you . . . they would surely be able to come together again. You could shine as brightly as you did before, in the time of peace."

I sensed, rather than heard, a deep sigh. The light from the little beings wavered, then steadied again.

"Ane thing I'll say for ye, ye hae hope enow for a hundred lassies," the unseen being observed. "Whatever drives ye, 'tis a force tae be reckoned wi'. Ye ken the winter's almost on us. Were ye plannin' on stayin' here at the Beehives through the dark o' the year? Would the witawoo be catchin' mice and voles tae feed the twa o' ye? Would ye be makin' fire tae bring the king's men doon on us?"

"Whisper—my companion—seemed to believe this place was safe even from them," I said.

"There's a charm can be cast ower the Beehives when it's needed, aye. I wouldna want tae be puttin' it tae the test. Keepin' oot a troop o' king's men, that would once hae been naethin' tae me. These days, I canna be sure I'd hae the strength."

This shocked me. A Guardian, worn down so far that she doubted her own magic?

"If I could stay here and be reasonably safe," I ventured, "and if you were prepared to teach me, Whisper and I would provide for ourselves. The supplies we brought will last us a while, and we can fish and forage."

"Fish? Forage? For what?"

A fair question; there would be scant pickings in the cold season. "I will be honest with you," I said. "I came to the east expecting that there would be more Good Folk in the region, and that they would help me. Are there no others of your people living close by?"

"Nane in these pairts, or they'd be here wi' me. As for further afield, I havena heard sae much as a chirp or a squeak these fifteen years or mair."

"Then I can't ask you for more than a roof over my head for as long as it takes to learn what I must. I will talk to Whisper. He is resourceful; I think we can manage. I hope very much that you will help me. I can, at the very least, provide you with some company over the winter."

A ripple went through the tiny folk, undoubtedly laughter.

"I didna say I wanted company. I didna say I fancied a witawoo up on the hill yonder, spyin' on my wee folk wi' his big e'en. But I ken what ye are and what ye can do. I felt ye comin' closer. I dinna ken if I hae the strength tae help ye. But ye can come in the Beehives by day, and we'll dae some talkin'."

"Thank you," I breathed. This was a great concession. All the same, my heart sank. If Whisper and I must sleep beyond the safe area of the cairns, and if making fire was likely to attract unwelcome attention, how could we get through the winter?

"I dinna want ye here by night," the Lady said. "I canna abide folk squirmin' and snorin' and disturbin' my sleep. And I canna feed ye; there's nae provisions for human folk in this place."

The fact was, I would need human help to get through the winter. But I could not reveal my presence to anyone. "My friend brought me here by . . . unusual means. I did not have a chance to see how the land lies around these cairns. How far are we from Winterfort?" Winterfort lay in the territory of Scourie; to the south, over the border in the territory of Glenfalloch, there was a rebel group. The chieftain of Glenfalloch was one of those who had secretly pledged their support for the rebellion. But I did not know how far away the rebels might be, or whether we were on Glenfalloch or Scourie land. Keldec's entire court would be at Winterfort now. If Winterfort lay to our south, anyone carrying a message would have to pass it to reach the rebel group.

"Ye'd best be awa' tae your friend oot there and hae a wee

chat. Mak' a few plans tae see ye through. As for *where*, 'tis no' sae near and no' sae far. Why dinna ye send the witawoo flyin' ower tae tak' a look? Bid him catch his supper while he's well awa' frae my wee folk. Awa' wi' ye, then. In the mornin', I'll talk tae ye again."

CHAPTER THREE

WHISPER WAS BACK, AND HE WAS NOT ALONE. Beside him, up on the hill by the rocks, a dark-haired girl stood shivering, her face blanched, her eyes haunted. She held her shawl hugged across her chest.

As I came up the hill, I saw that she was familiar: she'd been among those women performing their ritual at dusk. I judged her to be about twelve—the age I had been when the Enforcers swept down on my home settlement at Corbie's Wood.

Whisper spoke quietly as I drew near them. "Neryn, there's ill news. Come, sit down and I'll tell you."

The girl didn't say a word. The look on her face spoke for her. I had felt like that myself once, as if my world had been wrenched apart before my eyes. I wanted to offer a hug of reassurance, but she was wound as tight as a harp string, and I did not try to touch her.

It was a sorry tale indeed. While I had been talking to the White Lady, Whisper had flown east and come upon the aftermath of a night raid: the remains of a house still

50

smoldering, and bodies strewn about, some burned, some mutilated—a number of women and a dog. And this girl, whom Whisper had found drawing buckets of water one by one from a well to throw on the smoking ruins of the place, as if she might bring back the dead if only she tried hard enough.

She sat there, a silent ghost, as Whisper told the tale. "The lassie here, she was startled tae see me and tae hear me," he said at the end. "I bid her seek refuge wi' us; she has naebody else."

"What is your name?" I asked her. "I'm Neryn, as Whisper said." I had come on this journey with a prepared story and a different name to use, as the rebels always did when venturing out from Shadowfell. But it was too late for that. Whisper had given her my real name; he had shown himself. This girl had seen that I was traveling with one of the Good Folk, in breach of the king's laws. Burned. Murdered. Those women, so quiet and peaceful; the last place where the old rites were observed. I did not want to believe it.

"Can I trust you?" The girl's voice was a croaky whisper, as if her throat were swollen from weeping.

"There's not much choice," I said.

"The lassie willna talk tae me." Whisper sounded almost apologetic. "No' sae surprising. I dinna ken if it was king's men did this, or someone else. An ill night's work, either way."

"Scourie men," whispered the girl. "One of them I'd seen before, riding with Erevan's guard."

"Erevan—you mean the chieftain of Scourie? He sent them?"

"I don't know." A bout of shivering ran through her; she put a fold of her shawl up over her mouth.

"Will you tell me your name?" I tried to make my voice gentle, despite the anger that had flared in me at her words.

"Silva." It was a mere wisp of sound.

I looked at Whisper; he looked at me. Her presence was a danger to us, and ours to her. But he'd said she had nobody else.

"Silva," I said, "I understand how hard it is for you to talk right now. But you need to answer a few questions for me so I can help you. Have there been raids like this before?"

She shook her head. "Mostly they leave us alone. Erevan sends a man sometimes to talk to Maeva. She's our—She was our elder, our leader." Tears began to spill from her eyes; she scrubbed them away with a fierce hand. "They don't—they haven't—"

"Take a deep breath." I got out my waterskin, put it in her hands, waited until she had gulped down a mouthful. I tried to think as Tali might think, strategically. "Silva, I have to ask you this. I saw you and the other women yesterday, conducting your ritual down the hill there. Have all of them been killed? All your companions?"

A jerky nod.

"How was it you survived?"

"I was sleeping on my own; preparing for initiation. In the stillroom, by the herb garden. The fire missed the outhouses. They didn't find me." A sob racked her. "Lucky ran out, he was barking, trying to scare them away. . . . They didn't need to kill Lucky, he never hurt anyone. . . ."

"I'm sorry," I said, knowing no words were adequate. "Isn't there someone you can go to, family, friends? We could help you reach them."

Silva shook her head. "There's nobody."

Perhaps her family existed, and perhaps they were within reach. But she did not know me, and trust only went so far in Keldec's Alban, where brother might turn against brother to protect his own hide.

"The wise women were my family," she said.

My heart twisted. "Silva, is there a settlement close by the place of the fire? Will people come to see what's happened? To . . . set things to rights?" We could not leave those women lying where they had fallen.

"They'll stay away, more likely."

"I could keep watch for you," Whisper said to me, understanding what was in my mind. "'Tis a big job for twa lassies."

I wondered if Silva had the strength left to do anything at all. I would struggle to complete the job without her help. Whisper was not built for digging; besides, we'd need him on watch. "I'm going to ask you to be brave for a bit longer," I said to the girl. "We should go back there and bury them." I hoped there would be tools in those outhouses, something that had escaped the blaze. I could not bring myself to ask Silva. "Then we'll find somewhere safe to shelter."

She said nothing, only got to her feet and wiped her face on her sleeve.

"Whisper," I said, "she was there, at the cairns. I'll tell you more later."

"Oh, aye."

It took us all day to dig the hole, carry the bodies, lay them down, and cover them with earth and protective stones. Whisper maintained a presence above us, winging out on his patrols, circling back to report, heading off again. Nobody came.

When it was done, we went up to the top of the garden, where a stone bench was set under a leafless willow. I was too tired to do anything but sink down on the seat. Every part of my body ached. My clothing and my hands were filthy with blood and soil and burned flesh; I could barely think. I sat and stared out over the rows of newly planted winter vegetables to the dark shape of the burial mound under its blanket of stones. It wasn't the first time I'd had to do this. The memories of my home village, Corbie's Wood, had pressed close all day.

Silva got back up. "The chickens," she said. "I forgot to feed the chickens." After the long day's labor she looked like a wraith; a gust of wind might have blown her away. Her voice was a thread.

"I'll help you."

There were, it transpired, not only chickens to be fed but ducks as well, and a goat. I found the strength to follow her instructions. If she had the will to go on working, I must match her. The last in the row of decrepit outhouses proved a surprise. It looked empty, save for a few garden tools and a pile of old sacks. But Silva shifted the sacks to reveal a trapdoor, which opened to a stone-lined cellar packed with stores, evidence of a busy, productive household: crocks of honey, preserved eggs, dried fruits, cloth-wrapped cheeses, plaits of garlic and onions, tubs of fish layered in oil. There were sacks of flour and beans and oats.

"Maeva was worried about thieves," Silva said as she filled a pan with grain. "If folk came to the door, we'd give them food, but we always kept our stores hidden."

I followed her to the chicken coop, whose occupants were noisily informing the world they had been penned in all day, they were hungry, and it was time someone did something about it.

"Too late to let them out now," Silva said, tossing the grain over the wattle fence into the small enclosure. "Could you fill up the water trough, please?"

I did so from the bucket I'd carried from the well. I counted ten hens and one important-looking rooster, who eyed me suspiciously.

We attended to the five ducks, who came up from a stream at the bottom of the garden for their supper. We went to the goat in its walled field. Silva was calmer now; the company of the familiar creatures, the everyday tasks, seemed to reassure her. She greeted the goat with a rub on the forehead and kind words.

"Her name's Snow," she told me as she threw some hastily gathered greens into the goat's enclosure. "We've had her since she was tiny."

"She's lovely, Silva." Snow was hungry; I imagined her, on a different day, feasting on the leftovers from the women's table.

The animals were all fed; the job was done. "We'll need to go back to the Beehives before it gets dark," I said. "It'll be safer to camp close to the cairns."

Silva was silent a while, watching as Snow crunched on the greens. "I need to be here," she said. It was a simple statement of fact. "Someone has to give them their breakfast. Someone has to keep things going."

A child still, on her own, with the bodies of those she'd called her family lying ten strides away. *They come tae the*

Beehives, the invisible presence had said of the wise women. *If no' for that, I'd be a' gone awa'.*

"Silva," I said, "I have a lot to explain to you. A story I don't tell many people, but because you're on your own here now, you need to hear it so you can make some choices. But right now, what we need is a wash and a meal and some sleep. Considering what's happened, it would be safer if we didn't spend the night here."

"They won't come back." There was a core of strength in the uneven voice. "They came to kill, nothing else."

"How can you know that?"

"I heard their leader calling them off. When it was done. When they thought they had everyone. He gave an order to stop, and they rode away. If he hadn't done that, they'd probably have torched the outhouses too, and there would be nobody left to keep vigil tonight. But I'm here and that's what Maeva would expect me to do."

There was no arguing with this.

"Tomorrow I'll go down to the cairns and tell the Lady what happened so she can help Maeva and the others walk through the last gateway."

Her composure startled me almost as much as the implication that she knew the Lady was at the Beehives.

"There's a place to sleep in shelter here," Silva added. "Food and freshwater. You can stay if you want. And . . ." She glanced toward the ruins of the main house, where Whisper could be seen waiting on a stretch of drystone wall, wise eyes, white feathers, red felt boots. "And your companion, of course. He is . . . mysterious," she added with an attempt at a smile.

"Whisper comes from the north. He's part of the story. Let's go up and ask him what he thinks. Either way, you shouldn't do this on your own."

We washed in cold water from the well. We made a small fire and put together a meal from the wise women's supplies, though we had little appetite for it. Then we lit three candles Silva found in store. Down by the burial mound Whisper and I stood silent while Silva spoke prayers, naming each of those who had died. Her young voice speaking that litany of loss made me want to weep. It brought back my own losses: mother, father, brother, grandmother, comrades. It made me think of Flint, and the empty place that existed in me when we were apart.

"And Maeva, our leader, our mother, our sister. The Lady's light shone brightest in her." Silva's list was finished. But no: not quite. "And our faithful dog, Lucky, who died trying to protect us. Lucky, you were a good boy, right to the end." Her voice wobbled. "I'll miss you." For a moment, I saw the child she was as well as the composed, strong woman she would soon be. A tear rolled down her cheek, catching the light; she wiped it away.

We went back to our fire. After a while I asked Silva to tell us about the other women and the community—little stories about the good times—and she did. How Elen had been frightened of goats, and how Snow, most placid of creatures, had sensed this and gone out of her way to be gentle. How Maeva had told stories every night, tales from the old lore about the White Lady and the other Guardians, about battles and plagues, floods and fires, and how the people of

Alban had stayed strong in times of challenge and hardship. About the Good Folk, who had once been easier to see than they were now. Brollachans, trows, selkies; wee folk of the woods and glens. Fox-friends, fish-friends, bird-friends.

"How long have you been living here with the wise women, Silva?" I asked.

"Two years." She did not offer any information about her life before that.

"Guid place, this," Whisper put in. "But you canna keep it up on your ain, lassie."

"I must. There's nobody else."

We fell silent for a while. Today had been a nightmare; what I had seen, smelled, touched, would be forever imprinted on my mind. For Silva there had been last night as well—the screams, the smoke, the terror. She'd been as close to those women as a sister. How could I expect her, so soon afterward, to make wise decisions about the future? Besides, in a way she was right. Someone had to feed these animals. As for the ritual . . .

"Silva, I need to explain to you why Whisper and I are here. Perhaps we can help you; perhaps you can help us."

A nod. She sat hunched in her cloak, staring into the fire.

Information was dangerous; that was a lesson we rebels learned early. Anything we passed on could be repeated. The Enforcers would think nothing of torturing a child to extract what they wanted. I did not talk about the rebellion, only told Silva there were other people in Alban who wanted to see change, so that folk like her could observe the old rituals without fear. I told her I had the ability to see and speak with the Good Folk. That Whisper and I had come to the east to find the White Lady in the hope that I could spend the winter months with her, learning. And, though it felt risky, I told her about my conversation with the invisible presence in the beehive hut.

Silva listened wide-eyed. When I was done, she said, "Maeva told us she was there. Maeva can—could—hear her voice sometimes."

"Did Maeva ever talk of seeing anything?"

"Only the wee insects that fly around in that place. Like moths or grasshoppers, only brighter. Maeva said not to swat them away, because they were the Lady's messengers." She fell silent for a little. "I thought it was only a fancy."

"No fancy, but simple truth," I said. "Silva, I must be plain with you. If anyone discovers that I'm here, not only will I be in great danger, but so will a lot of other people. While Whisper and I are in this area, I'll need to be down in the beehive hut every day. Even with Whisper on watch, it will be risky for you and me to keep going openly between the Beehives and this place. If I hadn't seen you with the other women performing the ritual, I'd be suggesting Whisper take you away to a place of safety we know." He could transport Silva to Shadowfell quickly, using his magic. I could not see the girl as a rebel fighter, but she could set her hand to helping Milla and Eva with the myriad tasks that went into running the base. She would be safe there. "I'd be saying set the animals loose to find their own food and shelter."

"No!" Silva exclaimed. "I can't go away! There's the ritual—"

"Yes. And that's important; perhaps more important than even you realize. What she said—the Lady—was that the Beehives are the last place in the east, and maybe in all Alban, where folk still perform the seasonal rites. If the practice comes to an end, nobody will be able to find the White Lady any longer."

Silva made a little sound of shock and grief.

Whisper's eyes grew still rounder. "You mean . . . You mean if the lassie stops doing this, the Lady will be *deid*?"

The wee fire sparked in the chill evening breeze. The smell of burning flesh hung close even now; I wondered if I would ever be clean of it. "She implied that the last of her is in those tiny glowing beings. And she needs the ritual to keep her there. I don't know if she would die. But I believe the parts of her would be scattered so they could never be put together again. That is almost worse than death."

The silence stretched out. After a while, Silva buried her head in her hands, her shoulders quivering. I put my arm around her.

"We canna let that happen," Whisper said. "You canna let it happen, Neryn."

"I won't," I said with more confidence than I felt. "Among the three of us, we need to make a plan. But not now. Silva, why don't you try to sleep for a bit? We'll keep vigil for you."

But Silva would not. Weary to the bone, her face still wet with tears, she straightened her back and lifted her chin. "I must stay awake. That's what Maeva would expect. It's what the Lady would expect."

The next morning, the three of us returned to the place of the cairns. I waited with Silva while she spent some time in private, silent prayer. When she had finished, Whisper escorted her back to the ruined house. We hadn't made much of a plan, but it was obvious we could not survive the winter here without Silva's hospitality, and she in her turn would not consider leaving her duties of tending to the animals and maintaining the women's rituals. Whisper and I would have to trust that the natural magic of this place would keep me safe. We were agreed that Silva should not be left on her own.

When they were gone, I crept into the beehive hut. No sooner had I seated myself on the earthen floor and begun the slow sequence of breathing than a host of tiny presences swarmed down from somewhere in the arched roof to settle on me, their little lights painting the ancient stones with a many-colored glow.

"Ye hae a sorrow on ye," came the voice, softer today. "What is it that's happened?"

I told her, keeping to the facts, trying for a calm tone. "There's only the one young girl left—Silva—but she's sworn to keep the ritual going on her own," I said at the end.

"The wee lassie, aye. She'll be grievin'. 'Tis a sorry place, this Alban o' yours, sad and sorry."

"And yours," I felt compelled to say. "It may be sad and sorry now, but it's the same Alban where wise women once observed the high days openly; where they walked among their communities, teaching and healing, and were viewed with respect. My grandmother was one such. An herbalist."

"Oh, aye? And what became o' her?"

"An enthrallment that went awry. She died less than a year later."

"Oh, aye." I heard compassion in her voice. "And ye'd hae been a lassie around this one's age when it happened?"

"I was, yes."

"'Twillna be easy for ye, if ye must care for this lass and keep her safe, and follow your ain path, both at the same time."

I had not yet told Silva that as soon as my training was complete, we'd have to move on. "I know," I said.

"Aye, weel, ye willna be headin' off tomorrow. There's time for ye tae think things through. I see ye ken the five steps o' breathin'. Wha showed ye that?"

"The Hag of the Isles."

"That auld creature! Is that selkie fellow still by her side? Took up wi' him when she wasna mair than a lassie, she did. But then, she always did gae her ain way."

Her words brought a smile to my lips. I pictured the Hag as a young woman, tall and strong, swimming in those turbulent western waters alongside her selkie lover. I had learned, over the spring, that he had hidden depths. He was a gentler soul than the Hag; they complemented each other. "Yes, Himself is still there with her. I spent a good part of last spring with the Hag, learning. The day I first met her, she put me and my companion out on a skerry and left us there. First the two of us, then only me. It was a testing introduction to the magic of water."

"Were ye no' expectin' tae be tested?" I imagined the Lady raising her brows; the small bright beings made a sound like laughter.

"I expected the learning to be difficult. But I thought I had proved my physical endurance by then. I discovered, rather too slowly for my peace of mind, that what the Hag needed from me was not a demonstration of strength, but a recognition of the power of water in all its forms."

"Oh, aye. And what then?"

"After a few days on the skerry alone, I performed a ritual based on my understanding of water. It must have been good enough, because she came in her boat to collect me and take me back to my friends. Later, she taught me what I had traveled there to learn."

"Friends? Didna ye say there were twa o' ye?"

I felt my cheeks grow warm. "My guard and companion, Tali, one of the rebels. She had been on the skerry with me, but had been taken back to the bigger island while I slept. And . . . another friend."

"Ye dinna trust me enow tae tell me?"

"Of course I do. But I've become accustomed to keeping secrets. It still feels odd to speak openly of the rebellion and of my past. My friend . . . He plays a particular part for the rebels, a part that puts him in constant danger."

"Oh, aye," said my unseen companion. "Tell me, then, what did ye learn frae the Hag? What did the Lord o' the North teach ye?"

"From the Hag, I learned to make myself open to natural magic; to be the conduit through which it flows. When I use my Caller's gift, it's not my own power that brings the Good Folk to me and allows me to guide their actions, it's the power of earth, fire, water, and air. My openness to the natural world allows me to find uncanny folk and to speak to them in a particular way; the strength of the elements runs through me when I call."

"Go on."

"The Hag taught me to single out one among many. She taught me that sometimes my gift will result in harm to the one I call, and that I must accept those consequences if it's for the greater good." I fell silent, remembering the small deaths in the sea around Far Isle as I worked with the magic of water. "I still find that difficult. Before I began training with her, I used my gift a few times without really understanding how it worked, and folk died because of what I did. That's a heavy burden to bear."

"And yet, ye plan tae stand up before this king o' yours and challenge him and his Enforcers tae a fight? Ye canna be sae simple that ye dinna ken how many would fa' in such a battle. Or were ye thinkin' the Guardians would come tae the rescue and set a' tae rights wi' a quick pass o' the hands?"

If only they could. "Not at all. This king is of humankind, and it is for humankind to pay the price of removing him from power. But he has workers of magic in his household, folk with canny skills. At the last midsummer Gathering, a man from the court set wood on fire with a simple gesture, or so it seemed. Imagine what harm that could do if unleashed against an enemy."

"Dinna your rebels hae canny folk also? Wouldna ye set their talents against whatever the king's folk can offer?"

"We have a few folk with canny skills, but nothing that would alter the course of a battle. Apart from my gift."

"Aye, a Caller's gift. So your plan is tae use the Good Folk tae fight for ye. Fight and die for ye."

I had been presented with this argument almost every time I had explained the rebellion to a clan of Good Folk. "That's why I am traveling to each Guardian in turn and asking for training. So that I can control my call. So that I can enlist the Good Folk as allies to our cause, not draw them into the conflict against their will."

"'Tisna natural for your kind and mine tae be allies," the Lady said. "Cooperation isna the way o' the Good Folk. Ye must ken that by now."

"I do. But I have also discovered a will for change among your kind. Many have been helping us, spreading word of the rebellion, letting their clans all across Alban know what's coming. The Lord of the North has promised the support of his fighters. Smaller beings are working beside us too. Many have overcome their natural reluctance to work with other clans, and with human folk."

"Oh, aye? Then ye've wrought great change. Or is it that they canna say no tae ye, because o' what ye are? Isna that the nature o' a Caller?"

"I don't want to force anyone into anything. If I could learn to call only those willing to fight for the cause, that's what I'd do. If learning the magic of air will help me refine my call further, or make it stronger, or ensure it does not draw beings who would be quickly destroyed by Keldec's army, I will be deeply grateful."

"Oh, aye."

"While I was in the Lord of the North's hall, he had me work with his warriors. I am able to use the call more strategically now. I learned to call folk from a long distance, and to call beings I had not seen before, only imagined from a description. I practiced directing the actions of several folk at once, in a mock combat, for instance. That was not so hard, given that the beings concerned were willing volunteers. The Lord's folk have a good understanding of what is at stake for all of us."

"What o' the south, and the magic o' fire? If this king

has a fellow can conjure wi' flame, ye'll need a defense against it."

"I intend to visit the Master of Shadows when I leave here, not only for that, but to ask for a defense against cold iron. Unless we can protect them, many of the smaller Good Folk, the forest dwellers in particular, will soon perish if they are part of our challenge to the king. We've planned it for the next midsummer Gathering. Every troop of Enforcers will be at Summerfort, along with the personal armies of the chieftains of Alban. Our own fighters would soon be cut down if they could not use their iron weaponry. If there were a spell that could be cast over all those who fought against the king . . ."

"Ye dinna imagine," the Lady said, "that if the Master o' Shadows had such a spell he would gie it tae ye for free?"

"He seemed well disposed toward me," I ventured. "He is a volatile being, yes. Changeable, full of tricks. But . . . wouldn't he consider the cause of freedom important enough? I must at least ask him."

"Ye're crazy."

There was nothing I could say to this, so I sat quietly instead, practicing slow breathing.

" 'Tis a lot for a lassie to take on herself," the Lady said eventually. "A grand big task, sae grand a body can hardly get a picture o' it. Ye've got a stubborn streak in ye, that's plain. Comes frae that grandmother o' yours, nae doot."

Sudden tears sprang to my eyes. The wee bright folk murmured among themselves, and the one on my right shoulder flew up to brush my cheek with its wings.

"Ye miss her."

"My family's gone. I wouldn't wish them back; not into Alban the way it is today."

"Oh, aye. Now, tae the matter o' what I can teach ye. This rebellion, this challenge . . . at the Gatherin', ye say? Wi' a great army against ye, an army well trained and loyal tae the king. Hae ye considered what might happen when ye stand up, a wee lassie like yourself, and speak words o' defiance before that crowd? Once they start tae fight, it'll be a' stirred up like a pot o' porridge boilin' on the fire. Ye willna be able tae tell friend frae foe. Sheer bloody carnage, it'll be. This king, he willna wait for ye tae finish your speech before he orders the killin' tae start. As for callin' in uncanny folk tae help ye, the best Caller in a' the history o' Alban wouldna be heard ower such a clamor."

I gritted my teeth, swallowing those weak tears. "We have allies," I said. "Human allies as well as Good Folk. Three chieftains of Alban and their men-at-arms. On the day, our uncanny allies will be close enough for me to be able to call them easily, but concealed by magic. I'll need to get the timing exactly right."

"Let's suppose ye get tae Summerfort in time," said the Lady. "Let's imagine your folk are a' in position as ye planned. Ye stand up and say your wee speech, and the king's men attack ye. Your rebels rush intae battle, and find they canna prevail—there's nae human army can beat the Enforcers. Ye ca' the Good Folk tae help your rebels. They come to ye and join the fight; they use what magic they can. The king uses the magical abilities o' his canny followers. Folk start tae fall. Folk start tae die. Humankind and Good Folk alike. And there ye are, the Caller, wi' everyone waitin' for ye tae act.

But what ye see before ye isna a neat strategic plan. It's a field o' folk hackin' and maimin', a field of shouts and shrieks and sufferin'. What will ye dae?"

By now I was cold with misgiving. "I must learn to see order in chaos," I said, thinking that might be impossible. "To see clearly . . ." A sudden memory came to me. In the subterranean well where the Master of Shadows had tested my strength, I had heard the White Lady's voice. "I must see with the clarity of air," I said, repeating her words.

"Guid. Easy tae say, no' sae easy tae put intae practice, o' course. But mebbe there's time enow. New ways o' seein', ye'll work on. New ways o' hearin'. And shapin' the call tae the circumstances. Ye willna hae time, in this battle, tae look at ane fighter here and another ower there, and call tae each whatever will help him win. 'Tisna possible. The gift o' callin', 'tis a powerfu' weapon, but nae the sharpest or most precise. We hae much work ahead o' us, Neryn. When ye gae back tae the house o' the wise women, ask the lassie if there's a drum that survived burnin'. If there is, bring it wi' ye in the mornin'."

"A drum?"

"The magic o' air isna only seein' clear. There's hearin' the way a bird hears, or a dragonfly, or ane o' my wee bein's here. There's understandin' the moods o' air, frae the gentle breeze stirrin' the reeds tae the roarin' gale that snaps an ancient oak like a twig. Air's slow and quiet, and it's quick and hard. Ane day it carries the lark on her flight; the next it topples the tree wi' her nest o' wee ones in it. The drum will speak to ye o' air, if ye open your ears tae its voice."

*   *   *

Our lives fell into a pattern. Silva and I spent the nights in the stillroom, with Whisper on watch in a tree outside. In the mornings we fed the animals, then made our way to the Beehives, where Whisper and Silva waited until I was safely down among the cairns before returning to the ruined house.

All day, Silva tended the garden, planting, weeding, harvesting. She let the chickens out to roam. She cooked and stored food. We could only pray the smoke from her fire did not attract attention; with the winter weather setting in, we could not manage without it.

Before dusk each day, the two of them returned to the Beehives to fetch me. Sometimes they came early, and I assisted Silva with a ritual while Whisper stayed on the rise with his head turned away. Silva taught me how to help her, and I carried offerings, chanted responses, and paced formal paths with increasing confidence, honored that I could be part of something so sacred and so old.

We learned from Silva that Winterfort lay only a few days' walk north from the Beehives. The border with Glenfalloch was farther south. No messenger came from Tali—unsurprising, since it was winter and she did not know where we were—and I had no way to send word to her or to get in touch with the southern rebel group. Whisper was our protector and must stay with us. I could not ask the wee folk of the Beehives. It was inconceivable that any being so tiny and frail could endure a long flight out in the cold.

It was a perishing season. As the days and nights passed, and Silva kept us alive with her little fires, her vegetable broths, her flatbread and onions, I knew we owed her a debt that might never be repaid. For the Lady could not save us from hunger and cold. She could not protect us from the intrusions of ordinary folk, should they choose to ride over here and investigate who was living in the burned-out house. She had once been a powerful presence. Now, it seemed, she was reduced to the wise voice and the tiny bright beings who allowed it to be heard. I wished I knew what she had once been. And what of her people? Had they all faded away for want of folk who believed in them?

Diminished the Lady might be, but she could still teach. I spent hours with the drum, watching a pinch of earth dance on its ox-hide surface in response to my gentle tapping. I sang and made the skin vibrate; the grains of earth bounced and made mysterious patterns there, answering my voice. By placing my ear close to the drum skin, I learned to understand the tiny high speech of the wee folk, who would fly above it as they spoke, though, in truth, they preferred to give me their opinions in dumb show, as on that first day. For approval, leaping and clapping of hands. For disapproval, hands placed dramatically over eyes, or the back turned, or simply flying away. For excitement, dancing, somersaults, shrieks. I came to believe they were both independent of the White Lady and linked to her. After all, I thought, this was not so different from the household in the north, where the Lord was surrounded by retainers so loyal that they had waited three hundred years for him to wake from his enchanted sleep. Perhaps they too would die if they lost their Guardian. Perhaps it was the same in every Watch—the spirit of the Watch existed not only in its Guardian, but in every one of the folk who lived there, something that was shared among them, so although they were separate, they were at the same time one. That felt like a wondrous, deep knowledge; the thought filled me with awe.

Winter advanced. Somber clouds blanketed the sky. The wind beat on our modest refuge. The rain hurled itself against the walls as if to topple them, or came straight down in drenching sheets, turning the farmyard to a quagmire and forcing us to bring Snow and the chickens inside with us. The ducks were untroubled, finding shelter among the reeds that fringed the now-swollen stream.

There was a brief dry spell, and Silva dashed out to pull the last of the root vegetables and dig her broken beanstalks into the soil. The respite was soon over. On a day of howling gales and heavy rain, a day when it would have been foolish to attempt a walk to the cairns, the three of us huddled in the biggest of the outhouses with the animals, waiting for the worst to pass. I had insisted Whisper join us; surely no one would be abroad in such a storm. We had a little fire burning in a brazier, but the wind poked icy fingers between the shutters and under the door. The chickens perched in a row up on a shelf, muttering to each other and casting nervous glances at Whisper. Snow was bedded down on straw in a corner, content to be out of the weather.

It was time to be more open with Silva. Whisper and I had agreed, earlier, that she should not be left on her own, and we had kept to that. But we could not stay here forever; when my training was complete, we would have to move on, and she would indeed be alone. Her hard work and generosity were allowing us to survive here; I owed her as much of the truth as I could risk telling.

"Silva."

"Mm?" It was unusual to see her idle; even in moments of relative repose, her hands were usually busy with something: plaiting onions for drying, shredding herbs, mending a torn garment. Today she was sitting quietly by the goat, her shawl hugged around her shoulders, and I was reminded of how alone she really was.

"I need to explain more of my story to you. Mine and Whisper's."

She turned her gaze on me; it was very direct. "I've guessed some of it. I think I know where you come from. People whisper about that place. I won't say the name."

That surprised me. "Maybe it's the same place. I told you before that there's hope there, a plan to change the future. Winter's passing, and you need to know more about that plan and where I fit into it." Despite the storm, despite our isolation, I lowered my voice to a murmur. "You understand how dangerous it is to speak about these things. If I haven't told you everything earlier, it's been because the more you know, the more it endangers you." Silva nodded, saying nothing. "The plan comes to fruition next summer. My part in it is critical. To be ready in time, Whisper and I must travel south before then."

"South? You mean to Glenfalloch?"

"Possibly." The Master of Shadows could be anywhere. Whisper and I had not discussed how we would set about finding him. But Tali had wanted us to make contact with the rebels in the south, and that would be a good first step. "Certainly, we must be away from here as early as we can."

There was a silence, then Silva said, "You need not worry about me. I'll be fine on my own."

"I'm not sure you will be. We're eating our way through your supplies, using up what could have kept you going for a long time. However hard you work, you can't set away enough to feed yourself and the animals forever. What about grain for the hens? Where does that come from?"

"I'm not a child." Her chin went up. "We bartered for it at the village market. Sometimes with eggs; but mostly we offered cures and remedies. Folk were happy enough to trade with us and not ask questions." A pause. "That was before."

"And now? Would you go openly to the market in spring, after what happened here?" She'd be betrayed and handed over to the authorities before she bought her first sack of grain. Besides, how would she find time to make remedies to sell?

"Lassie." Whisper spoke at last, keeping his voice soft. Above us on the shelf, the hens ruffled their feathers and shifted their feet. "We ken you hae work here, work that's important tae you. But you need tae see things clear. Faith only takes a body so far when there's king's men bearing down on her wi' big swords in their hands."

"If you must go, you must," Silva said. "And I must stay here; there's no other way."

Spending all day inside the cramped confines of the beehive hut was taking a toll on me, body and mind. But my learning progressed. Now I could hear the subtlest of differences in the vibrations of the drum, and in the movement of the small folk inside the hut and outside, in the broader area of the Beehives. I could detect the movement of one bird in the elder trees, out there beyond my vision. I could identify one insect crawling out from cover at a distance of twenty paces.

Without needing to be out in the open, looking, I knew when Whisper came early to collect me; I heard the rustle of his wings up the hill, even when the howl of the wind must surely drown it.

"This new awareness will help ye," the Lady said. "If ye can hear the voice o' a wee crawlin' creature even when a storm's ragin', mebbe ye can gather your wits in the clamor o' battle and send a message tae the ears that must hear it. Do ye no' think?"

I imagined the battle: my friends and allies falling, dying before my eyes; the noise of clashing metal, the crunch of bones breaking, the screams. I had only witnessed one such conflict. This one would be ten times bigger, twenty times. "I can only pray I have learned enough to do it."

"Aye, weel, 'tis no' a thing ye can practice. Ye wouldna be lookin' for the king's men and givin' it a wee try. But there's ane mair thing I can teach ye. A storm, that's a bit like a battle, all bluster and turnin' things upside doon. The next time we hae a real gale, wi' thunder and sleety rain, ye can practice callin', and no' simply callin' your friend the witawoo neither. Ye should try callin' a fighter or twa. Or better still, call someone who can help ye. A messenger, mebbe. Didna ye mention ye wanted tae send word south?"

"Yes, but . . . the uncanny messengers we've used in the past . . . they've been birdlike in form. If I called such a being, it would have to fly here through the storm."

There was a silence. The wee folk were all clustered in one of the niches within the cairn, the glow of their lights turned on my face. Their scrutiny was uncomfortable.

"And when that battle comes," the Lady said eventually,

"willna folk need tae hear your ca', and follow your orders, through a storm o' swords and clubs and sprayin' blood, a whirlwind o' shoutin', screamin' fighters? 'Tis the best way for ye to learn, Neryn. Ye'll be havin' tae mak' choices. Which is mair important, winnin' the battle or keepin' your folk alive? Ye'll be havin' tae let some gae. Ye willna be able tae spend time savin' ane life or another. Ye dinna win a war wi'oot losin' good comrades. 'Tis the nature o' things."

I knew this, of course. That didn't mean I had come to terms with it. "Is this a test?" I asked her. "Calling a messenger to me during a storm?"

"'Twould be mair testin' for the one who's bein' called, seems tae me."

"I mean a . . . a formal test, to show I have learned enough to move on."

"You wouldna be wantin' tae move on in a storm. Unless you were half oot o' your wits." When I said nothing, she went on, "Could be ye mak' your ain test, Neryn. Think on that a while. But no' too lang. The storm's comin' soon enow."

Maybe she meant a storm with thunder, lightning, and rain. Maybe she meant another kind of upheaval. When I crawled out of the cairn, knowing it must be time for Whisper to escort me back to our place of shelter, the light was fading and there was no sign of him. It was the first time he had not come to fetch me before dusk.

I walked back on my own, hoping nothing was wrong. Just before I reached the spot where I'd be visible to anyone down at the burned-out house, I stopped walking. I lifted the drum, holding the ox-hide surface horizontal and putting my ear close. I used my new learning, tuning myself to every small vibration.

A voice came. Not Silva's, not Whisper's. A man's voice. My skin prickled; my heart thumped. Go forward or flee? Risk discovery or leave Silva in danger? I knew what Tali would say. I was Alban's salvation, or would be when I was fully trained. My safety must always come first.

But Tali was not here, and Silva was my friend. She had offered her support without reservation; she had shared all she had with us, virtual strangers.

"Can't stay here . . . ," the man was saying. He sounded young. ". . . dangerous . . ."

"I can manage." Silva's tone told me this was someone she knew, and knew well. "I don't need help. You shouldn't have come here, Ean."

"Why didn't you let me know where you were? I could have—"

A flurry of wings, and Whisper was on the path beside me.

"Who is it?" I hissed.

"Fellow came not lang since. I would hae fetched you, but I wanted tae be sure he was on his ain. Her brother, I'd be guessing. Like twa peas in a pod."

The young man spoke again. "Listen, Silva. I can get you safely away. . . ." His voice went down to a murmur, and the only word I caught was *Glenfalloch*.

"How much has she told him?" I whispered.

"She spoke o' the deaths o' her friends." A pause, then he added, "The door was open. He couldna fail tae see someone else was living here. She told him there were twa survivors:

76

herself and another woman, and that her companion was at the cairns. If no' for that, I'd hae told you tae keep under cover until he was gone."

"There's a storm coming," I said. "Or so I've been told."

"Aye." Whisper gave me a direct sort of look; in the dim light, his big owl-eyes were bright with knowledge. "But no' before morning. You'd best gae in and introduce yourself. I willna let him see me save as a creature, unless there's trouble the twa o' you canna handle. The fellow willna gae anywhere tonight; it's near dark." He paused for thought, then said, "He'd be doing us a favor if he took the lass awa' tae a place o' safety, as he's offering."

A shiver ran through me, as deep and cold as a river in winter. "If Silva goes, the Lady is no more." Could even the downfall of Keldec justify such a loss?

"A knotty puzzle," observed Whisper. "Could be there's mair than a single way tae untangle it."

The rain had ceased for now, and Silva had built her cooking fire in a sheltered area between the stillroom and the outhouse that we'd made into winter quarters for Snow and the chickens. She and her visitor were standing in the fire's glow, arguing. The young man was dressed for traveling and had his back to me; Silva saw me coming before he did. Whisper had flown up to the tree close by. Perching there, he looked exactly like an ordinary owl.

"Neryn, you're back!" Silva said as I approached—a warning that she had given the fellow my real name.

The man turned. He was younger than I expected; only a few years Silva's senior, and so like her that he had to be a kinsman. The dark wavy hair, the big eyes, the slender build, the heart-shaped face—he was surely her brother. He gave me a very direct look, sizing me up.

"This is my brother," Silva said. "Ean. I've offered him shelter for the night. Your prayers kept you at the cairns late."

I came up to the fire, trying to look natural. "Greetings, Ean," I said. "My name is Neryn." *I can get you safely away,* he'd said. And I was almost sure I'd heard him say Glenfalloch. That didn't make him a rebel, or even a friend. It could be sheer coincidence. "Need help with the supper?" I asked Silva.

"It's all ready." Silva's cook pot stood beside the fire, and now she filled three bowls with barley broth—Whisper would have to wait. A savory, comforting smell wafted through the chill air. There were hunks of flatbread to dip. The hot food was bliss after my cold, cramped day at the cairns, and although Ean's presence meant I could not relax my guard, eating did take away the need to talk. As we shared the meal, I wondered what had brought him here now, nearly three turnings of the moon after the fire. If he lived close by, surely he must have known where Silva was. Why hadn't he come looking for her as soon as he heard what had happened?

"Ean wants me to go south with him to a safer place," Silva said at last, setting down her empty bowl. "I've said no."

Ean's dark gaze moved to me, then back to her. He said nothing.

"I explained to you, Ean," Silva added. "I can't leave Neryn on her own. There were twelve of us before this happened. It's not a job for one."

Ean wanted to say something, I could see that, but he

didn't trust me. It was written all over his face. Fine; the feeling was mutual.

"You can talk in front of Neryn," Silva said.

But he couldn't, any more than I could tell him the truth about what I was. He might go straight out and denounce me to the authorities. If he was somehow associated with the rebellion, or even if he was prepared to risk helping Silva when he knew she was flouting the king's law, he took the same risk in being open with me. I looked directly at him.

"How can you be sure Silva would be safer in the south?"

"This place is a ruin." Ean's flat tone served to emphasize that this was the simple truth. "You'll run out of food for yourselves and the stock."

Neither of us said a thing.

"You know the risks of what you're doing, unless you're stupid." Ean's voice dropped to a murmur. "The folk of the settlement know there's someone here; that's how I found out where Silva was. They know someone survived. So far, they've kept clear because that's safer for you and safer for them. But you'll be found. Sooner or later, someone will come looking. You need to get away before that happens." He looked at me. "You shouldn't have kept Silva here. She's only young."

And what was he, I thought, fourteen? Younger than me, most likely. A painful memory of my own brother came to me. Farral had believed himself a man at fourteen. At the hands of the Enforcers he had died a man's death.

"This is not Neryn's doing," Silva said. "It's my choice to stay here. It's good to see you, Ean, but you shouldn't have come. What's dangerous for us is dangerous for you too."

Ean made a sound indicating exasperation. "You're a child," he said. "You have no idea—"

"Have you forgotten what happened here?" I asked him. "Or did the villagers not explain to you why this house lies in ruins and there are only the two of us left? Of course Silva understands the risk." I stopped myself from saying more. If Ean was trustworthy, and if he really did have a safe place to take her, it would make complete sense for her to go with him. But there was the White Lady. We could not walk away and let her fade.

"I can't go and I won't go." Silva folded her arms. "There's no need to talk about it anymore. Did you bring a bedroll? If you want to stay tonight, you'll have to sleep in with Snow and the chickens."

"I'm staying until you see sense," said Ean.

Chapter Four

At Winterfort, with the entire court in residence, no-where was safe from scrutiny. When a man already lay under suspicion, the slightest hint of error was sure to reach the ears of the king. Or, more likely, those of the queen. Varda had her eye on him. He was becoming more sure of that every day. And if the queen wanted someone made an example of, the king ensured it was done. It had been so since the day they were hand-fasted. If Keldec had never met Varda, would he have become a different kind of man? What if he had married, instead, a kindly woman with no ambition? Per-haps such women never wed kings.

Over his years at court, Flint had seen how the queen shaped her husband's thoughts and influenced his decisions. Varda liked spectacle. Blood excited her. She enjoyed watch-ing people suffer. Above all, she thrived on being in control. And since a woman could not rule in her own right—the an-cient laws of Alban forbade that—she made sure her husband ruled in the way she would.

The Caller was a new plaything for Varda, magnificent in his ability to provide her with diversions. Flint had seen him at work soon after the court moved back to Winterfort. A young man, twenty at most, nothing startling in looks—he might have been any farmhand or fisherman. The queen's agents in the south had found him in company with a fire creature, all flame and smoke. Brydian, Varda's councillor, had realized immediately what they had, since Brydian was something of a scholar and versed in ancient lore. So the young man, Esten, had not been summarily executed for breaking the king's law. Instead, he'd been apprehended, questioned, and brought back to court. Not a traitor. Not a miscreant. Esten would be a tool unparalleled in the queen's hands. Through him, she would show the people of Alban how much power the king could wield, not only over his human subjects, but also over the Good Folk.

For a tense few days, Flint had thought the king would order him to enthrall Esten, so the Caller's loyalty could be ensured. What other reason could there have been for Keldec's insistence that his right-hand man return from the foray to Wedderburn within as short a time as possible? Despite his very public failure at last midsummer's Gathering, Owen Swift-Sword was still the most reliable of the king's Enthrallers. The episode with Tali had been the only time his craft had been seen to go awry. Each of the other Enthrallers, less skilled, improperly trained, had a number of disasters behind him: victims whose minds had been destroyed by the process. Most settlements in Alban housed at least one such damaged individual, a grown man or woman turned witless and wandering by an enthrallment gone wrong.

It was no wonder ordinary folk called the Enthrallers mind-scrapers. So, Esten had arrived at court. The days had passed, and he had not only been welcomed and made much of, he had been quickly embraced by the queen's inner circle. The court had made its customary move from Summerfort to Winterfort as soon as the season changed, and no request for an enthrallment had come, either to Flint or to anyone else. It seemed the young man was willing to do whatever he was asked to do. It was hard to believe that Esten's canny gift was the same as Neryn's. They were worlds apart. Neryn put her talent to work for the good of Alban, for freedom, for change, for a brave new future. She would not dream of using it to gain power or to wield terror. Neryn loved and respected the Good Folk. She understood them in all their various and wondrous forms. She used her gift only to seek wisdom, to bring folk together, to . . . No longer accurate, of course; he was deluding himself. There was a battle looming, if, of course, Tali managed to pull the disparate elements of the rebellion together by midsummer. When the time came, Neryn would have to call the Good Folk to fight, to wound, to kill, to die. Whatever path next Gathering's confrontation took, she would come away from it carrying a heavy burden. If she survived. If any of them survived.

And he . . . He was trapped here, surrounded by comrades loyal to the king, under constant scrutiny. If Queen Varda was not watching him in person, she had her people doing it. He suspected there were some of his own kind, Enforcers, who were doing the same job when the troop rode out.

Perhaps he was foolish to hope for a message. None of the Good Folk would approach Winterfort, since the place was full of iron. Even when Stag Troop was out on patrol, uncanny folk would not come close, for the nature of the work meant everyone went heavily armed. He gave them opportunity when he could, walking out into the woods on his own with his weapons rolled into his cloak, but even then there was nothing. Yet Sage had approached him twice in the past when he was bearing knives.

The onset of winter made it unlikely Tali would use human messengers. It was a long way from Shadowfell to Winterfort, with a mountain pass to cross. Too far in the cold season, even if Tali had a chain of reliable folk all the way. Too risky, unless the matter was of utmost importance. And if messengers did not come to him, he could not send word back again. The rebels did not know about Esten. He could not warn them; Neryn could not prepare. Esten's presence would turn next midsummer's confrontation into disaster. It was the difference between an unlikely but possible victory and certain defeat. Worse than defeat. Annihilation. They'd all be done for, brave Tali, his beloved Neryn, the band of rebels who had shaped his destiny since he was little more than a boy, the chieftains who had pledged to stand up beside Tali's rebel army, and the men who followed them. And the Good Folk; those whom Neryn would call to fight alongside them. They too would be destroyed, perhaps by their own kind. It was unthinkable.

He was sure what Tali would want, if she knew about this. She'd expect him to kill Esten, despite the risk that he would be discovered. A straightforward assassination: a task well within his capabilities, if not for one thing. Brydian too had a canny gift, a highly unusual gift not known to many. He could throw a cloak of protection over a person, an unseen armor that no physical attack could penetrate. He used it to shield the king during his public appearances—for instance, at the Gathering.

Now Brydian was staying very close to the Caller, and Flint suspected he was under orders to keep Esten protected at all times. Unless and until Brydian let Esten go far enough from him to render the charm ineffective—the councillor's gift did not work over a long distance—there would be no quick and covert dispatch of the Caller.

He could account for Brydian first and then kill Esten, of course, but he was unlikely to get away with that, and the repercussions would be dire. Tali would expect him to sacrifice his own life for the good of the cause; it was part of the rebel code. But he'd need to be quite certain of his ability to stay silent under torture, or his will to use the packet of hemlock seeds they all carried for such an extreme. No point in this double murder if he then betrayed the tightly held secret of the planned rebellion. So. First Brydian, then Esten, then himself. He'd need to be constantly alert, ready to seize the opportunity. As for dying without seeing Neryn again, he could not let himself think of that.

He was in the stables, grooming Lightning. One or two other men were about, engaged in the same task—many horses were kept here. There were stable hands to do the job, but most of the Stag Troop men preferred to tend to their own mounts. It strengthened the bond; helped rider and horse to work as a team. The steady movement of the brush, the warmth of Lightning's presence close to him, the relative quiet of the stables, helped calm his racing thoughts. And if, even here, someone was watching him, ready to report back to Varda—perhaps that boy over there oiling harnesses, or the fellow from Seal Troop on the far side working on his horse's hooves—he would, for a little while, pretend it was not so. He would allow himself to remember last summer, and the night he and Neryn had spent lying chastely in each other's arms, alone in a cottage with the sound of the murmuring sea beyond the shutters. His last night of peace. Her hair soft against his naked skin; her hands touching him with such tenderness. That night, he had glimpsed a future that now seemed an impossible dream.

The king had made Esten demonstrate his skill before all of them. The Caller had conjured three of the smaller Good Folk out of nothing, or so it had seemed; he had, perhaps, called them forth from somewhere in the wooded hills around Winterfort, but the three of them had not walked in through the fortress gates. They had simply appeared beside Esten, looking bewildered. Two were human-like in form; the third had a long snout, big eyes, and a soft coat of dark fur. Under the wild applause of the assembled onlookers, the three had shrunk back. The furred one had screamed when the king approached to prod and examine them. Keldec had been wearing a knife at his belt. Even sheathed, it would have hurt them.

Nobody had attempted to engage the small ones in conversation. Instead, the queen had asked her Caller if he could make them dance; if he could make them fight; if he could make one of them attack an Enforcer. The resulting spectacle had been . . . He could not find the right word for it.

He only knew it would have brought bitter rage to Neryn's heart if she had seen it. He'd wanted to step in, to stop it. Instead, he had stood there watching like all the others, with his jaw clenched tight over a torrent of furious words. Others too had found the spectacle offensive; he had seen it on their faces. But nobody had spoken out.

The three small folk had survived their ordeal, though two had been injured. Now they were locked into one of the punishment cells, with an iron chain on the door to prevent their escape. Wolf Troop had the job of guarding prisoners. The special captives had been in custody awhile. The word was, the queen went to visit them every day, with Brydian and Esten. It entertained her to toy with the small folk. All three were weakening. How could he endure this until midsummer? The days were all edgy pretense, the nights a torment of agitated wakefulness or, worse, darkly violent dreams. How had he managed to be what he was, to do what he had to do, for all these years? How had he shut down his conscience for so long?

In the past, he'd been a master of shielding what he felt. Since that day at Wedderburn, when he had so nearly escaped this travesty of a life, it had become ever harder to maintain his detached look. Now he saw a question in his comrades' eyes as they glanced at him. Whether it was because the king had ordered him to prove his loyalty at the Gathering, or whether it was the delay in returning to court after the trip to Wedderburn—only a short delay, thanks to Rohan's intervention, but noticed all the same—he felt he was under scrutiny even by the men of his own troop. Midsummer seemed a long time away. And yet, it would come all too quickly.

"Owen?" Rohan was right beside him, arms folded. "The king wants you. Now, in the small council chamber."

"Any idea why?"

His second-in-command shook his head. "Here, give me those." Rohan took the horse brush and the rough cloth. "You'd better get cleaned up before you present yourself."

They looked at each other. Many times, Flint had been a hairbreadth from confiding in Rohan, whom he increasingly believed had more than an inkling that his troop leader was living a double life. But he had never risked it. If he was wrong, taking such a step would not only ensure his own death, it could bring down the entire rebel movement. If he was right, of course, then he had a valuable ally, someone who was prepared to live the lie with him rather than see him destroyed. It had been Rohan who had suggested Flint go alone to the isles, and thereby helped him save his old mentor. It had been Rohan who'd helped him rescue Tali and Neryn at the Gathering and not asked a single question afterward. It had been Rohan who'd come for him when he was on the verge of quitting the king's service. Each time, Flint became more convinced that these were his comrade's own choices, not those of a king's lackey trying to trick him into betraying himself. Still, he would not speak openly.

"Go on, then," Rohan said.

The small council chamber had two guards on the door, men from Wolf Troop. Inside, there was only Keldec. The king was seated at an oak table, frowning at a manuscript spread out before him. A map, the south of Alban from coast to coast, done in meticulous detail. Flint could see rivers, islands, mountain ranges, a fortification with a banner atop its tower, a lake in which a grotesque sea monster swam. Keldec was tracing a path with a dry quill. He appeared to be deep in thought.

Flint came to a halt a few steps from the table and waited in silence. The king ignored him. Well, two could play at that game. He stood breathing slowly, hoping to be ready for whatever Keldec might have to say to him. The silence drew out.

Finally, "Of what use is a Caller, Owen?" the king asked. "You've seen those fey folk, how puny and helpless they are. Touch them with the smallest knife or bracelet or buckle and their flesh swells and weeps as if burned. I thought my Caller would bring me warriors. Instead, he brought toys. Living poppets for the entertainment of women and children. And yet, in the old tales, Callers are instrumental in changing the course of battles. Callers aid in the conquest of new territories. They enable leaders to wield enormous power. So Brydian tells me. Esten . . . I see the fellow's potential, of course. But his reach seems quite limited. I had hoped for better things, far better."

"I'm sorry, my lord king."

"Sorry? You're sorry?" Keldec cast aside the quill and jumped up to stride over to a narrow window, where he set his hands against the wall on either side and stared out toward the east. Winterfort stood on a hill; a fortress wall encircled that hill, and below it a substantial settlement had grown up. "In what way is this your fault, Owen? I am musing, only musing." The king's shoulders were tight. "When word came to me that a Caller had been found, my mind leapt to what we might do, what we might achieve, with such a tool in our hands. We might build an army such as nobody in all Alban possessed; we might create a force capable of wiping out any opposition, however handsomely equipped, however expertly drilled. What I see now is an army of little folk, an army of squirrels and martens and children who will shriek and collapse if they see so much as a paring knife. I have not reprimanded Esten. The queen believes he will learn to do greater things. I am not sure how she can know that. To tell you the truth, old friend, I am somewhat disappointed."

At least the disappointment, this time, was not with Flint himself. Unless he was missing something. Keldec was fond of springing surprises. "Yes, my lord king."

"Are there not grander folk, stronger folk, giants, trolls, and the like, whom a Caller might summon? Creatures that can fight?"

"My lord king, I am no expert on such matters, but I believe folk of that kind are mentioned in the ancient stories. Brydian and the other councillors would be better able to advise you."

"I'm not asking Brydian. I'm asking you." Keldec turned, half seating himself on the stone ledge below the window. Cold winter light spilled in around him, but his face was in shadow. "I need a battle leader's advice, Owen, not a scholar's. If you were in my position, how would you turn a Caller into a strategic advantage? How would you ensure he was up to the job? Is it even possible to build an uncanny army of the kind I hope for?"

He longed to answer no, it was not and never would be. He longed to say that the king might as well abandon his plans to use Esten in such a way. Unfortunately, while Keldec himself might swallow that argument, Varda and Brydian would not. Keldec was a straightforward thinker. His wife was clever and unscrupulous, her councillor learned in lore and unswervingly loyal to her.

"My lord king," he said, "it's my understanding, from my limited knowledge of the lore, that a Caller can draw human and uncanny forces together against a common enemy. I imagine that if more powerful beings such as those you mentioned—trolls and the like—still exist in Alban, they might be summoned and commanded to fight alongside, say, your troops of Enforcers. The men would find it . . . challenging. The Caller would need to exercise a great deal of control. I would imagine such a person would need to spend time learning military strategy beforehand."

"We could do it, then." Keldec's eyes had brightened; there was a new note in his voice. "I was right, this is possible after all."

Flint's heart sank. "These small folk will never be warriors, my lord king. But yes, it might be possible with stronger beings. It would be a huge undertaking to find such beings and persuade them to cooperate."

"But a Caller removes the requirement for persuasion, Owen. We need only find these folk and bring them here."

"Yes, my lord king." Flint chose his words with particular care. "A grand endeavor indeed. The bigger folk may be in distant parts of Alban. Hidden deep. It could be the work of years."

"We must see what Esten can do. An expedition . . ."

Briefly, Flint let himself imagine Esten taken somewhere far away, hunting for elusive Good Folk; Esten gone from court until after midsummer. Too good to be true, he feared. "Yes, my lord king."

"As for the three we have in custody, my wife is tired of them. They no longer provide her with good entertainment."

"Will you cull them, my lord?" He kept his tone calm.

"The queen has suggested a course of action for their disposal. It involves you."

A test of his loyalty, no doubt; he waited for Keldec to order him down to the Hole to make an end of the three little folk. One of these days he would reach breaking point. One of these days he would refuse a direct order.

"We wish to send a clear message to all uncanny folk that our authority stretches over them as well as our human subjects; that we can do as we wish with them, and that if they fail to satisfy our needs, there will be dire consequences. So yes, they will be culled, but not here at Winterfort. On their own home ground. Brydian is of the opinion that these are folk of the forest. I want them taken out there, at a time when others of their kind may be close by, and executed. You will remove them from the cells at an appropriate time, convey them to a suitable spot, and carry out the culling."

Flint worked on keeping his expression bland. "On my own, my lord king?"

"What, frightened of three small folk no higher than your knee?" There was a twinkle in the king's eye. "My redoubtable Stag Troop leader?"

"Frightened, no, my lord. Surprised, yes. I will do it, of course."

"You wonder why this is a job for one man, and why I allocate it to such a senior Enforcer? Brydian believes that if several men go out, the other Good Folk are less likely to come close and witness what occurs. He also said your wisdom and experience will allow you to choose the right spot."

Wisdom and experience. That, from Brydian? This was some kind of trap. At the very least, a test of his loyalty. "I see, my lord king."

"It's been suggested you might take them out at dusk, around suppertime. I concur with that. Let us not make a performance of this."

So Keldec did not want his household to witness what had, in fact, been a dismal failure. "Yes, my lord king."

"Do it today, Owen. Brydian tells me the captives will not last much longer, and we don't want fate stealing our chance to make an example of them."

Not long before dusk, he went down to Winterfort's place of incarceration. The Hole—an unofficial name, but one that had stuck—lay between the outer and inner walls of the fortress. The cells were small; the place was dark. There was a lamp at the guard post, and here and there a fist-sized opening had been pierced through the outer wall, as if to tantalize the inmates with faint hope. Without the air these chinks admitted, prisoners would have succumbed too soon for useful questioning. The Hole was shadowy, damp, noxious. A man might die there of the stench, the biting insects, the watery gray substance that passed for food. Or he might perish from sheer despair before the king took any interest in him.

Before he reached the top of the narrow stairs that led down to the cells, he heard the screaming, a high, thready, exhausted sound. He descended, breathing slowly, allowing the practiced mask of calm to spread across his features.

Brocc from Wolf Troop, one of the enthralled men, was at the guard post. He saluted—right arm across breast, fist clenched—showing appropriate deference to Flint's status as a troop leader.

"Owen."

"Brocc. I'm here to take the small folk away."

Brocc lowered his voice, making it hard to catch his words above the sound from the cells. The crying was underscored now by a rhythmic rattling and thumping sound. "I was expecting you. Got the orders earlier. But . . ."

"But what?"

Brocc frowned. "The queen came down. She's in there now with the prisoners. Said she wanted some time with them before you took them out."

"How much time?" There wasn't long left, from the sound of things. "I need to get them out before the light goes."

"She hasn't been there long." Brocc was edgy, torn between the king's orders and the physical presence of the queen in the nearby cell. "Owen, I can't just walk in there and—"

An enthralled man was faultlessly loyal to the king. Brocc was therefore bound to obey the original orders. But only a man with very little imagination would dare slight the queen.

"I'll go in." Flint had already set aside his weaponry; it had not seemed appropriate to bring sword or knives close to these particular prisoners, even though Brocc had a sword and there were iron bars on the cells. He drew a deep breath, walked along the narrow way between the two rows of cells, stopped before the barred opening to the one where the screaming was coming from. Had come from. Varda was there, a small, upright figure in her red gown, with her dark hair piled high and her features alight with perverse pleasure. She had an Enforcer in the cell with her, another of the Wolves. He was the one who had been administering punishment; the queen had most likely been giving orders.

"Owen Swift-Sword." The queen's voice was a little breathless. "Here to clear out our rubbish? Such promise when Esten brought them in, and such a disappointment when we got to the real test. . . . Never mind. No doubt there are plenty more where these came from. Come in, don't stand on ceremony. We were just leaving." She brushed past him, her lips curving in a smile that did not reach her eyes. "I'm afraid you're just too late for this ugly little thing. But at least it's quiet now; my head was aching. Take them, Owen. That's what the king ordered." The voice was hard metal coated in syrup; she made no secret of her dislike. "Ardon, find Owen Swift-Sword a bag in which to carry this . . . remnant." She strode out of the cell, leaving the grilled door open, and swept away toward the steps. Ardon asked a question with his eyes; Flint shook his head, and the Enforcer followed the queen. He had a heavy chain over his shoulder and an iron bar in his hand.

I cannot afford anger. I cannot afford the luxury of feeling. There is a job to be done. Do it. "Brocc?" he called when the sound of the others' footsteps had faded away. "Can you bring the lamp? And an old blanket?"

He stepped into the cell. The furred creature was limp on the stone floor, broken, clearly dead. The manlike being was at the very back of the cell, pressed into a corner, visible only as a patch of darker shadow. The little woman was kneeling by the fallen one, holding its limp paw, murmuring, "Rise wi' the flame. Soar wi' the eagle. Swim wi' the selkies and rest in the fairest field o' flowers. Ye're safe at last, laddie. The dark night's ower; day's dawnin' fresh and fair."

Brocc came with a tattered blanket under one arm and the lantern in his hand. Warm light spread across the dank cell, showing the little woman's chalk-white face, her deep-set eyes, the pool of blood spreading on the stones. It illuminated the bruises, the broken limbs, the marks where iron had met flesh.

"Black Crow save us," Brocc muttered.

The wee woman's prayer was finished. She lifted her head and spat with some accuracy on his boot.

"I'll do what needs doing here," Flint said, taking the blanket. "Could you unlock the outer door? Leave me the lantern, will you?"

When Brocc was gone, Flint crouched by the woman, not too close. She hissed at him, giving not an inch of ground. Her eyes were those of a cornered wildcat, ready to fight to the death.

"My name is Owen." He kept his voice to a murmur. "I'm under orders to take you out of here. I'll see you safe into the woods, well away from this place. We need to go now."

The woman did not move. He had never seen such a baleful glare.

"Please," he said after a glance over his shoulder. No sign of Brocc, and he knew the other cells were empty. "I'm a friend. Let me help you."

"A friend. Ye tell me that, wi' the king's stamp all ower ye? Why would I trust ye in the slightest particular, when I'm shut up here wi' my friend lyin' deid in my arms?"

"You'd trust me because the alternative is staying in this place until you're dead too. Let me take him. Let me wrap him up and carry him out. Can you walk, the two of you? Are you injured?"

"Ha!" She released her hold on her dead friend's hand and got stiffly to her feet. "Ye could say we were injured, aye. But tae get oot o' this foul cage, we'd walk even if we had twa legs broken and our heids on the wrong way roond. Handle him gently or I'll lay a hex on ye," she added sharply as Flint spread out the blanket beside the broken creature.

Every instinct told him to be quick; to get them out before someone realized he had no intention of killing them. But he took his time, lifting the sad corpse onto the blanket with careful hands, swathing the creature as if it were a sleeping babe. The wee woman watched him, gimlet-eyed, until the job was done.

The little man had not moved from his dark corner. He had not uttered a sound.

"We need to go," Flint said again, looking at the woman. Brocc would have unbarred the door by now, and outside it would be almost night.

"Aye," the woman said. "Aye." She went over to the corner—she was limping badly—and slipped an arm around the little man's shoulders. When he tried to pull away from her, she held firm. "Time we were gone, laddie. Come ye wi' me now. We'll be hame soon. Come on, lad, ane foot after the other. Ye can dae it."

Flint went first, carrying the body. She came after, the lame supporting the lamer. Past the iron grille; along the narrow way between the rows of cells; past Brocc, who was coming up from the outer door, his knife at his belt. Iron everywhere.

The wee woman was singing under her breath. "Oh, hushaby birdie, and hushaby lamb . . ."

When they reached the outer door, the lullaby ceased. "Ye speakin' true?" she asked, looking at Flint. "They're fond o' tricks here. Ye're no' takin' us oot tae be done tae death like vermin?"

"Shh," he warned. "No talking until we're well out into the forest."

"If ye plan tae set us free, why dinna ye simply put us oot the door and be aboot your ain business?"

She was as stubborn as Sage. He could not miss the bruises on her fair skin; she was walking as if she'd endured a beating. But she held herself straight, and her arm was firm around her friend. "Quiet," he said. "We must move on. There's barely enough light to see the way."

"That's nae matter tae the wee fellow," she said. "He canna see at a', since your queen got the notion that an iron poker in the e'en would mak' him jump higher."

The light was not good enough to show him the wee man's features clearly, but what he could not see, he had no difficulty imagining. There was nothing to say. *Sorry* did not begin to capture the wrongness of this.

"And dinna ye dare apologize," said the woman, as if reading his mind. "Nae matter how gentle your hands might be or how soft your words, ye're like the others. Like her. Like that fellow who brought us here whether we wanted tae come or no. A breaker. A destroyer. Worse; ye hae the token o' fell magic aroond your neck, I see it."

His Enthraller's amulet; the dream vial on its cord had swung free of his tunic as he maneuvered through the little door. With both hands supporting the wrapped body, he could not push the token back into concealment. "Hush," he hissed. "No talk until we're safely away."

The moon was rising, near full, and cold light fell over the landscape before them. From this side of the hill there was no view of the settlement that lay below Winterfort's wall. Instead, there was a wooded slope, broken in places by the track that wound its way down to meet a northern road. Farther away the land rose and fell, with pockets of woodland becoming, at some distance, a dense forest of pine and oak. He knew the way. One bridge, two sentry posts. He hoped the fellows on duty had been told he had the king's permission for this. He might have a troop leader's authority, but a shadow of doubt lay over him now. Folk had viewed him differently since the Gathering, when the king had called his loyalty into question. It did not matter that he had proved himself to Keldec's satisfaction. Once hurled, mud had a habit of sticking. Today's events wouldn't help.

"Owen?"

He started; the little man gave a whimper of fright. Brocc had come back down the steps to loom up behind them, a solid dark figure.

"Mm?"

"I'd best lock up behind you. When you get back, hammer on the door and I'll let you in."

The edge of the forest lay within clear sight of Winterfort. Farmers took pigs to forage there; troops of Enforcers used the area to hone their tracking skills. Women gathered herbs by the streams that ran under the trees, carrying mountain water down to the loch. He'd need to take the two survivors past that area and well into the forest, so they'd have at least some chance of getting away.

His burden meant he could not help the survivors, and both of them were hobbling. The wee woman led the wee man; he leaned on her. The last of the daylight was gone. By pale moonlight they made a slow progress down the hill, across the bridge, and on toward the greater darkness of the forest. Twice the sentries challenged them; twice Flint identified himself and explained his purpose, and they were allowed to pass. He began to wonder who was following them; who was watching. Would not this be a perfect opportunity to walk away, to set it all behind him, as he'd tried to do once before? He could simply vanish into the forest along with his companions. He could find a way across the mountains to the Rush valley and thence to Shadowfell. He could escape.

Too easy. Too perfect. This had to be a trap. Why else give this task to him, and to him alone? He doubted the queen or Brydian suspected he might want to spare the prisoners. No; what they expected was that he would run, bolt for freedom as soon as he had the chance. Try it this time and the trap would surely be sprung. Had Rohan talked? He could have sworn that when Rohan spoke to him in the stables, he'd simply been passing on the message from the king. All the same, this was too odd to be taken at face value.

The moon was high by the time they reached the edge of the forest. The wee man's breathing had turned to wheezing sobs; the woman's face was a grim mask. They halted at the foot of a great oak, and Flint set down the creature's body.

"Off wi' ye." The wee woman's voice was flat with exhaustion.

"What?" Surely he had not heard right.

"Gae hame tae your friends wi' their iron bars and their fires and their hard words. We dinna need ye and we dinna want ye."

He drew a careful breath. "I must take you farther in. There will be folk about here, human folk, if not now, then in the morning. Your friend is hurt; you're exhausted. I must get you to a place where you can safely spend the night."

She fixed her eyes on him, and he thought how like Sage she was; it was as if she could see right inside him. "Ye deaf?"

His mind filled with questions he would not ask. "I could help you bury your friend," he said quietly. "Let me do that, at least."

"Bury him? Usin' what?"

There was a silence. "A branch. My hands. I want to help."

"Ye're late in offerin'." She gestured toward the blanketed form on the ground. "Too late tae save the wee man's sight."

The little man muttered something; Flint could not make out the words.

"What did he say?"

The woman glowered. "He says, if ye were expectin' tae be diggin' a grave, why didna ye bring a spade?"

Flint found himself looking over his shoulder; scanning the moonlit landscape for signs of concealed listeners. He lowered his voice. "Wooden spades are a rarity at Winterfort."

A longer silence. "Ye're bearin' nae iron at a'." There was, perhaps, the very slightest softening in her tone.

"I must hope I do not need to defend myself against armed attackers on the way back," he said.

"Nae weapons. Stupid, are ye?"

"That's for you to judge." He had indeed made himself vulnerable, setting his knives aside before he went to the Hole. The presence of cold iron would have shut off any hope of talking to the prisoners; it would have made a mockery of their release.

He squatted down beside the lifeless form in the blanket, for once unsure of how to proceed. Quite clearly these two were too weak to be left. The wee man might die before morning; if his injuries did not carry him off, the winter chill would. There was no way they could dig a hole adequate for the body of their companion. But he could not force his help on them, not in the face of such excoriating judgment.

"Ye ken there's twa men followin' ye?" The woman had come close, murmuring in his ear.

"Two, you think? Yes, I heard movement behind us. Saw them once or twice."

"And ye wi' nae means tae defend yoursel'."

"Spies, not assassins." The queen's men; he'd stake his life on it. Waiting for him to break; waiting for him to betray himself. "Never mind that. How can you—"

"We dinna need ye mair. Be off wi' ye—" The woman faltered; her eyes were on his amulet again. "That isna like the others," she said in a different tone.

"No." His was not the glass replica worn by the other Enthrallers. It was the true sign of a mind-mender, a shard from

Ossan's secret cave in the isles, the recognition that he had completed the long years of training in his ancient craft. His mentor had given it to him. Around its silver mounting was wound a lock of Neryn's honey-colored hair. "It is not the same."

"The one who taught ye . . . He'd be sad tae see what ye've come tae, sad and sorry."

He bowed his head. When she said no more, he got to his feet and realized that not far into the shadow of the forest tiny lights could be seen, like miniature lanterns. It seemed these wee folk had help at hand after all.

"Since you don't need my services, I will take your advice and go." There was one more thing he must say, one more risk he must take. "I have a question."

She waited.

"Do you know a woman named Sage? One of your own folk, from a clan that lives in the forest near Silverwater, west of the place where the Rush spills into the loch."

"A Westie." The tone was scornful, but her eyes told him the name meant something to her.

"I'm in no position to ask a favor, I know. But if you can make sure Sage hears the tale of what befell you here, I will be most grateful. The whole tale, in all its detail. The Caller, the queen, how you were treated, the way you got out."

Now she was staring at him as if he were talking gibberish. "Supposin' I can find this Sage, who do I say wanted her told this tale?"

"Tell her a king's man. She'll know who I am."

The woman made no reply. Behind her, the little man was sprawled on the ground at full length, one arm up over his damaged eyes. Whoever was holding the tiny lights under the trees, they had come no closer. Flint realized his presence was likely delaying these folk's rescue. Worse, if he stayed with them longer, he might draw the trackers up here. He was the one they were following; he would head back to Winterfort and take them with him.

"Be safe," he murmured. And he thought, *I'm sorry,* but he was too ashamed—of himself, of the sad world he lived in, of the cowardice and cruelty and misguided loyalties of humankind—to speak the words aloud. In the face of the wee folk's silence, he turned away. Under moonlight, he led his trackers home by the most circuitous route he could devise. He was not attacked. He was not stopped, save momentarily at the sentry posts. As he came out of the last cover and headed toward the little door in the fortress wall, whoever had been tailing him melted away into the night. He hammered on the door, and a yawning Brocc let him back into his prison.

CHAPTER FIVE

THE STORM CAME WITH A VENGEANCE. FIRST massing, ink-dark clouds; then spears of lightning and thunderclaps like giants playing drums; lastly, fierce winds and driving rain that made the downpours of earlier in the season seem like gentle showers. Beyond the barred door of the outhouse where we were huddled alongside Snow and the chickens, things were blowing about, crashing, falling.

It was morning, but when I opened the shutters a crack to look out, I saw only whirling dark. Things hurtled past—perhaps branches, perhaps timbers from the ruined house, perhaps birds snatched by the gale from their safe roosts. I fought to get the shutters closed again; Ean came to add his strength. Silva had the little brazier alight and was warming food in a pot. She seemed all orderly control, but as she wielded the ladle, her hands were shaking.

Whisper had required less persuasion than I'd expected to join us inside. He was perched opposite the chickens, keeping a close eye on Ean. I'd explained his presence by saying he was a domesticated owl, kept in order to control the rats.

Silva ladled out her concoction of oatmeal and herbs, and we ate it. We wiped our bowls and set them aside. The storm raged on unabated. There would be no going out; we'd be shut in here until it was over. Ean's presence made this awkward, and not only because of the need to hold our tongues on certain matters. While we were shut inside, our only privy was a bucket in a corner.

There was not much point in trying to talk; the voice of the storm drowned anything below a shout. We sat listening as the time passed, trapped in our small space with a weight of uncertainty. My mind wrestled with one problem after another: Ean, the White Lady, the ritual, the need for me to prove myself before I could move on. Had I been too quick to dismiss the challenge the Lady had set me? Perhaps, if I did not attempt it, I would fail at midsummer.

As the storm blustered outside, I fought a war within myself. If I called one of the Good Folk, it might die as it tried to reach me. If I did not call, I risked losing the final battle because I had not practiced this particular skill. I had come here to complete my training. This was a vital part of that training. On the other hand, the Lady had said something about making my own test.

I lay down on the pallet and closed my eyes. If I was quiet, if I prepared myself, perhaps the answer would come to me. Let Ean and Silva think I was asleep, so there would be no interruptions. I went through the patterns of breathing, as if readying myself for a call, and I opened my mind to the many moods of air. I reached out through the storm, thinking of wind and rain and hail, of cold and terror, of wings scarcely able to beat for the tempest that tore at them. I imagined air at its most powerful, and how easily a small being could be destroyed by what also helped keep it alive.

The White Lady had taught me to single out one sound among many; to be aware of the smallest rustling in a field of wind-tossed grasses, the tiniest footstep of a beetle among the stones. I would not call. For now, I would simply listen.

The shutters creaked. The wind howled around the outhouse. Beyond the door, objects crashed about, thrown hither and thither. Ean said something to Silva, perhaps that he would make a brew.

For some time I lay there, until, unmistakably, I heard a voice amid the tumult. Not words; not anything that would reach the ears of Ean or Silva. A high, high voice, a thin, faint screaming. Oh gods! The tiny folk from the Beehives! One of them was out there in that chaos of wind and rain and lightning. They were as fragile as the long-legged spiders that danced across the surface of ponds in springtime.

My heart galloped; I wanted to leap up and rush out into the storm to find the little one and bring it to shelter. But my long training helped me overcome that impulse, and I stayed immobile, eyes closed, holding on to the sound, holding on to the awareness. I hardly thought of tests and skills. Only that I must help this lost one find its way home.

Carefully, then; with such a frail being I could afford no errors. It was close by, as close as those trees that grew between the farm and the Beehives. But in the dark confusion of the storm, it was too frightened to tell up from down.

I made a picture of the cairns in my mind. The guardian trees; the domed shapes like a circle of wise old crones; the beehive hut that was the wee folk's haven. I thought of the

White Lady's wry voice, her chuckle of amusement. I called, and in my call was the image of a tiny bright being winging its way out from its place of hiding, down the hill to the cairns, and in through the low doorway to the circular chamber. Air holding it up, helping it fly. Drafts in the stone-lined space, setting the little lights of its fellow creatures aflicker. Silva drawing breath and lifting her voice in the ritual prayers, on another, calmer day.

The piercing scream ceased. *Home,* I willed the being, with my thoughts on shelter, rightness, peace. *See, it is not far off. Fly home.* And I sensed that the little one had heeded the call; for a moment I felt the beat of its fragile wings.

Sudden exhaustion came over me, as it so often did after I called. I would not know if the being had reached safety until the weather was calm and I could visit the cairns again. I lay quiet, realizing that I had used the same skill for this call as I would have employed to bring a messenger to me through the storm.

I drifted into an anxious half sleep in which images of Flint came to trouble me: Flint grim-faced in a moonlit forest, Flint carrying something wrapped in a blanket, Flint arguing with a little woman of the Good Folk, not Sage but someone I had never seen before. Waking, I knew in my heart that his burden had been a body; that something dark and terrible had happened. I lay there unmoving, waiting for my heart to slow.

While I'd slept, it seemed the worst of the storm had passed. The wind still moaned, the rain still fell, but beyond the shutters the day was brightening, and I no longer feared that the roof thatch would be ripped away, leaving us exposed to the elements. Silva was on the floor beside Snow, stroking the goat's head and murmuring to her. Ean was on the bench, feet apart, elbows on knees, head down, apparently lost in thought.

"We might be able to go outside soon," I said, realizing I could actually hear myself now. "See what's left of the garden and check on the ducks." I got up and walked over to the window, thinking to risk opening the shutters just a little. As I reached out, lightning flashed anew, its white brilliance visible through every crack and chink. And almost straightaway there was a deafening boom of thunder and a distant, rending crash.

There was only one tree I knew of whose destruction would make such a sound. My eyes met Silva's.

"The cairns," she whispered, and I nodded understanding. Nothing we could do. Only wait until the storm was truly over. Outside, the rain was falling again, a great roaring voice. Snow was quivering, her little eyes wild with fear. The chickens had balled themselves into one tight mass of feathers. Whisper had not moved; he looked half asleep, but I knew better.

It was late in the day before the storm finally died down. The rain had diminished to a series of short, sharp showers; it would be just possible to keep one's feet against the wind. The lowering clouds made it hard to guess how long we had until full dark.

I took my cloak from the peg where it was hanging, wondering how I could explain to Ean that we must go down to the cairns, even if it meant wading through a flood. He came up beside me, reaching to take his own cloak, and I saw something sewn or pinned to the woolen folds, on the inside. The dried-up head of a small thistle. My heart skipped a beat. He was one of us. What else could this mean? I folded back my own cloak, uncovering the embroidered thistle that Eva had sewn on for me before I left Shadowfell. This season, we were all wearing the emblem of rebellion; we would fight and die by it.

"You wear the thistle," I said, staring Ean in the eye.

"As do you."

"Why is that?"

"I might ask you the same."

"Give me a name," I said, "and if it's the right one, I'll tell you."

I saw him take a deep breath. I realized he was feeling exactly the same doubt as I was. One of us would have to take the first step.

"Shadowfell," he said.

"All right." It was hard to be open with him, thistle or no. There had been so many betrayals. "The place you mention . . . It's where I've traveled from. I'm not one of Silva's wise women. I arrived here not long before the community was attacked. I stayed partly so Silva wouldn't be alone, but mostly for my own purposes. Whisper is my guard and companion on the road."

Ean paled as Whisper flew down from his perch, no longer an ordinary owl but part bird, part young man, part something entirely Other.

"Greetings, laddie," Whisper said, fixing his startling eyes on Ean. "You're a man o' the thistle, then. Tell us where you came frae, and why, and dinna hold back. Neryn needs tae know everything."

Ean turned to look at me. When he spoke, his voice was shaking. "Does this mean—"

"Tell your tale," said Whisper, "and be quick about it. There's nae time tae spare."

"Ean," I said, "Silva has a job to do here, something that's so important to her that she isn't prepared to leave this place even when her life is at risk. And I have work to do here as well. You don't need all the details, only that I've been developing my abilities in preparation for . . . the future."

"For midsummer, you mean." Ean gathered himself visibly, taking a deep breath and squaring his shoulders.

"You know about that. How?"

He opened his mouth and closed it again. Looked over his shoulder, then toward the door. I knew exactly how he felt.

"Why are you here, Ean? Tell me the truth, or as much of it as you think safe."

"I didn't know we had a . . . someone like you. Someone who could talk to the Good Folk. That could make all the difference."

"It's not something our leaders want widely known. That information, in the wrong hands, could spell disaster."

He nodded. "I understand."

"You haven't heard it from anyone else? What I am, and that I'm in these parts?"

"No, Neryn. I didn't come looking for you. We didn't know you existed."

"We?"

"The group at Callan Stanes. Part of Shadowfell. Part of the uprising." At the look on my face, he added hastily, "I'm a man of the thistle, Neryn. I know the code of secrecy; I wouldn't speak of this in other company."

"You didn't answer the question. Why did you come here?"

"I was looking for Silva. We . . . we went our separate ways, two years ago. With this change coming—what's planned for midsummer, I mean—I needed to make sure she was safe."

"Neryn." Silva's tone was urgent. "We should go." As the rest of us talked, she had lit two lanterns from the brazier, and had put on her cloak and boots.

"Callan Stanes," mused Whisper. "Would that be on Glenfalloch territory?"

"A few miles from Gormal's stronghold," Ean said. "And you know, I suppose, that Gormal is . . . not unfriendly to our cause. The Stanes—it's an old place, and folk stay away now that the king's forbidden the rites. There's a farm close by, with room for all of us."

"How many?" I asked.

"Twenty-three at last count." There was such pride in his tone that I swallowed my disappointment that there were not more of them.

"Neryn!" Silva was waiting by the door. "We have to go *now*."

"Aye, the lassie speaks true." Whisper gave Ean an assessing look. "Best you dinna come wi' us, laddie. The Beehives, they're a women's place."

"What about you?" Ean challenged.

"Oh, stop it!" Silva opened the door, admitting a blast of cold air. "Bring the other lantern. When we get there, you wait with Whisper while Neryn and I go down to the cairns. And don't waste time arguing."

Outside our place of shelter, debris was strewn everywhere. Trees lay prone, roots torn from the soil; the garden was ruined. The stream had flooded. Water was lapping the burial mound, and pools filled every pocket of the land. My boots soon wore a heavy coating of clinging mud; my cloak failed to keep out the chill. The world was in eerie half darkness; in the distance, flashes of lightning could still be seen as the storm moved on.

The track to the Beehives was blocked by fallen trees; we climbed over the smaller ones and found a way around the others. Where a tiny streamlet had once trickled across the path, now a wide lake lay before us, and we had to scramble a long way upstream before we found a place narrow enough to get over. The corpses of birds lay where the wind had tossed them, broken by that last wild flight.

Before we reached the top of the rise, we saw that the great oak was gone. Silva and I had known it when we heard the sound. But knowing was not the same as seeing the giant uprooted, split to its heart by a lightning bolt there was no withstanding, not even for such an ancient and venerable guardian. Dead. Fallen. And . . .

Silva sucked in her breath. I felt my heart clench into a tight ball. Something else had changed here. I could feel no trace of magic, no tingling sensation across my skin, no sense of wonder. Gone. All gone.

"Laddie," Whisper murmured, "this is where you and I wait. Dinna be lang, Neryn; the walk hame willna be easy in darkness."

I looked at Silva; she looked back at me, white as a ghost. Then, as one, we headed down the hill. The beehive hut had been right in the path of the massive toppling oak. Against such a mighty blow, even the most carefully laid stones could not stand. I had seen at first glance that the hut was ruined; I found myself hoping, nonetheless, that somehow I was wrong. The White Lady was a Guardian. She was like a goddess. How could she . . . ? But the Beehives felt as empty as a tomb. I had called that little one to its death. Silva was murmuring a prayer: "Lady, guard and shield us. Lady, shine your light on us. Lady, sing of hope. . . ."

We stood by the place where there had been an entry; where Silva had placed her ritual offerings and I had crawled in each day to hear the White Lady's voice and receive her wisdom. A jumbled pile of stones lay before us. There was no way in. Silva's song became a sob; she set down the lantern and put her hands over her face.

Be strong, Neryn. I made myself walk around the broken hut. Here and there, sections of the drystone walls stood almost intact. Between those remnants the walls had caved in, leaving the inside exposed. There was no sign of life.

"She's gone," Silva whispered. "I can't feel her at all. It's finished. It's over."

"Don't say that." I reached under my cloak and brought out the drum. "Hold the lantern high, Silva. Yes, that's it— over toward that gap in the stones."

"But—"

"Shh."

I was well practiced in listening now. If there was anything of the Lady left, I would surely hear it. Even with the wind still stirring the grasses; even with Silva so close; even with the broken remnants of the sacred place right before me, making a mockery of my hope.

Silva had never seen me working at the Beehives; she had

never come inside the hut with me or heard me speaking to the Lady. But she was a wise woman, or soon would be, and she stood still and quiet as I listened. The dusk faded to night. The lantern made a glowing circle around the two of us. Up on the rise, Whisper and Ean waited in silence.

Nothing. Not the least stirring of the drum skin, not the slightest sign of movement among the ruins. I might stand here all night in the cold, keeping my companions from their rest, and all because I could not bear to accept the truth. The truth . . . the song of truth . . . I had thought I would never call a Guardian, save at the last extreme. But this would not be calling the Lady, not exactly; I would reach out to any of those tiny beings that might have survived the storm. Besides, if the death of a Guardian was not the last extreme, I did not know what was.

"Silva," I murmured, making the drum vibrate in my hands, "we should sing. Do you know the forbidden song? The song of truth?" She nodded, wide-eyed. "Will you sing it with me?"

Our voices rose together through the drizzling rain and the darkness, across the tumbled stones and out through the circle of leafless elders. I did not sing as well as I had when I had used this same song to rouse the small folk of the Beehives, but I did my best. By the time we reached the third verse, our voices had been joined by two lower ones: up on the rise, Whisper and Ean were singing too.

> White Lady, shield me with your fire;
> Lord of the North, my heart inspire;
> Hag of the Isles, my secrets keep;
> Master of Shadows, guard my sleep.

115

I held up my hand, and the others stopped singing. The drum skin stilled; all was quiet. I thought of the wee folk, as fragile as butterflies, lovely as spring flowers, bright as sunbeams. I remembered their curious dumb show, the high tinkling that was their laughter, the way they had flown down to gather on my shoulders when they thought I needed comfort. I imagined them clustered on the stone shelves in the cairn, or dancing in firefly garlands around the heads of the wise women as they enacted the ritual. I remembered the wry, wise voice of the White Lady.

This call would not be delivered in ringing tones, a summons to war. It would be as light as thistledown in the wind, as subtle as moon shadows.

"If you're there, come out, wee ones," I whispered against the drum skin. "It's safe now. Look, your priestess is here; she is faithful to you. And there are three of us with her, three friends of the White Lady. Your home is ruined; your great tree is fallen. But we will find you a new home, a place where the rite can continue, and we will take you there. I give my solemn promise." I took a breath, then as softly as I could, I sang the next few lines:

> I am the mountain, I am the sky,
> I am the song that will not die,
> I am the heather, I am the sea . . .

The silence drew out until I could hardly bear it. Perhaps I'd been foolish. Long ago, my grandmother had told me one thing that the Good Folk hated was to hear a song or poem unfinished. The likelihood was that if a human singer stopped before the end, a wee voice would pipe up and supply

116

the missing lines. That was probably just a fancy, something Grandmother had invented to amuse me. This, now, was life and death: the loss of a being so old and precious she was part of the very fabric of Alban, the strength and hope that kept us all fighting for what was right. I laid my hand on the drum skin, knowing there would be nothing, knowing I must check anyway before we turned our backs on this place and walked away.

Under my palm the drum skin was vibrating. It was the very slightest of movements, the tiniest sign of life, like the weak pulse of some little forest creature wrenched from its safe place and left to die. I bent my head again, but I could not hear a voice.

"Show me where you are," I breathed. "Can you make a light?"

The skin shuddered and went still. *Don't be dead. Please don't be dead.*

Silva put her hand on my arm, making me start. She said nothing, only pointed down among the broken stones, beyond the circle cast by our lamp. In the shadows, a faint light flickered. Something after all; something to be saved.

I motioned to Silva—*Don't reach in, don't say anything.* That first day, my voice and movements had scared the tiny beings. Now, with the cairn broken apart, the drum might help me speak to them. I whispered against its surface. "You know me. I'm Neryn, the Caller. Will you come out? I will look after you, I promise. Find you somewhere safe. Take you there." At the back of my mind a plan was forming; I hoped I would not make a liar of myself.

Silva sucked in a sharp breath. A tiny hand had appeared on the edge of a broken stone. Another hand followed, then a small form pulled itself up from the darkness. Its wings were torn, its wispy hair stood up in wild disarray; it clung to the stones as if the next raindrop might be enough to dislodge it. This was the wee one who had been full of fun, miming my own probable demise from cold. Now it seemed at the last gasp of exhaustion.

"Come," I whispered against the drum. "Come with me. Bring the others. It is night, and you need shelter."

The fragile being struggled to its feet, a forlorn, defeated scrap. It opened its mouth and sang, or I guessed it did. Its voice was as before, too high for me to make out more than squeaking, but I was in no doubt that it had emerged to provide the last line of the song: *My spirit is forever free.*

"Where are the others?" I murmured, pointing toward the hole from which it had emerged. "Your friends?" I passed the drum to Silva, then tried to show what I meant, making a play of counting on my fingers and raising my brows in question.

The small one shook its head, then shrugged, spreading its arms wide. *Gone. All gone.* It pointed toward its own chest, then held up a minuscule finger. *Only me.* There followed a mime of flying, of being buffeted by powerful forces. The being touched its ear as if listening, indicated me, gestured to the broken hut. *You brought me home.*

One left. One tiny scrap of all that had once been the White Lady, Guardian of the East. How it had survived I did not know, since I had called it home before the tree fell. But here it was, without home or comrades, without any help but us. I heard Tali's voice in my mind: *Get on with it, Neryn. Don't waste time on might-have-beens.* I cupped my hands together, placing them where the little one could reach. "Come," I said. "You can't stay here on your own. Come with us."

A sudden, strange shiver of wind passed through the place of the cairns, stirring every tree, making the lantern flicker, blowing Silva's dark hair across her face. The little one stepped onto my palm and I lifted it, cradling it against my chest. It was as light as thistledown.

"Good," I said softly. "Now we're going home."

We made a bed in the egg basket, lining it with an old, soft cloth. To my surprise, the wee one curled up there and went straight off to sleep. The four of us gathered around the brazier, drinking Silva's herbal brew, and held a council.

Ean had been shocked into silence by what he had seen. Silva was quiet too—the loss at the cairns was a kind of death to her, and I thought she would have liked time alone to grieve, but that was not possible. As for Whisper, he was calm, though somber. He understood the magnitude of what had happened; whether he would agree to my half-formed plan remained to be seen.

As simply as I could, I explained to Ean that the tiny being was vitally important to the participation of the Good Folk in the rebellion, and indeed to the future of Alban.

"I can't explain to you exactly what the wee one is, but it is the last of its kind here; there were more of them before the storm. They've been safe here because of . . . an ancient magic, a protective power maintained by the wise women's rituals. After the fire, after the other women were killed, Silva kept that going by herself."

Ean raised his brows. "What about you?"

"Neryn helped me," Silva said, frowning at him. "But she's not trained in the rituals. And she had her own work to do." When he made to speak, she added, "She's needed for the end, Ean. For midsummer. Don't you listen?"

The show of temper was a good sign; anything was better than the aching sorrow I had seen on her face when she realized the Lady was gone. "I've had my own work here." I kept my tone even. "But now that there is only one of these beings left, that work has changed. My next task must be moving the little one to a place where it can be safe, and where Silva or someone else can continue the appropriate rituals."

"But, Neryn," said Silva, "this was the last place."

"That's what I was told, yes." It was what the Lady herself had believed. "But don't you think if we have faith and hope, and if we take steps to mend what's been broken, we can change that? Maybe we can bring the magic back."

The others stared at me, uncomprehending.

"The sanctuary is gone," Silva said flatly. "The tree has fallen. The Beehives are no more."

"Besides," put in Ean, "Silva can't stay here, not after this. She needs to come south with me. If you have any sense, you'll pack up your things and do the same." He glanced at Whisper. "At least, you will, Neryn."

"Silva," I said, "there is one left. We can't give up hope while one survives, even such a small and fragile one. And maybe it's not the place itself that matters so much as a . . . a meeting of things: time and place, hearts and minds, hope and belief. When all comes together, the magic is born. In my grandmother's time and before, people performed rituals all over Alban, on hilltops and in caves and out in the forest.

120

In their own houses, sometimes. Think about the song we were singing; the magic is present in every part of Alban, if only we look for it. Sometimes it's hard to find. Sometimes it's hidden away. Sometimes we don't have the strength to keep on looking. But it never really dies. It never really goes away."

"Are you saying we should take the little being away from here?" Silva's voice was hushed with shock. "Wouldn't it die?"

"If it's left behind on its ain," said Whisper, "it surely willna survive."

"But, Neryn," protested Silva, "if the wee beings are what you said they are, we can't . . . I mean we shouldn't . . ."

"If we're stopped on the way and anyone sees that thing"—Ean nodded in the general direction of the egg basket with its small occupant—"we'll all be hauled up before the authorities. You know that, I suppose?"

"All too well," I said levelly. "Fortunately, the being is small enough to be easily hidden. I wasn't planning to carry it on my shoulder like a pet bird." I caught myself before I went any further; Ean was only asking the questions I might ask if the situation were reversed. "Ean," I said, "you told me you were living at Callan Stanes. And you said something about ritual. How did that place get its name?" I prayed that my hunch about this was right.

"The Stanes? Well, that's what it is, an old stone circle. Sometimes called the Giants, though there's more giants lying down now than standing tall. All covered over with moss and brambles. Godforsaken sort of spot. Nobody goes there anymore except rabbits and mice and a crow or two."

I saw dawning comprehension on Silva's face, and on

Whisper's. "A stone circle," I said. "And you said the rebel base is at a nearby farm. How near?"

"A short walk. Farther from the stones to the settlement. The Giants are not straightforward to find. There's a tale about them."

"Oh yes?"

Ean's face was rosy in the light from the brazier; his expression softened. "People say the stones move around as they please. The Slow Dance, it's called. Each time you go there, you'll find them in different places. And . . . at certain times of year, at sunrise and at sunset, they say you can see them dancing. You can't watch the stones directly or they'll freeze in place. You have to watch their shadows."

As her brother spoke, Silva's eyes came alight. I felt my own heart beat faster. He had told me exactly what I wanted to hear.

"It's only a story," Ean said, looking at Silva. "But I thought you'd like it."

"Aye," said Whisper. "A pleasing tale. You say naebody visits this place save the wee field creatures? But you tell it as if you ken the spot weel. The brambles and the fallen stanes and all."

Ean cleared his throat. "One or two of us have been there. The folk from the farm, I mean. Cut away some thornbushes, set one of the smaller stones back upright. There's a girl knows some of the old prayers. The folk from the settlement don't go there, and we haven't cleared the path."

Now all eyes were on him.

"It felt right," he said. "That is, I thought it was what Silva would have wanted me to do. Back then, I didn't know where she was. I didn't know if she was dead or alive."

Silva put her arms around him. "You did well," she murmured. "You did a good thing." He gave her an awkward hug in return.

"It's plain we need to move on after what's happened," I said. "Silva's reason for staying here is gone. Besides, as Ean pointed out, it's far more likely folk will come out this way to have a look as the weather improves. What's to stop them reporting back to the local authorities? We should go—all of us—to this farm near Callan Stanes. It sounds as safe for you as anywhere can be right now, Silva. The wee one might survive at the stone circle if you're there to conduct the rituals. The girl Ean mentioned, the one who's been offering prayers, might be able to help you."

"And you?" asked Ean, looking at me.

"Whisper and I were planning to link up with your group when we left here anyway. Once we've spoken with your leaders, we'll move on to the south."

"Just one thing," Ean said.

"What?"

"Whisper," Ean said. "And you. You talk about moving away from here because of folk reporting to the authorities. But you intend to travel together. That's a sure way of getting yourself turned over to the Enforcers."

"Are you volunteering to take his place as my protector?"

A flush rose to his cheeks. "You want me to put it more bluntly? I will, then. I came here to find Silva and bring her back across the border. I wasn't expecting you, and I certainly wasn't expecting *you*." He nodded toward Whisper. "You've helped Silva, and I thank you for that. I do understand that you need to come to Callan Stanes and talk to my group, if not now, then sometime soon. But traveling with you and him together isn't going to make Silva safer. The opposite, more likely."

"Neryn gaes wi' me," Whisper said. His tone made it clear there would be no further discussion.

"And Silva must go with me," I added. "Because I'm the one who has promised to take the little being to Callan Stanes, and her prayers are needed to keep it alive on the way. So, like it or not, if you want to escort Silva to the south, you'll be traveling with all of us." Seeing his jaw tighten, I added, "Ean, arguing among ourselves is a waste of precious time. We're all on the same side. We have a shared purpose. You know the way to Callan Stanes. We need you to show us."

"How soon were you thinking of heading off?" Ean was still frowning, but it seemed he had accepted my argument. "Erevan's got patrols in place all the way to the border. When I came the other way, I saw king's men on the roads too. There's far more activity than last winter. Almost as if they're expecting trouble."

Let that not mean the king had somehow got word of the impending challenge to his authority. One of the great strengths of our plan was its secrecy. But as the day drew closer, and the word spread more widely among both human folk and Good Folk, the risk increased that someone would break their silence. "We'll wait for the weather to clear, of course. And Silva will need to do something about the animals." Silva was holding a chicken on her knee now, gentling it as if it were a cat or little dog; her thin fingers moved steadily, stroking the tawny feathers. "Perhaps there's some way of getting them to a nearby farm without being too obvious."

"We could take Snow with us," Silva said.

"What?" Ean was incredulous.

"She can walk to Callan Stanes, if we don't go too fast for her. If we had her, we'd pass more easily as ordinary farm folk."

"Ordinary farm folk with a walking, talking owl."

"Did you no' spot the wings, then, laddie?"

It took a moment before Ean realized this was a joke. He drew a breath, then visibly relaxed. "I'm sorry," he said. "It's been . . . It's been hard. Of course you would fly, and I've seen how you can change your appearance, become more . . . unobtrusive. I've been discourteous."

"We're all slow to trust," I said. "With good reason. Now, are we agreed that we'll head for Callan Stanes together? That we'll go as soon as the weather improves?"

Everyone nodded assent.

"Good. Time enough to talk about goats in the morning. We'd best try to get some sleep." I moved to peer into the egg basket, which we'd set in one corner on a stool. All I could see of the tiny being was its wispy white hair; it was tucked in deep. With a careful finger I lifted the bedding so I could check that it was breathing. "I have no idea what they eat, or even if they do eat," I murmured to Silva, who had come up alongside me.

"It's so little," she whispered. "It's hard to believe that something so tiny . . ."

"Mm."

"I suppose we'll find out how to look after it as we go," said Silva. It was the voice of the girl who had tended to her garden and her animals and, eventually, Whisper and me as well, without ever questioning whether she could manage it all.

"I suppose we will." Indeed, we must. My instincts told me how important this was; in its own way, it was as vital as the challenge to Keldec. If a Guardian perished, the end of Alban was surely nigh. But I would not talk about that now. Ean would be useful for getting us to Callan Stanes, but his part in my journey went that far and no farther. He would therefore be told what he needed to know and no more. *Good, Neryn,* I imagined Tali saying. *You're starting to think like a warrior.*

CHAPTER SIX

ONE STORM ENDED ONLY TO BE FOLLOWED BY another and then another, and we could not leave. We were wet, tired, and ill tempered. Ean did more than his share of work around the place, tackling the heavy jobs that were beyond Silva and me. But his anxiety made him sharp, and when he could not throw his pent-up energy into hard physical activity, he was either snappish and quarrelsome or silent and brooding. His presence did nothing to lighten my own mood. Several times Whisper had seen some of the local men on the track between the settlement and the Beehives, and it seemed only a matter of time before we had visitors.

Ean had been with us for nearly a full turning of the moon before winter began to release its grip on the land. It was still bitterly cold. There were more wet days than dry, and the mud was everywhere. But little by little the sun began to show its face, and the first tentative shoots of bluebell and snowdrop appeared under the trees, and at last it seemed we would soon be on our way.

From the dwindling stores, Silva prepared hard bread and other supplies for our journey. She packed a healer's bag containing salves and lotions, bandages and useful implements—between us, she and I had enough skill to tend to all but the most serious ailments and injuries.

The hens were already gone. Ean had suggested, earlier, that if we slaughtered one every few days, we could have good eating while we waited for fine weather. Neither Whisper nor I would have dreamed of suggesting this to Silva. The look on her face had silenced Ean immediately. So, Whisper had flown off to find a suitable place to leave the birds, and had spotted a tiny farmstead where an old couple was eking out a living. It had a chicken run, well fenced, with a small flock in residence, and no rooster. Silva had been quick to raise difficulties: what if the other hens picked on hers, what if the old couple decided her hens would be for eating, not laying, what if they reported the sudden arrival to the authorities? But when the time came to take the birds, by night, to the farmstead and slip them into the enclosure, she cooperated with dry eyes and no further comments. She had accepted that this was the best we could do for her beloved flock.

The next day she was very quiet. But she had something else to keep her busy. The wee one, last remnant of the White Lady, had to be tended to. Since we had no way to discover its name, we were calling it Piper.

Piper did eat and drink. It liked honey water, dried fruit cut very fine, and tiny pieces of cheese. Our supply of cheese was low; there would be no more before we reached the rebels at Callan Stanes, and perhaps not even then. Piper slept in its basket, traveled about on my shoulder or Silva's, and kept its distance from Whisper. Ean's knives did not seem to trouble it. We were fortunate in that. On the way to Callan Stanes, Ean and I might both need to use our weapons.

The burial mound had been damaged by the flood, and one of Ean's first tasks had been to build it up securely. He had carried larger stones to cover it, laying them in a pattern of Silva's devising. At dawn and dusk, Silva took Piper down there and murmured her way through the ritual prayers. If the little one could not understand her human voice, that hardly mattered—she was continuing the wise women's practice, the very thing the White Lady had said kept the last of her alive.

Sometimes I spoke to Piper, using the drum. I told the little one our plan; explained that Callan Stanes was another place of ancient ritual, sacred, quiet, safer now than the Beehives. I said that Silva would stay there, and that I would move on. I whispered my hope that in Piper the White Lady still existed, that in the wee one her great light still burned, and that maybe it could grow strong again.

We were not really sure if Piper was male or female, but I began to think of the small being as a he; his sense of fun suggested a cheeky boy, and his garb was a leafy tunic with openings for his wings, diminutive trousers, and a fine gossamer cape. He accepted my explanations with unusual gravity, bowing with arms crossed on his chest, and sometimes replied in dumb show, which he seemed to enjoy. Could this be part of the White Lady and at the same time a lad? Perhaps, so long ago that it was beyond human remembering, all the little beings together had made up Lord and Lady, man and woman, male and female.

Snow was still with us; none of us had managed to persuade Silva to part with her. There was, in fact, a strong argument for taking the goat south when we left. Snow was well known in the district of the Beehives. She'd been mated several times with other farmers' billy goats, and her offspring had fetched good prices at the market. Her sudden appearance on someone's farm would surely call attention to our departure, and while it was possible nobody in the settlement would care one way or another, we wanted to be well away from the Beehives before anyone knew we were gone. All rebel groups kept their existence secret, either by living in a remote location like Shadowfell, or—more usually—by maintaining an ordinary life as well as their covert one. The group at Callan Stanes was on an isolated farm. The last thing Ean would want was to attract notice to them.

We left on a crisp, fair day, just after dawn: two young women, one young man, an owl, and a goat. Ean, Silva, and I had staves and packs; Ean also bore his weaponry, and my knife was in my belt.

The mood was sober. Silva was leaving a beloved home and a place whose sacred rites had been the center of her life. She was also walking away from those who had been her sisters, her family; leaving their grave untended. Ean had his jaw set firm and his gaze straight ahead, but I knew his responsibilities lay heavily on his young shoulders. As for me, I had done as Tali would have wanted, making a plan and acting on it as soon as I could. But inside, I was full of doubt. Could it really be right for me, a human woman, to remove Piper from the Beehives and transport him south on the basis of a hunch? The more I thought about it, the more outrageous it seemed. I longed for Sage to be here, so I could talk to my wise friend and seek her counsel. As for Whisper, he'd had very little to say in recent days, but that was nothing unusual in the company of Ean. Once we'd reached Callan Stanes, I told myself, once we'd seen Silva and Piper to their place of safety and had a word with the Glenfalloch rebels, we'd be on our own again, just Whisper and me. I was surprised to find myself looking forward to that.

At first we made good speed. This was not like crossing country in the Rush valley, or traveling along the wooded hillsides that fringed the chain of lochs running west to east from Darkwater to Brightwater. The danger lay not in precipitous slopes and perilous bridges, or in dense forest and hard-to-find ways, but in the benign nature of the land, gentle grassy hills and valleys, small copses of birch or elder, and broad fields dotted with farm buildings. Faster to cross; much harder to do so unseen. There were long stretches with no cover beyond the drystone walls that marked out the fields, and those were only chest-high. Many folk were about, in the fields, coming in and out of their houses, moving stock or driving carts along the tracks. We were not the only people taking advantage of the fine weather.

At midmorning we paused to rest atop a small hill. A cluster of hawthorns offered some concealment. Drinking water and sharing some of Silva's waybread, we took stock of the land around us.

"There's a settlement to the south there," I said to Ean.

"And twa mair beyond," put in Whisper, who had just returned from a foray southward. His doubts about Ean as a protector had had to be set aside so he could do the invaluable job of spying out likely problems ahead. "When you came the other way, laddie, did you skirt around all of those, or pass through them?"

"It's possible to go around, but only by crossing farmland. When I was on my own, it was easier to avoid attention. I had a story; once or twice I used it."

"I'll be glad if we don't need to go into any settlements," I said. "And even happier if we can reach the camping spot you spoke of before dusk today." The plan was to reach a certain secluded valley and stop there for the night. Ean said it was three days' walk from there to the Glenfalloch border. Once across, we should be safe from Erevan's patrols, though the king's men might be anywhere.

Silva was scraping morsels from a wizened apple and passing them to Piper, who perched on her shoulder. She had made a traveling nest for the little being in a pannier strapped to Snow's back, and we had expected he would want to hide away in there while we moved across country. But Piper was becoming more adventurous the farther we traveled from his home. He would call to us in his high, incomprehensible voice as we walked, and one of us would have to get him out and let him ride on a shoulder or—even more to his liking—on someone's head, clutching their hair for purchase. Silva and I took turns, glad our small companion was apparently happy and healthy. Indeed, the frightened, wretched scrap we had seen crawling out of the broken cairn was quite transformed.

"You'll need to keep him hidden when we move on from here," Ean said now, frowning at Piper and Silva. "And keep him quiet. That squeak of his can only draw attention, and not in a good way."

"I'll explain it to him if I can." I did not like using the drum for this purpose with Ean and Whisper close by, for that way of speaking and listening was surely secret, a wisdom the White Lady had shared with me for her own purposes.

"We gae across the farms, then?" Whisper sounded dubious.

"Better than walking through the settlement. Be ready with the story," I said, knowing the story would take us only so far. "And we leave the talking to Ean, unless there's no other alternative."

I was not entirely happy with this part of the plan. Could Ean tell barefaced lies and get away with it? Our story had him and Silva as the brother and sister they were, and me as their cousin. We lived on Glenfalloch land, working a small farm; our parents were dead. We had traveled north to pick up this fine breeding goat, promised to us by an acquaintance in the Scourie region. My brother, Fergus, was tending to the farm in our absence. Where was the farm? South of Gormal's stronghold by some two days' walk. The story placed our home in a region Ean knew fairly well. If anyone chose to question us about the details, he could furnish them. Silva and I would be shy country girls, leaving our kinsman to do all the talking. As for Whisper, he must remain at a distance unless a calamity befell us. His presence put all of us at greater risk. But at the last extreme, his magic might save us.

Before we moved on, Silva and I went a short distance down the hill to relieve ourselves in privacy. I took the drum; Silva brought Piper. We sat together on the grassy slope, Silva with Piper on her knee, I with the drum held level and my mouth close to the skin.

"Can you hear me?" I whispered. "Can you understand?"

Piper spread his arms, gave a nod.

"Good. We're heading into an area where there may be lots of people. Humankind. Folk who may be suspicious of us, perhaps ask us awkward questions. We must make sure they don't find out about you. Can you stay hidden in the pannier, and not make any noise? Your voice would draw attention quickly, even if all you did was sneeze."

Piper seemed unimpressed by this. He mimed, rapidly, being squashed into a small space, feeling trapped and uncomfortable, being overcome with a desperate need to sneeze, and fainting under the overwhelming pressure of holding it back. He lay prone on Silva's knee for a count of five, then bounced back to his feet and took a bow.

"We will stop and let you out when we can," I murmured. "For meals, and to stretch your legs. I know it's a lot to ask. But it's vital, Piper. Not only to your safety but to ours as well."

He made the shape of a flying bird with his hands, pointing back up the hill, then shrugged with outstretched arms. I could almost hear the Lady's dry voice: *And what about the witawoo? Whaur's his basket?*

"Whisper can pass for an ordinary owl. He'll stay close but not too close, and intervene only if there's no other choice. We're hoping nobody will be interested in the three of us; we look like ordinary folk."

Piper laughed, a high buzzing sound that made the drum skin shiver.

"*Shh,*" hissed Silva and I together.

The wee one clapped his hand over his mouth, his big eyes round with exaggerated horror. I smiled despite myself.

"I mean it," I whispered against the drum. "Completely quiet from the moment you go back into the pannier until we open it to let you out. Promise?"

All I got was a waggle of the wings and a shrug.

"Promise, Piper. Please."

He nodded, tiny features suddenly somber.

"Good." I put the drum aside and got to my feet. "Silva, you go first. I'll hold him for a bit."

But Piper rose from her knee, his wings flashing in the sunlight, and flew away from us. I sucked in a shocked breath; what if we couldn't get him back? My promises would be for nothing. He was so small, a thrush could eat him in one mouthful.

"You go first," Silva said calmly. "I'll keep an eye on him."

"But—"

"He just needs to stretch his wings and enjoy the air. When it's time, he'll come back."

She was right; when we were done, Piper swooped down to land on my shoulder, where he seated himself cross-legged. Back in the pannier, he bedded himself down and shut his eyes. "Be safe," I whispered as I fastened the lid over him, but I did not have the drum, and my words most likely made no more sense to him than the sound of leaves stirring in the breeze.

We were still well short of our planned stopping place when the light began to fade. We had bypassed the first settlement with no trouble, exchanging a nod or a word with other folk on the paths, but keeping ourselves to ourselves. We were plainly dressed; we matched our story.

It was Snow's exhaustion that made us camp where we did, on the bank of a stream not far from a stone wall marking a farmer's field. Within the field there were cows; Snow answered their plaintive calls with her own distinctive cry. Piper had kept quiet, as requested. A goat, especially a hungry and footsore goat, was not so easily silenced.

"She can't go any farther today," Silva said. "We have to stop here."

Ean said nothing, nor did I. It was less than ideal: too close to several farmhouses, too exposed to the eyes of passersby, too open to be easily defended. But we had seen none of Erevan's fighters on the road, nor any Enforcers. With luck the local farmer would be behind closed doors by this hour. By the time he emerged in the morning, we would be gone.

The sun went down and the cold crept in on us, a deep chill that felt almost malevolent. In the fading light we collected wood, made a rudimentary hearth from stones, and built a small fire. A risk, maybe, but I was not prepared to face the alternative, which was to die of cold before we'd even reached the border.

For once, Ean did not argue, but helped with the fire and shared out rations. Later, as Silva settled to sleep snuggled against the goat, he spoke to me in an undertone. "Neryn?"

"Mm?"

"Promise me you'll get her there safely."

"What?"

"Silva. Promise that if anything happens to me, you'll see she gets to the others."

I stared at him. The firelight flickered across his face; he looked deadly serious. I opened my mouth to say something, but before I could utter a word, Whisper flew across from the stone wall and landed abruptly between us.

"Dinna ask Neryn any such thing, laddie," he said. "Her ain safety comes first; there's nae arguing wi' that. If we dinna hae her, the rebellion's doomed."

Ean stared at him. "Doomed? That's a strong word."

"Ean," I said, "we're all traveling together. We all face the same risks. If something happened to you, of course we'd try to keep Silva safe. But the only promise anyone can make is to do their best."

Now Ean was eyeing me narrowly. "What does he mean, doomed?"

"I hae ears o' my ain, laddie, and a tongue tae answer wi'. Neryn's close tae the leaders o' this whole endeavor. Everyone has a part tae play, but hers is a part naebody else can take. And I'm her guard; my job is keeping her alive. I canna put it mair plainly."

After a pause, Ean spoke again. "It's to do with this, isn't it? You and him, traveling together. And that little creature, Piper. Your . . . gift. Your affinity with them."

"How long have you been with the rebels?" I asked him bluntly.

"Since autumn."

"You're new to it, then."

His jaw tightened. "I'm not a child. I can play my part."

When Whisper began to speak, I motioned him quiet. "I know that, Ean, and I respect you for it. One thing I learned early, and never forget: what a person doesn't know can't be beaten out of them. We share only what's necessary as a matter of strategy. We don't ask personal questions and we don't offer confidences. You've been careful; that's good. I have to be careful too." I stared into the little fire, watching the flames dance. "It doesn't get easier," I said. "We're all torn between our personal loyalties and the cause. Even those who are older and have been doing this for years." Flint, kneeling by another Enforcer slain in battle, ashen-faced. Tali, wrapped tight around her pain after Regan was killed. The terrible tale of Andra and her brother. "But Whisper is right about me. Like it or not, I'm indispensable to the cause. Nobody can take my place."

"So if you had to sacrifice Silva to save yourself, you would." His voice was flat.

"Let's hope I never have to make that decision. Now, I suggest we try to get some sleep. It'll be an early start tomorrow."

On the third day we ran into trouble. The weather had stayed fair, and the border was so close we could almost smell it. We had made up the time lost on that first day, and were hoping to be on Glenfalloch land by nightfall. Our spirits were high; even Snow was walking with a spring in her step.

Perhaps we relaxed our guard a little; maybe we were just unlucky. Whisper had flown ahead as usual, and returned to warn us that there was a checkpoint across the track, and men in Erevan's colors questioning travelers. We took evasive action, heading off across a field housing a small flock of sheep. It was necessary to open a gate to get Snow through, and then to do some pushing and shoving, as she seemed not to like the look of the sheep at all. I seized the opportunity to lift the lid of the pannier and check on Piper. He was holding on like grim death, and made a shrill protest the moment he saw me.

"Shh," I warned, putting a finger against my lips. I closed the lid and made sure the strap was done up.

The sheep announced our presence by scattering with loud bleats of panic. We got through the gate on the far side, beyond which lay a narrow pathway between high banks. Since there was no other choice, we clambered down and headed on. Nobody spoke. When Snow was startled by a shadow, Silva hauled her on with less than her usual gentleness.

We rounded a corner, the pathway opened up, and there was a farm shed. Two men came walking out of it, with swords at their belts and purposeful looks on their faces. Whisper, who had been flying close by us, veered off to the south and out of sight.

"Halt!"

We obeyed.

"You!" The taller of the men addressed Ean. "State your name and purpose!"

At least they were not king's men. Maybe they'd just check us and send us on our way.

"Gruan, son of Arden. Been up north to collect the goat; heading home."

"And these women?"

"My sister. My cousin." Ean was doing well, his tone calm, his stance relaxed.

"Names?"

"Lia. Calla."

"Must be a difficult sort of goat if it needs three keepers."

"A good breeder. Valuable."

The man looked Snow up and down. "Mm-hm."

"Goatherd, are you, then?" asked the shorter man.

"I've my own smallholding. With my cousins."

"Oh yes?"

Ean stood quiet. He met the fellow's stare.

"You girls haven't got much to say for yourselves," the taller man said, and now both of them were giving us a look up and down, the same way they had sized up Snow.

Ean's hand moved very slightly toward the hilt of his knife, and they saw it.

"Fighter, are you?"

"I try to keep out of trouble," Ean said. I heard the edge in his voice. "My weapons are to defend myself and my family, that's all."

"Weapons. Knife and what else?" The taller man's whole demeanor had changed. A chill went up my spine. This was why they'd stopped us. They wanted a fight.

"Knife. Staff. Bare hands. Only if I have to. All we want is to get on home with the goat. My sister's tired. We've been walking a while."

"Your sister can sit down over there and take a rest. The other girl too." He motioned to the side of the track, by the hut, where there was a patch of grass. "I'm not interested in them." He whistled, and two more men came out of the hut, striding toward us with purpose. My stomach clenched tight. Whatever this was, it didn't look good.

"Take the goat," the man said.

Silva opened her mouth to protest and shut it again as I

dug her sharply in the ribs. We had to keep calm, whatever happened. Where was Whisper? Could he see us?

The newcomers ripped Snow's leading rope from Silva's hand; she could not suppress a sound of shock.

"Give it up, little lady," one man said. "We've got authority to take what we need. King's orders." With that, they led Snow away. She disappeared, pannier and all, behind the hut. I wrapped my hand around Silva's; she was shaking.

"Right, now," said the taller of Ean's inquisitors. "Let's see what you're made of. Staves first, I think, and you can shape up to my friend here; he's more of a height with you."

"I've no wish to fight you," Ean said, shifting his grip on his staff. "We just want to get home with the goat. Folk are expecting us."

"It's not up to you, laddie." Swift as a diving hawk, the shorter man swung his staff around, aiming straight for Ean's head. Ean's own staff came up to parry the blow. It seemed there was no choice but to fight.

Silva was holding back sobs; I could only clutch her hand and hope this was no more than a couple of guards amusing themselves before letting us go on our way. Perhaps they'd bring Snow back when they were done. Perhaps they wouldn't search the pannier. Perhaps, perhaps . . .

"Piper," whispered Silva, her eyes brimming with tears. A moment later there was a gurgling bleat from behind the hut, abruptly cut off. The blood drained from her face.

I tightened my grip on her hand and gave the smallest shake of my head. *Don't say anything. Don't do anything.* If Snow was gone, she was gone. Protests of outrage would not bring her back. Besides, there were four of them. Of us three, only one was a fighter. I could not use my gift, not here with so many eyes on us. *You're our secret weapon, Neryn,* Tali said in my mind. *Put your own safety first.*

They fought with staves, then with knives, then with bare fists. Two things became apparent. First, Ean was good at this; Tali would have recruited him on the spot. Second, this was no impulsive act by the guards, carried out purely for their own entertainment. They were testing Ean. First one and then the other took him on, stretching him hard but always holding back at a certain point, as if to avoid doing him any real injury. They were adult men, well trained and well disciplined; this was the kind of bout the new recruits at Shadowfell undertook time after time in the practice yard, earning their place among Regan's Rebels. Why would these guards bother to put a passing farmer through his paces?

The fight ended; the guards stepped away. Ean bent over, hands on knees, getting his breath back. He had a few bruises; so did both the others.

"You sure you're a goat farmer, lad?"

"My cousin's a fighter; he taught me." Ean gasped in a breath. "Can we be going now?"

"As to that . . ." Without any apparent signal, the two other men reappeared from behind the hut, moving in so that our exit was blocked. One of them had blood on his hands. Silva stood rigid beside me; I sensed she was trying not to be sick. "Your kinswomen here can be on their way. You, we'll be needing to keep a while longer."

"A while? How long? And why?" Ean glanced at us, looked quickly away. He must know, as I did, that making a bolt for it would be pointless. Silva put her balled fist up against her mouth.

"Long enough so your womenfolk shouldn't bother waiting around for you."

"Why are you treating Gruan like this?" It wasn't hard to make my voice sound shaky and frightened. "He hasn't done anything wrong. And what about our goat?"

"The goat's been confiscated. There are hungry men to feed and supplies are short. As for your kinsman here, we're offering him an opportunity. A rare one. We're recruiting your Gruan for a brand-new venture. King's special forces. If he does well, he'll be richly rewarded. If he fails, he goes back to the goat farm. But you won't fail, young fellow, will you? Not with these two lovely ladies depending on you." He ran his eyes over us again, and now there was a different look in them, one I did not like at all. Had that been a threat? "Come on, then, lad. There's a couple of king's men over at the other checkpoint who'll be wanting a word with you."

I saw Ean consider putting up a fight and deciding it would only make the situation worse. "Don't wait for me," he said, squaring his shoulders. "Head on home. I'll come when I can."

King's special forces. What in Black Crow's name was that? What kind of special forces could be made up of young men gathered at random on the road?

I picked up Ean's pack and passed it to him. "Safe journey," I said, doing my best to sound cheerful and confident. "We'll see you back at the farm. Come on, Lia."

"You killed my goat," Silva whispered, her eyes brimming with tears. "You killed Snow."

My heart ached for her, and for Ean, and for all those caught up in the wretched place Alban was today. "We have to go, Lia. Take my arm, here."

"Want your basket back?" inquired one of the men.

My heart thudded. "Yes, please," I said.

He went back behind the hut and returned with the pannier, bloodstained and gaping open. He tossed it at me, and I managed to catch it. If, by some unlikely chance, Piper was still in there, he must be clinging like a limpet.

"Thank you," I forced myself to say. "Gruan, good luck."

Silva gave Ean one anguished look before two of the men seized his arms and took him off. One of the others made a curt gesture, waving us on along the track.

"Come on." I set off briskly, almost dragging her with me. "Quick," I muttered when we were out of earshot, "before they change their minds." As we walked, I checked the pannier, trying not to be too obvious in case we were still being watched. Snow's blood was everywhere, and there was a strange hole in the wickerwork, as if it had been burned. Piper was gone.

"Piper," Silva gasped. "Ean . . ."

"Keep walking. There's nothing we can do right now." I knew just how she felt: as if she were being torn in two. It was so wrong to leave them, so wrong to step back and abandon them to their fate, when we should be . . . what? We could not have rescued Ean. If I had used my canny skill, or if Whisper had intervened of his own accord, the whole mission would have been in jeopardy. As for fighting our way out, Ean had understood straightaway, as perhaps Silva had not, that he had no chance of prevailing against such odds. He'd have to go along with whatever they had in store for him and try to escape later.

"Snow." Silva spoke on a wrenching sob. "They killed Snow."

"Shh," I whispered. "If the Lady has a good place for goats, be sure Snow's there munching on sweet grass. Try to think of that." Sudden tears sprang to my eyes, startling me. Snow was a small loss in the pattern of things, an innocent victim of the times. But there were so many losses. We all bore our share of wounds, the ones that marked our bodies and the ones we carried inside where nobody could see. It could be hard, so hard, to keep sight of the goal. "Ean was very brave," I murmured. He had been braver than Silva probably realized, choosing compliance so she and I could make a clean escape. He had shown the strength of a true rebel.

We reached a fork in the path and took a side track southward. There was a little wood not far off, birches and beeches still naked from the winter; it seemed a good spot to wait for Whisper. As we drew near, he flew over us, winging toward the trees, and relief flooded through me.

By a trickling stream, under the half concealment of the bare trees, we told him our story and heard his.

"There are riders everywhere," Whisper said. "Men in Erevan's colors. Knocking on doors, stopping folk on the road or in the fields. Gathering men. Fit young men. I've seen Enforcers in the next settlement and on the road too. I canna tell you what they're aboot, only that it looks well planned."

"One of the men we encountered mentioned the king's special forces; said he was recruiting Ean for that."

"Mebbe this is the start o' something new," Whisper said

grimly. "The fact is, we canna help the lad. We should be on our way before there's mair o' them on the roads."

"But Piper," protested Silva. "We can't leave him behind."

Piper, last piece of the White Lady. I had promised to get him to safety. If he perished, she was gone, and with her, part of Alban's spirit. And was not that, in truth, what the rebellion was all about?

"We canna gae back," said Whisper quietly. "But you could ca' the wee fellow, Neryn. Risky, I ken, wi' sae many folk close by; but Piper's sma'. What's ane wee grasshopper or butterfly crossing a field?"

Ane bite for a witawoo. I heard the wry voice as if the Lady were right beside me.

"You'd want tae be quick," Whisper said. "The sooner we're awa' frae these parts, the better." Then, to Silva, "Come on, lassie, let's we twa move awa' a bit, give Neryn some room."

The drum; I should use the drum, or Piper would not be able to understand the call. But no. The drum only worked if we were both close to the vibrating skin. Piper might be anywhere. He might already have perished, trampled underfoot without a thought, or crushed and broken as the pannier was ripped from the goat's back. Or, if he still lived, he might even now be crawling through the long grass with damaged wings, or flying blindly about, dazed and distressed.

Stop it, Neryn. Stop thinking the worst. Though this was bad enough, with Ean taken and Piper lost. *Stop it. You are a Caller.*

I knew how to do this. Piper was a being of air, part of the White Lady. The White Lady had taught me the many moods of air; she had taught me to shape the call to the circumstances. There were Enforcers as near as the next checkpoint; there were armed men on the roads. And Piper could not understand my speech anyway. Like the call I had made back at the Beehives, in the storm, this must be silent.

If I had been a mage, I would have conjured up a breeze to waft the wee one safely to me. But I had no magic of my own. I must find the magic of air; I must use its strength for the call. I shut my eyes and thought of the wondrous moment when the small, bright beings had swarmed around the heads of the wise women, crowning each with light. I made myself an image of Piper and the others in the cairn, seated on my arms and shoulders and in my lap; I remembered the wry, wise voice of the Lady. I breathed, using the slow patterns the Hag had taught me. I set aside Ean, the Enforcers, Silva, the long walk still to be completed before we would reach the safety of Callan Stanes.

I thought of an easterly breeze; felt its cool fingers brushing the skin of my cheek. The breeze brought the distinctive odor of sheep, the fresh scent of grass, the smell of smoke. I imagined Piper's tiny, bright form, his beady eyes, his delicate wings. He was the last one. If we lost him, we lost something irreplaceable.

I thought of the Guardians, and how they were part of the very fabric of Alban. Take one away, and all would surely fall. The White Lady was wind and storm. She was the hoot of an owl, the howl of a wolf, the scream of a dying man, the hum of a mother singing her babe to sleep. She was breath. She was life.

I shaped words with my lips, but did not speak them

aloud. I pictured Piper winging his way toward me, crossing the fields of grazing sheep, the drystone walls, the farmhouses and barns. The armed men on the tracks, the Enforcers in their masks and black cloaks. Evading the keen eye and sudden talons of the hawk. The call went out without a sound. *Fly safe. Fly true. Fly home.*

I opened my eyes; trees and rocks swirled around me. My knees gave way and I collapsed onto the ground. I had done my best.

"Neryn!" Silva's voice as she ran over to me. "Are you all right?"

Before I could find my voice, a shrill sound split the air, and a moment later Piper flew out of nowhere to crash into my chest, where he clung, quivering. My ears rang with his shrieks. Silva knelt beside me; Whisper hovered close. Still the screams went on, loud enough to alert every farmer for five miles around.

"Hush," said Silva. "Piper, you're safe now. Shh!"

The drum, where was the drum . . . ? Gods, I was so tired. I cupped my hands around Piper's shaking form. Was he hurt? There was blood on his little tunic and on his hands. But perhaps it was Snow's.

"Here," Silva said. She held out the drum, level, ready.

I whispered across its surface, though how Piper would hear me through the piercing sound of his own voice, I did not know. "Hush, little one. You're safe now. You found us. Hush." I went on in this mode for a while, holding him close to my body, until his cries died down to shuddering gasps. This, I thought, was not only the shock and terror of the goat's violent death and of being lost. If Piper was anything, he was resilient. There was something more here. "Show us," I breathed against the drum skin, heedless now of Silva and Whisper watching me. "Show us what is troubling you."

He tried, miming the goat standing uncomplaining on her rope, then sweeping his hand, an imaginary knife clutched in it, across his own throat. Then a sequence of movements suggesting being trapped, fighting to find a way out. A gesture I could not interpret, a complex movement of the hands almost like the casting of a spell. Then he clutched his head with both hands and opened his mouth in another scream, this one mercifully silent. He pointed one way, then the opposite way, then toward his head again, using both hands. He finished his performance by crouching down on my palm and wrapping his arms over his head.

"You're safe," I whispered again. He was upset by Snow's death and he had a monstrous headache, that much I understood. That was not all of it, I was sure, but I would not push him further. And we had to move on.

"Thank you, Silva," I said, struggling to my feet. I felt as weary as if I had been running all day. Calling might seem to other folk to be merely a matter of standing still and concentrating, but it drained both body and spirit. "I won't use the drum anymore now. We must go. Can you take him in your pocket?"

Without speaking, Silva reached out for the little being and placed him carefully in the pouch at her belt. She untied her kerchief and tucked it in after him.

"Neryn," said Whisper. His tone chilled me; it was full of trouble.

"What is it?"

"The wee fellow isna alane wi' his sore heid. There's a . . . an odd feeling, a kind o' pull in the air. Setting my ain heid all a-scramble."

I felt nothing at all. "What do you think it is? Some kind of magic?"

"I dinna ken. When we move on, mebbe it will fade."

"Without Ean," said Silva, "we don't know the way to Callan Stanes."

"Once we're over the border, Whisper can fly ahead and find it for us."

"Leaving you wi' nae guard?" protested Whisper. "That wasna the arrangement we made, back at Shadowfell."

"Silva and I will manage. We'll have to."

Farther south there were just as many folk on the roads, and we had to dive into the bushes once to avoid being seen by a group of Enforcers riding past. My heart did not slow until they were well out of sight. We skirted another village and saw, at a distance, a group of men being addressed by a fellow in Erevan's colors.

Later in the day, as we passed by a farm, a woman feeding chickens in the yard offered us freshly baked bread. I accepted, giving her two coppers from my small supply.

"Thank you," she said, slipping them into her pouch. "It's hard with the lads gone. Every bit helps."

"The lads—your sons?"

"Aye, three of them, all gone off with the chieftain's men. An opportunity, the fellow said." She pursed her lips. "They'd need to come home with a full purse to make it worthwhile. Tending the place on my own isn't easy."

"Maybe it's not for long," I said, trying not to sound too inquisitive.

"The fellows that came for them, they weren't saying much. I'm hoping the boys will be back before summer. Special forces, that was what the fellow called it. Sounded like fighting."

"Do your sons have fighting skills, then?" I asked the woman.

"I raised them to be farmers, not fighters. But they're strong, the three of them. Big, sturdy lads. Nobody who knows them would dare speak to their mother the wrong way." There was a weary pride in her voice.

"I hope they'll be back soon, safe and sound. Now we'd best be moving on. Thank you again for the bread; it smells wonderful."

"I baked more than I can eat on my own." She gave a crooked smile. "I forget, sometimes, that they're gone. Big boys, big appetites. Travel safe."

We crossed the border onto Glenfalloch land. The terrain became hilly, with more vegetation and therefore better cover. From atop a rise I thought I glimpsed a fortress tower, perhaps the stronghold of the regional chieftain, Gormal, whom we knew to be a supporter of the rebel movement. Ean had said Callan Stanes was not far inland from that place.

With the goal in sight, we took even greater care, keeping right off any major tracks. Being over the border did not mean everyone we met would be a friend. The king's men visited all parts of Alban; they had eyes and ears everywhere. Besides, Silva and I were two young women traveling ostensibly alone, with no men to guard us. Neither of us was of strapping build. Whisper's concern was justified. When he was not close by, we were vulnerable.

We had another problem: Piper. Since the day of Snow's death and Ean's departure, the little one had been restless. He was hardly sleeping, and he often clutched his head with both hands as if the pain were a monster threatening to eat its way out. Silva tended to him as best she could, but the need to keep on walking meant Piper was confined to her pouch for long periods of the day. We'd be going along quietly when he would suddenly shriek, making us both jump. Or he would break into plaintive squeaks that sounded like sobbing. This was perilous for all of us, for his voice was penetrating and strange. It could not be explained away as a mouse or a little bird or a strange insect.

Whenever we stopped to rest, I spoke to him, using the drum, reminding him how important it was that he keep quiet, asking him to show me again what was wrong. He tried, repeating the same sequence of gestures, but I could not understand. Something was making his head hurt, something that came from two directions at once. Beyond that, I could not make sense of it. Whisper too was disturbed. His head felt odd, he said; aching and confused. But he assured me he was well enough to get us safely to the rebel base.

We reached a place that offered good cover, on a hill forested with beech trees showing their first spring green. The only path forward was up over the top, where the terrain became open and rocky. Before we went on, Whisper said, he would fly ahead and search out a path all the way to Callan Stanes.

He left early. Silva and I refilled our waterskins from a nearby stream, then rested in the shade of the trees, taking turns to stay alert for trouble. Piper dozed on Silva's knee. The sun moved higher; the day warmed. I dreamed of the farmhouse Ean had spoken of, and how good it would be to eat a hot meal and sleep under proper shelter, even if it was only for a few nights. Once we'd delivered Silva and Piper safely there, Whisper and I would be moving on south, seeking out the Master of Shadows.

The Master was full of tricks. I knew that; I'd met him. Perhaps he did have the key to protection against cold iron. But perhaps he wouldn't want to give it to me. Maybe he'd been lying all along and there was no such charm.

Time passed. The sun came close to its midpoint. I'd expected Whisper back long ago. And something else was troubling me.

"He should be here by now." Silva was feeding Piper, dipping her finger in honey water and letting him lick it.

"Mm. I'm going to climb the hill and see if I can catch sight of him. You stay here with Piper."

"Neryn."

"Yes?"

"Can you smell smoke?"

I had been able to smell it for a while. "I'll go up and have a look," I said, keeping my voice calm. My mind was already racing ahead, and I did not like what it was telling me.

I made my way up the hill. Above the tree cover the air was full of floating ash, and there was a strange haze in the sky. After a challenging climb—Tali would have been proud of me—I reached a level area at the top and looked south.

There was a broad valley before me, lying east to west across our intended path. Smoke lay over that place; down there, something was burning. Some distance beyond the valley, the fortress tower that was our marker came in and out of sight through the haze, like something from a half-remembered dream. My skin prickled; I felt the familiar touch of magic. There was no fire in the valley, but something else, something moving, something out of place. I could not make sense of it. I only knew it terrified me.

I made myself breathe slowly, though my heart was thudding. I called upon the Lady's teaching. *See with the clarity of air.* What was that? It moved like a great river; but it was not water. As it passed, trees fell, rocks crumbled, birds flew up screaming in fright. *Breathe, Neryn. Make sense of this.*

"By the Lady," I murmured to myself. "By the powers of good. By freedom and justice." It was not quite a prayer, not quite a charm. But it steadied me, and I looked with new eyes.

The dark tide was a crowd of folk moving on the valley floor. Marching along, at least a hundred strong. An army. An army not of men but of Good Folk. A trio of imposing warriors led them, beings in form almost human, but far taller than any man could be. Behind them smaller folk moved. Their voices came to me, not raised in the kind of song warriors might use to give them heart on a long march, but moaning, gasping, muttering, wailing as they passed.

A whip cracked; a chain rattled; a staff thumped on unprotected flesh. My heart turned cold. There were Enforcers riding on the margins of the dark uncanny throng, their horses wild-eyed and sweating. The king's men had their blades unsheathed; they were using iron to keep the great flow of beings in order. Even the strangest of the Good Folk, the creatures of smoke and fire, the tiny winged ones and the lumbering stony ones, were held by it. And there, along with the uncanny army, marched young men, row on row of them, their faces white with terror. They were not clad as warriors; there was a leather cap here, a breast-piece or set of gauntlets there, but most had no protection against flame, steam, and the carelessly carried weapons of their uncanny companions. Some of the lads were limping; some wore makeshift bandages. Some were supporting flagging comrades as they walked. A young man fell as I watched, and the tide of beings simply flowed over him.

I stood rooted to the spot as the throng moved eastward along the valley. My mind refused to accept what this must mean. I stayed there until the end of the procession passed below me. Last in line was a group of human folk riding together, with a guard of Enforcers all around. Not prisoners; I did not think so anyway, for at least one of them I recognized. He was surely the confidant I had seen sitting beside Queen Varda at the last midsummer Gathering, whispering in her ear, laughing with her as act after depraved act of cruelty unfolded before us. The other men with him I did not know, but they were clad like courtiers, not common folk. At the very end of the line rode a pair of Enforcers, and . . . oh gods! Between them, dwarfed by the king's men on their horses, was a familiar friend. His big eyes blank, his snowy feathers dappled with red, his feet in their little felt boots moving him forward with the rest, there marched Whisper.

My throat ached with sorrow. My heart bled. I watched until they were out of sight. Where they had marched, the ground was scorched, blackened, ruined. Their passing left a wasteland where surely nothing would ever grow again. I stood motionless, stunned with shock. Good Folk and humankind together. Good Folk and humankind, Good Folk and *Enforcers,* marching side by side as one army. Even Whisper, so strong, so stalwart, had been drawn away from his true purpose. This could mean one thing only. There was another Caller, and he was doing the king's bidding.

CHAPTER SEVEN

"Owen?"

Rohan Death-Blade's voice was held low; at Winterfort, a word incautiously spoken could mean death.

They were in the stables. With Lightning and Fleet in adjacent stalls, the routine of tending to their mounts allowed brief opportunities for private conversation. There was an understanding between them these days, never put into words, but strong for all their reticence.

"Mm?"

Rohan's voice dropped to a whisper. "You're being watched. I don't mean right now, but generally." He glanced over his shoulder. They were the only two men in the stables, save for a couple of grooms over the far side, out of earshot. "Brydian's folk. Perhaps the queen's orders."

"I know."

"Just wanted to warn you. Be careful. We'll keep an eye out."

The brush went still in Flint's hand. "We?"

"Couple of us. It's safe."

Flint turned to meet his companion's eyes. "No, it's not," he said. "You and who else?"

"I won't name names."

He could not press it further. It had come to him over a period of many moons, the realization that Rohan had guessed what he was. It had taken a long time for him to accept that Rohan was sympathetic to the cause, not on a mission to trick him into revealing that he was a spy. The implication that others might be involved shocked him. The more people who knew he was less than perfectly loyal to the king, the more likely it was that someone would be coerced into betraying him.

"It's since the prisoners were released," Rohan said. "No witnesses to what happened afterward, out in the forest. Questions being asked in certain quarters. Be on your guard, that's all I'm saying."

He drew a breath; composed himself. "I'm always on my guard," he said. "As for you, you put yourself at risk every time you warn me."

"I know," said Rohan simply.

Flint's memory showed him the men of Boar Troop, lying in their blood after the ambush near Shadowfell. Chests staved in, bodies hacked, heads crushed into a pulpy mess unrecognizable as part of a man. "You should step back," he murmured.

"Step back," said Rohan, "and it keeps on going." And when Flint, shocked that his comrade would speak out thus, made no reply, Rohan added, "Just know you're not quite on your own."

Flint put a finger to his lips. "No more," he said. Then nodded, as if to say, *Friend*.

Hound and Bull Troops had ridden south as soon as the spring thaw allowed it. With them had traveled the queen's councillor Brydian and the Caller, Esten, along with a party of court officials. Details of their mission had not been made widely known, and after their departure Winterfort had filled with wild speculation about the possibilities. Esten's summoning of the three fey beings and the queen's experimentation with them had fired the court's imagination. Theories on the ensuing expedition ranged from a mass cull of the Good Folk to the raising of an uncanny army. Varda had put a stop to the talk by issuing an edict that anyone caught discussing the matter would be whipped. But everyone had a theory about the mission to the south, and another about what the party might bring home when it returned.

What Flint knew, he shared with no one. The king had told him in confidence, and what he had learned terrified him. The mission was the next step in Keldec's quest to build an army no enemy could resist. The men of Hound and Bull Troops had gone south to gather not only fit young men to swell Keldec's fighting forces, but a body of uncanny folk who would be brought to Winterfort and trained up to stand alongside the human contingent, using their magic as a weapon. Since Esten, the young Caller, was himself from the south, that region was to be visited first. Esten would use his gift to call the uncanny folk in, control them on the way back to Winterfort, then ensure they continued to comply with the king's orders.

It was a plan riddled with flaws, the product of a mind crazed with the desire for power. Keldec believed this force would give him almost limitless might. He was confident that it would allow him to prevail against the most recalcitrant chieftain. The pretender in the north would be annihilated, he'd said, meaning Lannan Long-Arm, whose continuing absence from the annual Gathering had been duly noted and interpreted. More than that: the king would use his new army to cross the borders of Alban and conquer the territories that lay beyond. He would be the greatest ruler not only in the entire history of Alban, but in all the lands of the north.

It had been impossible for Flint to talk to Keldec honestly about his grand venture. Any attempt to point out its weaknesses would have offended the king. It might also have revealed that his loyal Owen knew more than anyone would expect about Callers and the Good Folk. He must not endanger Neryn. He must not draw attention in any way to the rebels' plans for midsummer, or to the links already established between humankind and Alban's uncanny inhabitants. So, while a bright-eyed Keldec enthused about his plans for the future, his most trusted confidant listened quietly and limited his contributions to the occasional "Yes, my lord king."

All the while his mind conjured up possibilities, and every one of them was disastrous. What lay most heavily in his thoughts was that the army Keldec hoped to create, the peerless fighting force made up of human and fey warriors working side by side, was essentially no different from the force Regan's Rebels planned to bring to Summerfort for the Gathering. The fact that one army would fight for power and dominance and the other for freedom and justice seemed almost immaterial; their clash would set a dark stain on the soil of Alban, a blight that would linger for generations. That was not what Regan had planned. It was not what they had worked for, all these years.

But then, was there any such thing as a clean fight? The best one could hope for was that the opponents might be evenly matched, and that in the end honor and compassion would prevail. He remembered the two from Seal Troop who had fought to the death at the last Gathering, as punishment for trivial infringements of the king's rules. It had gone on a long time; too long. One comrade had fallen at last. The king had refused the winner a knife with which to dispatch his vanquished opponent; he'd had to do it with his bare hands. Later, away from the eyes of the crowd, away from everyone, the victor had hanged himself. Keldec's need for total control had lost him not one but two peerless fighters that day. It was then, Flint thought, that he'd begun to see a new look in some of the men's eyes.

He wondered what the Caller thought of the job he was expected to do. At court, the queen and Brydian had kept Esten on a tight rein; nobody had spoken to him beyond a greeting. The lad looked ordinary enough. Indeed, Flint wondered if he would be able to summon the great army Keldec wanted. Bringing those three small folk in to be incarcerated and tortured was one thing; this was a far grander endeavor.

He felt a mad urge to speak plainly to the king and queen, pointing out that the scheme was cruel, misguided, overweening. To spell out the truth—that under Keldec's rule, Alban had already been ruined, and that if this venture went ahead, the kingdom might never recover. He had to check himself, often, as the desire to speak out warred with his long-practiced self-control. At such times he reminded himself that he had sent a message. Against the odds, the little woman of the Good Folk might have passed it on to Sage, so it was possible Tali and the others had received it. Neryn might have been warned. There might be something she could do to avert disaster. By now she must be close to completing her training. Of course, the little woman might have gone to ground, keeping his message to herself. There'd been no reason for her to do him any favors. He was a king's man. His people had shown her the face of human cruelty at its very worst.

You should step back, he had told Rohan, wishing his friend might somehow be protected, stay safe. But there was no stepping back; whatever was coming, it would engulf them all.

The day after I saw the dark army, we moved on toward Callan Stanes. Without a map, without a guide, with our hope in tatters, we made our way down the hill, across the broken and blackened wilderness left by the strange troop's passing, and into the forested area beyond. We spoke little. The shock of losing Whisper and the overwhelming blow of what I had seen had robbed us of easy words.

The task of tending to Piper steadied Silva, and as I watched her feeding him or settling him in the pouch, her face soft and her hands gentle, I realized what it was he had been trying so hard to convey to me with his desperate gestures, what had caused Whisper's headaches and confusion. Torn two ways. *Called* two ways. Piper knew me. He had been drawn out of the ruined cairn by my call; he had shared the road with me and knew me well. But he had also heard that other call, the one powerful enough to bring out a great crowd of Good Folk and coerce them in one direction, flanked by Enforcers. Powerful enough, at closer quarters, to draw in even Whisper, so good, so wise, so strong in magic. Very likely, Piper's being with us still, safe from that other Caller's power, was due not so much to me as to the fact that Piper was part of the White Lady. Tiny and frail-looking as he was, in this test he had proved stronger than Whisper.

After she heard my story, Silva asked me only one question: had her brother been among the men marching? I told her I did not know, had not seen. I thought it more likely Ean would be gathered up in the throng as it moved north, but I did not say that. Her white face told me she had worked it out for herself.

We reached a farm that must have been the one Ean had spoken of, for it was the only dwelling anywhere near the ring of standing stones, which we'd glimpsed from a rise as we approached the area. The farm was guarded; a young man with a pitchfork and a young woman with a staff met us on the track some distance short of the house, barring our way. I showed the thistle embroidered on my cloak; Silva did the same. The guards did not move, but one whistled, and another man walked down from the house. His eyes widened when he saw Silva.

"You got a brother? One who looks a lot like you?"

Silva nodded.

"Works for a fellow called Regan," I said.

The man looked me up and down; turned his attention back to Silva. "Is Ean with you?"

Tears spilled from Silva's eyes; she reached up a hand to scrub them away.

"We have news of him," I said. "We've shown the thistle. Let us in and we'll give you the full story."

"And you are?"

I felt my lips curl in a grim smile. "Another one who works for Regan."

The man nodded. He was broad-shouldered, stocky, strong-looking. Perhaps twenty, perhaps older. Flame-red hair cut short; penetrating green eyes. There was a look of Regan about him.

"This is news you'll want to hear," I said. "Most of it's not good. I hope you'll trust us enough to let us tell it."

At that moment Piper decided to add his voice to the conversation, offering a series of shrill squeaks from the depths of Silva's pouch. The guards, startled, raised their weapons; the red-haired man took a step back.

"Shh!" hissed Silva, peering into the pouch. "Stop it!"

"What in the name of all that's holy is that?" the red-haired man asked.

Piper popped his head up over the edge of the linen, all staring eyes and wild cobweb hair. The woman muttered an oath.

"We're tired," I said, realizing just how exhausted I really was. "Silva and the little one here need rest, and I could do with a brew and somewhere to sit down. We're on our own; we've made sure nobody's following."

The guards lowered their weapons. The red-haired man folded back the collar of his shirt to show the thistle sewn there, crude but immediately recognizable. "I'll take them in," he said to the guards. "Come, this way."

Within the farmhouse and its outbuildings was an orderly community. Their leader, red-haired Foras, had built up the numbers slowly. They knew about Shadowfell; they knew that Regan had died in the course of the rebellion, and that we continued our fight in his name. They knew, in broad terms, what was planned for midsummer. And they knew we had a spy at court, though not his identity.

Their work was not quite like that of the Shadowfell rebels, for Foras's team was not a fighting troop. Their principal work was gathering information and carrying sensitive messages, often for Gormal, chieftain of Glenfalloch. I understood this. The chieftains who supported the rebellion could not afford any slipups, for the first murmur to the king that a certain leader might be breeding dissent would bring the Enforcers down on the traitor immediately.

If I had not seen that army on the march, if I had not known there must be another Caller, I might have been less open with Foras. But everything had changed. Whisper was gone; the old plan was in tatters. I had barely enough time to find the Master of Shadows, undergo further training, and get to Summerfort for the Gathering as it was. The looming disaster of a second Caller, the horror of that captive army, could not be set aside while I did so.

I knew what Tali's solution would be. She'd say the king's Caller must be eliminated. Whoever performed that act would pay for it with his life. The rebel code was harsh; it had to be, or we could not have survived for so long. If Tali ordered an assassination, Flint would carry it out. Of that I had no doubt. But it felt wrong to me, deeply wrong, and not only because Flint was dear to my heart. I could not think about that other Caller without seeing myself in his shoes, my gift twisted and warped by the king's will, my good intentions forced askew and used to make the innocent suffer. Perhaps that Caller was not evil in himself. Perhaps he was only another victim of Keldec's tyranny. Silva was too tired to attend any sort of council. A tall girl with fair plaits came forward, introduced herself as Creia, and led her away to rest. Piper had fallen mercifully quiet. Perhaps he sensed how close we were to the standing stones, another place of ancient spirit. Perhaps the uncanny army had traveled far enough away so he no longer heard the other call.

I sat with Foras and a small group of others in the farm kitchen, where I was given food and drink and time to finish both before I told my story. When I was ready, I gave them an honest accounting. I explained who I was and what I was, and discovered that they had already heard of me, thanks to a strange birdlike messenger who had visited them earlier in the season. They had an idea of the part I was to play at the Gathering. If I'd known that before I saw the fey army marching under duress, it would have troubled me. Now I was simply glad that it made my explanations shorter. I told them about Ean; I told them the king's men were gathering local lads and taking them away under the pretext of offering an opportunity. I told them what I had seen on the way here and what it implied.

"By all that's holy," breathed Foras. "Reports have been coming in for a while—strange fires, odd folk about, increased numbers of Enforcers in the region. We've had a few theories about what it might mean, but this . . . It bodes ill for midsummer, doesn't it? Or do I not fully understand your role in that?"

"If I go ahead with what's been planned and if nothing is done about this other Caller, we could have two armies made up of both human and fey folk facing each other at the Gathering. How can we call our allies to fight their own kind?"

Murmurs around the table. Nobody made comment.

"And there's another thing. It seems that when there are two Callers using their skill, the Good Folk may be open to both calls at the same time. I believe that Piper, the small creature you heard squeaking before, could feel that other Caller commanding the folk in the valley. And he could feel my presence too; I need not actually call to draw the Good Folk to me. It made Piper confused and distressed. I think it caused him severe pain. And our fey companion, Whisper . . . He was taken from us." I shut my eyes; the memory was like a fist to the gut. "He marched away with them. Whisper was my guard. He was strong in magic. That doesn't augur well for the future."

"And you know nothing about this other Caller?"

"Only that he or she must be working for Keldec."

Foras looked me in the eye. "What do you need from us?" he asked quietly.

Gods, it was good to be back among friends. These folk were like the people of Shadowfell, calm, capable, strong. Quick to understand. Which was just as well, because a mad idea was growing in my mind, an idea that flew in the face of what everyone at Shadowfell had told me—that I was the rebellion's secret weapon, and that I must always put my own safety first.

"Tali would want this Caller killed," I said, looking around the circle of grave, attentive faces. "I'm in no doubt of it. And we have a man at court—you possibly know that—who could do it if we could get a message to him. Only that's tricky at present. Our man has fallen out of favor with the king, and may be under suspicion."

"That would be a suicide mission," said Foras levelly.

"I know." A shiver ran through me. "And I'm not sure it's the best way to deal with this, even if we could get a message into Winterfort." As I thought of Whisper and that sad crowd of Good Folk marching as if to the grave, every instinct told me my crazy plan was the right one. It meant throwing away the opportunity to find the Master of Shadows; sacrificing the chance to learn from him and perhaps get the answer to the threat of cold iron. Above all, it meant putting myself in peril, which was completely counter to Tali's orders. And yet, I knew it was what I must do. "If I had to get inside Winterfort and attach myself to the king's household," I said, "how best could I do that without attracting the wrong kind of attention?"

One man gave a long whistle; another muttered an oath.

"You're asking that seriously," said Foras.

"I am." I made myself take a slow breath. "I think it's what I must do."

"You don't seem the obvious choice as an assassin," said Foras. "And didn't you say you were heading on south?"

"I was. But it's different now. You didn't see what I saw. It was an abomination even by Keldec's standards. And my instincts tell me I may be the only person who can stop it."

"Your instincts are all very well," said a woman, "but

marching into court? All you're likely to do is get yourself killed."

"Can't help agreeing with that," said Foras.

I could see they all thought I'd suddenly lost my wits. "I'm a Caller," I said simply. "I can't let this happen. It's taken a long time for any of the Good Folk to set aside their wariness of humankind and join us as allies. But they have, in the north and the west. That's largely because I've convinced them it's the right thing to do. The king has just demonstrated to the Good Folk how a Caller can use terror to force their compliance. He's treated them as nothing more than raw material to be manipulated to his own gain. When the news of this gets out, why wouldn't our fey allies turn their backs on us in disgust and walk away from the whole endeavor?"

"But won't you be doing the same thing when midsummer comes?" asked one of the men. "Using these folk to fight our fight?"

I made myself breathe slowly; held on to my temper. "Not quite the same. I've used my gift to bring the Good Folk to our councils; it has played a role in their agreeing to be our allies. I've never used it to make someone fight against their will, and I don't intend to. At present they are supporting us of their own choice, because we've persuaded them to believe in the cause. When it comes to the battle, I need to be there to help our fey allies cooperate among themselves—something the Good Folk don't do naturally—and work with us. But I'll be guiding people, not . . . enslaving them."

"Say you got in," said Foras. "What could you achieve before midsummer without giving yourself away?"

"I won't know that until I get there; until I see what is

being done with these folk and find out what the other Caller's role is. I'll do whatever I can to put an end to the cruelty, but I'll stop short of revealing what I am too early. I know that would be disastrous."

"Tali wouldn't like this," said Foras.

"I know that. But she'd leave the final decision to me. She trusts my judgment."

"You wouldn't last a day at court," said one of the women flatly.

"She might, with the right story," said a big, dark-bearded man. "Got any special skills, beyond calling Good Folk? Something they might have need of in that place?"

"Not really," I said. The skills I had learned over my years of living rough and fending for myself, the skills Tali had taught me over the long winter at Shadowfell, included nothing that would win me a position in the royal household. The only outstanding ability I possessed was the one that would imperil me every moment if I went to court.

"Ask yourself," Foras said, "what kind of folk the king might be wanting right now."

"Fighters," said the dark-bearded man after a moment.

"That hardly helps, Brenn," put in the woman, "since Neryn quite clearly isn't built to excel in that area."

"Besides," I said, "neither Keldec nor Varda believes in female fighters. That was proved at the last Gathering."

"You were there?" The woman was impressed now, her voice suddenly hushed.

"I was, and believe me, whatever tales you may have heard about what it's like, the reality was a hundred times worse. Foras, when I left Shadowfell, Tali had planned to send one of the men with me as a bodyguard. Circumstances meant it was Whisper who came with me instead." I glanced at the dark-bearded Brenn. "But maybe I could gain admittance to court if I were attached to someone the king found desirable. For instance, a fighter."

Foras gave a grim smile. "That'd be the way in. I have grave doubts about the wisdom of what you're proposing. It makes far more sense for us to send one of our own people in, get a message to the contact at court, and make sure the Caller is eliminated."

"Both the person you sent and our man at court would die."

"They can be replaced," said Brenn. "You can't."

I felt cold all through. "I promise I'll give this further consideration. But right now, let's assume I'm going to court. Who would you send with me?"

"We have several men here who'd be selected immediately for training if they offered their services," Foras said. "Not in this makeshift force you mentioned, but as Enforcers. Once in, our man would have a place at court at least until midsummer. You could go as his wife. I don't believe celibacy is one of the requirements for an Enforcer. Though how such a man's wife could bear to live with him, I do wonder."

"They're well paid," someone said a little sourly.

I looked around the circle of somber faces. "Whoever went with me would face another risk," I said. "The authorities might decide he needed to be enthralled to ensure his loyalty. That's worse than death."

There was a silence; then Foras said, "We're aware of that, Neryn. I wouldn't ask for a volunteer until I knew you were absolutely sure about this. Sure it's the best way. If you do this and you're discovered, you could be tortured for the information you hold. Both you and whoever goes with you. What if someone decides *you* should be enthralled? Then the king would have two Callers at his command."

"I know that, Foras. I understand all the risks, and I still believe I should go. There's a lot I don't know about this other Caller, but I've seen how powerful his gift is. To draw so many folk after him . . . his ability is frightening. Yes, I know assassination is the obvious choice. But imagine we did send someone in and the Caller was killed. What do you think Keldec would do with those captives?"

"He'd have them culled," Brenn said.

Nobody challenged this flat statement.

"Exactly—that would be absolutely in keeping with the way he does things. And that arbitrary culling, on top of the act of cruelty that's taking place now, would be enough to set our people and the Good Folk at enmity for generations to come. The rebellion is meant to be the start of a new age of justice and peace."

"We should sleep on this," Foras said. "You won't be wanting to head north while that force you saw is still on the road. Give it a few days; give us time to think it through. You look as if you need a rest."

"Thank you. I am hoping Silva can stay on here. The little being she's carrying, Piper . . . he needs a particular kind of safe place, and I believe Callan Stanes is such a place. And he needs Silva to look after him. I can't explain fully, it's a secret matter of the Good Folk, but Silva must continue the old rituals as she did when she was living in the north. If you accept her into your community, she will be an asset. She's not a fighter like her brother. But her work is equally important."

"We'd take her in anyway," Foras said. "She's Ean's sister. One of our own."

"Ean is a fine lad," said the dark-bearded man. "Pigheaded sometimes, but a promising fighter and a good comrade. Knowing he's caught up in this wretched business . . . I don't like it. It angers me."

They gave us beds in the women's quarters, warm water for bathing, and clean garments to wear while ours were laundered. After she'd rested, Silva went out to the standing stones while it was still light enough to find the way, along with Creia and a curly-haired girl who gave her name as Danna. When they came back in, Piper was not with them.

"He's safe," Silva said. "As soon as we got to the stones, he was off, up into a hollow at the top of the tallest stone, and so quiet I wouldn't have known he was there except for his little light in the dusk. We went through the evening ritual, the three of us. When it was time to walk back, Piper flew down and circled around us, then went up into the stone again. I'm sure he'll be safe."

It was one less thing to worry about. Still, when the household settled for sleep, I lay on my bed with my thoughts in disorder. Staring up at the ceiling, I thought of being at close quarters with the king and queen, whose ruthless cruelty I had witnessed at the Gathering. I would be in the same household as Flint, and we'd both have to pretend convincingly that we were strangers. My being there would put him in additional danger. If that other Enforcer was at Winterfort, the one who'd helped Flint get us away from the Gathering, he would surely recognize me. Last but not least, if the king found out I was a Caller, the entire rebellion would be in jeopardy.

Against those arguments was the pressing urge to reach Winterfort before too much damage was done. What I had seen had been the stuff of my worst nightmare. It had been so deeply wrong I could hardly believe it had happened, even knowing what I did of Keldec. Undoing that could not wait until midsummer. Those folk might all be dead by then. And who was going to change things, unless I did? Flint might kill the Caller, if we could send the order, and our plans for midsummer might then go ahead unaltered. But this dark happening, this twisted use of a gift that was twin to my own, would do such damage that even if we won our battle, the Good Folk would rightly shun us thereafter. The hard-won trust would be gone forever.

And I wanted a solution that spared the Caller, who must be a person very like me. What if I had been the one found by Keldec? What if I had been prevailed upon to use my gift in his service, or enthralled into loyalty? Would I then deserve death, or only pity?

You're too soft, said Tali's voice in my head. *It's a war. People die. This Caller is both evil and powerful. Why should he be spared?*

I had no argument to offer; only that, deep down, I knew there must be a better, wiser way.

Silva and the other women who shared our chamber were asleep. From beyond the shuttered window came soft nighttime sounds, a cow lowing in the field, sleepy chickens jostling for space in their coop—Silva would like them—and the muted voices of some of the men who were on guard outside. This was a good place. A pity I would not be staying long.

I realized that I had forgotten something earlier. I did indeed have a talent that might get me into Winterfort. Before my grandmother had died, she had begun to teach me the skills of a healer and an herbalist, and at Shadowfell I had often helped Fingal in the infirmary. With the so-called special forces perhaps being trained at Winterfort, there could well be a need for additional healers.

My heart was thudding now as I lay still on the pallet. We would be a desirable pair: the husband an outstanding fighter desperately keen to join the Enforcers, the wife competent in the healing arts. This was in fact possible. It might really happen. I might be in the same house as Keldec. In the same chamber as Queen Varda. I might be stuck in an infirmary, unable to reach any of the captive Good Folk. I might find myself powerless to do anything but watch, day by day, from now to midsummer, the hideous results of their experiments with this new Caller.

Stop it, Neryn. There must be no guilt, no panic, no dwelling on the worst that could happen. If I decided to travel to court, I must do so in the confidence that what I could achieve outweighed the terrible risk I was taking. There was another argument in support of my plan. Keldec and his entourage would move to Summerfort in the warmer weather. Most likely my warrior husband, as an Enforcer in training, would travel with them, and so would I. I would be exactly where Tali needed me to be for the Gathering. *Breathe, Neryn. This is within your reach. You can do this.*

After a night spent going over and over the possibilities, I fell asleep before dawn and dreamed of Flint. The dream was confused, unclear. He seemed to be looking out of a tower window, gazing southward. But then he was in the dark, his eyes patches of shadow in a face drained of color, and there were iron bars between him and me. I reached out my hand, and he put his fingers up against the bars on the other side, but however hard I tried, I could not quite touch him. I tried to speak, to tell him it was all right, I was here, right here in front of him, but I had no voice. *Neryn,* he said. *Neryn, where are you? I can't see you.* And then, *It's too late.*

I woke with my face all tears. Light was creeping in around the shutters; it was morning, and across the chamber Silva and Creia were already up and dressed.

"Neryn?" Silva came to sit on the edge of my bed. "We're going up to the stones for the morning ritual. Why don't you come and help us?"

She'd noticed, no doubt of it. And she was wise. Better by far to be out of doors, walking in the sunlight in company with friends, than lying here while my mind churned with unwelcome thoughts. I got up and reached for my clothes.

"One day at a time," murmured Silva, passing me my tunic. "That's what I keep telling myself. Go on for one more day. Be brave for one more day. That's easier than thinking about a whole turning of the moon, a whole season, a whole life." She reached to help me fasten my skirt. "Now I've made you cry again."

"It's nothing." I dashed the tears from my cheeks. "A bad dream, that was all." I thrust my feet into my boots; twisted my hair into a makeshift knot. "I'm ready."

The Callan Stanes were well protected against intrusion. Between them and the farm boundary there grew every plant best designed to cut, scratch, stab, or otherwise damage anyone who went that way. Brambles. Thornbushes. Nettles. There would be few casual visitors here.

We emerged onto a flat grassy sward. There they were: nine of them in a rough circle, the tallest twice the height of a big man, the smallest only as high as my shoulder. More lay prone, sleeping. In the dawn light their shadows spread long and gray behind them on the grass, like trailing capes. The stones were old. Mosses softened their crevices, and lichens splashed their surfaces with purple and gold and brown. Around them was a profound stillness, as if the ground within their protective circle were set apart from the ordinary world.

I walked with the other girls in procession, joining in the responses to Silva's prayers, but my thoughts were full of Flint's white face, his hand against the bars, his anguished voice saying, *I can't see you.* I reminded myself sharply of where I was and what I was doing, and moved through the cycles of meditative breathing the Hag had taught me. I made my mind open, empty, ready for whatever wisdom might come. Silva's voice, sweet and clear, was echoed by the chirping of meadow birds in the grass around the ancient stones.

We had brought offerings: a bowl of clear water, a sprig of rosemary, a little honey cake. These we placed on a stone slab that lay in the center of the circle.

"Accept our gifts, White Lady," Silva said. "We make this offering in love and in hope. Bless this sacred ground with your presence. May this be a place of calm and learning in our troubled land."

When the ritual was complete, we turned to walk away,

and Creia gave a gasp of shock. From high on the tallest stone, a small form came flying to circle around Silva's head, gossamer wings glinting in the morning light. Piper was here; he was indeed safe. And now it was my turn to catch my breath, for following him down from the rock came two others, one shining silver, the other deep rose red, crowning Silva with a three-part dance. We left the circle, and as we passed between the stones, the small beings flew back up to their aerie and out of sight.

I was crying again; what was wrong with me? I scrubbed a hand across my cheeks.

"Neryn," said Silva quietly. "It's all right to cry." Her own eyes were wet. "We've done a good thing."

She was right; we had done a remarkable thing. We'd taken an immense risk, and because of that, the White Lady was still here among us. Alive; growing stronger already.

"I know." Perhaps this was the time for tears, while I was safe among friends. At Winterfort, I would not be able to cry. I'd have to be strong. Fearless. I'd have to set aside the chill terror that gripped me at the very thought of what lay ahead.

Once Foras's people accepted that I would not change my mind, the plan took shape with frightening speed. Foras was a leader, like Tali—he understood what needed to be done and how to do it. He knew how to make things happen.

"This isn't a simple matter of a couple walking into Winterfort and telling the authorities the fellow wants to join the Enforcers," he told me as we sat in council on the third day after my arrival. A few others were with us, including the dark-bearded Brenn, who had been chosen to accompany me. "If a man has outstanding fighting skills already, the first thing the king's people will ask is how he came by them, what household he's been attached to, why he's leaving, why he hasn't sought a position among the Enforcers before. The good old *I grew up on a farm and learned from my brothers* isn't adequate in this situation, not when a man knows how to use weapons no farmer would have lying around. Brenn could claim he's from beyond the borders of Alban and learned in some other king's army, but he'd have to be good at an accent, good enough to fool the king's councillors, I suspect. Be hard to keep that up all the time."

"Fortunately," put in Brenn, giving me a shrewd look, "we have another idea. May I explain?" He glanced at Foras.

"Go ahead."

"You'll know that our chieftain, Gormal, is a supporter of the rebellion. He's treading a perilous path, and the closer we get to midsummer, the more dangerous that path becomes. It'll be the same for any leader who plans to stand alongside us at the Gathering. Gormal's already had to divulge his strategy to his master-at-arms; we know that. Most likely also to other members of his household, those who need to know. His men have to be prepared for what's coming. But Gormal shares a border with Erevan of Scourie, who's loyal to the king. Gormal can't risk Erevan's folk getting word of his treachery, as Erevan would see it. That means he has to let the king's men ride across his territory in this mad quest to gather a new fighting force for Keldec. He must stay quiet; he can't afford to attract attention before midsummer. That's not to say he can't help us, in a small way."

"You can't tell Gormal about me," I protested, horrified. "That would be risking the whole rebellion!"

"All we need tell him is that we want a cover story," said Brenn calmly. "He can provide that. His master-at-arms, who's a friend of ours, will back him up if required. We'll be supplied with items of clothing and weaponry that fit the story, which will be that I've been released from Gormal's service, with his blessing, to follow my dream of becoming an Enforcer. Why now? Because I'm recently wed and keen to be a good provider for my new wife, who just happens to be a skilled healer."

It was neat. Almost too neat. "And how does my background story tie in with yours?" I asked.

"Once they get a demonstration of Brenn's fighting skills, nobody's going to be interested in you," said one of the women, Marnit. "Choose an obscure part of Glenfalloch as your home region, say your old grandmother taught you everything you know, and I doubt anyone will ask you further questions. It's a weakness in their defenses. Useful."

"How long will it take to speak to these people and obtain the clothing and weapons you mentioned?" I asked.

"You don't want to be crossing paths with this uncanny army on your way north," said Foras. "I've sent folk out to track them; it seems they are headed in the general direction of Winterfort, but we'll wait for confirmation that the way is clear before you set off. We want Brenn to offer himself as an Enforcer, not be swept up in these so-called special forces. While we wait for further intelligence, we'll arrange the cover story."

I nodded agreement, knowing this was the best plan

anyone was likely to come up with in the circumstances. "If another bird comes when I'm gone," I said, "a messenger from Tali, I mean, you should send it back with word of what's happened." Tali had said she would send Gort too, by less magical means. He might already have come down the valley, since the turning of the season should allow that by now. But he had no way to find me. He was hardly going to come looking within the walls of Winterfort.

"I have a question for you," said Marnit. "On that first day, when you were telling your story, you said something about Good Folk being drawn to you even when you weren't calling them. You told us the little creature who came here with you was torn between you and the other Caller, feeling the influence of both. If that's true, why didn't those folk you saw marching along the valley know you were up on the hillside watching as they went by? Why didn't they feel your magic?"

"It's not magic. Or, at least, it's not my magic. The call comes from what already exists: earth, air, fire, and water. And from spirit, deep within. Maybe they felt my presence that day, even though I made sure I didn't call. But the other Caller was far closer to them than I was. And there were Enforcers armed with iron weapons all around them." I saw unspoken questions on the faces of my companions.

"We're only going to have one opportunity to win this, and that will be at the Gathering. When I get to court, I won't be calling the prisoners to rise up against the Enforcers. I won't be testing my gift against the other Caller's—not before midsummer. But I want to let them know they're not alone; that freedom is coming." I thought of Whisper marching at the end of that column, his great eyes blank, his snowy feathers dappled with blood; Ean drawn into those ranks of terrified young men; the Good Folk, big and small, powerful and weak, forced into this cruel and destructive game. "I want to bring them hope."

Our supplies were prepared: clothing and weaponry, food for the road, a bigger and better-stocked healer's bag than the one we had brought from the Beehives. Steps were taken to alter my appearance, though there was a limit to what was possible. Creia cut my hair off level with my shoulders and dyed it a dull red-brown with a walnut shell and beet juice concoction. Once at Winterfort, I would need to repeat this process when the natural color began to show. The clothing provided for me was of richer fabric and more elegant cut than anything I had worn before. This was consistent with Brenn's status in Gormal's household. The women of Callan Stanes made me practice walking like a lady and showed me how to put my shorter hair up in a smooth roll with not a single stray strand. I perfected a graceful curtsy. I reminded myself that at Shadowfell we did not use the word *impossible*.

Word came in from Foras's people that the road was clear; the makeshift army had tramped its way north to Winterfort and entered the fortress gates, fey warriors, farm boys, and all. Brenn guessed the Enforcers would be given the job of transforming that throng into some kind of fighting force. Very likely they'd have limited time for training new recruits, but they'd be wanting men like Brenn, who had a high degree of discipline already, to take on the more straightforward responsibilities—guard duty, for instance.

My traveling companion's matter-of-fact manner should

have reassured me. Instead, it made me wonder if he knew what we were heading into.

"Have you ever been to the Gathering?" I asked him the night before we were due to leave the farm.

"Managed to avoid it thus far, Neryn. But I've heard enough."

"I thought I had too. My father used to talk about it. But nothing could have prepared me. And . . ."

"And what?"

"Even before midsummer, you could be asked to perform acts that go against everything you believe in. Terrible acts of violence and cruelty. For this to work, you'll have to obey orders without question."

"I know that." His tone was kindly, as if he were speaking to a child. "I've been part of Foras's group for years."

I thought of how the years of living a double life had scarred Flint; the heavy burden he carried day by day, the bleak look that was often in his eyes. My last troubling dream of him was never far from my thoughts. "You haven't done *this* before," I said. "It'll take a toll. On both of us."

Brenn was regarding me soberly now, his dark eyes narrowed in his strong, bearded face. "I have an idea what might lie ahead."

At that moment Foras came in with something in his hand. "You'll need to carry these," he said, passing a small packet to each of us. "You know the rule, Neryn, I imagine?"

"I have my own supply," I said. Hemlock, a fail-safe means of escape from torture. The rebel code meant a person would kill herself rather than be forced into betraying secrets.

"Take it only in the last extreme. Now that Keldec's using

the Good Folk, your role is even more vital to our success. I have to say, despite going over and over the arguments, I'm barely convinced that you're making the right choice. Even with Brenn, you'll be vulnerable at court. I'll be holding my breath until the Gathering, wondering if my poor strategy has ruined any chance we had of winning this."

I forced a smile. "Not your poor strategy, Foras. Mine."

"Well. Are you ready?" His cheerful tone was unconvincing.

One day at a time, I thought, remembering Silva's words. *Be brave for one day. Go on for one day.* "As ready as we can be," I said.

The next morning I went to the stones with Silva, only the two of us, and I took the drum. Silva spoke a prayer, and we laid fresh-picked flowers at the foot of the tallest stone. Then Silva moved back a short distance, and I sat cross-legged on the ground with the drum in my hands.

The day was cold, the sun hiding behind clouds. If the little birds were out and about searching for choice morsels in the long grass, they were doing it in silence.

I sat quiet. I did not call. At Winterfort I would have to shut my gift down. When in company with my own kind, I would have to appear as ordinary as possible. I would be a young woman delighted and a little awed to find herself within the royal household. Awed but not scared, because that too might attract unwelcome attention. And yet, what young woman in that situation would not be in terror of setting a foot wrong? I had seen how the king and queen treated folk who made mistakes, even trivial ones.

After some time I whispered against the drum skin, "Are you there? I've come to say goodbye." There wasn't much time. Now that the way was clear, Foras wanted us over the border as quickly as we could manage it. We wouldn't be walking, we'd be riding, or at least Brenn would be, with me up behind him. In a matter of two days, if all went to plan, we would be at Winterfort.

I saw Silva look up suddenly, and a moment later three—no, four—small beings were flying down to land, two on my shoulders, two in my hair. I had not held great hopes that the Lady would speak to me here at Callan Stanes, with so few of the wee folk left and no enclosed place to bring her voice forth. But as I watched, breathless with wonder that another of them had appeared, the little ones crept down my arms and placed themselves two on each wrist, right by the drum. Piper mimed for me, lying down on my palm, laying his head against the goatskin, then sitting up with a grin of surprise and delight. I found myself smiling in response.

I lifted the drum and put my ear close, careful not to dislodge the little beings. I breathed slowly and waited.

The voice came, cracked and faint, but undeniably hers.

'Tis a dark path lies before ye, lassie.

"I know," I whispered. "But the only one."

There's a choice ahead fit tae break your hairt. At the end, your faith will be stretched thin as a thread o' silk. Dinna lose your belief in yoursel', Neryn, or ye canna dae this.

I could not speak.

Ye did guid, lassie. Ye did fine. Dinna forget tae see wi' the clarity o' air. Even when all around ye is smoke and fire, blood and death. Even when your heart's hurtin' and your e'en are blinded wi' tears. See through the terror. See through the sorrow tae what's true and guid and worth fightin' for.

The wise voice faded away. Piper and his companions flew a few exuberant circles around me, moved across to salute Silva in the same way, then were off up to their aerie atop the tallest stone.

I was torn between joy and tears. She had spoken to me; the White Lady was here and growing stronger. Here in this sacred place, here among devoted friends, her light still shone in benighted Alban. And now I must leave this haven and head north again, north into the gathering dark.

CHAPTER EIGHT

FLINT WAS UP ON THE WALKWAY WHEN BRYDIAN'S expedition arrived back at Winterfort. Word had come in that they were bringing a contingent of captive Good Folk, but nobody had known quite what to expect. His vantage point let him see the grim procession climbing the hill, the prisoners herded along by Enforcers with iron weapons, a group of young men marching behind them, and Brydian riding triumphant at the rear with the Caller beside him. There was a disquieting rumor afoot about those young men. Someone had hinted that Keldec considered them more or less disposable; that they would be used in place of Enforcers while the uncanny army was trained.

The young men didn't even reach the fortress. A mile or so down the road, a team from the escort, Bull Troop men, split the party up, dividing humankind from Good Folk, then led the young men off along the track that branched up to Seven Oaks Farm, where most of his own men were currently deployed training would-be Enforcers under Rohan's capable leadership. So those lads, at least, would be safe for a while longer. Seven Oaks was often used when Winterfort was full to capacity; it had spacious, if basic, accommodations and plenty of room for training.

The throng of Good Folk was driven ahead and through the great gates into the courtyard below him. He could not see the king or queen, but he guessed they would be on the steps down there to welcome their Caller home and remark on his feat. One or two of the Good Folk tried to bolt for freedom and were prodded back at spearpoint. The heavy gates were swung shut, trapping all of them within.

Flint gazed down to the courtyard, silent, as a kind of madness descended on those who found themselves thus enclosed. The Good Folk were suddenly deaf to the shouted orders of the Enforcers. They wailed, shrieked, wept, collapsed. Three strapping beings were held back from attacking their guards only by a forest of spears pointed in their direction. Others struck out at random, screaming and clawing at their own kind and their captors alike. Around the edges of the yard, wooden items began to smoke and smolder and catch alight. The men of Hound and Bull Troops struggled to keep themselves and their horses safe.

In the chaos, he'd lost sight of the Caller. But now, with four of the Hound Troop men around him, Esten stepped out. And there was Brydian, not far away, with his own guards. He shouted something at the Caller over the noise, and Esten raised his hands in response, palms up. As far as Flint could tell, he did not cry out or chant or do anything that might be interpreted as a call. He simply stood there looking out on the scene of disorder. But a silent shock seemed to pass through every uncanny being. While the Enforcers on guard held their ground, the Good Folk collapsed like felled trees or shrank down with their arms curled over their heads. Those whose natural form was fiery wavered and dimmed. Smoke arose to shroud the courtyard and its occupants. When it cleared, the men of Hound and Bull Troops remained standing, weapons in their hands, but the Good Folk were cowering down, hunched, defeated, terrified. The place had fallen silent save for a thready whimpering. Esten sagged at the knees; one of his guards caught him before he hit the ground. Whatever spell he had cast, it had robbed him of all his strength.

Flint did not wait to see more, but headed down the steps. When he reached the great hall, senior members of the household were gathering around Brydian. The king had ordered that two full troops of Enforcers were to be stationed in a ring around the captives at all times, with their iron blades unsheathed. This was a temporary measure. A council would be held tomorrow that every troop leader and deputy was required to attend. The king wanted a plan for security and a plan for training. They were all to bring solutions.

Flint sent a messenger to summon Rohan back from Seven Oaks. He did not go out into the courtyard to observe the captives, but spoke to some of the men from Bull and Hound Troops who had brought them from the south. When the guard changed that first evening, he heard that several of the smaller beings had collapsed and died within the circle of swords and spears, though none of the Enforcers had touched them. Others were reported to be shivering continuously, as if in great pain.

He tried to think strategically. The king wanted solutions. Could any solution be found here that would not only satisfy Keldec—or, more importantly, the queen—but also do the right thing by the Good Folk?

He made himself treat it like any other tactical problem. Even with the constant guard, the uncanny folk presented a danger to the king's household. They needed to be moved. And the king wanted them trained. The first step was to get them away, somewhere they could be held securely without the ring of iron and the high enclosing walls. The next step . . . The next step was beyond him. Could Esten persuade these Good Folk to cooperate? Could they learn to fight alongside human warriors? If that happened, if he was complicit in it, he would be sharpening a tool to use against his own allies. He would be undermining the rebellion.

Thirteen Enforcers attended the council: each troop leader and deputy with the exception of Wolf Troop's second-in-command, Finan, who was at Summerfort overseeing the small contingent that wintered there. Owen Swift-Sword and Rohan Death-Blade came into the chamber with the others to find both king and queen already present, along with Brydian and his fellow councillor, Gethan, a man with a powerful canny gift involving fire. Esten was seated between the queen and Brydian. He looked as if he hadn't slept for days.

"Sit," said the king.

The troop leaders seated themselves; their deputies stood behind. The anticipatory silence lasted a little longer than was quite comfortable.

"This won't take long," Keldec said with a smile Flint did

not find reassuring. "I had expected that the arrival of these folk at court would be a triumph. Instead, we have something close to catastrophe. I want this addressed quickly." He glanced at Esten. "I mean no criticism of the Caller. If his talents are as yet limited, no matter. He will learn."

Implicit in that, Flint thought, was the threat of what might befall the Caller if he failed to learn well enough, or quickly enough. But Esten looked relieved. He did not yet know the king as the rest of them did.

"As troop leaders, you are my right hand," Keldec said smoothly, making sure his gaze traveled over every one of them. "I rely on you to maintain security and order. Everywhere in my kingdom. Under every possible set of circumstances. I hope you have given due thought to this problem. I hope you have brought me solutions."

What did he think they were, a gathering of mages? Everyone was carefully avoiding meeting anyone else's eye.

"Of course, my lord king." Flint spoke into the silence, his voice betraying nothing of the conflict within him. "Might we first hear from the Caller? We have been impressed by his efforts to control these folk since their arrival here. But none of us fully understand the extent of his abilities. Our solutions might be better shaped to the problem if we were more fully informed on this point." Keldec had not confided in him before calling this council, as he had so often done in the past. Such conversations had their own special peril, but they did provide Flint with clues to the king's thinking. This was like trying to steer a boat through stormy waters without oars or sail. "Or if you prefer," he added, "one of your councillors might provide us with some further details."

Galany, leader of Bull Troop, cleared his throat. "My lord king, I support Owen's suggestion. With your permission, if we might also put some questions to the Caller, that could prove most helpful."

Flint was watching the queen. Watching her eyes narrow; seeing the way she examined the face of one man after another as if to divine his true thoughts. When her gaze came to him, he met it steadily.

"I want this done quickly," Keldec said. "While we waste time with questions and answers, those folk are running amok out there. I will have no uncanny army left."

"My lord king, our solutions can only be effective if we have the information required to make them. We would not prolong the discussion unnecessarily." The smooth tone still came easily, despite everything. Flint hated himself for it.

Keldec regarded him, and for a moment there were only the two of them in the chamber. Flint wondered, not for the first time, if the king sometimes wanted it all to go away: his ambitious wife, his self-serving councillors, the whole edifice of power and cruelty he had built up over his fifteen years on the throne of Alban. Given the opportunity, would Keldec prefer to be a different man, a scholar, a shepherd, a hermit?

"You speak wisely, Owen," the king said. "Brydian, is our Caller able to answer for himself?"

Brydian wore a frown; the queen's lips had tightened. "Yes, my lord," the councillor said. He gave Flint a long, assessing look.

"Very well, let us hear what he has to say."

Esten rose to his feet. He was not a tall man, and the robe they had given him to wear sat loose on him. He looked sick, wretched. But his voice was steady. "Thank you, my lord king. My lady." A glance toward Varda and a small inclination of the head. This was no gauche country lad. "I apologize for what has happened. I had thought . . . I had hoped I could keep control of these folk once we reached Winterfort. It seems not. I am . . . mortified. Aghast." He looked around the council chamber, and the thirteen Enforcers gazed back at him. "It will perhaps be easier if you tell me what you want to know and I attempt to answer." A sideways glance at Brydian. "If you permit, my lord king, my lady, may I sit down? Until now, until we rode south, I had never exercised my gift for so long a period. I'm afraid it has weakened me. . . ." He sank back onto the seat.

"Yes, yes," Keldec said, waving a hand as if the request were mere time-wasting.

Brydian was solicitous, leaning toward the Caller, laying a hand on his arm. Gethan poured mead from the jug on the table, then passed the cup to Esten. The queen did not react; her eyes were still on the circle of men, her expression hard to read. Waiting, Flint guessed. Waiting for one of them to slip up, to say something she did not care for, to express even the slightest criticism.

"Ask your questions," the king said. "Time is running short."

There was a silence. Every one of the Enforcers knew the price of speaking too frankly.

Rohan cleared his throat. "May I speak?"

This to his troop leader, in accordance with the protocol for such councils. Flint nodded, trusting that Rohan would be careful.

"I am Rohan Death-Blade, second-in-command of Stag Troop." This was for Esten's benefit, since everyone else present knew him. "I understand little of how your gift works, Esten. My knowledge of uncanny folk is also limited. What I know, I know from childhood stories."

"Get on with it," muttered Brydian.

"It seems some of these folk may have powerful magic," Rohan said. "Perhaps the ability to travel in ways unlike those of humankind. Many of them bear some resemblance to creatures of one kind or another, including birds—I saw several winged beings among them. I understand that you called them to you in the south and compelled them to follow you here. Did you do that from a distance, or was it necessary to seek them out, to be within sight or earshot, before they would respond to your summons? Would your gift be strong enough to bring Good Folk here from a place some miles away? Or even farther?" He hesitated. "I was thinking that if they could fly, or perhaps move in magical ways, they might travel the distance more easily. And a great deal more quickly."

"If that were so"—Brydian's tone was scathing—"do you not imagine we would have performed the exercise thus and avoided a long, weary trip to the border and back?"

A little silence. Rohan seemed on the point of speaking again, perhaps to say—at some peril to himself—that this was no answer to the question, but the king spoke first.

"Let the Caller respond to this."

"When I am well rested, when circumstances permit, I can summon folk from a certain distance," Esten said. "Some of you witnessed my first call at Winterfort, when I brought three beings here from . . . another place. I had not seen them; I had . . . I had felt their presence close by. What I do . . . It's not a call in the usual sense, a shout or a cry, or a charm spoken aloud. It is more of a feeling, something that is inside, in my mind and body."

Several Enforcers spoke at once.

"Well rested. What do you—"

"How did you come by this—"

"But if you can do that—"

Brydian lifted a hand and the voices died. "Esten, you might explain to these men how you learned to use your skill."

Esten chewed his lower lip and stared down at the table. He looked as if he would rather not speak. When he did, his tone was almost apologetic. "A man is born with such a gift," he said. "You all know this, I imagine, and you know that the exercise of such talents in the community is against the king's law. Growing up, I used to see things, hear things I knew I should not. Beings out in the woods; creatures following me, speaking to me. I told nobody. I did my best to shut my ears and eyes to it, knowing it was wrong. When Master Brydian found me, I was working as a scribe's assistant, grinding pigments, making parchment, shaping quills. But . . . for a Caller, it is not possible to sever that link with the Good Folk. I have only to wander out of doors, by a stream or down a forest path, to hear their voices on the wind. I have only to use my eyes to see them. Master Brydian came knocking on my master's door, asking questions. I had wandered out to the fields to take my midday meal of bread and cheese. When Master Brydian first saw me, there was an uncanny creature nearby that had approached me unbidden. I had not used my gift of calling; not once. My very nature draws them to me."

"But you have used your gift now." This deep voice was that of Frossach, leader of Seal Troop.

"Yes, I . . . Master Brydian explained to me what he was looking for, and after that I . . . practiced."

That was it? The fellow was completely untutored, yet a brief period of practice had rendered him skillful enough to draw that huge group of fey folk after him, surrounded by iron-wielding Enforcers, all the way to Winterfort? The expedition had lasted barely long enough to ride to the border and back. Something was missing here. Was Esten lying, and if so, who knew the truth?

"My lord king, I'm aware of the need for haste," Flint said, "but clearly we will not solve this very real problem without Esten's assistance. He is the only Caller we have, and he appears exhausted. Preserving his health must be a priority. I have a question; possibly Brydian is better placed to answer it than the Caller himself."

Brydian folded his hands on the table before him. He narrowed his eyes.

"What can you tell us of the lore concerning Callers?" Flint went on. "It is such a powerful gift, it seems likely there must be some kind of training required before a man has full mastery of it." He had to tread carefully, lest his words endanger Neryn. He needed to know what Esten was holding back; whether Esten had indeed completed the training Neryn had said was necessary, but for some reason was not saying so. "I would imagine it might take as long as the training required to master the craft of enthrallment, or even longer." That seemed safe enough, since everyone here, with the exception of Esten, knew that he had learned his own craft the old way.

"I don't see the point in this," Brydian said shortly.

"We seek a way to keep better control of our . . . captive army," said Flint, working on a calm, detached tone. "Our Caller is tired, he's struggling, and the king has asked us for a solution. One solution might be for Esten to seek out further training; to polish his skills and his strength under the tutelage of . . . an expert."

"What expert?" The king was beginning to sound impatient.

"That I cannot tell you, my lord king," Flint said. "But Master Brydian is the most learned member of this household and known to be skilled in the interpretation of ancient lore. What do the old tales tell of Callers, Brydian? Perhaps they provide advice on harnessing the Good Folk to work for human rulers."

"There is a very old story of a Caller bringing out an army of brollachans to fight alongside humankind against a common enemy," Brydian said.

"Brollachans," said the king flatly.

"Yes, my lord king. Only a tale, of course. In that story, the Caller traveled away from home as a youth and did not return until he had learned his craft. Where he went and who taught him, the tale does not tell."

"Did they win their battle?" the king asked.

"Yes, my lord king."

"Esten." Queen Varda spoke for the first time, her voice low and pleasant. She did not look at the Caller but across the table toward Flint and, behind him, Rohan, who had asked

197

the first question. "Do you know anything of such training? Do you know who might offer it and where? Or how long it might take before your skills were sufficiently polished to provide the king with exactly what he needs?"

"No, my lady. What I can do, I do by myself. Nobody knew of my gift before Master Brydian found me."

Whether this was true or not, it would take more than polite questioning to find out. And one thing was certain: nobody was going to get the chance to apply pressure to the king's Caller.

"Thank you," Flint said. "My lord king, as you've said, the current state of affairs cannot be allowed to continue. I believe Rohan Death-Blade was going to suggest the uncanny folk be moved away from the fortress, to a place where they can be held safely. Somewhere they can receive training without presenting a daily obstacle to the functioning of your household. Should it be possible for Esten to exercise control over them at a distance, from a place where he could not see them, that could be achieved quite quickly. Otherwise, Esten would need to accompany them and remain close at hand while they were trained." *Stop there,* he told himself. But the next part had to be said sometime. Surely the king had realized what this meant. "The Caller would need to be present every time these folk were deployed in battle, my lord king. That would be quite a heavy burden for him."

Several of the troop leaders spoke at once and were silenced by the king's raised hand. But it was Varda who responded, her tone silken smooth. "Are you volunteering the services of Stag Troop to oversee this exercise, Owen? Making sure that under your capable hand everything is done as well as it possibly can be, including taking appropriate steps to safeguard our Caller's welfare?"

He swallowed, made his features calm. "Stag Troop is currently training a group of aspiring Enforcers, my lady. And Rohan tells me we'll also be responsible for the human contingent of this new force. The uncanny folk, I believe, will need to be housed and trained separately, at least until we have a better idea of their potential as fighters. That would be best done away from Winterfort. We will, of course, follow the king's orders."

"Where would you put them?" asked red-bearded Corb, leader of Eagle Troop. "You've seen what a rabble they are. You'd need somewhere very secure. And you'd need to house and supply them; they can't live on air."

"It would tie up at least two troops," said Frossach, frowning. "That might leave us short of men to perform the usual patrols, my lord king."

"It's tying up two troops now," said Rohan. "I concur with Owen. The uncanny folk should be trained separately. Completely apart. And not at Seven Oaks with those young lads, who'll have enough difficulty shaping up as half-competent fighters without needing to do it alongside Good Folk. If they're to be mixed up later, so be it. But let's get the lads up to a good standard of skill before we complicate things."

"Makes sense to me," said Frossach. "Whichever troop is given the task of making that mob in the courtyard into some kind of fighting force, they're going to do a better job if they need not also concern themselves with an ongoing threat to the king's household. Provided Esten can keep control—and it does sound as if he'll need to be right there, alongside whoever's doing the training, to achieve that—this has at least some chance of success." He paused, then added hastily, "No criticism intended, my lord king, my lady, learned councillors. It's a worthwhile venture, new, bold, exciting. A challenge we all look forward to."

They had become expert liars, every one of them, Flint thought. There were no enthralled men among the troop leaders. Enthrallment rendered a man faultlessly loyal. It also reduced his capacity to think for himself. Every Enforcer in this chamber knew that the king's plan was a grand folly, a venture more likely to end in disaster than the brilliant display of might Keldec anticipated. But not one of them was prepared to say so.

"I have a question, my lord king." Galany of Bull Troop spoke.

Keldec nodded for him to continue.

"The Good Folk are afraid of iron. More than that, it's a kind of poison to them. Weakens them, hurts them, can kill them. Seems the tales are true in that respect, at least. We've used that weakness to keep them under control. But what about when they're fighting *for* us? The first sniff of a knife and they'll be falling like ninepins."

"I hope you are not suggesting the entire venture is misguided, Galany." The king's tone was all frost.

"No, my lord king. There must be an answer to this, of course, if we're to believe the old stories. If an army of brollachans fought alongside an army of men and vanquished their enemy, those brollachans must have been resistant to iron. Unless men in those days carried weapons made of wood or bone."

There was a ripple of amusement around the council table; not quite laughter.

"I brought you here to provide solutions," said the king. "Not to raise further problems."

"The issue of iron is easily dealt with," said the queen. "Whichever troop is given responsibility for training these creatures must first test each of them for its ability to withstand iron. Those with good resistance will be retained. Those without such resistance will be culled."

A brief silence. The appropriate response was simple agreement. None of the Enforcers present seemed quite prepared to give it.

"May I speak?" Abhan of Horse Troop rose to his considerable height. His hair fell in twisted locks to his shoulders; his beard was equally luxuriant. Abhan had been a king's man since Flint was a boy. If anyone was going to offer the services of his troop to carry out such a cull, it would surely be this man.

Keldec waved a hand, making no attempt to conceal his impatience. "Go on, Abhan, we don't have all day."

"A cull might not be required," Abhan said, to Flint's great surprise. "The men we've got on guard down there will be able to tell you which of these folk have most resistance to iron; they'll likely be able to tell you which are the best natural fighters and which are the likeliest to cooperate. The rest of them . . . Why bother with a cull, and the messy business of disposal? Why not simply take them out the gates and let them go? They'd be off back home before you could so much as snap your fingers, my lord king. In my opinion, that would be the quickest and easiest way to deal with this."

"Where would the stronger ones be taken for training?" asked Frossach, leaving the issue of culling unresolved. "Could the young fellows from the south come back here, and these folk be moved out to Seven Oaks?"

Rohan saved his troop leader from having to reply. "Seven Oaks is too close to Brightwater settlement; there would be issues with the safety of the local people. And while the place is well set up for ordinary training, it's not secure enough for this."

"My lord king," Flint said, "you'll be aware that Stag Troop is generally responsible for the training and preparation of fighters. In view of our experience, I believe that Rohan Death-Blade and I may be best equipped to advise you on this particular matter."

"Go on," said the king.

"I suggest we shift the uncanny folk to Summerfort now, rather than waiting until the court makes its annual move." He lifted a hand for quiet as objections broke out among the listening Enforcers. "Hear me out, please. Esten would need to travel with them, and he'd have to stay there while they were trained. I know the Caller is tired. He has made a long journey; so have the Good Folk. But Summerfort has all the facilities required, including a large practice area that is safely walled without having the . . . the intimidating sense of enclosure that Winterfort may convey to our captives." He hated the whole thing; it was a cruel, misbegotten venture. But the king wanted answers. And this made a kind of sense. There was some chance that the presence of the captive Good Folk at Summerfort would be noticed and reported up the valley to Tali. A warning, allowing the rebels to prepare for a darker and more deadly encounter than anyone had anticipated. It would get the captives away from the queen, at least for a while. And it might provide what he needed: Esten away from Brydian, without his magical defense, a clear target. "I believe that if given a strong escort and due consideration for their welfare on the way, these folk could reach Summerfort in good condition, my lord king," he added, holding his voice calm over the thunderous beating of his heart. This plan would lead to his own death. Of that he had no doubt whatever. "And I am convinced moving them there is the best solution to our current difficulty. The young men from the south could remain at Seven Oaks until the rest of your court moves later in the season; that would allow the basic training Rohan mentioned to be completed before they were challenged further."

Keldec had been listening intently. His eyes were bright with enthusiasm. "An excellent idea, Owen. Well considered. What contingent of guards would you recommend to accompany these folk on the way?"

"My lord—" Brydian made to protest, but the king gestured him silent.

"Half of Wolf Troop is in residence at Summerfort already. I would suggest the remainder of the troop be deployed there, if Gill concurs." He glanced at the Wolf Troop leader. "I'd recommend sending another full troop with them. I believe that number would be sufficient to keep control on the way and to provide the necessary training, my lord king." There was one more question that had to be asked. "The task ahead of us is complex, as I'm sure you all realize. Training the Good Folk, whose capacity and limitations are as yet

203

largely unknown; training the young men at Seven Oaks, some of whom have almost no combat skills; combining the two forces and drilling them as a single army. Is there a requirement that this fighting force be battle-ready by a certain time, my lord king?" He kept his voice coolly detached.

"Let us be realistic about this," Keldec said. "This is only the first stage; we haven't the numbers yet for the kind of force I have in mind, and as you say, training these folk fully will take time. But I need the capacity to demonstrate what is coming; to ensure that my chieftains—the loyal, the not quite so loyal—are fully aware of how potent this new weapon will one day be. What I need is a display. A spectacle of harnessed power. We'll do that, obviously, at the next Gathering."

Flint's heart jolted; was there an unspoken message here? Could the king possibly have learned of the rebellion? The troop leaders exchanged glances, but nobody said a word.

"Brydian, bring out the letter," said the king.

Brydian drew out a rolled parchment, unfastened it, and laid it flat on the table before him, his long fingers holding it in place.

"The letter is from Lannan Long-Arm, chieftain of the north," Keldec said. "I will not ask Brydian to read it to you; it's somewhat wordy. But the message is clear enough. Next midsummer, Lannan plans to favor us with his presence at the Gathering. He will no doubt be bringing an entourage. *An expression of amity,* I believe those were his words. Amity from that man? Pah! As for why he's doing this now, after so many years of shunning our hospitality, I can only guess that it's a gesture of some kind, a show of power. The fellow is kin to the rulers of the northern isles; he has strong ties there.

Who knows what he's up to? When he gets here, I want to give him an emphatic reminder that I am the ruler of Alban, and that he'd be an utter fool if he ever thought to challenge that. It won't hurt the rest of my chieftains to receive the same message."

If he had believed in gods, Flint would have thanked them; it seemed the timing was only coincidence. "My lord king, do I have this correct? For the Gathering, you require a . . . a mock battle of some kind, demonstrating the Caller's capacity to maintain control when Good Folk and human fighters work as a team?"

"Correct, Owen. I require a public display of the might we can wield with the assistance of uncanny magic."

The timing was ridiculous, impossible. But at least Keldec was not suggesting this new force be ready to march out to battle somewhere; at least it was only a demonstration. Flint tried to weigh the arguments quickly, before someone else offered to do it and the whole mad enterprise lurched onward like an ill-balanced cart. If he wanted a chance to eliminate the Caller, he'd have to volunteer Stag Troop for this job. Could he bring himself to do that, even if it meant culling some of the Good Folk? Or should he let someone else go, stay close to the king, keep out of trouble? That way he would survive until midsummer. There was a great longing in him to stand up beside the rebels in the final confrontation, to show the king his true colors. Still, after everything, Regan's flame burned bright. *You have the king's trust, despite all,* his inner voice told him. *Make him believe in you. This is your most powerful weapon.*

"My lord king, I volunteer Stag Troop for this mission."

There was, at least, the satisfaction of seeing he had astonished both the queen and Brydian. "As I have said, my men are highly experienced in combat training, though this would be a new challenge for them. The decision is yours alone, of course. If you choose to honor us with this task, I'll leave my capable second-in-command at Seven Oaks for a short while to assist with the transfer of responsibility for the young men from the south. We also have a group of aspiring Enforcers in training. They'll come to Summerfort with the troop; the experience will only sharpen their skills." Black Crow have mercy; he hoped he would not regret this the moment the king said yes.

Keldec smiled. Briefly, there was nothing but simple pleasure on his narrow features, and Flint caught a glimpse of the man he might have been, if he had not been born to rule. If he had not wed as he had. If he had been blessed with wiser councillors. "Thank you, Owen," the king said. "That is exactly what I wanted to hear. This enterprise could not be in more capable hands." It was quite plain the queen wanted to interject, but the king was captured by his own enthusiasm and went on, not noticing. "Berrian, Hound Troop will take over the work at Seven Oaks—an easier duty, without any doubt. Think of it as a reward for the leadership you showed on the expedition south. Bull Troop will be similarly recognized." He rose to his feet; everyone else did the same. "We will leave you now. You'll have many practical arrangements to put in place. Get it done quickly. The sooner these folk are out of here, the better. Brydian, you will travel with Esten, of course. You will ensure his safety. And we will rely on you to send frequent reports. Midsummer is not so very far away. But I am confident none of you will disappoint me."

CHAPTER NINE

THE UNCANNY ARMY LEFT WINTERFORT IN THE same manner as it had arrived there: surrounded by men with naked blades. Once well clear of the fortress, Flint called a halt and ordered his men not to intimidate their captives with iron. Unless their leaders gave a specific instruction, the men of Stag and Wolf Troops were to keep their weapons sheathed and rely on the Caller to maintain control.

Brydian protested. While Esten was capable of doing what was required, it was foolish to travel without the additional precaution of iron. Hadn't Owen seen what happened in the courtyard at Winterfort? Flint heard him out. Then he told Brydian to stick to his own job, which was to look after the Caller's welfare, and let him deal with matters of security.

They proceeded with their iron shielded. Esten had not said a word. He rode beside Brydian, just behind the last of the Good Folk. The Caller looked frail, like a man with a mortal illness. Would Neryn too, in time, become a wraith with haunted eyes, shrunken by the practice of her craft? Or would her innate goodness keep her strong?

This, with the iron, was less of a risk than it appeared, since the men could reach their concealed weapons quickly enough if Flint gave the order. It had seemed important to establish some small element of goodwill with these folk as early as possible. He had yet to decide what approach he and his men would take once they reached Summerfort. Unless he laid down his arms and walked away, inviting a knife in the back, he'd have to go through the motions of training Keldec's uncanny army in conventional fighting. They were unlikely to cooperate of their own free will. The only way to secure their obedience thus far had been to compel it, using the Caller. Do that, and Brydian would have control. Nobody spoke to Esten without Brydian; nobody got close enough to have a conversation with the man, let alone take action to remove him. So much for the hope that Esten would leave his minder back at Winterfort with the king—he'd been a fool to believe that might happen. It had been all very well to overrule Brydian today, out on the road, on a mission with his troop around him. At Summerfort it would be different. Flint wondered, not for the first time, if he had dug a grave, not only for the hapless beings from the south, but for his comrades and himself. One official complaint to Keldec, one personal note to the queen, and he'd be relieved of his responsibility immediately. As disastrous as the current situation was, and with little prospect of his eliminating the Caller, at least if he was nominally in charge, he had some chance of altering the course of events before the Gathering.

They broke the journey on the shore of Brightwater; Enforcers from Stag and Wolf Troops took shifts guarding the captives. As ordered, they kept their distance. Iron weaponry remained sheathed. Flint knew his men well; should there be some kind of attack, they could be ready in an instant. The horses were led down to the loch to drink, then provided with oats. Food was distributed among both human folk and Good Folk: plain bread, cheese, dried fish.

Esten and Brydian had seated themselves on the bank, a little apart from the captives. The councillor was coaxing his Caller to eat. Brydian's face was set, his lips tight. He didn't need to say a word to show how he felt about Esten leaving Winterfort and the powerful influence of the queen. But when an idea caught the king's imagination, as had happened with his trusted Owen's solution to the courtyard full of unruly Good Folk, Keldec became deaf to the objections of all around him. Flint had often found this difficult.

If only this Caller had tried to do as Neryn had. If only Esten had treated the Good Folk as equals, beings with their own hopes and fears and desires, their own families and clans and territories, to be respected, if never fully understood. If only Esten or Brydian or one of the troop leaders who'd ridden out on the expedition had bothered sitting down to talk to them. Instead, the Good Folk had been seen as a commodity to be taken and used as their captors saw fit, and discarded if they proved inadequate to the task.

And now, Flint thought as he watched the great crowd of them on the shore, circled by guards and picking without enthusiasm at their rations, it was probably too late. The Caller had used his rare and wonderful gift to hurt and intimidate them. That he had done so under Brydian's orders made this no less heinous. Which of them would listen if Flint tried to talk to them now? And what was there to say? He wore the king's colors. Step out of line, and Brydian's dispatch would be off to Winterfort with the next messenger.

They'd need to be on their way again soon. Some of these folk walked slowly; some had short legs. Many of the winged beings had perished in the courtyard at Winterfort before they could be moved on; this was a far smaller company than the throng that had marched in through the great gates. None now attempted to fly. Perhaps Esten pulled them to the earth. It was not clear in what way the Caller commanded them as they traveled. In the courtyard they had raged and fought until he'd performed his quelling magic. Now they seemed so weighed down there was little fight left in them. Perhaps they were in such dread of that particular call that they would comply with orders rather than endure it again. Not much of an army. But then, perhaps all Esten had to do was command them to fight and they would, using the magic Keldec believed he could harness to make himself great.

Flint glanced up toward the wooded hills that rose above Brightwater. Sage's clan of Good Folk lived farther west, but others of their kind might be watching. He hoped they would not be drawn by Esten's presence. There was a strong desire in him to break all the rules—to order his men to lay down their weapons and set the captives free. Would they obey? Not quickly enough to stop Esten from freezing the Good Folk in place, then making them march on.

"Chief."

He'd been deep in thought, too deep. Tallis Pathfinder was standing right beside him and he'd hardly noticed. "We should move on, yes?"

"They're ready." A hesitation. "Owen?"

"Mm?"

"Heard them talking. The three big fellows." Tallis gave a slight jerk of the head, indicating the formidable trio of fey warriors who had, all along, appeared the most likely to be useful in any future army.

"And?"

Tallis lowered his voice. "They were talking strategy. Exchanging theories about what you'd do, what Brydian would do, what lay ahead. Just the way we would if things were the other way around."

"Mm-hm."

"You don't sound surprised."

"Later. Get the horses moved back up and we'll be on our way." It was Tallis who had come with Rohan to stop him when he'd made his attempt to escape the king's service. Tallis must have some inkling that his troop leader was not the loyal subject of Keldec an Enforcer was supposed to be.

Stand by me and you walk into deadly peril, he thought, watching as Tallis strode off. *Oppose me and I might have to kill you. What sort of leader does that make me?*

Someone was watching him. Not Brydian, who had gone into the woods with Esten, presumably so they could relieve themselves. He felt the gaze as a prickling on his skin, a warning. The Stag Troop men, under Tallis's instructions, were fetching horses, stowing gear, preparing to depart. Gill's men maintained the guard over the captives. The Good Folk were rising to their feet. Flint narrowed his eyes, scanning the crowd.

There. One of the smaller ones, a creature like a bedraggled owl; it had perhaps been white before the turmoil of recent times had turned its plumage a tattered gray. Taloned feet, one clad in a little felt boot. Great eyes fixed on him in unwavering scrutiny. It was as if the being could see straight into his mind. Its face was owl-like, but with subtle differences that made it disconcerting. How had such a fragile creature survived the long journey from the south and the time of blood and fear within the walls of Winterfort?

He made a slight movement with his head, indicating the forest, where, surely, an owl could lose itself quickly. He checked that nobody was observing him, then mouthed, *Go*.

The creature blinked, then turned its gaze away. Even if it had been able to speak to him—and after meeting Sage, he had learned to expect surprises from the Good Folk—it was not close enough to make itself heard. Esten and Brydian walked out from under the trees, and the moment was over. Had the being been trying to tell him something, or was his imagination making him see what he so badly wanted to see, some sign that the captives might be prepared to speak with him?

They moved on. With the Good Folk on foot, they'd be needing to camp overnight at least once on the journey. Perhaps, while Esten and Brydian slept, he might try to speak with the Good Folk out of earshot of whoever was on sentry duty. He might tell them, at least, that there would be no culling on his watch. If there were any folk here who lacked adequate resistance to cold iron, he would set them free.

Perhaps, he thought as he watched the owl-like being limping along with the others, one foot shod, one foot bare, perhaps some kind of bargain could be made. He imagined the little creature flying free, purest white, gliding across a night sky spangled with stars. There was such beauty in Alban, such wonder. Under Keldec's rule, people had lost sight of that.

His hand moved to touch the talisman that hung against his breast, under his shirt: the dream vial worn only by those who had learned the ancient craft of mind-mending. When he lost faith in himself, this token pulled him back. When he came close to despair, it whispered of hope. He had been cruel, violent, destructive; his conscience would be burdened until the day he died. But the talisman spoke of good things. Neryn's love and courage; the wisdom of Ossan, his old mentor; Regan's bright flame of hope, shining in this ruined realm. *Until the vial is shattered forever, until the last drop of kindness drains from Alban, I must hold on to that.*

Two days after we left Callan Stanes, we rode across a bridge and into Brightwater village, a substantial settlement among wooded hills. The river we had crossed flowed eastward to the sea; follow it the other way, and a traveler would come to the chain of lochs that ran across Alban like a bright girdle. The village looked prosperous, with many stone buildings alongside those of mud and wattles. On a hill a short distance to the west loomed a high fortress wall of weathered stone. Atop this massive barrier were watchtowers, and I glimpsed the roof of a keep. Winterfort: King Keldec's main residence. We were almost there.

"Best if we find somewhere in the settlement to spend the night, and I'll make a few casual inquiries," said Brenn over his shoulder as we came into the settlement. "I daresay you could do with a good sleep."

"Mm." I had made sure I did not complain about my aches and pains, but my discomfort must have been obvious when we camped on the way here. Sometime in the future, I promised myself, I would learn to ride properly so I'd need never again be jostled around on the back of someone else's horse like a piece of baggage. The future . . . It was hard to imagine what Alban might be like if the rebellion succeeded. Regan had spoken of a place at peace, a realm without constant fear. I thought every rebel must have dreamed of that. But even if we did win, even if Keldec was deposed, Alban would not change overnight. When I tried to think about that future world, it retreated into a haze, as insubstantial as a dream. What I felt most right now, apart from my bruises, was the chill of complete terror. So close. The king, the queen, the Enforcers, the Enthrallers—everything I feared most was no more than two miles away, and we were heading straight into the middle of it.

"Not far now," said Brenn. "You all right?"

"Fine." What a lie that was. But I had to be fine, I had to be brave and confident and stick to the story, no matter what happened. He was Morven. I was Ellida. Married three months. Previously both in the household of Gormal of Glenfalloch, he as a man-at-arms, I as an assistant healer and herbalist. Each of us from a different, obscure part of the far south; each of us without living kinsfolk, though Morven had had an older brother who had fallen in Gormal's service. Now Gormal had given us his blessing to come here, so Morven could seek admission to the ranks of the king's Enforcers.

Neither of us with any sort of canny gift; neither of us with any knowledge of such things. The offering we brought, our key to acceptance, was Morven's outstanding fighting skill.

We reached an inn and clattered into the yard. Brenn lifted me down, spoke to a couple of grooms, ushered me inside. I was so stiff and sore I could barely walk; Brenn was as solicitous and tender as if I really were his new wife. His manner with the inn workers was easy and confident. This, along with his imposing physical presence—he was a tall, well-made man, his dark hair and beard helping draw the eye—meant folk provided for our needs swiftly and without question.

There was space for us in the communal sleeping quarters; the innkeeper apologized for the lack of privacy. A few coppers changed hands. A meal was supplied, with good ale. Brenn was reassured as to the welfare of his horse, Bolter. We sat on our own in the dining chamber, not wanting to be drawn into conversation unless we must. I made myself sit close to my husband and smile at him with what I hoped was convincing fondness, but all the while I was becoming aware of something odd, something I had not expected in this place full of humankind. A prickle of magic, a familiar sensation that told me Good Folk were somewhere near.

I was hungry after the long ride and enjoyed my hot supper. It was only after I had finished eating that I noticed a little dog running about the dining chamber, getting under people's feet as she hunted for scraps of bread or cheese or sausage on the floor. This creature was of striking appearance. All down one side, from nose to tail, her hair was night black; all down the other, pure white. The color might have been painted, so neat and exact was the division. Could there be more than one such animal? I did not think so. Last time I had seen this dog, she had been with the Master of Shadows.

Stay calm, Neryn. Don't make it too obvious you're looking. There were several old men in the chamber. Some were silently nursing their ale cups. Two were talking to the innkeeper. One sat alone in a corner. Was it the Master? If so, should I approach him? My heart thumped; my palms were clammy. There had been a question nagging at me since I had seen the captive Good Folk driven north under duress. I knew they were not the White Lady's folk; most likely they came from the Watch of the South, of which the Master was Guardian. He must know what had happened, surely. Had he done nothing to protect his own people?

"Here, girl." I clicked my fingers as the dog came near, wishing I had left some of my mutton pie. "Here, little one."

The dog let me scratch behind her ears, but once she realized I had no food, she was off into the crowd. Brenn had gone out to use the privy. I looked across the room again, and the old man sitting by himself raised his head to look at me. Or not to look, exactly, since he had the milky eyes of a blind man. But he saw me. I was in no doubt of that. It was him: the Master of Shadows right here in Brightwater village.

What now? Even if I hadn't been playing the part of a shy young newlywed, I could hardly walk over and confront him in public. But what if this was the only chance I ever got?

The old man's mouth stretched in a slow, mocking smile. He had not taken his eyes off me. And now Brenn was back, seating himself beside me again.

"One of the fellows said I should ask for Rohan Death-Blade when we get up there," he said. "But he said the troops are being shifted around, so they may not be taking on anyone new for a while. Hope that's wrong."

Across the chamber, the Master of Shadows had risen to his feet and picked up his staff. He whistled, and the little dog came to stand by him.

"I— What did you say?" Rohan. Could there be more than one Enforcer by that name?

"Rohan Death-Blade. In charge of training. He's the one to ask for."

The Master was heading out, tapping his staff to find the way, with the little dog going in front. Curse it! He knew I was here, I was sure of it. Last time I'd met him, he'd only been blind when it suited him. He was playing games with me. I half rose, then made myself sit down again.

"What?" murmured Brenn.

"Nothing. I'll tell you later." The Master was gone; I had missed my chance.

The innkeeper's wife came by with her tray, removed our platters, offered more ale. "Poor old man," she observed, glancing toward the doorway. Perhaps she had seen me watching him.

"Unusual dog," I said.

"Funny-looking creature," said the woman. "Goes everywhere with him. It's his eyes."

I'd have liked to find out how long the old man had been in Brightwater. But Ellida would not ask that question. "That was a fine supper," I said. "Thank you."

"Good luck to you," she said. "Enjoy your sleep."

*　　*　　*

We were lucky. While this inn did not run to such luxuries as private chambers, we were given our own little area at one end of the communal sleeping quarters, and because the place was not full, we were able to conduct a conversation without fear of being overheard. We lay close, as was appropriate for a couple not long wed, and spoke in whispers.

"There's something I need to tell you. You know there's one of ours at court."

"I do."

"You mentioned a man called Rohan. An Enforcer by that name saw me at the last Gathering, when I was with Tali." I had given the Glenfalloch rebels a brief version of that story. "Chances are it's the same person. I'll have to hope he doesn't recognize me."

"This Rohan's not our man?"

"No; but they're comrades. Our man is the Stag Troop leader, a senior Enforcer."

"A troop leader," he whispered. "Black Crow save us. Are you sure?"

"Would I tell you if I wasn't sure? I know him well. And . . . if you see an old man with a black-and-white dog, be careful."

"Old man. Black-and-white dog. Uh-huh. Going to explain why?"

"That's not something you need to know. This Rohan Death-Blade—he may be an ally, but it's far from certain. Don't take any risks with him."

He was silent for a while, then murmured, "A troop leader. I can hardly believe it. The man must have some bollocks."

"Mm."

We slept close to maintain our story, I with my head on Brenn's chest, he with his arm around me. It brought back memories of the night on the island, when I had slept in Flint's arms. I expected disturbing dreams, dreams of Flint in trouble, but I was so tired I fell asleep quickly, and if I did have dreams, when I woke next morning, I had forgotten them.

It was early. We washed, dressed, repacked our bags. After a quick breakfast, we fetched Bolter from the stable and were on our way up to the daunting wall and high towers of Winterfort.

The way was broad and well maintained. Of course, it would need to accommodate troops of horsemen going to and fro, not to mention the carts that would take in supplies for the king's household. The tingle of the uncanny was strong here too; did that mean the southern Good Folk had passed this way? Were they in there, just on the other side of that wall? What if I came face to face with Whisper? What if those folk felt what I was and responded to it, as Sage and her clan had done when I first met them?

We came up to a guard post and were halted by Enforcers with spears. We got down. I felt cold sweat breaking out on my body; my heart was thumping.

In response to a series of curt questions, Brenn gave our names and explained where we had come from and why. He mentioned Rohan Death-Blade. "I was told he's the man I need to speak to. I'm hoping he'll give me a trial, at least."

"A married man?" The Enforcer who was doing the talking lifted his brows.

"My wife's an experienced healer. She'd be an asset to any household."

The man spared me a glance. "Go on, then. Small door to the left of the main entry; tell the guard there that Sark of Seal Troop said to let you in. Good luck. Don't like your chances; your timing's unfortunate."

"Oh? Why is that?"

"Let me give you some advice. The fewer questions you ask, the better."

We moved on, and after another check, passed through the smaller entry to one side of a set of massive closed gates. The arched opening was just high enough to admit a horse; Brenn led Bolter through and I followed.

We found ourselves in a broad courtyard. It was full of activity, folk sweeping, scrubbing, busy with whitewash. There was a faint sensation of magic even here within the walls. I tried to fix my mind on anything but that. Ellida was accustomed to living in a chieftain's household and would therefore not be intimidated in a place like this. She had no trace of a canny gift. Never mind that the southern Good Folk might be somewhere nearby; never mind what my instincts were telling me. I must think as Ellida would.

We were questioned again, standing in the yard while people busied themselves around us. Whatever had happened here, it had done a great deal of damage. Burned timbers were being replaced; vigorous scrubbing was failing to remove certain dark stains from the paving stones. The Enforcer in charge took away Brenn's weapons; he surrendered them without argument. The man did not ask for my weapons, and I did not tell him about the knife that was wrapped up at the bottom of my bag. Brenn mentioned Rohan Death-Blade again. Whether the name meant anything to the Enforcer who was questioning him, there was no telling. Even here within the fortress he was wearing the half mask that was part of the uniform, and all we could see of his face was the eyes. He summoned an underling, who took us to the stables and showed us a stall where Bolter could be left. Brenn unsaddled the horse and rubbed him down.

I had seen this place in a dream; it felt strange to realize how accurate that dream had been. Flint had been here, tending to his horse and looking as if the burdens he carried were becoming too heavy to bear. There was nobody here now but Brenn and me, with the servingman hovering not far off. The place was big enough for a great number of animals, though many of the stalls were empty. Down at the other end were some long-legged black horses, Enforcer mounts. The stalls at Bolter's end housed more ordinary-looking creatures.

When Bolter was settled, our guide took us to an outhouse near the stables and told us to wait. We sat side by side on a bench. Nobody came to offer us food and drink or to tell us how long we might be here. Any conversation seemed fraught with peril.

It was a test, of sorts. A test of patience and a test of nerves. After a long time, we heard voices in the yard outside, and an Enforcer appeared in the doorway. It was not the man I knew as Rohan; I unclenched my tight fists.

"He'll see you now," the Enforcer said, and I was tense

with unease again. Brenn and I got up, and the man said, "Not you. Only him."

I sat. Brenn went out. He left the door ajar, and I heard someone speak outside.

"Morven. I'm Rohan Death-Blade, second-in-command of Stag Troop. I don't have much time. You're from Lord Gormal's household, yes?"

Brenn set out his credentials: he had skills in armed and unarmed combat, a good record in Gormal's service, a heroic dead brother. His tone was a convincing blend of quiet pride and modesty.

"We don't take men who just wander in and ask for a place," Rohan said. "You'd be naïve if you believed that."

"I'm prepared to go through any testing required. I expect no less. This is a lifetime dream for me, something I've worked toward since I was a lad."

"Why leave it so long, then? What are you, five-and-twenty?"

"Close to that. Seemed to me I'd have more to offer if I proved myself first. I've given ten years of loyal service to Gormal. He knew I wanted this; gave me his blessing."

"And he'll take you back if we don't accept you."

A pause. "I hope that won't be necessary."

"We do need experienced men, there's no doubt of that, and at any other time I'd give you a trial. But I'm not taking on any more recruits at present. My troop is at Summerfort, and I'm riding to join them today. Besides, the men we have in training have been with us for some time; you'd be well behind."

"But—"

"Go home to Glenfalloch, Morven. Next spring, if you still have a burning desire to be an Enforcer, come back and talk to me again." A short silence, then in a different tone, "I'm sorry. You've had a long ride. You and your wife."

Brenn sounded as if he was choking back tears. "They told you I'm newly married, then?"

"It is another reason why I am not offering you a trial. While there's no rule stating a king's man should be single, we do prefer that. Your mind needs to be on the job and only on the job. Besides, I doubt very much that your new bride will be wanting to get back on a horse and ride off to Summerfort this morning."

"This was partly for her," Brenn said. "For Ellida. I want to provide for her properly, and as a king's man, I could do that. She has something to offer too. My wife is a talented healer."

"We have healers already, both here and at Summerfort. You should rest overnight, then take your Ellida home. I'm sorry."

He'd be gone in a moment. No time to weigh this fully. The captives and the Caller might be here at Winterfort. Or they might have gone on to Summerfort. One thing was clear: unless Rohan could be persuaded to change his mind, Brenn and I would not be staying at either place. With my heart threatening to leap from my chest, I got up and walked outside. Rohan Death-Blade was clad for riding, from the black boots to the traveling cloak. He was not wearing an Enforcer mask. He looked at me and his amiable blue eyes narrowed.

"My lord," I said, "I am Morven's wife, Ellida. I'm sorry, I could not avoid overhearing what you were saying. May I add my voice to my husband's? He's a fine warrior and deserves a chance. You're right, I am not especially keen to ride out again today, but I will do whatever is required to allow Morven that chance. As for being behind the others, you might give him the opportunity to prove he can catch up." I clasped my hands together behind my back, lest he see how badly they were shaking. Had he recognized me, or did that assessing look mean only that he was wondering what to make of me?

Rohan gestured the servingman over. "Tell Doman I'll be a little longer. He can check the supplies again." The servant left; Rohan turned back toward me. "What's your background?" The question was crisp.

I told him my prepared story. He did not ask questions that would have revealed the truth, such as why I said I was from Glenfalloch, when last summer I had told him Tali and I came from an isolated settlement south of Hiddenwater. He did not comment on my status as a married woman, when at the time of the Gathering Tali and I had been traveling on our own. He did not mention our previous encounter at all. Instead, Rohan Death-Blade asked me how I would treat ill humors in a wound. He asked what I would do if confronted with a man whose hand had been severed by an ax blow. How would I prevent him from bleeding to death, and would he thank me for it? He asked if I had the strength for bone-setting, and I answered honestly that I would need a strong assistant to set a broken limb, but that I could instruct such a person efficiently. He listened to my answers while Brenn stood by with a convincing expression of pride on his face.

"Capable rider, are you?" Rohan asked at the end.

I felt myself flush. "I'm afraid not. My method of riding is to go up behind Morven and hold on tightly."

"Long ride to Summerfort. Two full days, at least."

"If you give us this chance, my lord, I promise not to complain on the way."

"If you're going to be staying at court, you should learn to ride. We move between Summerfort and Winterfort every year."

"I understand, my lord." Was he saying yes?

"I'm nobody's lord, Ellida. I'm a fighter, not a courtier." He looked at Brenn once more. "You'll need a fresh horse; yours can be brought to Summerfort when the court moves later in the season. Talk to the grooms, get them to find you a mount suitable to carry your wife as well."

"Thank you." Brenn's tone was grateful without being groveling. He was good at this. I limited my thanks to a smile. It came to me that perhaps Rohan had said yes not in spite of my being the woman he had met at the Gathering under such suspicious circumstances, but because of it. If that was true, either he had rebel sympathies or he was setting a trap.

"Don't give me cause to regret this," Rohan said, sounding more like the Enforcer he was. "Not in any way, you understand? You'll find the situation at Summerfort somewhat confronting. You accept it, you deal with it, you perform your duties, and you watch what you say."

"We understand," Brenn said.

"I'm not sure you can understand until we get there." Then, to me, "There'll only be four of us riding out: myself, my comrade Doman, and the two of you. Morven, your weaponry will be returned to you before we leave. I'm bending some rules here, but in view of what the two of you have to offer, I'm prepared to do that. Make sure you don't betray the trust I'm placing in you. Now go and see the grooms. I want to be away from here quickly." He glanced over his shoulder, as if to check that nobody was close by. "We'll take it a little more gradually than usual. You may be confident in your ability to do this, Ellida, but in my judgment you'll be lucky to last the day out."

We made camp by Brightwater, in a spot that looked as if it might be frequently used for the purpose, since there was a fireplace among stones, a neat stack of wood beside it, and a stretch of level, sandy shore where the horses could be easily watered. Brenn lifted me down from the horse's back; I steadied myself against its flank, willing my legs to hold me up. I longed for nothing more than to lie down on my blanket and not move one inch until morning. But in the company of the two Enforcers, with Summerfort only another day's ride away, I did not want to show weakness.

"I need to stretch my legs, get rid of a few cramps," I said as the men began unsaddling their horses. I made my way with extreme care down to the shore, trying not to walk like an old woman.

"Stay in sight," said Rohan.

The light was fading; farther along the water's edge some geese had come ashore and were settling noisily for the night. I suppressed the longing to sit down on the ground, breathe deeply for a while, and think of nothing at all. I made myself do what Tali would do. Bend, stretch. Walk on the spot until the cramps eased. Tali would then have run along the shore and back again, not once but several times, each time a little quicker than the last. But Ellida would not run with three men watching, two of them virtual strangers.

I walked briskly until I was almost out of sight, then walked back again a little more quickly. Brenn gave me a smile as I came up to the camping spot; Rohan glanced at me but said nothing. The other Enforcer, Doman, was busy settling the three horses.

"Feeling better?" Brenn asked.

"Yes. What can I do to help?"

"You can make a fire," said Rohan.

"I'll do—" Brenn began.

"Of course." There was plenty of dry material about, and the stack of wood made the task easy. Brenn came over to break up some of the longer branches for me, but otherwise the men left the job to me.

It was as I moved about the area collecting material to get the blaze started that I felt the tingle of magic again. I did not think any Good Folk were close at hand, for the sensation was faint, but perhaps they had passed this way. I looked about more carefully. Here was a neat pile of tiny white stones, all perfectly egg-shaped. Here were five holly leaves threaded onto a willow stick. And here, half concealed by leaf litter, was a feather that had once been white, and now was gray with dust and spattered with what I guessed was blood. A message. Whisper.

"You all right, Ellida?"

I started at Brenn's voice; I had been standing stock-still, the feather in my hand.

"Mm, yes." They'd been here recently enough for these

traces to be undisturbed. It seemed the uncanny army was being taken to Summerfort, or somewhere close by. That meant the Caller would be there. And so, almost certainly, would Flint.

"Need help?" asked Brenn.

"Oh. No, I'm fine." I slipped the feather into my pouch, picked up the pile of tinder, and got back to the job of fire-lighting. This was no accident, I was sure of it. Whisper had known I was coming, had sensed it. And had managed to escape the other Caller's control for long enough to leave me a sign. After all, my friend was not quite broken.

Do not cry, I ordered myself. *Not one tear. Be like Flint. Play your part as he does, as if it were the only truth.*

Later, while both Brenn and Doman slept, Rohan kept watch. He did not stand with spear in hand but sat by the fire, staring at the glowing coals with a slight frown on his brow. I could not sleep, so I lay watching, and saw him get up every so often to patrol the camping area—he walked with barely a sound—before returning to his place.

My mind was too full to let me rest. What troubled me most in a whole sea of difficulties was that if Whisper had sensed I was close by and left me a token, the other Good Folk might also be aware of me. When we reached Summerfort, if indeed they were being held there, I might find I could not keep my gift concealed from them. I had visited three Guardians, had learned something from each of them, and had not once asked for advice on how to mask my ability from uncanny folk. The plan had always been that I would come to Summerfort with the rebels, conceal myself in the crowd with the others, and call in our fey allies when our leader stood up to challenge the king. We had never planned for a second Caller and a second army of Good Folk.

"Can't sleep?" Rohan's voice was quiet.

So he'd noticed I was awake. Being an Enforcer, perhaps he noticed everything.

"I'm making a brew," he said. "Join me if you like."

He was efficient, like Flint. The little pot on the fire, the handful of herbs from a supply neatly stowed in his pack, even a spare cup.

Rohan saw me sniffing the brew, trying to work out the ingredients, and said, "I am no herbalist. A healer made this up for me. Told me there's some skill required in getting the proportions just right."

Was he making polite conversation or testing me? "It's the rosemary," I said. "When it's made into a tea, a little is good for you. Too much, taken often, can kill you." I wondered why the healer had given him this particular mixture, which was effective in soothing troubled minds. Was Rohan also beset by whirling thoughts, dilemmas too difficult to solve? "I'd say this brew is mostly chamomile and peppermint, with only a touch of rosemary."

He smiled, and I remembered the day of the Gathering, when he had helped Flint rescue us. Until then, that day had been all darkness, a sickening show of what Alban and its people had become under Keldec's rule. Rohan's kindness toward us had been all the more memorable, coming after such cruelty.

"You did well today," Rohan said. "You hide your weakness like a warrior."

"I did promise not to complain."

"Someone has taught you to be strong."

"May I ask you a question?"

"Go ahead."

"You said something back at Winterfort about the training my husband will be doing; you said the situation would be confronting. What did you mean?"

His guileless blue eyes met mine. "That's rather direct," he said.

"I'm concerned for Morven. He's a good fighter, and quick-witted enough to get himself out of trouble. But *confronting* sounds serious. I'll be at Summerfort too. What should we expect?"

"I don't answer that kind of question, Ellida. Especially when it's asked by someone I met less than a day ago. Already I've skipped several checks that should have occurred before I let Morven ride with me. Don't make me regret that." His tone was still friendly, his manner unchanged, but the message was quite clear.

"I'm sorry," I murmured. "I won't, I promise." Stupid. All of Alban knew the peril of asking too much, or of revealing too much. Rohan's quick decision to let us come with him had been startling. I was sure people didn't get invitations to join the Enforcers, or to work in Keldec's household, without going through rigorous checking. Even at times when Summerfort needed every trained fighter it could find, there'd be hard questioning and the need to wait until the story was verified. Otherwise, someone would have assassinated Keldec years ago.

Rohan was the kind of man a person might want as a

friend, a man whose openness inspired confidences. But he might be an accomplished dissembler like Flint. The question was where his true loyalties lay.

At dusk the next day, we reached the spot where the river Rush divided into three and flowed into the great loch of Deepwater. There, at the southern end of the Rush valley, was Summerfort, surrounded by a defensive wall as Winterfort was. Beside the fortress lay a broad open area where men practiced the arts of war. This too had its wall, substantial but low enough to allow a glimpse within, provided a person had a vantage point such as that forested hill across the river, the place where Flint and Rohan had left Tali and me after the Gathering. Up there, Sage's clan of Good Folk had various bolt-holes and pathways.

Working as a healer, I'd need to gather herbs from time to time. If I could get into those woods on my own, I might be able to meet Sage or Silver or whoever was about, and send a message to Tali at Shadowfell. My heart grew a little lighter, though I could not look at Summerfort without remembering the Gathering in all its hideous detail. Nor could I ignore the feeling that magic was once again close. In the face of this stronghold, which must be full of iron, I sensed a powerful presence of the uncanny.

At the time of the Gathering there had been tents set up on the level ground between the fortress and the river. That temporary settlement had housed both ordinary travelers, like Tali and me, and the household retainers of Alban's chieftains. Only the guests of highest status were accommodated in the keep itself. When I'd passed this way at other times of year, the level area had held only rough grass dotted with the stumps of the lovely willows that had once grown there. Today the tents were back. Not only that, but campfires burned here and there among them, and I glimpsed folk moving about. Beyond the encampment, Enforcers stood guard.

"Not far now," Rohan said, giving me an assessing look. Before I could say a word, he and Doman moved their horses in on either side of our mount, effectively blocking my view. Had I actually seen Good Folk down there, sitting around a fire eating a meal? Or had that only been a trick of the light? Was Keldec's uncanny army housed *outside* the fortress walls, within a heartbeat of the forest?

"As you see," Rohan said, "Summerfort has some unusual guests at present. Don't comment, don't ask questions. Not at any time. Understood?"

"Of course," murmured Brenn.

"Understood," I said. My heart was beating fast. Flint was probably here; I might see him soon. Would I be able to guard my tongue and school my expression well enough?

The gate guards called a challenge; Rohan identified himself and Doman, said we were his guests, and told them to hurry up and let us in while there was still some supper left. There was laughter; evidently, they knew him well. A gate was opened for us and we rode through into the practice yard, which was empty. The magic was powerful here, for all that.

The men dismounted, and Brenn helped me down.

"Now some news you may not like much," Rohan said with a half smile. "There are no married quarters for Enforcers, at

232

least not until they're fully trained and allocated to a troop; at that point you can put in a request and it will be looked at." He pointed toward an annex of the keep, located near the inner gates. "Stag Troop sleeps and eats there; we work all day. That includes the new recruits, Morven. Ellida, I'll have a word with the household steward about you; he won't be expecting either of you, and I think a wife will be something of a surprise. The women's quarters are in the main part of the keep. When the queen's in residence, there can be a shortage of beds, but there will be plenty of room at present. In the morning someone will introduce you to our healers."

"Thank you," I said. And froze where I stood, because striding toward us from the direction of the annex was a familiar figure. Tears sprang to my eyes. He was here, he was well, my troubling dream of him imprisoned and blind had not, after all, been true.

"Rohan! You're here earlier than we expected. Doman, welcome. I trust you—" Flint saw me and came to a sudden, complete halt. *Say something,* I willed him.

It was Rohan who filled the dangerous silence. "Owen, this is Morven from the household of Gormal of Glenfalloch. He wants to train with our recruits. Morven arrived just as I was leaving, and in view of his skills and experience, I made an exception to the rules for him. This is Ellida, Morven's wife. An accomplished healer. I'm sure a place can be found for her here."

Flint managed a nod to Brenn. Now he was making sure he did not meet my eye. "A long ride," he commented.

"For Ellida in particular, since she's not a horsewoman," Rohan said. "Doman, you and Morven take the horses to the stables and settle them in, then you can show him the living quarters. I'll take Ellida into the keep and find someone to look after her."

"I'll do that." Flint had control of his voice again. "I imagine Toleg will appreciate another assistant. This is a period of intensive training for us, and that tends to mean a steady flow of minor injuries. This way," he said to me, offering an arm in the manner of a courtier.

"Your bag," Brenn said. "And your staff—here." He unstrapped my belongings from the horse's back and handed them over; Flint shouldered the bag. "Might be a while before I see you, from the sound of things," Brenn added, and bent to kiss me on the brow. "Be safe, sweetheart."

With my arm in Flint's and my whole body alive to his, I rose to my tiptoes and kissed Brenn on the cheek. Our story must be maintained at every moment; we must make no errors, even in the company of men who knew the truth or half guessed it. "And you be safe," I said. "I'll miss you."

Flint and I walked across the practice area, the place where so much blood had been shed last midsummer. *When we reach that doorway,* I thought, *I'll have to let go of him.* And I wished the walk were a hundred, a thousand, times longer.

"Don't say you're actually married to that man," Flint said under his breath.

"Of course not. He's one of us. Flint, tell me quickly, is the other Caller here?" It felt perilous to speak of this, even with a wide empty space all around us. In a place like this, I wondered if anywhere was truly safe.

"You know, then. My message got through."

"I know because I saw them marching north. That's

why I've come." We were halfway to the inner gates already. Torches burned in sockets to either side, and guards would be on duty in the tower. Even out of earshot, we had to be careful.

"It's so good to see you," Flint murmured. "But your being here terrifies me. The Caller, Esten—watch out for him; he's more powerful than he looks. And beware of the man who controls him, Brydian. In the queen's pocket, and quick to suspect anyone. Brydian is canny. His gift allows him to protect Esten while he's close; that reduces the possibilities."

He was speaking of assassination, telling me it couldn't be done while this Brydian was about. I said nothing, only nodded.

"Don't draw attention to yourself," Flint said. "You'll have seen what's beyond the walls. I'm . . . working on that. No more now."

We were still twenty feet from the gates, but someone had seen us coming. The gates were opened and two Enforcers came from within to stand one to each side, waiting for us to enter. I had the distinct sense that I was walking into a prison.

"Not far now, Ellida," Flint said, nodding at the guards as we passed between them. "I'll find someone to look after you."

"Thank you. May I ask your name?"

He smiled. "Owen. Owen Swift-Sword. I'm the leader of Stag Troop, and we have responsibility for the training of warriors, both the new and the seasoned. Your husband, I gather, is in the latter group. Still, there are aspects of an

Enforcer's training that a man cannot learn anywhere but here. I'm sure you understand that."

"I do."

"This way," he said. "I hope you're ready for this."

Weapons sharp, backs straight, hearts high. "I'm ready," I said.

Flint introduced me to Summerfort's steward, Brand, a man of about five-and-thirty who walked with a limp—I wondered if he had once been a fighter, for he had a no-nonsense briskness of manner—and his wife, Scia, a tall woman with freckled skin and nut-brown hair in a tidily plaited crown. Then he left me.

Scia was a sometime assistant to Toleg, Summerfort's healer and herbalist. During the busy summer months, she told me, she helped him all day; in the quieter time, when the court was at Winterfort, she managed the household with her husband and only worked in the infirmary when Toleg needed her. I felt awkward at first, wondering if she would consider my arrival a threat. But she seemed delighted, saying the extra pair of hands would free her for myriad other tasks.

Scia quizzed me on my experience. I'd had limited practice in some areas of healing, but my herb knowledge was good enough to have her nodding and smiling.

I would not meet Toleg until the morning, for he was engaged in a complex decoction and had ordered that nobody disturb him. "He's not the most even-tempered of men," Scia said. "But expert; he's taught me a great deal. If you keep quiet and get on with your work, he'll come around to accepting you."

She took me to a great hall for supper—a cavernous chamber barely warmed by the fire burning on its broad hearth. Of the five long tables, only one was occupied, and it was not full. The serving people were few. Among those seated there was a group of Enforcers; I counted ten.

"Men of Wolf Troop," Scia said, seeing me watching them. "They keep a complement here over the winter to guard prisoners, maintain the watch, attend to local problems. The rest of them are helping Stag Troop with the training. You won't see many of them in the keep, not now they've got the . . ." She hesitated. "You'll have spotted them, I imagine, as you rode in. Folk from the south, a different kind of folk, here to learn how to fight. Camped outside the wall; they come into the practice yard during the day. The less we say about that, the better. That man over there, the one in the dark robe, is Master Brydian, the queen's councillor. He's told us all to keep our mouths shut about it. If I could give you only one piece of advice, it would be this: never disobey an order from Master Brydian."

The councillor was sitting with three other men, quite a distance down the table from us. He was the man who had sat beside Queen Varda at the Gathering; I had seen him again escorting the captives on that terrible journey from the south. Two of his companions wore Enforcer black. The other was a young fellow; I guessed his age as no more than twenty. I was fairly sure he too had been riding behind the enslaved Good Folk, and from what little Flint had been able to tell me, I deduced this was Esten. He looked unwell. His skin was sickly pale and grooves bracketed his mouth, as if he was in constant pain. Brydian leaned toward him, murmuring something, and he answered. I made myself look away.

"You won't see those strange folk in the infirmary," Scia said, keeping her voice down. "When they get hurt, Toleg goes out to tend to them in the yard. He's not happy with the situation, but don't tell him I said that. It's not as if we don't have a steady stream of our own fighters coming in with sprains and bruises and cuts."

"I understand."

"I'm not sure anyone could understand, really, until they'd seen it. But I'm pleased you're here. Toleg will be too, especially if you can work without supervision. I can't always come and help him. My children are still small, and there's other work to do."

I asked her their names and ages; while she spoke of them, her face softening, I considered how appalling it would be to raise a family here, within the walls of Summerfort. Perhaps she and Brand sent them away during the Gathering. A child who witnessed such acts would surely be scarred forever. "Maybe, now that I'm here, you can have more time with them," I said.

Her smile was rueful. "I doubt it, Ellida. This new venture—it's testing us all hard. And once the court moves here, nobody gets a spare moment. But enough of that. Tell me about this new husband of yours. How did you meet?"

I did my best to be the blushing new bride, telling her the romantic and completely untrue story of how Morven and I had met, and how thrilled I was that Rohan Death-Blade had offered my husband the opportunity he'd longed for since he was a lad. Scia seemed happy to listen. It was a rarity, perhaps, for her to have another woman to talk to when the court was at Winterfort; here in the dining hall I could only see one other, and she was busy collecting platters. I talked about the clothes I had brought, and how I doubted they would be fine enough to wear once the king and queen arrived at Summerfort. Not that I would be seeing much of them, I supposed.

"Well, no," Scia said. "You'll be even busier when they get here, what with all the men filling the place up. By midsummer every troop of Enforcers will be in residence, and we'll be run off our feet stitching up wounds and dispensing drafts. That's not even to mention those folk out beyond the walls—" She came to a sudden halt, looking up over my shoulder. Her face had turned white.

"Idle talk, Scia." The voice was deep and soft. I felt the hairs on the back of my neck prickle. "And who is this? A new face? I did not know anyone was expected."

I rose to my feet; turned to look up into the dark eyes of Brydian, the queen's councillor, who had moved as silently as a wildcat stalking its prey. I could not read his expression, but his tone had alerted me. "I am Ellida from Glenfalloch, Master Brydian." I dropped my practiced curtsy, hating myself. "I rode here with my husband, who has been accepted to train as an Enforcer. Rohan Death-Blade came with us from Winterfort." I paused to draw breath, and when he said nothing, simply went on examining me as if he did not believe a word, I added, "I am an experienced healer, my lord. Rohan believed there would be work for me here, as well as for my husband. Scia was just explaining the duties to me."

"I see." A long pause. "Then Scia must make sure she keeps to that. She and her husband have been in this household a long time. How many little ones is it now, Scia, three, four?"

"Three, Master Brydian." Scia's tone was uneven.

"Ah, yes. I believe I've seen your son in the courtyard playing with a ball. So tender at that age, aren't they? Fragile as spring flowers."

Scia said nothing. I swallowed sudden rage. It had been a threat, clear as clear.

"We have rules here," Brydian said, his cool gaze back on me. "Rules designed for the good of every member of the household. Start with this: no idle questions and no gossip. Of course, that may be a little difficult for women to adhere to." He gave a wintry smile, which I did not return. "But we expect obedience. Complete obedience. I hope that is understood."

I made myself speak courteously. "It's understood, Master Brydian. Morven—my husband—and I are here to work. We know it's a rare opportunity. We won't give you any cause for concern, I promise."

He smiled again. "Good, good. Make sure you don't forget." He turned on his heel and was gone, back to his place beside the Caller. I would not ask Scia about him. I hardly dared ask her about anything, lest I put her and her family at risk.

We sat in silence, finishing our meal. Only after Brydian arose to leave did Scia murmur, "The winters are easier."

"Mm. Fewer people here?" No Brydian. No king and queen. Only a half troop of Enforcers, who, under the circumstances, would perhaps be somewhat more relaxed.

"That's right. Now, if you're finished, I'll show you the

women's quarters. Almost empty at present; you'll have a choice of beds." Her manner was briskly cheerful, but her face was still pale.

As we went out, I looked across the hall and saw Brydian and the Caller leaving through another door. Brydian had a hand on Esten's shoulder as if to steer him along. Flint had said Brydian was in the queen's pocket. I had observed Queen Varda at the Gathering. I had seen how often the king turned to her for advice before making a choice; I had seen how often she chose the cruelest, the most repellent option. No wonder Esten looked like a man plagued by nightmares. A shiver of utter terror ran through me. Here, within the walls of Summerfort, I was only one step away from discovery. If Brydian guessed what I was, if anyone did, I could find myself in Esten's position, a pawn in the queen's perverse games. A tool for the king's ambition. Before that could happen, I would use the hemlock I carried with me. Better no Caller than a Caller forced to the king's will.

"Feeling cold?" Scia glanced at me as we walked along one of Summerfort's many hallways. "I'll see about getting you another shawl, maybe something more suitable to wear in the queen's presence, later in the season. She likes a certain standard at supper. Your things are perfectly suitable, but she can be . . . fussy." And, when I made to protest, "It's all right, we do have a few garments set by. Her ladies leave behind whatever they're tired of; nobody seems to mind if we make use of those items. I may even find you a gown or two, though you're very slight. Perhaps we can make some alterations."

"Thank you. That's kind of you." *Just don't give me anything that was worn by Queen Varda herself,* I thought. The queen was of a similar height to me, though considerably more shapely. The thought of touching any garment of hers, even something as small as a ribbon, repulsed me.

Scia gave me a warm smile. Now that we were well away from the hall and Brydian's watchful eye, her cheeks had more color. "It's a pleasure, Ellida. Here are the sleeping quarters. You can claim any bed that doesn't have someone's possessions stored under it. There's a little yard with a privy out the door there, and a pump for washing. I won't see you again until the morning—Brand and I have our own quarters. As for idle gossip"—she looked over her shoulder, as if Brydian might have followed us like a dark shadow all the way from the hall—"you won't find much of it here. Everyone knows the penalty if they break the rules. Besides, by the time the women finish their work for the day, they're too tired to want anything but sleep."

There were only four other women sharing the long sleeping chamber, and Scia was right: when they came in sometime after she had left me, they greeted me without a great deal of interest, told me their names, then rolled into their beds and fell asleep.

For me, sleep came less readily, and when it did, my dreams were full of all I feared most. In the morning I woke still weary. I washed and dressed; most of the other women were already gone to kitchen duties, but a girl who looked after the household mending walked to the hall with me. The keep was large, the steps and hallways and outbuildings many and confusing. I must learn my way about quickly.

After breakfast, Scia took me to meet the healer, Toleg. He had not come to eat in the hall, but Scia said that was nothing unusual. Toleg was most content in his own domain, and often had someone bring him a meal of bread and cheese rather than bothering with formal dining. So I met him in the infirmary, which consisted of a roomy chamber with several pallets and a well-stocked stillroom.

I had plaited my hair tightly, not a wisp astray, and over it I wore a neat cloth that one of the other women had found for me. A clean apron covered my gown. I'd made sure my hands were well scrubbed.

Toleg was a small person, not much taller than me, and quite old, his hair and beard gray, his face marked with deep lines around the brow. He wore a long robe something like Brydian's, but of brown homespun, and over it an apron similar to mine. The sleeves of the robe were rolled up.

Scia introduced us. "This is Ellida from Glenfalloch, wife of the new Enforcer in training. You'll have had Brand's message about her. Another assistant for us. Ellida, this is Master Toleg, who taught me most of what I know about healing."

"Did I say we had need of an unskilled helper, Scia?" Toleg's brows went up.

"Master Toleg," I ventured, "I am not unskilled. I've been working in the household of—"

"Yes, yes, I've been told all that," Toleg said dismissively, reaching for a cloth to wipe his hands. He had, it appeared, already started work for the day. A tray with an untouched platter of bread and cold meat stood at one end of the workbench. On a board were tidy heaps of finely chopped herbs, and on the small hearth a kettle steamed. There were no patients in the infirmary, but tools of surgery were laid out in meticulous order on a side table. "How can you be skilled? You're not much more than a child."

"I'm sixteen, Master Toleg." This was not like talking to Brydian. Here, I could prove myself if he gave me a chance. "I'm a married woman. My grandmother taught me herb craft from an early age. For the last two years I have been assisting the healers in Gormal of Glenfalloch's household. A large household with many men-at-arms. I can perform most of the everyday duties you must require here."

He said nothing, only went back to chopping his herbs. The scent was powerful, spreading through the warm air of the chamber.

Scia had put on her own apron, which was hanging from a peg, and was tending the fire.

"Everyday duties," Toleg echoed with his back to me. "Can you deal with a suppurating wound? Set a broken bone? Deliver a child from a dead mother?"

I swallowed. This was somewhat more testing than Rohan's inquisition. "Ill humors in a wound? That would probably require surgery, Master Toleg, and I would be lying if I claimed I could do that, though I am very keen to learn. I would be able to assist you without fainting. In a less severe case, the problem might be solved, at least in part, by the use of maggots to eat away dying flesh. I cannot set a bone on my own, but I have assisted with it several times and, given a helper with strong arms, I can ensure the process is carried out correctly. The delivery of a child after the mother's death would also be a matter of surgery. I hope I never have to help with such an event, but if I had to do it, I would. The child would have to be cut from the womb. Its chances of survival would be slim at best."

"What am I making?" He shot the question at me, arrow-quick.

My sense of smell was good; I hoped my memory was as good. "I would guess someone has a skin condition, a severe rash, an itch, and that you are making a curative wash. Or you may be preparing a poultice for a tumor of the skin."

"And the components are?"

"Figwort, mandrake, speedwell. Perhaps other herbs in quantities too small for me to identify."

"What other possibilities might one investigate for such a tumor, assuming this is a poultice?"

I thought fast. "All parts of slippery elm, Master Toleg. Heather twigs and flowers. But I understand mandrake root, if it can be found, is the most effective."

"Mm-hm. Scia, show Ellida where we keep everything." He turned. "It's a trial only, understand? Anyone can spout theory. Show me you can stay calm when there's a man screaming under the knife, and I might consider keeping you."

"Thank you," I said. "I'll work hard."

"Work hard and work well," said Toleg. "Now go and learn where to find things quickly. Would that this might be a place of peace, where there was time to teach a new assistant properly. But it's quite the opposite, as you'll soon discover. We must be ready for anything."

I wanted to act without delay: to talk to the captive Good Folk, to find out if Whisper was all right, to know if Ean and the other young men from the south were safe. I wanted, oh so badly, to talk to Flint again.

Instead, I spent my days between infirmary and still-room, keeping quiet and making myself useful. Toleg was terse at the best of times, but to the extent that such a man could thaw, he did so day by day, thanks, I guessed, to my ability to work hard, learn quickly, and show honest respect. I was far from an expert healer, but Toleg soon realized I knew enough to be genuinely helpful.

There were small milestones of trust: the first time he let me make and apply a poultice unsupervised, the first time he left me in the infirmary alone while he went to tend to one of the Good Folk who had been injured. The first time he sent me, with the key, to his locked cupboard to fetch substances too dangerous to be stored where idle hands could reach them. I brought exactly what he'd asked for and locked the cupboard after me.

As the days passed, Toleg began to entrust duties to me that had been Scia's, and increasingly, when she came to the infirmary to ask if he needed her, he'd tell her to go off and see her children. She didn't speak of them much; perhaps Brydian's threat had stopped her tongue. But she and Toleg had worked together a long while, and he would sometimes ask her about them, revealing a softer side of himself that was seldom on show. Scia kept her answers short, but her tone was full of love and pride. She might as well enjoy her time with them now, Toleg said, as once the royal party arrived, none of us would have a moment to ourselves.

I did not see Brenn and I did not see Flint. The household guards from Wolf Troop were the only Enforcers who took their meals in the hall. When Stag Troop was afflicted with a vomiting and purging malady, an Enforcer named Tallis came to the infirmary to request a large quantity of the draft Toleg made up for such problems. He needed sufficient to dose everyone, he said. I risked asking after my husband, and was told Morven was as sick as a dog like the rest of them, but otherwise doing well—Owen Swift-Sword had commented recently that his newest recruit hardly needed training.

I had no plausible excuse to go beyond the inner wall that guarded the keep. A large kitchen garden was maintained within that wall, including an herb patch to supply us with the more commonly used plants. Toleg would go out to the woods every so often with a basket over his arm and come back with wild-harvested herbs. He never said anything about what he had seen out there, and neither Scia nor I asked him. I thought escaping the stone walls and enjoying the smells and sounds and sights of the forest would lift a person's spirits. But when Toleg returned from these trips outside, he was more taciturn than ever, his shoulders hunched in a posture that said more plainly than any words, *Leave me alone*. It was blindingly clear that he did not like what was happening at Summerfort. But he too obeyed Brydian's rules.

I had hoped there might be a high vantage point somewhere within the keep, a window, a patch of flat roof, from which I could get at least a partial view of the Good Folk's encampment by the river mouth. Given the right spot, I should also be able to see down into the practice yard, where Stag Troop would be doing their training. But while such places undoubtedly existed—the lookout tower, for instance, where guards from Wolf Troop were stationed on watch—I could not get to them without drawing suspicion.

I did not dream of Flint now. Perhaps his being so close, yet out of reach, had altered the way our minds worked together. He had not told me much about his canny skill of mind-mending. From the first, I had shrunk from that, since I had more reason than most folk to loathe and despise what it had become: the vile art of enthrallment. But I knew that Flint's gift, used in the way it should be, would allow him to heal tormented minds, bring comfort to the grieving and peace to the troubled. It had made our dreams of each other especially vivid, often reflecting something of the truth. The dreams could be disturbing, but also useful. It was a dream of me alone out on the windswept skerry that had brought Flint rushing back to the isles and allowed us our only night together, a beautiful night we had spent in each other's arms. We had not lain together as husband and wife; we would not take that final step until Alban was free and we could believe in a future spent together.

Seeing Scia's situation, I was even more glad that we had made that choice. We had made ourselves vulnerable enough by falling in love. To add a child to the picture would make our situation untenable. I understood, better than I ever had before, why soft feelings were forbidden among the rebels of Shadowfell. For Flint and me, those feelings had grown despite our efforts to stop them; they had been like a tenacious plant that sets down roots between the rocks and shoots up high, raising a triumphant flower to defy the autumn frost, the winter gale. A smile came to my face as I thought of it. That plant would be a thistle, strong-stemmed, spiked with defensive prickles, holding aloft its purple bloom. And that was only right, since Regan's Rebels had chosen the thistle as their emblem. A love as strong as Alban itself. A love as enduring as the glens and mountains and silvery lochs of this poor, damaged land of ours.

Chapter Ten

Barely two moons had passed since Gill had taken over as leader of Wolf Troop, after the unfortunate death of Murad from a wound turned foul with ill humors. Gill was still establishing his authority with his men, and was far more ready than, say, Galany or Abhan would have been to let Flint take the lead in handling the near-impossible job the king had given them. That made things easier.

Then there were his own men. Rohan he trusted with all but the most perilous secrets, and he suspected his second-in-command had an awareness even of those. Tallis could be relied on not to rush off to Brydian every time Flint took a risk or bent a rule. The others still seemed to respect and trust their troop leader, even after what had happened at the last Gathering.

Flint had not been the only Enforcer called on to perform that day, though he was the only one still standing. Keldec had no idea what a profound effect that fight to the death between Duvach and Buan had had on the men; all the Enforcers, even the enthralled ones, went quiet when someone spoke of it. Since he'd come back to Summerfort, Flint had seen how the men went to the spot where Buan had hanged himself after the fight. There'd nearly always be one or two of them there, keeping silent vigil as if to reassure Buan's shade that they understood he'd had no choice. Every Enforcer present that day had seen him kill his comrade as quickly and mercifully as he could. What he had been obliged to do, he had done well; his fellow warriors would have forgiven the act. But Buan had not been able to forgive himself.

Something had changed in the men's attitudes that day, not only in Seal Troop, from which those two comrades had come, but in most of the fighting men. It extended even to the troop leaders; Flint had sensed it at that council before he left Winterfort, when Abhan, a combat veteran of many years, had supported his suggestion that the captive Good Folk not be culled. Perhaps the change would be short-lived. For now, he welcomed it. If it helped him convince his men that the Good Folk could be spoken to, listened to, negotiated with, and perhaps made into something like allies, so much the better. A plan was forming in his mind, a plan that would allow him to continue with the king's work while at the same time preparing for the rebellion. For it to succeed, he had to stay one step ahead of Brydian.

He'd been shocked when Neryn arrived at Summerfort, though, to his immense relief, she'd come with a convincing cover story. She was never far from his thoughts, no matter what he was doing. He believed she'd approve of his plan. It was a pity there was no opportunity to explain it to her, but her coming to court was so fraught with risk that it was probably just as well his duties kept them apart. He could have manufactured excuses to visit the infirmary, but he did not; surely, however well the two of them dissembled, someone would see how it was between them. As for why Neryn had taken the perilous step of coming here so early, with only the one companion, he did not understand that at all. He could not see Tali approving such a plan. But he had been out of contact for a while. Maybe the situation had changed.

For his own plan, he took advantage of suppertime. Brydian and Esten always ate in the relative luxury of the keep. Stag Troop took its meals in the Enforcers' communal living quarters, entered through the practice area. The Good Folk, under Flint's rules, were responsible for preparing their own food; the household provided them with rations and wood for their fires. They took their supper in the encampment.

Esten was so worn out by each day's work, Flint judged he would only leave the keep after supper if there was an emergency, something nobody else could settle. Brydian might, he supposed, take it into his head to spring a surprise visit, but generally where Esten was, Brydian was also. Thus had arisen the idea of the Twilight Councils.

The first few evenings he went on his own, without a scrap of iron on him. The usual contingent from Wolf Troop was guarding the camp. While Esten slept, it was necessary to maintain control with iron, distasteful as that was; if he ordered the men of Wolf Troop to set aside their own swords and knives, he suspected these captives would overwhelm their human guards and escape before reinforcements could arrive. In practical terms, setting them all free would not serve the cause well. It would see him, and probably Rohan too, either executed or imprisoned. Besides, now that he had Esten, the king could simply order that a new army of Good Folk be formed to replace the others.

His own plan was far subtler. If it worked—and with Neryn at Summerfort already, he thought perhaps it might— then the hideous thing Esten had been made to do could be turned on its head; these captives might, in the end, be called to fight, not as a display of the king's might, but as part of the rebellion. Could he do it? There was no telling, but Sage had spoken to him of her own accord, not once but twice. He could at least try.

During his visits to the camp, he ordered the Wolf Troop men to back off a certain distance, hoping that might reduce the discomfort cold iron caused even the strongest of these folk. This did not win him instant trust among the Good Folk; he had not expected that. But he took his own food, day by day, and waited to be invited to their fireside. He asked one after another, much as he might ask his own men after a long day's hard fighting, how they were faring, whether they were well, whether the rations were proving suitable. Many of the captives were in a bad way, damaged in body or mind by the constant presence of iron. Of those still strong enough to answer, some offered growls or invective, some spat at him, some threw stones. But as the days passed and he kept up a steady pattern of visits, first one, then another, was prepared to give a nod of recognition when he came among them.

On the seventh evening, the owl-like creature flew over to walk by him as he crossed the open ground from the practice area.

"Time's short," the owl being said. "So I'll give you my name. I'm Whisper, and I come frae the north. These folk are Southies; they hae a good resistance tae iron, or they wouldna hae lasted sae long. But even a Southie has his breaking point. There's folk wi' maybe three, four more days in them before they fall victim tae its destructive power. Is that what your king wants, an army o' dead folk?"

"Thank you for talking to me, Whisper. I am Owen Swift-Sword, as you know."

"Aye, I heard that was ane o' your names."

Flint gave the being a sharp look. Both of them stopped walking.

"I have a question for you," Flint said, lowering his voice, though none of Wolf Troop was within earshot. "I know little about how a Caller uses his gift, but I see the influence Esten has upon all of you. He can make you act against your true nature, I believe." He looked straight into the big owl-eyes, wishing he could be sure it was safe to speak. Any one of these folk might pretend a truce, then report every word he said back to Brydian.

"Aye," Whisper said. "The Caller can dae that. You mentioned a question. But you didna ask it."

He lowered his voice still further. "By night, when the Caller is asleep, is your mind free of him?"

Whisper said nothing, only dipped his head in a half nod.

"What of the others? Would they flee if there were no guards? Or no iron?"

"I canna answer for Southies. They make their ain rules."

"You could give me an informed guess."

"The iron keeps them in, aye. There's fighters among

254

these folk who could overpower your guards, if there wasna sae much iron. But . . . we all fear the Caller. You've seen what that fellow can dae. He's got a charm that can turn a body tae jelly wi' pain. Tae rise up against your folk is tae risk that man coming oot here o' a sudden, or calling frae within those walls, and setting his terror on us. When he does . . . It's the pain o' your worst nightmare, like having your skin peeled off bit by bit, or finding yourself trussed up ower a fire, slowly roasting tae death. And at the same time your heid blasted tae splinters. The threat o' that, even when the fellow's awa' inside and fast asleep, is enow tae keep the bravest among them obedient." Whisper fell silent a moment, glancing around the encampment.

"But you're not obedient. You're saying things that could get you in a lot of trouble."

"Aye."

"So you're capable of thinking and acting for yourself, even with that threat over you. Why don't you fly away, over the heads of my guards, out of reach of their weapons?"

Whisper looked especially grave. "Wi' me, it's a bittie mair complicated. I could, aye. But I wouldna. There's a responsibility, you ken?"

"To the Southies?" From what he had heard of the Good Folk, this sounded unlikely. Could Whisper be hinting that he was an ally? Part of the rebellion?

"A bigger responsibility than that, laddie. As for how it is that I can speak my mind, it wasna that way when the Caller first dragged us under his influence. It scrambled up my heid; I lost myself awhile. But something's changed; I started tae feel it as you were bringing us along the loch. Someone coming close. She's here now, at Summerfort. A friend I was parted frae when I was taken. A body whose voice I hear even when she doesna speak. Wi' her sae close, my mind's clear again. The others are no' sae open tae her; they're well beaten doon. But . . . if she called, chances are they'd hear."

Flint's heart was pounding. Neryn. Whisper meant Neryn. "Don't breathe a word of this to the others," he said. "You risk her safety if you do."

"Nae need tae tell me that, laddie. I'm nae fool." A pause; they regarded each other. "I hae a wee suggestion, if you care tae listen."

"I do." Flint squatted down to be nearer Whisper's level.

"If you want something frae a Southie, dinna ask him straight out for a favor. Offer him a bargain, a deal. Food and firewood and the absence of stone walls, that's a first step, aye. They ken that's your doing, and you hae that act o' kindness tae thank for your chance tae walk among them wi'oot getting your head ripped off by one o' those three fellows, the biggest ones. You're looking for fighters? Believe me, they've shown you only the smallest part o' what they can dae, Caller or no Caller."

"I see. Offer them something, you say. What would they want? I cannot send them all home." No doubt that if he put the question to them, every one of them would say freedom. And that was something he could not give; not yet.

"Freedom for those likely tae perish under the iron before your king can make use o' them; cooperation frae the others as the price. And a skerrick o' hope, if you can get that in wi'oot spilling any secrets. Simple. And I can tell you which tae put the proposition tae."

"The three you mentioned, the big warriors?"

"Them first. Leaders among their own clans. Not natural allies, but drawn intae a kind o' alliance by adversity. Call a council; make it formal, though it'd be only yourself and them, unless you hae others o' your kind that willna slash out at the least sign o' disobedience."

"It has to be out here, at dusk or later."

"While the Caller sleeps, aye? And his minder."

Flint nodded. From down in the encampment, many eyes were now turned in their direction; he could not see the Wolf Troop guards, who were in the shadows beyond the firelight, but he imagined they too were watching and wondering. He must bring the conversation to an end quickly. "Thank you," he murmured. "And if it helps, I can reassure you that at present the friend you spoke of is safe and well. But I have little opportunity to speak with her. I have one last question for you."

"Aye?"

"Esten. Controlling the Southies, and yourself, with the threat of using his especially painful call. If word got to him, or to the minder, that you and I had been talking at length, could he not extract the details of our conversation from you by using that same call?"

"I might ask you the same question," Whisper said. "There's a lot o' your guards wi' their e'en on us, nae doot wondering what we might find tae say tae each other."

"Enforcers answer to their troop leaders, not to councillors. I am the troop leader. Those men—carefully chosen men—respect my way of going about things; they share my view that the preparation of fighters is not the work of a councillor, or indeed of a Caller. I trust them not to tell; and if they break that trust, I am ready for what might follow."

"Why doesna that surprise me?" The owl-eyes held the trace of a smile. "As for me, if it came to it, I might dae as you suggested: fly oot o' trouble. I wouldna tell. I gie my solemn word."

Flint nodded acceptance.

"Come wi' me, then," Whisper said, "and we'll hae a word wi' those big fellows."

The meeting that followed was the first of the Twilight Councils. The guards from Wolf Troop were too far away to hear, and he explained it to them later as a discussion of how they could all cooperate better over the training, which was the truth, as far as it went. With Whisper smoothing the way, he spoke to the three big warriors, each shaped much like a man, but with certain features that marked him out as something else. One had a pelt like little flickering flames; he gave his name as Scorch. Another possessed the normal complement of eyes, nose, and mouth, set in a face that resembled a chunk of rock, complete with crevices and holes from which, from time to time, jets of pungent steam emerged; he was called Fume. The third had feet like those of a huge bird, the toes tipped with scythe-like talons, and on his head a crest of exuberant crimson feathers in place of hair. His name was Blaze. Each of them was fearsome in combat, capable of destroying a human opponent in moments. As a result, all three had been subject to Esten's tightest control, and none greeted Flint with any enthusiasm. It was, Flint suspected, only Whisper's moderating presence that stopped them from burning, steaming, and ripping him to death without a word spoken.

Knowing the opportunity might come only once, he set out the situation clearly for them, then made his offer. He told them the king had no immediate plans to send them into battle, but wanted them to put on a display at the Gathering, one mixed troop of fey and human warriors against another, demonstrating their skills. He had no doubt, he added, that they had the capacity to deliver this, provided everyone was prepared to work together.

"After what's been done tae us," Fume growled, "why would any o' us be wantin' tae work wi' ye? Or did ye miss the fact that we've been hauled up here against oor will? That we've been forced tae stand by while wee folk were tortured and murdered a' alang the way? That we've been fenced in wi' cold iron, mocked, shamed, and tormented till some o' the little ones went oot o' their minds? Why would we trust a word ye say?"

"Because I'm here, outside the walls," Flint said quietly. "Because I came on my own, without any weapons, knowing you could kill me if you chose to. Because the alternative is to go on with what you just described until even more of you are destroyed. And because I have something to offer you."

"Oh, aye?" Scorch's tone was of complete disbelief. He folded his massive arms. "And what might that be? Extra rations tae nibble on while we watch oor folk drop deid under the Caller's evil spell? A wee pat on the heid before ye deliver us up tae this *king* o' yours?" He spoke the word as if it were poison on his lips.

"You might give the laddie time tae explain," said Whisper. He seemed not in the least intimidated by the giant trio.

"In return for the cooperation of your strongest folk, those capable of fighting well and of resisting iron, I will release your weaker ones. I will order my guards to let them slip away by night and find their own way home. We'd do it over the next few nights, so the drop in numbers is less obvious."

A silence. They were surprised, at the very least.

"The plan's no' sae bad, so far as it gaes," Fume said eventually. "But what aboot the rest o' us? Dinna expect us tae believe this king o' yours will watch oor wee display at this Gatherin', then thank us kindly, toss us a few coppers for oor pains, and bid us be off hame."

Now it became perilous. "Would I expect you to believe that, when I myself know how unlikely it is?" Flint said. "I'm asking for your cooperation only until midsummer day; until you are asked to step up and prove yourselves at the Gathering. We'll rehearse the mock combat; we'll all go into it with every move prepared. The human contingent, fighting alongside you, will be made up of young men who are still undergoing basic training; they will be at Summerfort within a turning of the moon, and we'll practice this together. When we step out before the king, at midsummer, the Caller will be there. I cannot control that. But . . ."

"Spit it oot, laddie!"

Flint looked at Whisper.

"What he tells you," Whisper said, "it's no' for sharing, understand? You've seen the fellow that watches ower the Caller; you've seen the look in his eyes. There's folk willna be happy tae find the number o' us reduced night by night, and no' ane corpse tae show for it, aye?" He glanced up at Flint, who nodded, stunned at the small being's perception. "And the plan—there's some parts o' that better not spread abroad.

I canna see that fellow lowering himself tae chat tae us, but if he does, we're deaf and mute."

"What aboot the Caller, curse his evil heart? If he bids us talk, we talk whether we want tae or no'."

"As tae that," said Whisper, looking up at Scorch, "it's possible you may find the Caller's hold ower you weakening as time passes. You may find you can resist it a bittie mair."

"Oh, aye?" Scorch glanced at the smaller being in plain disbelief.

"Aye," said Whisper. "It's the truth. Open yourself up tae a change; see if you can feel it. I canna explain further."

Enough; this conversation was sailing into dangerous waters. "Do I have your word that you'll keep this quiet, as far as you can?" Flint asked. "Not only the plan, but the fact that it is my plan?"

"A promise, wi'oot kennin' what it is ye havena told us yet? Ye think we're half-wits?"

Flint smiled. "Far from it. I think you are fine warriors, with excellent judgment; fighters whom, under different circumstances, I would be honored to have as comrades. I believe you capable of passing on to the rest of your folk here what they need to know—and keeping to yourselves what is too risky to share. But I need an undertaking from you before I put the last of it into words."

"Aye," the three rumbled.

"It's my informed belief that midsummer will mark a great change in the affairs of Alban," he murmured. Even that seemed too loud. Every word was fraught with risk. His palms were clammy and his heart beat hard. "The pattern of events will not be as folk expect." He drew an unsteady breath.

"Blood will be shed." Whisper too was keeping his voice low. "There'll be risk, aye; risk o' death or maiming. But we face that risk already, day by day, as prisoners o' the king. Take up the laddie's offer and there's a real chance o' getting hame. I dinna mean the notion you scoffed at, the king patting us on the back and saying, *Well done.* I'm speaking o' gaeing hame and living in peace, wi' nae chance o' this happening again."

The three stared at him in amazement.

"Is that right?" Blaze said, turning to Flint. "Is the Northie speakin' true?"

"He is," Flint said.

"Ye're lyin'," Fume said, scowling. "The Caller can order every move we make; he can play wi' oor thoughts, mak' us dae what we'd rightly be shrinkin' frae. And ye said the Caller will be there, at the Gatherin'. Ye canna be tellin' us the fellow will turn against the king?"

"No," Flint said. "But I must ask you to take this on trust. To tell you more would be to take one risk too many." He was prepared to risk his own safety in order to win these folk's trust, but not Neryn's. Without her, the plan he was putting in place could not succeed. All depended on her ability to override Esten's call; to take control not only of the forces Tali would bring to the Gathering, but of those he was preparing. *Let her be strong enough,* he prayed. *Let my plan not destroy both her and the rebellion.*

"Aye, weel," said Scorch, "we'd be needin' tae put it tae the other folk here. Escape for some at the price o' cooperation frae the others."

"Of course. You'll need time. But not too much time, I

hope, because we have work to do, and I want the weaker folk safely away before I challenge you further."

"Ane question," said Fume, whose craggy brow bore wrinkles of perplexity.

"I'll answer it if I can."

"Why would ye care? Ye're a hard man, a king's man, a leader among your ain kind. You'll hae done what a' king's men dae. What changed ye? What softened your hairt, so ye care aboot the wee folk here? Or are ye only usin' that tae win us ower?"

"I don't deny I'm using it to bargain with you. It seemed to me I was in a particularly weak position to ask you any favors. As to why I care, I won't go into the reasons. I will tell you only that I am loyal to the great, free kingdom of Alban, and that every decision I make is based on that loyalty."

"Dinna make the laddie tell mair." Whisper spoke with calm authority. "Push him too hard and the whole thing falls in pieces. And dinna take all night tae make up your minds. Why dinna you gather the others together now, while he steps back oot o' earshot? I'll wager you willna get much argument frae them, if they ken the alternative is mair o' the same."

"Wha put ye in charge, ye wee scribbet?" challenged Blaze.

"The king's man here's in charge. I'm only speaking common sense. I hope Southies are no' deaf tae that."

Fume released a stream of vapor in Whisper's direction; the owl being stepped swiftly to one side.

"Will you speak to them now?" Flint asked.

"Aye, we will," said Scorch. "Move awa', so ye dinna frighten them off."

Flint went up to have a word with the guards, who had been watching with a certain amazement. To approach these folk without the protection of an iron weapon, to sit down with them and hold a long conversation without the Caller present to maintain control—they were amazed and impressed that Owen Swift-Sword was able to do these things, and they told him so.

He turned the talk to ordinary matters—the new weapons being made from bone and wood, and how effective they might be; a suggestion that Stag Troop might take a share of the guard duties. How soon the king and queen would arrive at Summerfort with the rest of their court, and whether the rations would improve.

Down by the campfire, the three fey warriors had called in all of their fellow captives. A great circle of folk sat around them, folk of many kinds, from those who looked almost human to the odd wispy beings and the ones that seemed to wink in and out of their shape. All were intent on Blaze as he spoke. Whisper had placed himself at the back of the crowd, perched on a stump, making himself only one among many.

Twilight turned to full dark, and eventually the meeting by the fire broke up. Blaze beckoned; Flint went back down.

"They agree wi' the proposition," the big warrior said. "Ye'll be wantin' a bittie time tae explain this tae your men, aye? Say we hae the first group ready tae slip awa' tomorrow night? Dae it ower three nights?"

The flood of elation within him was tempered by fear. "Thank you. Releasing them in three groups will work well. And yes, I will ensure whoever is on duty down here tomorrow night knows the plan, and that they'll keep it quiet. You

264

understand, I imagine, that if word gets out about this, we cannot go ahead with it."

"Aye. Ye better be sure ye get this right, king's man, or your heid will be the first tae be staved in."

As he'd anticipated, at a certain point there was a cold, furious argument with the queen's councillor. They met behind a closed door, just the two of them.

"We set out from Winterfort with over a hundred." Brydian's voice was all frost. "I'm not blind, Owen. The number has been reduced by as many as thirty. Yet I haven't seen one of them killed in the practice yard."

"Brydian. I am a war leader and have been for some years. I'm expert in strategy and in the training of warriors. The king has requested that these folk be ready to display their fighting skills by the time of the Gathering. He has given me the responsibility of making that happen. You are a councillor; my equal, but not my superior. It would be unfortunate if your interference made it impossible for me to meet the king's request. Most unfortunate."

"You cannot be threatening me." Brydian was white with rage.

"You'll interpret my words as you choose, of course."

"You've let them go. The smaller ones, the weaker ones. Haven't you? You weren't prepared to cull them. When? When did you do this?"

"Did you not understand me? The king asked me to prepare this fighting force for him. He entrusted the mission to Stag Troop, under my leadership. I make every decision with that in mind. What do you imagine the king wants, a force of sixty beings all capable of resisting iron, of learning to fight as a disciplined unit, of obeying orders and meeting challenges, or a hundred-strong assembly in which almost half are incapable of doing the job? We're wasting time even discussing this."

"You forget the one most important element, Owen: the Caller. Esten is not under your command, he's—" Brydian fell short of saying: *He's under mine.* "He's the king's Caller. He reports to me. And without Esten, you have no control over these folk at all."

"Esten will continue to be present, of course, while we conduct training," Flint said. "And yourself, if that's what you wish. But no more interference without consulting me first. No exercise of Esten's more . . . destructive abilities unless you get my agreement that it's required. Folk don't fight well when they're forced into it. I want to win their cooperation."

"Cooperation, pah!" Brydian made a sound of utter disdain. "You've gone soft, Owen."

"Another thing." Flint kept his tone calm and controlled. "You should ensure your Caller is getting enough sleep at night if you want him at his best during the day. Toleg could give him a sleeping draft. It'd need to be something relatively mild, since Esten has to be up bright and early each morning, ready to do his work. But it would help him. He looks unwell."

Brydian's hands were balled into furious fists; for a moment, Flint wondered if the councillor would strike him. "How dare you?" No angry shout; the chilly undertone, barely more than a whisper, was far more threatening. "How dare you meddle with this, when you've long been under suspicion of—"

"Watch your words." Flint had his own quiet voice for such times. There were only the two of them in the chamber; Brydian knew, surely, that Flint could kill him in an instant. "A king's councillor does not accuse a man without evidence. Stay out of my way, let me get on with my job, and the king should be pleased with both of us. The Caller is your responsibility, yes. All the rest of this is mine, and I've no intention of allowing you to make a shambles of it. This conversation is finished. I have work to do."

The morning after that interchange, Brydian sent a dispatch to the king. Flint had his sources of information within each of the royal households, and word of this reached him soon after the messenger told the stable master he'd be needing a horse. Flint held a quick and covert meeting with his senior men, pointing out how much harder it would be for them to meet the goal the king had set them if Brydian were given the control he so clearly wanted. His men knew his plan; they understood that to achieve the impossible, it was necessary to go beyond the conventional methods. A party was sent to ensure the message never reached its destination.

The king's return to Summerfort drew ever closer. Every day I showed Toleg how reliable I was, how hard I could work, how little supervision I required. Sometimes he was called down to the practice yard to tend to an injured man who, for one reason or another, could not be brought to the infirmary. I waited for a chance to go with him, so I might get a glimpse, at least, of the captives. But Toleg did not ask me to come.

He did leave me in charge, on my own, when he was absent during the day. Where once he would have called in Scia to supervise me, now he gave me a list of tasks to get on with, and trusted me to tend to anyone who might come seeking help while he was gone. This was a big step, and made me glad I had not rushed things. But time was passing swiftly. I'd had no chance to see if Whisper was with the captives, or to speak with Flint, whom I had not seen since that first day.

The temptation to use my gift was always there, though I kept it in check. I could try to call Whisper to me; I could learn if this was possible while Esten was close at hand and exerting his own influence over the captives. I could call one of our fey allies, Sage or Daw perhaps, and seek their advice. By now the news that Good Folk were being held at Summerfort and trained to fight must have made its way up the valley to Shadowfell; Sage's folk would be able to see what was happening from the wooded hill. Unless the iron kept them away. Unless fear of being drawn in by Esten's call had driven them far from their home forest. That was all too believable.

There came a day when Toleg had headed out early with his herb basket and knives, leaving me with two infusions and a salve to prepare before he returned. Should I be faced with anything beyond my abilities, he said, I was to send for Scia. I suggested, in modest fashion, that next time he might allow me to do the herb gathering in his place, since I had younger legs.

"We'll see, Ellida," he said. "That husband of yours might not be well pleased if I let you wander about in the forest on your own, not to speak of the need to cross the encampment out there twice over."

"I did it regularly at Glenfalloch, Master Toleg, and Morven raised no objection."

"Then the man's a fool. If I had a pretty young wife, I wouldn't be letting her tramp around hither and thither all alone, not with Alban the way it is these days. Now you'd best get started on that salve; it takes a while. And I'll be off."

I worked for some time uninterrupted. I completed the first infusion and was fetching beeswax for the salve when there was a knock on the infirmary door. I opened it, and there was the Caller, with Brydian like a dark shadow behind him.

"You," Brydian said, plainly far from pleased. "Where is Master Toleg?"

"He's gone out to gather herbs, Master Brydian. Please enter. I will help you if I can."

"When is Toleg due back? This is most unfortunate." He made no move to come in. One look at Esten told me he was in severe pain, most likely from a headache.

"You should sit down," I said directly to Esten. I put my hand under his arm and led him to a bench. "Sit here. I can help you." I looked toward Brydian, who was still in the doorway. "Master Toleg will be away until late afternoon."

"We'll return later," Brydian said. "Esten, come."

The healer in me wanted to tell him that was both foolish and cruel. The strategist in me might have pointed out that keeping his Caller fit and well would surely be the king's priority. But I remembered Scia's warning and said nothing. It was Esten who spoke, raising his head to look up at the councillor. His face was a death mask, the eyes bright with pain.

"I can't," he said. "My head . . ." He bent and put his hands to his temples.

I crouched down beside him, ignoring Brydian. "How long have you had this pain?"

"A long time," Esten murmured. "Since . . . since before I came here. But . . . much worse now. I . . ."

I recognized the look on his face and dived for a bowl before he could be sick all over the infirmary floor. He retched helplessly while I held it in place. As soon as the spasm was over, Brydian came forward.

"Thank you for your assistance. Send word as soon as Toleg returns. Come, Esten."

The healer won out over the spy. "Master Brydian," I said, "your friend is not well enough to be moved. By all means, wait for Master Toleg, who is much more experienced than I am. But let Esten wait here on a bed, in comfort. He's in severe pain. I'm able to make an infusion to relieve that, and I can also give him something to help him sleep. Master Toleg left me in charge."

"Where is Scia?"

"She's helping Brand prepare for King Keldec's arrival. Master Toleg is not expecting her in the infirmary today."

Brydian replied by stalking back to the door and rapping out an order to someone outside. Had they brought guards with them? "Fetch Scia here!"

We waited in awkward silence. Esten was on the verge of fainting from the pain. I struggled to hold back a protest.

When Scia arrived, looking flustered, Brydian said, "If Toleg's away, you should be available when needed. I have a sick man here. What were you doing?"

"Now that Master Toleg has Ellida to assist him, I don't work here every day, Master Brydian." Scia managed to sound calm and capable; I was impressed. "Brand has me in charge of ensuring the king's and queen's apartments are perfectly prepared for them." She glanced at me, took in the wilting Esten. "Ellida is a skilled herbalist and capable of dealing with all but the most difficult situations. Everything I can do, she can do. If she needed help in Master Toleg's absence, she would call me."

"I see." Brydian sounded less than impressed. "Since you're here, take a look at Esten and tell me what you would recommend."

There was no point in being offended. In fact, Scia had far more practical experience as a healer than I did; she had exaggerated my capabilities. She spoke to Esten quietly, peered into his eyes, touched his brow, and asked him where the pain was worst. She examined the contents of the bowl into which he had vomited. She asked the same question I had, and received the same answer.

"Ellida can make up an infusion to relieve Esten's pain and allow him a good sleep," Scia said. "He'd be best staying here awhile so she can keep an eye on him and make sure he is not disturbed. And when Master Toleg returns, he can see him straightaway."

There was a brief silence.

"Very well, Scia, you can go. You"—Brydian jerked his head in my direction—"do what you have to do, and keep your questions to yourself, understood? You'll remain in the infirmary until Master Toleg is back."

"Yes, Master Brydian. Of course . . ." I hesitated.

"What?"

"There are some questions a healer must ask her patient, those that relate to the symptoms and the duration of his ailment. I understand the need for discretion."

"Make sure you do." Scia had departed, but Brydian made no move to follow her. I wondered if he planned to stand there watching me all day. Flint had said the councillor had a canny gift; that he could protect Esten from attack. Perhaps he never let the Caller out of his sight. "This is not just any patient," Brydian went on. "Esten must be restored to himself as quickly as possible. We need him. The king needs him."

"Yes, Master Brydian." I was helping Esten to a pallet, finding an extra pillow. He hardly had the strength to set one foot before the other.

"One more thing. Any potion you dose him with is to be tasted first."

I straightened, momentarily unable to guard my features. There was a drug in Toleg's locked cupboard that would kill Esten quickly, and its effects might possibly be taken as a sudden worsening of his current illness. Oh, so easy. But the risk was too high; I'd likely be dead myself before nightfall if I tried it. Besides, it felt wrong. It felt as wrong as coming here to court had felt right, and still did, despite my failure to speak to the Good Folk.

"I can't stay here all day. I have matters to attend to," Brydian said crisply. "I'll leave a guard at the door; Osgar will be your taster."

"Very well."

"I hope you will recover quickly, Esten. Young woman, make sure I'm informed the moment Toleg returns."

"Yes, Master Brydian."

The door closed behind him and I let out my breath. Esten lay prone on the pallet with one arm up over his eyes. I fetched a stool and sat down beside him.

"I will start making the infusion soon," I said quietly. "It won't take long. But first I need to ask you some questions. This headache—is it troubling you all the time? Is your sight affected?"

"My sight . . . Yes, sometimes. A dizziness; spots dancing before my eyes. Once or twice I have fainted. And I can't sleep. When I do, it's all nightmares, and I wake in a cold sweat. I'm so tired. . . . Sometimes I think I will die of the pain. . . ."

"When did the headaches begin?"

"I . . . I don't think I'm supposed to tell you that."

"If I'm to help you, you'll need to give me some answers. I promise you, nothing you say will go beyond these four walls." A lie, almost certainly; I hated myself for it even as I knew fate had delivered me a gift today—not the opportunity to kill this man, but the chance to hear him talk, away from his minder.

"They started on the journey north. When I was required to . . . to do certain things. You know, I suppose, that I am a Caller."

"I do know, though I'm not exactly sure what that means. I've heard you are able to control those strange creatures that are being trained here." After a moment I added, "I imagine that is difficult. Tiring."

He made no reply.

"I'll go through into the stillroom now and fetch what

273

I need for the infusion. The sooner you take it, the longer you'll be able to sleep before Toleg comes back."

"Sleep . . . I have almost forgotten what a dreamless sleep is like. Will this really work? Can you really make the pain go away?"

"For a while, at least. I'll do my best."

I wondered, as I measured out the ingredients for the draft, taking extra care lest an honest error should make me a target for Brydian's wrath, why it had not occurred to Esten to use his skill to his own advantage. I'd seen him growing sicker and more exhausted night by night as he took his place at the supper table. Brydian was always there, always close, controlling whom his Caller spoke to and who spoke to him. And, of course, protecting him from attack. It surprised me that Brydian had been prepared to leave his charge here with me, even with a guard on the door. The councillor's manner was not that of guardian to precious charge, or of senior courtier to junior, or of mentor to student. It was more like that of jailer to valuable prisoner. Esten was being manipulated, he was being worked to exhaustion, he was being made ill by their demands on him. And he, meek-mannered and quiet, was simply going along with it. Yet he possessed a bargaining tool second to none.

When I went back into the infirmary with the draft in a cup, he was sitting up on the pallet. The febrile glitter in his eyes was troubling. This man desperately needed sleep; I hoped I had made the infusion strong enough.

"You could say no," I suggested quietly. "You might have done that long ago, before this made you so ill."

He stared at me. I had shocked him.

"If you go on like this, it will kill you," I said. "That is my informed opinion as a healer. I think Master Toleg will tell you the same."

"You don't know what you are saying," Esten whispered. "Refuse an order from the king's representative? How could I do that?"

I wanted to tell him, *With a lot of courage,* but I had already said too much. If he chose to report this conversation to Brydian, I would have to say he'd been in a feverish dream and imagined it. "Here, drink this."

He was raising the cup to his lips when I remembered the taster and snatched it from his hands. "Not yet, sorry."

The guard, Osgar, was tall and broad, with yellow hair in plaits and a beard to match. He sipped the brew, uncomplaining, then wiped his lips with the back of a large hand. "Can't say I care much for the taste, but it hasn't killed me. How about a proper brew later on? You're Morven's wife, aren't you?"

"That's right."

"Good fellow, Morven. Quick on his feet. You must be missing him."

"I am. Now I must give this to my patient." I was turning away when I realized I had been presented with another opportunity. "As for a brew, if I manage to get him off to sleep, I'll make something more palatable. Long day for you."

"This? It's an easy duty, lassie. What's your name?"

"Ellida. Yes, I suppose by comparison it is."

While Esten slept, Osgar and I enjoyed a brew and shared the food Toleg had forgotten to eat at breakfast time. Osgar would not sit down, but I persuaded him to move a bench close to the door he was supposed to be guarding, and I sat there while he leaned on the wall beside me. He did not forget his job; I could see how he watched the hallway outside, through the part-open door.

We spoke in lowered voices, mindful both of the sleeping man and—in my case anyway—of the possible return of Brydian.

"Good brew. Reminds me of one my mother used to make."

"It's simple enough. Mostly mint and honey."

Osgar glanced over toward the pallet where Esten lay still under his blanket. "What you gave him seems to have worked. Sleeping like a babe."

"Mm." Here was another Enforcer like Rohan, outwardly the kind of man anyone would want as a friend. I must not for a moment forget what he was and where his allegiance must lie. "I suppose they all work hard. Morven too."

"Our leaders keep us up to the mark, yes."

"You're from Wolf Troop, aren't you? I've seen you and some of your comrades in the hall at meals. But not Stag Troop—isn't that the one Rohan Death-Blade belongs to? He accepted Morven for training and rode here with us."

"We're stationed here mostly for guard duty. But there's an extra job on now; big need for training. Both troops are busy. Of course, when the court moves here, it will all change again. The king likes to stir things up."

That was an admission I had not expected. I must tread very cautiously. "It's hard for me with Morven having to live separately," I said. "I mean, I did expect that might happen while he was being trained, but not that I wouldn't see him at all. Do they ever let people go out to watch the men being put through their paces?"

Osgar grimaced. "Different situation right now, as I suppose you know." He glanced over at Esten. "Under more normal circumstances, the fellows might put on a display for the household from time to time, mock battle, shooting at targets—a fighter needs to learn to block out distractions such as a lady he admires sitting on the sidelines cheering him on, or a crowd of children making noise. But there's a bigger job on here than training men for the Enforcers." He stuck his head out the door, looked up and down the hallway, turned back to me. "You'll have had one or two of those odd folk in here with injuries to be tended to, I imagine."

"Not since I got here. But Toleg goes out to patch them up sometimes."

"The fact is, Morven and the other recruits are doing more teaching than learning now. Especially your husband. Big strong fellow, lot of skill—and he's good with those strange folk. Not everyone has that knack."

"Knack?" I could not stop myself from glancing toward Esten.

"Not like that fellow. Just the knack of getting them to listen. Like Owen, the Stag Troop leader. Has a way of dealing with them that seems to get the best out of them. But I'm talking too much. You'll have things to do. Don't let me keep you from your work."

"There's more of the brew, if you'd like another cup. And a few dried plums here—I don't think Master Toleg ate any breakfast at all."

"Thank you, Ellida, don't mind if I do."

I refilled his cup, then went to the workbench to resume preparing the salve Toleg had told me to make. Osgar was right; I needed to get my duties done before Esten woke.

For some time neither of us spoke. Osgar stayed at the door, watching while I made a strong infusion of the herbs Toleg had specified, combined it with a pure oil, and heated it until the mixture was a rich gold in color and no longer steaming. I lifted the little pot off the brazier and set it on the bench to cool while I melted the beeswax to thicken the salve. Esten had not stirred. Indeed, at one point I went over to make sure he was still breathing.

"You know," Osgar said, his voice held quiet, "there is a spot where you can get a good view of the practice yard. Most folk wouldn't be aware of it. We know it, of course, since our job is to be familiar with every corner of the place, in case of attack. If you wanted a look at your man in action, I could show you."

"Really?" I tried not to sound too excited. "That would be wonderful—but only if it doesn't get me in trouble. Or you." I gave him a smile.

"Not breaking any rules, as I see it. Does the old man keep you hard at work all day?"

"He does let me out for meals. Master Toleg is the only one so wedded to his craft that he would rather eat in here. I might be free for a little in the middle of the day. Not today, of course."

"Tomorrow, if you like. I can come by and take you up there. Then, when you do catch up with Morven, you can surprise him with a compliment on his fine work."

"Thank you," I said. "That is very kind. If you're quite sure about not breaking rules."

"I wouldn't go announcing it to all and sundry," Osgar said. "We don't want half the household up there. I hope you're not scared of heights."

A powerful memory came to me, of Brollachan Brig, and Hollow holding me by one ankle as I dangled above the abyss. "I'll be fine," I said.

Before either Brydian or Toleg came back, Esten began to wake from his sound sleep. At first it was gentle, a rolling to his side, a murmur or two, a sigh. Then, as the effects of the draft faded, a restless tossing and turning and a sequence of muttered dream-troubles. "No . . . I can't . . . not again, please no . . . Die, die now, quickly. . . . Take your hands off me! . . ."

His ramblings were disturbing; I could have spun a tale from them, but in truth there was no guessing just what the pattern of his dreams might be. The only thing clear was that he had not slept anywhere near long enough. Could I risk dosing him again? I completed the salve, sealing it in jars. I prepared the second infusion Toleg had asked for and cleaned up after myself. Esten's nightmares continued; I sponged his brow with cool water. There was still a cupful of the sleeping potion in the jug.

When he woke fully, the first thing he said was, "More. Please."

"The mixture is potent." The look in my patient's eyes made me wish Toleg were back. "This is not the answer to your problem, or at least it is only a short-term answer, relief for your symptoms. What you need is . . ." I hesitated. My position at Summerfort was crucial to the rebellion. Helping the king's Caller get well enough to lead an army against us was not part of the plan. "Rest," I said. "Not drugged rest; natural rest. A man cannot go on working the way you do, day after day, without paying a price. Master Toleg will agree with me, I am certain."

"Please," he said again. His voice was ragged; his skin was clammy. "Just a little." He gave a furtive glance toward the doorway, but Osgar had gone out into the hall. "They need not know. Just enough."

"The more you take, the less effective it will be."

"Please, Ellida. There's nobody to help me."

"A very small dose," I said, weighing his distress against the risk that I might give him too much and make him worse. "Not enough to send you back to sleep, but sufficient to ease the pain for a while longer. I am not the chief healer here, only Toleg's assistant, and a very new one at that." I fetched the jug, poured him a small measure, put the cup into his shaking hands. "Drink it slowly. A draft such as this must not be misused. I will not give you more than Master Toleg would recommend."

"Thank you," he whispered, passing back the empty cup. "If I . . . could I . . ."

"Even once a day would be too often. You would become accustomed to it; reliant on it. The longer you used it, the harder it would be for you to stop taking it. You would find it impossible to fall asleep without its help. Master Toleg will tell you the same thing, Esten. But perhaps he can recommend something a little milder that will give you easier sleep by night without inducing a . . . need."

Voices in the hall outside: an Enforcer named Ardon

280

had come to relieve Osgar on the door. Ardon had brought food for us, but he was not inclined to talk. He stayed outside the half-open door and kept himself to himself. Esten did not want to eat. I made him swallow a few mouthfuls of the baked fish and some root vegetables, which I mashed up as if for a baby. It was hard to believe what Flint had said: *He's more powerful than he looks.*

After we had finished the meal and I had made an ordinary brew for myself and Ardon, I sat on the stool beside Esten's pallet. He would not sleep again, and that was perhaps a good thing, since slumbering all day would give him another wakeful night.

"Why is this so exhausting?" I asked. "What you do, I mean. I don't really understand."

A flush came to his wan cheeks. "Master Brydian has said that I should not speak about it," he said.

What now? Step back or press further? Our voices were held low, but I could not be sure Ardon was out of earshot. "I understand. Only . . . you seem very troubled by this. Talking about what's wrong may help. Anything a patient says to me remains within these four walls, Esten. I promise you that."

He sat quiet for a little, then he said, "How can it help?"

"Troubles bring headaches; headaches bring sleepless nights. Talking may help you find your own solutions to your troubles." It was glib, and I hated myself for it.

Esten gave me a very direct look. "You can't understand, or you would not ask this," he murmured. "The penalties for speaking out are . . . They're unthinkable."

I understood all too well. "This is not speaking out," I

said. "It's between you and me. Or you and Master Toleg, if you would prefer to wait for him."

There was a long silence, during which I moved to the doorway and said to Ardon, "There's a draft coming in—do you mind?" Before he could answer, I shut the door. I went back to the bedside, sat down again, put my hands in my lap.

"Why should I trust you?" Esten's eyes were full of trouble. Even after the sleep, he looked worn out.

"Nobody in all Alban can give you an answer to that question," I said. "The best I can do is remind you that I am a healer and bound by a healer's codes. It's my job to find ways to help you. I think talking is one of those ways. I will understand if you don't wish to tell me whatever it is."

"I hardly know what it is," he said. "Only that I was promised power, wealth, and recognition, and that I find myself trapped in a nightmare of my own making. Sometimes I think I would rather die than do what is required of me. But . . . I have been nothing in the past, insignificant, overlooked. And when I use this gift, I feel powerful, I feel fully alive, I feel . . . I feel like a leader." He dropped his gaze. "I know what I do is wrong. I know it is cruel. But I cannot stop doing it, Ellida. It's like what you said about the draft; the more of it you have, the more of it you want. Even if it makes you do terrible things. Even if it sets a burden on you that you can hardly bear."

Black Crow save me. I struggled to find words.

"You wish now that you had not asked me to speak," he said.

"No, though what you say is . . . disconcerting. Esten,

when did you start using this gift? Folk with canny talents are born with them, I know. How old were you when you realized what you could do?"

"I don't remember. A child. But I didn't know what it was, only that I heard strange voices calling me, out in the woods, and sometimes saw odd things I thought might be mere tricks of the light. I never spoke of it to anyone. There were . . . reasons. Everyone knows that."

I judged he was four or five years my senior. Esten's early childhood would have been before Keldec came to the throne and outlawed the use of canny gifts outside his own court. "And later?" I ventured. "It sounds as if your gift is very powerful. How did it develop?"

"I hardly used it. Nobody knew about it. Once or twice, when I was out of doors on my own, one of them—the Good Folk—would appear and try to talk to me, and I would do my best to pretend I could not see it. They are trouble. The king's law is wise, forbidding us to meet and mingle. What is happening to these folk now—they brought it on themselves. They should have left me alone."

I could not tell him he was wrong; I must judge each question with utmost care. "I have heard the story—that you traveled to the south with the king's expedition and brought them back. Many of them. So they followed you against your will?"

He shook his head. "I called them. I made them come. That was what the queen wanted. That's what a Caller is: one who can compel and command these folk. Make them follow. Make them fight. Make them do whatever I want."

Or whatever your masters want, I thought. "I don't

understand," I said. "Didn't you say they should have left you alone? But if you were the one who called them forth . . . ?"

"It was one of them that started all this," Esten said in a whisper. "If not for that, nobody would ever have known what I could do. Even I would not have known. I was doing exactly as the law requires, not using my gift, not acknowledging it in any way. Then, one day when I was out in the woods, I met an old man with a dog."

I went cold with horror. He'd been trained. He'd met the Master of Shadows. It meant . . . it meant . . . But the Master was a trickster. Perhaps this was not what it seemed. "Go on," I said, struggling to sound calm and encouraging.

"I thought he was an ordinary man, of humankind. He was carrying firewood, too much for an old fellow to manage, and I offered to help him get it to his hut. And when we reached the place . . . he proved to be something other than human."

"You mean—he was one of *them*? How could you tell?"

"He . . . changed. The dog too. Now one thing, now another. And he told me about my . . . my gift, my ability. . . . I didn't want to speak of it, because of the law, but the old man seemed to know all about me, how I could see and hear those folk, how I had held back, tried to pretend it was nothing. And . . . and he told me what power I could wield. The magnificent things I could do. Stand at the king's right hand. Command great armies. Make folk perform wonderful magic. Become . . . become someone." A wretched silence. "I told him I would not listen; that it was dangerous nonsense. I walked back home, ate my supper, went to bed. Spent the whole night thinking about it, about how it could change my life, how it could transform me into someone different, someone people looked up to, someone they feared. The next day I went back to the old man's hut, and the next, and many times after that. He . . . he showed me things. Not as much as I wanted, but . . . enough for me to start. One day, when I went to find him, he was gone. The man, the dog, even the hut had vanished as if it had never been. But I knew what I could be and what I could do. I was . . . I was practicing when Master Brydian came by and saw me."

"And brought you to court, just as you had hoped." By all that was holy. The Master of Shadows had not only shown himself to this Caller, he had trained him. Had Esten too demonstrated the seven virtues? When could he have done that? And what about the other Guardians? Why would the Master do this?

"Just as I had hoped," he said on a sigh. "Only . . . I have proved weaker than I should be. Inadequate to the task the king needs done. The headaches, the nightmares, they were not so bad at first. The queen had faith in me. Master Brydian was kind to me, took time for me. But here . . . I get so tired. I can still do it, but the call I use to quell unrest . . . it drains my strength and I cannot go on. They have stopped asking me to call. For some time now, the fellow in charge of the fighters, Owen Swift-Sword, has said that he doesn't need me there. He says he can keep the Good Folk in order without me."

"Really?" How could that be possible?

"Queen Varda will be disappointed in me. That is what Master Brydian says. He wants me cured. He wants Master Toleg to restore my strength before the king and queen come to Summerfort." He turned anguished eyes on me. "If I could have the sleeping draft at night, perhaps I could perform as I should by day."

I pitied him despite myself. "I explained to you why that is not possible. Any healer would tell you the same thing. But we'll talk to Toleg and ask him for advice—"

"No!" he said sharply. "You promised! What I told you is secret—"

Gods, he was strung tight as a harp string. "Of course I will not tell him anything without your permission," I said. "I won't tell anyone. I gave you my word. But we must at least explain to Master Toleg about the headaches and the lack of sleep, since that was the reason you came to see us. You should lie down and rest again until he comes. Practice breathing slowly and making your body limp. Try to think of good things."

"Good things," he echoed. "I have forgotten what they are, if indeed I ever knew."

And I wanted to tell him he had brought that on himself, with his desire for power, but I held back. Esten had wandered into perilous clutches: first the Master of Shadows, then Brydian, dark representatives of Alban's two races. Not to mention Queen Varda. If I had been in his shoes, I hoped I would have had the strength to say no. But I could not be sure.

He lay back as I had suggested and closed his eyes. I busied myself with various tasks, all the while struggling to come to terms with what Esten had revealed. I had believed the Master of Shadows supported me, in his own peculiar way. He had warned me to expect tricks; he had told me to practice playing games before our next encounter. Was that what this was, an elaborate game whose purpose I had failed to understand? Or had he decided Esten made a more promising Caller than me, more powerful perhaps, less cautious about what damage he might do along the way? This was like trying to walk across shifting ground where at any moment a solid surface might turn to sucking bog. There were no rules; there was no map. A Caller who both feared his own gift and loved what it might deliver him was truly a dangerous weapon. Dangerous not only to his enemies, but to his friends as well. Most dangerous of all to himself. I gazed at his still form on the pallet and considered that if our positions had been reversed, Esten would not have hesitated to ensure his draft rendered me not peacefully asleep but dead and cold, a threat no more. His craving to be a different, more powerful person had delivered the king exactly what he needed—a Caller prepared to set aside his scruples. How much damage could Esten do before his gift destroyed him?

"Up here," Osgar said. "Take care, it's steep."

We had come to the end of a long hallway on the upper level of the fortress. Ahead was an odd half wall, and behind it a hidden stairway, ladder-steep, leading up into total darkness.

Osgar climbed; I followed, feeling my way. He took the steps with apparent ease. My legs were soon aching.

My companion reached up, pushing aside a trapdoor and admitting a sudden shaft of light. He climbed out; I clambered up behind him and found that we were on a narrow ledge, at most one stride from back to front, with just room enough for the two of us to stand side by side next to the opening. The low barrier, not even knee-high, would do little to protect us from a long, long fall to the courtyard below. I pressed my back against the stone wall of the keep and told myself to be calm.

"All right?"

"Yes, fine. It is very high."

"Secret lookout. Comes in handy occasionally. Look that way."

Our vantage point provided a clear view into the practice yard, where Enforcers in uniform were working with two groups of fighters, each group wearing tokens in either green or blue—a scarf, a ribbon, a kerchief tied around the neck or arm. The scene looked strangely ordinary, as if the Enforcers were conducting standard combat training. Yet at the same time it was the opposite of ordinary, for Good Folk were down there mingling with the warriors in training. Big folk, smaller folk, folk of many different forms and kinds, including some that seemed to be alight or smoking, and some with wings. There were onlookers too, seated in the raised area to one side, the place from which the royal party had watched the Gathering. Not Brydian, and not Esten, whom I knew to be resting on Toleg's orders. A group of young men sat there. A big group. And there alongside them was a small winged being with feathers of snowy white. Whisper. Not fighting; only watching. As relief flooded through me, he turned his head and looked straight up at us.

Don't look at him, Neryn. Don't think about him, don't reach out to him. Now is not the time.

"Morven's over there near the main gates," Osgar said,

pointing. "Sparring with one of those big brutes, the fellow with a head like a rock."

"Oh." I did not have to pretend concern. The being Brenn was grappling with was both tall and broad, and seemed to be spurting steam from various parts of his body. Surely he could topple Brenn in an instant if he chose to. But as the bout progressed, I realized that this was indeed only practice; the two combatants would reach a certain point in the fight, then an Enforcer—Rohan—would step in and separate them, speak to them awhile, then watch as they set to again.

I had seen Flint the moment I looked down there; I would always recognize him, even at such a distance. He was not fighting, but stood to one side with his legs apart and his arms folded, keeping an eye on things. Another king's man stood by him, but this one I did not know.

"Orderly work," Osgar observed. "Not like the early days. Those folk were all spit and defiance then, needed the Caller to make them comply, and a ring of iron to stop them from bolting. And they didn't seem to know how to fight. Odd, really, seeing as they've got magical powers, throwing flame and that kind of thing."

"What has changed, then, to make it so well controlled now?"

"Owen Swift-Sword's doing. The troop leader, down there at the side with Tallis. I know he had the armorers make some special weapons, not your usual iron, but wood, bone, other materials these folk can handle. Not sure what else he did, but he's got them cooperating quite well. Which is fortunate, seeing as the Caller's out of action for now. Did Master Toleg have any answers?"

It was no more Osgar's business than the training of Good Folk was mine, but I would provide an answer in the hope of getting one from him in return. "He's given Esten a different sleeping draft, one that he can use every night. And another potion for his headaches. But what Esten really needs is a proper rest; he needs to stop calling for a while."

Osgar looked at me sideways. "Just as well, then, that Owen's got these folk eating out of his hand. So to speak."

"Mm." I did not think Brydian would be interested in giving his Caller a long rest. Esten himself would only agree to it while his exhaustion overcame his drive for power. I guessed that within a day or two, he and his minder would be back out there again. "Osgar, I thought nobody was allowed to watch while these folk were being trained. Who are those people there?"

"The young fellows? New recruits. They just got in today from Winterfort, with some men from Hound Troop. Owen's going to have his work cut out."

It was as I had suspected. Those were the young men from the south, the other part of the king's special forces. It was all falling into place. I could not see if Ean was among them. "Work cut out doing what?" I hoped this question was artless enough. "How long will it be before I can see Morven again, do you think? See him properly, I mean, to talk to."

"Can't answer that. I have heard, just quietly, that there are plans for the Gathering; some sort of show the king wants put on, using these folk. After that, who knows?"

"You mean I might not see him until after midsummer? That is a long time."

"I'd say count yourself lucky Morven's doing so well. I'd

guess he'll be posted to Stag Troop in due course. Maybe even before midsummer. But it's not for me to say. And best not discussed openly in the household. You're new here; you probably don't quite understand."

"Thank you for warning me. I won't say a thing. And thank you for bringing me up here; it's wonderful to see my husband, even if only for a moment or two."

"Might do it again. Some other day. We should go back down now."

The most astonishing thing my trip to the lookout had shown me was that Flint was not only safe thus far, but was somehow managing to train his uncanny charges without need of either iron as a deterrent or the Caller's presence. How he was achieving this I had no idea. As far as I knew, he possessed no particular affinity with the Good Folk, and I could not understand their compliance. If he could do this, if he could keep it up, then all we needed at midsummer was to make sure Esten was out of action, perhaps with a judiciously administered sleeping draft, something that would fell him without killing him. That part seemed almost too easy. Once we dealt with Esten, I could use my own gift to rally those folk down there to fight, not for the king, but against him.

Not only was Flint unharmed and working miracles, but Brenn was still safe as well, and so was Whisper. Perhaps Ean too, among those hapless lads. That gave me four allies at court. My spirits lifted; I went back to my duties in the infirmary with a smile, and had to explain my mood to Toleg by saying I'd had word my husband was acquitting himself splendidly at training.

"You fancy life as an Enforcer's wife," Toleg remarked, not turning from where he was working at the bench.

"I don't know," I said, watching my words. He would be quick to see through my lies. "But it is what Morven wants. It's what he has wanted for years. And I love him. If this is the life he has chosen, then it will be mine too."

"You'll be spending a lot of your time waiting for him while he's away on one mission or another. You know that, I suppose."

"I do. And I think it is just as well I have my own work to keep me busy."

"Well, you've proved useful enough, I'll say that. It can't have been easy dealing with young Esten on your own. I'm not sure I'd have risked what you did. Too much of that particular draft can kill a man."

"I was careful with the dose. He wanted more; I gave him only what I knew was safe."

"You judged it well, yes. I'll show you another draft, the one they use for enthrallments—if it happens again, that would be safer. The Enthrallers call it Oblivion. Sends folk to sleep almost immediately, and there's a quick-working antidote if required. The components are in the locked cupboard; when I'm finished here, I'll go through it with you."

"Thank you." The idea turned me cold. Twice I had seen a person enthralled, though with Tali it had been pretense. The draft forced down the throat, the rapid descent into deep sleep, and later, the sudden, terrified waking. I was not sure I could bring myself to use such a potion, even for a different purpose.

"Don't thank me, just learn," Toleg said, and although he

still did not turn, I heard a smile in his voice. "Since it sounds as if you're going to be underfoot here even when that husband of yours has finished his training, you need to develop your skills as fast as you can. How about sweeping the floor while I'm finishing this?"

He had thought the safeguards he'd set in place would be sufficient to keep things in balance. Brydian could not insist his Caller intimidate the Good Folk when there was no need for it. He could not insist on the use of iron when the captive army made no attempt to run riot, bolt from the practice area, or attack those who fought alongside them. The truce, the arrangement Whisper had helped him set in place, had held thus far. And with luck they still had as much as a turning of the moon before Keldec brought his court to Summerfort.

Esten's illness made things even easier. Nobody wanted him and Brydian there all the time, watching every move, stepping in to exercise control whenever they chose to. Brydian was no warrior. Esten had a gift of fearsome power, but he only used it on the councillor's orders, and the men did not respect him for that. They were happier working with their own kind, fighting men, and so, it became apparent, were the Good Folk. As for the dispatches Brydian sent at regular intervals to the king at Winterfort, Flint had had one or two intercepted, and had found they contained nothing dangerous. It seemed even Brydian realized the value of Flint's approach, though he did not say so in his dispatches, only that the exercise was progressing well.

As the season advanced, Flint began cautiously to hope

that they might all survive until midsummer, when everything would change. That hope was ill founded. One bright, cloudless morning three men of Bull Troop rode up to the gates with an urgent message. It seemed Keldec had grown tired of waiting to see his special forces in training. The king and his court were on the way to Summerfort.

Chapter Eleven

With the king's arrival, everything changed. The women's quarters filled to capacity, with extra pallets laid on the floor and people sharing. Toleg offered me a bed in the stillroom—if we had patients overnight, we'd need to be close by anyway—and I accepted gratefully. He had a tiny chamber of his own, with barely enough room for a pallet and a little chest, reached through a low archway behind our workbench.

With Keldec and Varda had traveled a vast number of retainers: stableboys and grooms, scullions and cooks, seamstresses, personal maids, councillors, and, of course, a large contingent of Enforcers. The stables were packed. There were dogs too, some kenneled, some wandering about. The queen had a tiny white terrier. One of her waiting women carried it around for her.

And she had a son. I had forgotten, sometimes, about this child, whom the king wanted to make his successor, against the ancient laws of Alban, which determined that only sons of the royal women could contest the kingship. The old law meant the kingship usually passed from uncle to nephew, cousin to cousin, or, sometimes, brother to brother. The true heir, the person Regan had considered to have the strongest claim to succeed Keldec, was also a little boy. He was hidden away somewhere so Keldec could not take steps to eliminate the child he saw as his son's rival.

The king's boy was called Ochi, and he was three years old. I first saw him crossing the courtyard one day as I was gathering herbs in the kitchen garden; he was attended by a pair of solicitous nursemaids, with a guard following at a short distance. From this group of attendants I would have guessed who the child was, even without the richness of his clothing. For all that, he looked like an ordinary little boy, dawdling to examine a beetle on the stones; running back to point out something to the guard, who squatted down to listen; staring over toward me in the garden. *Who's that?* I imagined him asking, and one of the maids saying, *Nobody.*

Maybe that child would be his father all over again, and maybe he would not. Maybe Ochi would prove to have the same fears, the same streak of cruelty, the same weakness. Or he might become a quite different kind of person. One thing was sure: it was better that Keldec's son never became king. Better for Alban, and better for himself.

With so many more folk at Summerfort, there was enough work to keep not only Toleg and me but also Scia busy all day. We had a constant flow of folk into the infirmary: fighters with combat injuries, cooks with burns, people with all manner of ailments for which they needed a draft or lotion or salve. I took to snatching meals when I could, as Toleg did, but he insisted I stop work in time to have supper in the hall.

Now all the tables were full. Keldec, Varda, and their inner circle sat at a raised table, where they could look out over their household; Brydian and Esten were close to them, along with the man whom I had seen using fire at the last Gathering, another councillor. Men from Wolf Troop were on guard by their table, and I soon realized the Enforcer who stood behind Keldec was acting as the king's taster.

My table was occupied mostly by women—not only the queen's attendants, who did not join her at the high table, but lesser members of her household, such as laundresses, seamstresses, embroiderers, and so on. I usually sat beside a young woman named Devan, who had striking golden hair in a long plait down her back and a sweet, sad face. Devan was a spinner. When she told me that, it brought back a sharp memory of the Gathering, and the man who had won a grueling contest of strength. His prize had been to protect his talented daughter from the Cull, but at a cost—the queen had wanted the fine spinner as a member of her circle, and when her father had explained that she was expecting a baby, he'd been told the child would have to go elsewhere, as Varda wanted no squalling infants in her household. I could not ask Devan if she was that young woman, whose father had tried to explain that her talent was not canny in nature, but had come down to her through generations of fine craftswomen. I had seen, at the Gathering, that this king and queen heard only what they wanted to hear.

Under different circumstances, Devan and I might have become friends. As it was, we were limited to exchanging a few pleasantries while we ate our meal. Folk's conversation was even more guarded than before, as if there might be hostile ears everywhere.

So many Enforcers were now in residence that they took their meals in shifts. I heard from Osgar, who dropped in to have a word whenever his duties brought him near the infirmary, that three troops were sharing the annex, which was bursting at the seams thanks to the need to accommodate the young lads from the south as well. Another three troops were housed within the keep—the men's quarters were far more capacious than the women's. Part of Eagle Troop had stayed behind as security for Winterfort; the rest of that troop had been sent on an unspecified mission. They would all ride to Summerfort in time for the Gathering.

Soon after the king arrived, the training took a turn for the worse. We began tending to many more injuries than before, and those injuries included some unlikely to have been inflicted during a practice fight such as the one I'd seen from the secret lookout, conducted under the watchful eye of senior Enforcers. Strange burns. Peculiar cuts. Bites. When we had Enforcers as patients, they tended to be short on explanations, but I heard "That creature did it, the one with the teeth like a saw" and "He burned me, the poxy wretch, lit up that pelt of his and scorched my skin right off."

The Good Folk were being injured too. An Enforcer would come to the door and motion to Toleg, and after a consultation in lowered voices, Toleg would pack some items into a bag and go off, promising not to be long. But sometimes it was long. Sometimes he came back pale and silent, and responded to our expressions of concern by shaking his head, turning his back, and finding work for his hands. At those times, he chopped his healing herbs with unnecessary violence.

If Summerfort had been a place of caution before, now its inhabitants watched every step. I was lucky Osgar had befriended me earlier, and luckier still that his duties gave him an excuse to speak to me so often. He'd taken me up to the secret lookout twice more in those earlier days, but now we were all too busy, and I did not ask to go. But I wanted to see. What had happened to disrupt that orderly training? Why would anyone want to change things when they had been going so well?

I could climb up to the lookout by myself, supposing I could get to the steps without being seen and then manage to lift the trapdoor. I was fairly sure Osgar had broken a rule by showing me the place, but possibly it was known only to Wolf Troop, whose job had long been household security. I resolved to seize the first opportunity that came my way.

But when an opportunity did come, it was of another kind. We were running low on herbs, not the common ones that grew in the garden, but the kind that must be wild-gathered to use while fresh. And we had a very sick man in the infirmary, Ruarc from Bull Troop, who had taken a mighty blow to the head and needed not only Toleg's experience in the management of such injuries, but the presence of two fellow Enforcers to restrain the patient when his pain and confusion sent him into a raving frenzy, which was often. Toleg could not go anywhere. Scia and I were busy handling the other work of the infirmary. But we could not do without the herbs, and nobody else had the knowledge to find and gather them.

"You'd better go, Ellida," Toleg said during a spell of blessed quiet while Ruarc was sleeping. "Once you're across the river, you'll find a path up the hill. Stick to the main track until you reach a stream, and then head westward along the bank. Most of what we need can be found within an easy walk from that point." He glanced at Ruarc's two comrades, who had taken the opportunity to sit down on a bench and drink the ale Scia had brought for them earlier. Both were white-faced, somber, and silent. "You should take a guard," Toleg added. "Ask Brand to find someone to go with you."

"Mm-hm." My heart was beating fast. At last, a chance to get out of this place and speak to the Good Folk of the forest without drawing them too close to Esten's influence. I could not be away long; I must use this opportunity wisely.

"And, Ellida?" Toleg spoke as I fetched my basket, my cloth-wrapped knife, my staff.

"Yes?"

"Take care crossing the encampment out there. At this time of day, our visitors will probably be in the practice area. But go cautiously, all the same."

"I will."

If Summerfort had not been so full and everyone so busy, I'd never have managed to get away on my own—someone would have insisted I take an escort, even if it was only the most junior of stable hands. As it was, the gate guards were Wolf Troop men and knew me. They accepted the perfectly true explanation that Toleg could not leave the infirmary while Ruarc was so ill—the news of his grave injury was known to every Enforcer I had met since it happened, and seemed to overshadow everything else for them. One guard said he was sorry he could not offer to go with me; the other warned me to walk around the very edge of the practice area, as there was a mock combat in progress.

They opened the inner gate. As I stepped through, the noise hit me. Groans, cries, shouting. The mock combat had gone terribly wrong. Injured fighters, both human and uncanny, staggered about or lay on the earth, with folk clustering around trying to help them. A big creature, the one with the pelt like flickering flames, was bellowing defiance while crouched down with both hands clutched over what looked like a gaping wound in his belly. His fiery pelt was dulling, turning to ash gray even as I looked. I saw Flint go over and reach out to lay a hand on the wounded being's shoulder. One of the other big fighters, a creature with a head like a rough stone, moved in and shoved him aside, snarling.

Flint turned to face Brydian, who sat at the front of the raised seating with Esten beside him. "I specifically ordered that the Caller not exert his control without my consent!" he shouted. "This is the work of warriors, and I am still in charge here! Take your Caller and get out of my sight. Your interference has done more than enough damage!"

All my instincts called me to rush in and help. There were folk out there bleeding, suffering, dying. Why else had I come to court early but to try to undo some of the evil caused by Esten's call? But I couldn't. Not here, not now. To run out there and attempt to aid the wounded Good Folk with Brydian and his Caller looking on would be to risk everything. Already one or two of them had lifted their heads to look in my direction. In my mind I offered an apology to my grandmother, who had taught me the healer's craft, and another to Toleg. I lowered my gaze and headed for the outer gate.

"Can I believe my ears?" Brydian's voice; it was under better control than Flint's. "You're countermanding the king's direct orders?"

A sudden clamor drowned the rest of Brydian's speech. And I was at the gate. The guard on duty—a man whose twisted ankle I had tended to not long ago—came over to speak to me. While I explained my business to him, I risked a quick look over my shoulder. The injured being had risen to his feet; a stream of fluid was issuing from his wound. He took two staggering steps, then fell to lie motionless, face-down. A deep, sobbing sigh arose from all the Good Folk, a recognition not only of this loss, I thought, but of wrong heaped upon wrong.

I caught a glimpse of Flint's face. The tight guard he kept on his expression was gone; he was incandescent with rage. "The orders that led to this," he said—and now his voice was cold and clear—"are orders I can no longer follow."

"I should be back fairly soon," I said to the guard. My voice shook like a willow in an autumn gale.

"Sure you're all right to go on your own?"

"I'll be fine."

"We'll be looking out for you." He glanced over toward the scene in the practice area, his face grim, but made no comment. He opened the gate, and I went out.

I crossed the encampment, forded the river, and made my way up into the woods almost without noticing. My mind was full of what had just happened. Flint had ordered Brydian and Esten off the field. He'd said he would no longer obey the king's orders. He had just condemned himself to death.

Up on the hill, under the shelter of trees now resplendent

in their summer finery, I sat down on a stone and allowed myself to shed tears: tears for Flint, tears for that fallen being and all the others, and a few tears of sheer panic. But not for long; I had to call Sage, and for that I wanted to be farther away from the fortress and that scene of carnage. Besides, it would not help anyone if I was late back. Whatever happened to Flint's part of the mission, and surely that was at an end now, I had my own part to play and I must keep to it.

I found the stream and followed it westward, making sure I gathered all the herbs Toleg had asked for. I was nearly far enough from the path to try calling Sage. As I cut a last supply of woodruff, I heard a dry little cough behind me, and whirled to see a familiar figure there, her beady eyes fixed on me, her hair a wild green-gray fuzz around her wise face. There was no need to call; Sage was here.

I dropped my basket, scattering the herbs, and knelt to embrace her. "Sage! I've missed you!"

"Aye, lassie, aye." She patted my arm. "Dry those tears now, we dinna have much time. There are weighty matters to consider."

"Flint—I have to tell you about Flint!" The words burst out of me. "He's done something terrible, something that means he will be— When I left, he was— He spoke out against the king's orders, he—"

"Take a deep breath, Neryn. Sit down here. Aye, that's it, lassie. Now, then."

She was not alone. From under the trees others of her clan came forward: delicate Silver; the wizened elder, Blackthorn; Gentle, the little healer in her blue cloak. No sign of Red Cap.

Sage guessed whom I was looking for. "Red Cap is safe," she said. "I bid the wee fellow go to ground until this is all over. He took his bairnie and went off into the deep parts of the forest."

"I'm glad to hear that. Sage, Flint has put himself in terrible danger—"

"One step at a time. Take it slowly."

I made myself breathe steadily. I tried to assemble my story in a way that made sense, though I thought maybe my heart was breaking. "Sage, Silver, everyone—you know there is another Caller at Summerfort?"

"We know it." Silver managed to speak in a tone like little chiming bells and still sound dour. She was a lovely creature, all flowing hair and graceful floating garments, but she had been slowest of Sage's clan to accept me. "We feel it; we see it."

"Whisper, who was with me before—a Northie—he was caught up in it. Swept along by Esten's call in the south, even though I was close by. And now he's in there with that band of captive Good Folk, and Flint and his troop were supposed to prepare an army for the king, your kind and humankind, just the same as we are trying to do, only—"

"Slow down, lassie," Sage said. "We know of the captive Southies, aye. Their camp's plain enough to see from up here. And we feel the call of that other fellow, but not so strong that we canna hold out against it. If we were closer, or if he reached out straight to us, it might be different. We willna put that to the test before we must."

"The other Caller, Esten—he seems to hate what he does, but he can't stop himself. He craves power. And he's under the control of the queen's councillor."

"Aye, we've seen what the fellow can do. His call is crushing. Shrivels up hope. Sets despair in the bones."

"Just as I went out from the fortress, I saw one of the Southies die. Flint was blaming Esten and the man who controls him, Brydian. And he—Flint—said he wouldn't obey the king's orders anymore. He was so angry I think the words just came out. They'll kill him, Sage." My chest ached; I felt as if I had a knife in my heart.

"Why now?" Blackthorn asked, turning his dark eyes on me. "After keeping up his pretense so long?"

Sage answered, her voice very quiet. "He was ready to walk away from court before the winter. I told him he should stay. Then, of course, his comrades came and took him back. Maybe I should have bid him follow his heart. Even the strongest man has his breaking point."

I swallowed my tears. We had little time, and I must get some answers from them. "I had a chance to watch what Flint and his troop were doing before the king came to Summerfort. From a secret lookout. That day the Caller was not present and Flint's troop was working with the captive Southies quite amicably, going through practice bouts—I've heard they are preparing for some kind of display at midsummer. Doesn't it say in the lore that humankind and Good Folk can't work for a shared purpose without a Caller to lead them? That's the reason I have done all my training—so I can rally this combined force at the Gathering. But Flint was getting them to work together without a Caller—at the time, Esten was sick. No Caller and no iron. And one of the other Enforcers spoke of it too, how when these folk first arrived, it was chaos, and how Flint somehow managed to make that chaos into order."

"There was no sign of the Caller," said Silver, "when Flint went out to the camp to meet with the Southies, night by night, earlier in the season."

"He did that?"

"He did; we saw it."

"So it is possible for our kind and yours to work for a shared purpose without a Caller. How can the lore be wrong?"

"It isna wrong, Neryn," said Sage. "There's no grand purpose here, only a practical bargain. Your man let a goodly few of the Southies go early on, after those meetings in the camp. The smaller ones. The weaker ones. My guess is, the rest of them offered their cooperation in return for that. And now it's all gone wrong. Since the king and queen came, we've been seeing far more folk injured. And it can only get worse. After this, it'll be back to controlling the Southies with iron and with Esten's call."

"As I understand it," Silver said, "at midsummer we'll be battling these Southies. Why would you be wanting anyone to do a good job of training them? It's to our advantage, and that of your human rebels, surely, if things do fall into disarray down there."

I swallowed an angry retort. "I see the sense in that. But—it's cruel. It's wrong. Folk are suffering and dying for no good purpose. Besides, I don't think this is as simple as it sounds. I doubt the king really wants no more than a sort of mock battle, which is what everyone says they are preparing for. And Flint . . . He must have had a plan, but I can't ask him what it was. I haven't even been able to talk to the man who came here with me, the one who's pretending to be my husband."

"I'm sorry Flint's in trouble." Sage gave a crooked smile.

"I ken how sorely that must hurt you. But you must set his needs aside. You know that, deep down; it's what Tali would tell you. Midsummer is close, you're in Summerfort for a reason, and you must let nothing get in the way of that. Look for this Caller's weak point. Learn what he can and cannot do. And when the time comes, make quite sure you are the stronger."

I was cold all through. The terrible dream came back to me, Flint and me on opposite sides of a barred door, our hands palm to palm, and Flint saying, *I can't see you.*

"It may cheer you to know that Tali and her folk are moving down the valley now, in twos and threes," Sage said. "It's been planned so they can all be in the area by midsummer without attracting attention. If they can get anyone else inside Summerfort, they will. Tali's concerned about you. She got a message from your folk in the south; she knows you're already here. She's wondering where you'll be when it all happens, and whether you can stay safe long enough to do what you must do."

"On the day, it's quite likely I'll be expected to stay in the infirmary to tend to anyone who is hurt. But I'll find a way to get out."

"You'll need a good vantage point, where you can watch everything unfold and keep control of it. But protected, so they dinna put an arrow through your heart the moment they see what you're doing."

I said nothing. Now that I was talking to them, now that I knew Tali and the rebels were on the way, midsummer felt far too close. I could not afford to be afraid; but after what I had seen in the practice yard, I was full of doubt.

"You can do it, lassie," said Gentle. "We hae faith in you. Dinna lose faith in yourself."

Their words of confidence suggested they did not know my training was yet incomplete. It was a delicate point; I no longer had time to go anywhere else before midsummer, and my work here gave me the perfect reason to be present at the Gathering. But without the wisdom of all four Guardians, I fell short of a fully trained Caller.

"I have to tell you," I said, "that I have not visited the Master of Shadows yet, and he is the only one who may have a charm to protect you against cold iron."

"But you saw the White Lady?" Gentle's voice was full of awe. "You spoke to her?"

I nodded, not wanting to tell them how diminished the Lady had been, or how tenuous her existence was even now. "I did. But when I saw the captive Southies on the march, I made the decision to come straight here. So I did not seek out the Master. Only . . ."

"Only he's here already?" Sage sounded grim. "We heard some rumors."

"I saw him at the inn in Brightwater. I don't understand how he could let his folk be captured like that. How can he stand by while they are hurt and manipulated? What is he doing?"

"Playin' games," said Blackthorn. "That's his favorite pastime. The Master thrives on trickery. This'll be more than it seems, mark my words."

"I discovered that Esten had met him and perhaps even had some training. If the Master supports him at the Gathering, I have little hope of overriding his call. I thought that the Master would support me as the other Guardians have."

"Mebbe he will," said Blackthorn. "Mebbe the game's trickier than we imagine. He might have decided it needed to be harder for you. Harder for all of us, so we'd learn something that stuck."

"But that's—that's just wrong!"

Sage gave me one of her shrewd looks. "Then you must make it right," she said. "Now, time's passing. Do you have what you came for?"

I crouched down to gather up my scattered harvest. "Can you let your people know," I said, "that I still have no solution to the problem of cold iron? When the time comes, I will try to call only those strong enough to survive the battle. But I can make no promises."

"Aye, we ken that," Sage said. "The battle willna be won without losses. A body would be a fool to think different."

"I'd best go." I did not want to see the aftermath of that scene in the yard. I dreaded learning what had happened to Flint. At the same time, I was desperate to know. And Scia would be needing me.

"Farewell, Neryn," said Sage. "They're bad times, but it isna long till midsummer, and we have faith in you. Hold the flame high, lassie, and keep on forward."

The others bid me farewell in their turn; even Silver gave me grave kisses on either cheek. Then they faded back into the forest and I was alone once more.

The encampment beside the river was ringed with Enforcers bearing iron weapons. There were sad sounds coming from within that cordon, sounds that filled me with fury—at the king and queen, at Brydian, at Esten, most of all at myself. Why in the name of the gods had I insisted on coming here early? I'd let my self-appointed mission divert me from the last part of my training; I'd rushed to court hoping to undo some of the wrong Esten had inflicted. But I hadn't done anything for the captives. I had failed to find an opportunity to talk to them. Today I had walked right by as they lay wounded in the practice yard, and now I was walking by again. Yes, it was the right choice for the cause. But it felt deeply wrong.

Nobody stopped me as I skirted the camp and headed for the gates. There was no one in the practice yard except the guards at the entry. The earth in the center was gouged and scraped; a great dark stain marked the place where the fiery being had fallen. The guards told me I'd find the infirmary busy. Things were not looking good for Owen Swift-Sword; the word was he'd been summoned to appear before King Keldec.

In the infirmary, Ruarc was raving, struggling in the grip of his two comrades while Toleg tried to get a draft down his throat. Scia was stitching up a knife wound in an Enforcer's arm, a job Toleg would usually have done. Her patient sat stoically as she performed her meticulous work, but his gaze kept darting to the tormented Ruarc. There were seven other men waiting in the hallway, one of whom was Brenn.

I gave him a quick greeting before I went in; no time for more. I put the herb basket on the bench. In the stillroom, I stowed my cloak and staff. I took off my shoes, which were soaked from the river crossing, and put on the indoor slippers I had acquired from the household collection of cast-off clothing. I took a few deep, slow breaths. Ruarc was sobbing now; the sound made me want to weep along with him.

"Scia," I said as I came back into the infirmary, "I'll use

310

the stillroom; that will make it quicker to see everyone." And it would be farther from those terrible noises, but not far enough to shut them out. If Ruarc survived, he would be forever changed. Perhaps he'd be like that young man I had met in the Rush valley, the one enthralled against his will, a lost child in a strong man's body. There was a question over Ruarc's long-term care. Thus far, we'd avoided talking about it.

Scia glanced up from her work and nodded. She looked drawn and weary. "Galany of Bull Troop is next," Scia said.

Brenn and I exchanged a somewhat forced smile as I called Galany through, leaving the stillroom door open for propriety. My meager personal possessions were stowed under the pallet; I kept the place scrupulously tidy, as much for my own satisfaction as Toleg's.

"Wrenched my back," Galany told me. "Heavy blow to the shield arm, caught me off balance; should have been more careful where I put my feet."

He was in a lot of pain; I felt gently up and down his spine and saw him trying not to flinch when I touched the sore spot.

"I can give you a draft for the pain. You'll need rest. Don't move about too much or lift anything too heavy until it feels better."

He half smiled and got up as if to leave.

"I'm serious." I gave him my sternest look. "Unless you want this to get worse every time you take a knock of that kind, you need to give it long enough to mend."

"How long?"

"As long as it takes. At least three days of complete rest, and then only light duties until you're not feeling pain."

That little smile again. "New here, aren't you? We don't ask for time off. Just give me the draft. It'll dull the pain for a bit. That's all I came for."

Clearly my sternest look was not stern enough for an Enforcer. "Tell your troop leader that unless you rest this injury, you'll soon be unfit for active duty. Yes, I am new, but Toleg would say exactly the same thing."

Both of us glanced through the stillroom doorway to where Toleg was now seated on the edge of Ruarc's pallet, peering into the injured man's eyes. One of Ruarc's comrades held him still with an arm around his shoulders; the other was dipping a cloth into a bowl, ready to wipe his tearstained face.

"That was a fine man," muttered my patient.

"He still is."

"Not much left of him, poor bastard. As for telling the troop leader I need a rest, I am the troop leader."

"Oh. Then tell . . ." Tell the king?

"Just give me the draft, lass, and get on to the next man, will you?"

So it went, with Scia tending to one man in the infirmary while I looked after another in the stillroom. My final patient was the man my companions knew as Morven, my husband. I was too tired to think straight, and nearly called him Brenn. I hardly knew whether to show concern or pleasure that he was here.

"Anything serious?" asked Scia, who had just sent her last patient off with a salve for his severely bruised toe—he had insisted on putting his boots back on, grunting with pain as he did so.

"A boil," Brenn said. "Simple enough to fix, I expect.

Only it's on . . . er . . . a delicate part of the anatomy." His eyes passed over Scia, who was tidying the workbench, and Toleg, still with Ruarc. "Prefer not to pull my trousers down in front of an audience."

"I'll deal with it," I said. "Come through to the stillroom." A boil was easy; I'd lance it first, then apply a poultice. Since I'd have to make that fresh, we should have some time to talk. "Scia, I'll spare Morven's blushes by closing the door, but just knock if you need anything. Could you pass me that little knife, please?"

He did, in fact, have the beginnings of a boil. I was beyond being embarrassed by such things, and made him lie facedown on the pallet while I tended to it. We spoke in murmurs.

"What happened to Owen Swift-Sword? I was walking past when he shouted at Brydian."

"Hauled off to account for himself to the king. That can't be good. There were some mutterings in the troop; they're loyal to Owen, even though he's a man who likes to go his own way. Rohan took charge. But the word is Wolf Troop will be given the job of training now, and Stag Troop will get guard duty. The men aren't happy about any of it. Everything was going smoothly until the king arrived."

"Shh, keep your voice down. Brenn, I went up to the forest. Tali and the people from Shadowfell are on the way down the valley. And our allies among the Good Folk will be ready too. I need a good vantage point for the Gathering; I need to make sure I'm not stuck in here when it happens. Somewhere very close, but as safe as possible. If you think of anything, let me know. Have you seen Ean? Silva's brother?"

"Ouch!"

"I'm being as gentle as I can. I'll just clean this a bit, then it's the poultice. Awkward spot for a bandage."

Brenn turned his head, managed a smile. "Ean's training with the rest of them and trying not to show how good a fighter he is. No chance to talk to him privately. Those young fellows are going to be mincemeat in any combat, Neryn. The whole idea's crazy. Owen has managed to keep them on the sidelines thus far, but that can't last."

"What will they do to him, Brenn?"

He did not answer straightaway. I was busy assembling what I needed for the poultice, and had my back to him. But he had heard something in my voice. "You and him," he murmured. "What's between the two of you?"

"Nothing."

"If you say so. My guess is the king will make an example of him. Whatever punishment Keldec decides on, it won't be pretty."

My belly was tight; my throat felt as if it would close up. A flood of tears waited just behind my eyes. *The cause. Think of the cause.* "What about you?" I asked. "Are you still being trained, and if so, for what?"

"Enforcer training has been more or less abandoned. The seven of us are doing what the rest of Stag Troop does, just without the pretty silver badge. So if the whole troop's relegated to guard duty, that's what I'll be doing." A pause. "Could be useful."

"Will you see him, do you think?" The question came out despite my better judgment, and my voice shook. "Owen?"

"I don't know. There's a place of incarceration here, but I'm not sure exactly where it's located. Wolf Troop's special preserve. The Wolves take pride in their work. They may not be so pleased if they're ordered to hand over responsibility. Of course, if Owen's locked up in there, the king's hardly going to want his own troop guarding him. My guess is they'll use enthralled men to keep this particular prisoner under control."

"I don't suppose we can do anything to help him. But . . ."

"He's one of ours," Brenn said soberly. "And not just any one. I know the rebel code: the cause must always come first. But I'd hate to see Owen Swift-Sword swallowed up by the king's wrongheaded desire for faster, crueler, showier results before we even get to midsummer. If ever there's a man who deserves to be present when we declare Alban free at last, it's him." A pause. "But you know that."

His tone told me he had guessed that the bond between Flint and me went deeper than that of comrades in the fight, but he held back from saying anything more.

"You don't really need this poultice," I said, "but under the circumstances I'd better apply it for a bit, at least."

"Don't take too long or Scia will be imagining all kinds of things."

"All the more convincing. We're newlyweds."

Before they'd locked him up, they'd given him a thorough beating. Hard enough to render him unconscious, not hard enough to break anything. His assailants had all been enthralled men. They'd have been given precise instructions, designed to ensure their victim would be fit enough to stand up at the Gathering and face whatever public humiliation his king had in mind for him.

He lay in his barred cell, waiting for whatever might come next. They'd given him water, which he'd vomited back up. He couldn't stop shivering. There'd been a blow across the face at some point, and his eyes hurt. His body felt disconnected, a jumble of bones thrown at random into a bag. There would be more beatings. He'd seen it all before; he'd watched his own men carry out the king's orders in precisely the same way. Was Keldec hoping to extract information from him? The interrogation, earlier, had not suggested that. There had been no hint that anyone else was under suspicion; no indication that the king or his advisers knew anything about the coming rebellion. His outburst in the practice yard had been taken as an individual act of defiance. At least he would die knowing he had not betrayed the cause.

If he had been alone with Keldec, he might have told how he'd gradually won the Good Folk's trust, and how that had seemed the best way to meet the challenge his troop had been set. He might have argued that fear was not the best tool for building a loyal fighting force. But not with Brydian at the council table, cold-faced and hard-eyed; not before the queen's small, chill smile. So he had remained silent, save for the necessary "Yes, my lord king" and "No, my lord king." If he survived until midsummer, if he lasted so long, then he would speak. Before they finished him, he would make his voice a clarion call for freedom.

It was dark in here. Could it be night already? The pallet was hard and the cell was as cold as the grave. He tried to sit up and felt his stomach churn with nausea. Pain in his belly, in his back, in his neck. Most of all, an insistent throbbing in the skull, behind the eyes. He had been trained to endure, to set pain aside until the job was done. But there was no longer a mission. Not for Stag Troop, and not for its misguided leader.

Why had he done it? Why had he spoken out against Brydian? He had lost comrades before. Over and over, he and his men had laid down their dead friends and moved on; that was the nature of a warrior's calling. Why had the death of Scorch been different? The big fighter was not even of his own kind; they had known each other less than a season. And yet, this loss had felt worse than all the rest. He had offered the hand of friendship to these folk; he had made them a promise, and in return they had given him their trust, even after all that had befallen them. Even after the long march. Even after the cold iron. They had worked together, played out the intricate moves of combat together, sat around the campfire together. And in the end . . .

He still could not make sense of what had happened. The bout had been routine, king's men and Good Folk together. Scorch and his two comrades were strong, even without their magical advantages, so he'd pitted each of them against a pair of Stag Troop men. The rules of engagement were clear: back off when ordered to do so. And even if that order did not come—for he and Rohan could not watch all of them at once—back off before anyone got seriously hurt.

Brydian must have believed Scorch was out of control, or he would not have ordered Esten to use the quelling call. He had done so behind Flint's back, with no warning, and in the moment when shock made Scorch freeze in place, a spear had pierced his belly. A wooden spear, since there were no iron weapons on the field; but the damage was done. Oddly, what stayed strongest in his memory was not the big warrior falling to his knees, trying to hold his guts in place, but what came after: himself moving forward to help his stricken comrade, and Fume's powerful arm coming out to push him away. The furious words, delivered in a bitter undertone: "Back off! You're nae friend o' his, and you're nae friend o' mine."

He had no right to be hurt by those words—he deserved them. He was troop leader. He had been in charge when it happened. That made Scorch's death his responsibility. He had seen Brydian and Esten come out to watch earlier; he should have known what could happen. He could have called off the training. He could have spoken to Brydian, requested that Esten make no use of his gift. This rested on his shoulders. Whatever the king had in store for him, it would be no more than he deserved.

Some time later, as he lay in a restless half sleep, he heard the bolt slide open on the big door down at the end of the confinement cells. His body readied itself for another assault; the long years of training had their effect, even when his mind was a fog. He breathed deeply, sat up without a sound, tried to focus on the space beyond the bars. His eyes would not cooperate; everything was hazy. He listened instead. The door was closed and bolted again; two men—no, three—spoke in lowered voices at the guard post. One was Brocc from Wolf Troop. Brocc had not been among those who'd beaten him earlier. But Brocc was an enthralled man, and that made him faultlessly loyal to the king. The second was Galany, leader of Bull Troop. The third was Rohan Death-Blade.

Footsteps along the walkway.

"Keep it short," Brocc said. "I have orders, and letting in visitors isn't one of them."

"Can you unlock the cell? He's hardly going to make a run for it with all three of us here."

"Why would I unlock it?"

"Brought him a blanket." Rohan's voice. "And some ale."

"You can give those to me. And you can talk through the door. He's in there." A big, dark form that must be Brocc loomed beyond the iron bars. "Someone to see you, Owen."

He attempted to stand, and failed. Brocc retreated; the other two came to the bars. What was wrong with his eyes? He could hardly tell which was Galany and which Rohan.

"Owen?"

Ah. Rohan on the right.

"Brought you a blanket. Make sure Brocc gives it to you. Perishing cold down here."

A blanket would be good; perhaps it would stop this wretched shivering. "Thank you." He wanted to ask them what was going on out there, how the Good Folk were faring, whether the whole of Stag Troop was paying the price for his lapse in self-control. But getting the words out felt like swimming against an impossible tide.

"Got a few bruises there." Rohan was being careful, with Galany and Brocc both within earshot. "Has anyone had a look? Toleg or one of his helpers?"

"Hardly. Eyes troubling me. Nothing serious." This was not only about a blanket. Rohan might come solely to check on his welfare, but not Galany.

There was an exchange in murmurs, which he heard. Rohan saying he looked unfit to talk about anything; Galany saying it had to be now.

"What?" he managed.

"Listen, Owen," Galany began, and even through the fog

Flint could hear the awkwardness in the Bull Troop leader's voice. "I have a question for you, knowing you're the most skillful Enthraller we have. Knowing you learned the old art of mind-mending, the way folk say it was before."

This was unexpected. "I'm listening."

"Ruarc's still in the infirmary. That was a mighty blow to the skull, would have killed a lesser man. He's not himself. Raving, fighting anyone who tries to help him. Needs two men there just to stop him from hurting someone. And Toleg says that might not change. He says an injury like that can shake up a man's mind so badly there's no curing him."

A silence. Nobody said what they were probably all thinking: a man with a ruined mind was of no use at all to the king. Ruarc could not be safely returned to his home village and forgotten about, as was done with victims of botched enthrallments. This man had been an Enforcer; he was strong and skillful, and with his mind in disorder he would be dangerous.

"Galany and I were wondering if Ruarc could be helped by mind-mending," Rohan said quietly. "Wasn't it sometimes used in old times to bring a measure of peace to folk who were troubled?"

Flint did not answer. Behind this apparently simple request lay many, many questions.

Galany spoke in a murmur. "Come over to the door, Owen."

He found that he could rise, though everything tilted around him and his belly churned with nausea. His walk was a stagger; when he got there, he had to clutch the bars with both hands to stay upright.

"Can you do it?" whispered Galany urgently. "Can you help him?"

Oh gods. He was so tired. He felt as if he might lie down and never get up again. "I don't know," he whispered back. "It's been a long time since I used it in that way. If too much damage has been done, the best I could achieve would be to calm him a bit. And once might not be enough."

"But you could help?"

His legs gave up the attempt to hold him; he collapsed to the floor. Galany squatted down on the other side of the bars. Rohan stayed on his feet, perhaps keeping an eye out for Brocc.

"I'm in here. Ruarc's in the infirmary. Why would the king authorize letting me out?"

"We could bring Ruarc here. How long would it take?"

"At best, overnight. More likely several nights. You'd need Oblivion; he'd have to be in a deep sleep. Galany, this is not something you can do without anyone else knowing. At the very least, the guards would have to agree to it. And Brocc . . ." No need to finish this; Brocc's enthralled state meant he would feel obliged to report such an occurrence to the king.

"Keldec might be happy to see one of his best warriors restored to health and ready to return to duty," Rohan said.

"He might. And if this were yesterday, perhaps he'd agree to let me try what you suggest."

"Don't concern yourself with that," Rohan said. "Just tell us, if you got the opportunity, would you try this?"

He rested his head against the bars; closed his eyes.

"Galany," Rohan murmured, "go and have a word with

Brocc. Keep him occupied. Tell him he can drink the ale."
With the other man gone, Rohan crouched down beside his
leader. "Got a plan," he whispered. "Get you out of here."

Flint felt a thrill of terror run through him. "No! The
error was mine; I don't want anyone else paying for it. Don't
risk yourself or any of the troop." He drew a ragged breath.
"Are they all right? The rest of the men, and Blaze and his
folk? Are you still in control?"

"I haven't been officially relieved of my duties yet, but
it's only a matter of time. We're sure Wolf Troop will get
the training job, perhaps jointly with Bull, since time's running short. There have been no further losses as yet. Owen,
the men support you. They understand why you did what
you did."

"They should forget me. They should concentrate on
surviving."

"Until midsummer?" Rohan's voice was a thread.

The silence was full of the perilous unspoken.

"And what about you?" Rohan added. "Is that all you
want, just to survive?"

"My survival doesn't matter."

"And Ruarc?"

"I'm locked up and awaiting punishment. I'm too weak
even to stand up. I've lost the king's trust. I wish I could help
Ruarc. He was a fine man."

"You could bring him back."

"I might try it and fail."

"You'd at least have tried. Besides . . ."

Galany was back, and down at the guard post someone
was jangling keys. "Will you help?" the Bull Troop leader

asked bluntly. There was something in his tone that gave Flint pause. Something that reminded him of comrades fallen, of himself kneeling beside a dead man and whispering a half-remembered prayer. He thought of a line in the old song: *I am the warrior, sword in hand*. With Ruarc's life in the balance, how could he refuse?

"If you can set it up, I'll try. No promises."

"Thank you. Rohan said you'd help us. Don't know when, but be ready. We're almost out of time."

CHAPTER TWELVE

AT LAST RUARC WAS ASLEEP. SO WAS TOLEG, who had been so worn out by another morning's struggle with the injured warrior that he had raised no objection when I suggested he retire to his little chamber for a rest and leave me in charge. We'd been managing without Scia, who was unwell. Ruarc's two guards were taking a break, eating the food and drink a Bull Troop man had brought for all of us. I picked at my own share. Ruarc's ravings had us constantly on edge; times of quiet like this rarely lasted long.

And then there was Flint. Word had come that he was locked up in a secret prison within the walls of Summerfort, and that the king was so furious about the whole affair that he could barely speak. I'd heard talk that Keldec was planning a special punishment for his disobedient troop leader, to be delivered at the Gathering. Owen Swift-Sword was not universally liked. Folk thought him something of a rebel—if things had been different, I might have laughed at that. He was known as a man who went his own way, and who did not suffer fools gladly. Most of all, people knew him as Keldec's favorite, the one whom the king would forgive almost anything. This was a mighty fall from grace.

One of the guards came over to top up my mead cup.

"Thank you—" I began, then fell silent at the sound of a small child screaming from somewhere beyond the infirmary door. The screaming was getting louder by the moment.

Without a word, the two guards went back to Ruarc's pallet, one to each side. I made for the door. If I could stall whoever it was before they came in, perhaps I could prevent them from waking him.

The door slammed open, making me jump back. The noise was shrill enough to wake the dead. Ruarc sat up abruptly, shouting. A group of folk burst into the chamber. I swallowed my fury and took control. Or tried. The screaming child was the king's son, Ochi, thrashing around in the arms of a nursemaid, his face purple. Two other women were yelling at me, but over Ochi's voice and Ruarc's I could not catch a word. Something about his nose?

"Tell me calmly what's the matter," I said.

"Master Toleg," one of the women shrieked. "Where's Master Toleg? The queen won't—"

A cold resolve came over me. Toleg had not emerged from behind the closed door of his chamber. Just possibly he was so tired this had not woken him. If so, that was how it was going to stay. "You're not helping anyone with all this noise," I said. "Least of all the child. Take a deep breath and explain to me what has happened."

"Ochi— Can't get it out— The queen—"

The women were beyond speaking sense. The two Bull

Troop men were taken up with restraining Ruarc. But—ah, yes. Standing behind the gesticulating women was the guard I'd seen with Ochi that day in the garden, the one to whom the child had run to share a discovery.

"You," I said to the guard. "What's happened here?"

"Playing with beads. Somehow got one stuck up his nose. We tried to get it out, but . . ." He looked at the frantic scene, the screeching child, the dithering women. There was no need to explain why the attempt had been unsuccessful. "One of the maids went to fetch the queen," he added.

Black Crow save me. The queen on her way? I rolled up my sleeves. The first step was to get Ochi calm. That wasn't going to happen with his nursemaids close by, or indeed with Ruarc in the same chamber.

"Through here," I said, indicating the stillroom entry. "You—what is your name?"

"Maelan," the guard said. "I'll take him, shall I? Come on, Ochi, this nice lady's going to make it all better." He scooped the boy out of the nursemaid's arms and strode past me into the stillroom. The maids clustered around, wanting to follow.

"Just Maelan and the boy," I said. "The rest of you, find somewhere to sit down, and be quiet."

"But he's not—"

"But the queen—"

I shut the door in their faces.

Ochi was still screaming. Maelan put him up against his shoulder like a baby and patted his back. "All better soon, little man," he said. "Don't rub your nose, now. How about a story while the lady gets ready?" Without waiting for an answer, he launched into a tale about a mother cat that found a baby hedgehog among her kittens. The story was punctuated with dramatic meows and squeaks. Ochi's yelling subsided to hiccuping sobs; Maelan sat down on the edge of my pallet with the boy on his knee and began knotting a handkerchief, making it into a little creature with ears and a tail.

I found wax; melted a little over warm water and set it to cool. I cut a short length from a reed. "How far up?" I asked softly. "Left or right?"

"Left, and not far," Maelan murmured. "But sitting awkwardly."

"When it's time, the young man needs his back against your chest," I said in the same quietly casual tone. "One arm around his brow to hold his head still, the other around his body, pinning the arms. Very firm."

He nodded. "Just say when you're ready. You're Morven's wife, aren't you?"

"That's right, I'm Ellida."

"Good man, Morven." He made the handkerchief creature creep up Ochi's arm. "Then Malkin crept closer—*meow, meow*—and said to Snufflepig, 'You are no cat! Your fur is too sharp. Your eyes are too beady. And where is your tail?'"

The wax was cool enough. I stuck it firmly onto one end of the reed. I moved a three-legged stool close to Maelan and the child and sat down, holding the implement out of Ochi's view. "And what did Snufflepig have to say to that?" I asked, indicating with a nod that it was time.

Maelan wrapped his arms around Ochi, pinioning head and body against his chest. I leaned forward, looking up the child's tiny nostril, my wax-tipped reed in hand. Ochi opened his mouth to protest, and the door from the infirmary crashed open behind me.

"What are you doing to my son?"

327

Maelan, bless him, did not move a muscle, though Ochi squealed in fright. I called upon my training, breathing deeply, shutting out everything but the task. There was the culprit, lodged crosswise but within easy reach. I stuck the reed in and pressed the blob of soft wax firmly against the bead, trying not to push the thing farther in. With the queen's enraged presence almost palpable behind me, I made myself count slowly to five. I sent up a swift, wordless prayer and pulled the reed back out. The bead came with it.

Maelan relaxed his hold; the firm restraint became a gentle hug, a stroking of the wispy hair. "There, laddie," he said. "Brave boy. All gone."

I rose to my feet, the reed in one hand, the wooden bead in the other. I turned. She stood there: immaculately dressed hair, dark eyes in a flawless pale face, elegant gown with spreading skirts of a rich blue. Small, vivid, furious. The nursemaids were clustered in the doorway behind her, silent now. From here I could not see Ruarc, but his voice was everywhere.

"My lady," I said, making myself curtsy. To be so close to Varda chilled me; it took me back to the last Gathering, where I had seen how she fed off others' pain. "I am Ellida, one of Toleg's assistants. The prince had a bead stuck in his nose; I have removed it, and he is unharmed, though a little upset."

"Show me."

I opened my palm to display the offending object. The queen had made no attempt to speak to her son or touch him, and the sobbing Ochi did not reach out for her or say *Mama*. He was clinging to Maelan's shirt with one hand and clutching the handkerchief creature in the other.

"I see." Queen Varda turned her gaze on the guard. "How did this come about, Maelan? Who did this to my son?"

Maelan rose to his feet with Ochi in his arms. "My lady. The children were playing in the sewing room while the women worked. I was on guard at the door. I did not see exactly what happened. The maids could perhaps tell you more. Ochi is unharmed, as Ellida says. She did a good job."

She turned on me. "Why were you tending to him in here, with only Maelan present? Why was the door closed? Where is Toleg?"

I took a considered breath. "My lady, we have a very sick man in the infirmary, as you probably saw and heard when you came through. And the nursemaids were—less than calm. Your son needed a friend with him, and I needed someone who could hold him still and reassure him. I asked Maelan to do that job."

"And Toleg?"

"I'm here, my lady." He appeared behind the nursemaids, his gray hair tousled. "I'm sorry I was not at hand when your son was brought in. But it appears Ellida has coped admirably in my absence."

"And where were you?"

"Sleeping, my lady. Our patient requires constant supervision. It's my practice to sit up with him overnight so my assistants can get their rest. The place is busy at this time of year, as I'm sure you will understand."

"I see." Her voice was wintry. "This is unsatisfactory. What ails that man out there that he cannot be kept quiet when there are other patients requiring your attention?"

"A combat injury, my lady. Ruarc sustained a severe blow to the head; his recovery will take some time."

Varda turned on her heel and stalked through to the infirmary, brushing past Toleg as if he were not there. The rest of us followed in her wake. At the foot of Ruarc's pallet she halted. One of his comrades was holding him steady while the other sponged his red and angry face. "You say it will take time," she said coolly. "How much time?"

I could see Toleg wanted to lie. But this was the queen, and he told the truth. "I cannot answer that, my lady. We are still working on ways to help him."

"Out with it, Toleg. You are far from certain he will recover, yes?"

"I cannot be sure either way, my lady. But Ruarc is a loyal member of Bull Troop, one of the king's valuable fighting men. The king would surely want us to keep trying."

A delicate frown appeared on Varda's brow. "It is not up to you to judge what the king may or may not want, Toleg. One thing is sure: this man cannot stay here, shouting and screaming day and night and disrupting your regular duties. And these two should be with their troop, doing their work as Enforcers, not acting as nursemaids. I will send Brydian to make an assessment."

Toleg's jaw tightened. "Yes, my lady."

"You," Varda said, whirling and pointing a finger in my direction. My heart skipped a beat. "Your approach to your duties seems a little unconventional, but you have done well today."

"Thank you, my lady." The words came through gritted teeth; never had I wanted so badly to tell someone exactly what I thought of them.

"You!" She addressed the cringing maidservants. "Maelan

330

tells me my son was playing with other children when this episode occurred. What other children?"

"Brand and Scia's younger children, my lady." The woman's voice was trembling. "Dai and Eda."

"And which of them put a bead in my son's nose?"

It seemed to me quite likely Ochi had done it himself in a spirit of experimentation, but it was not for me to speak.

"I—I can't say, my lady."

"Were you not watching over my son?" The hushed tone was truly terrifying.

"Yes, but—I did not see what happened, exactly. It was so quick." The woman had clasped her shaking hands together.

"It would have been Dai," one of the other maids said. "Eda is only a baby."

"Maelan, take Ochi back to the nursery, then have someone summon Brand to my audience chamber. You three, report to the kitchens." She turned the full, chill force of her stare on the nursemaids. "At this time of year there's sure to be work for scullions. It has escaped you, perhaps, that my son will one day be king of Alban. A future monarch requires more responsible attendants."

It took time to calm Ruarc again once Varda and the others were gone. When he was reasonably quiet, we left the Bull Troop men to watch over him. Toleg prepared tinctures; I brewed more of the sleeping draft we were using to maintain precarious control over Ruarc's moods. Time passed, but for all our orderly activity, the infirmary was full of tension. How long did we have before Brydian came and declared our patient unable to recover?

I'd heard the others talking when Ruarc was asleep. I

331

knew what they feared. When an Enforcer was so badly wounded he could no longer perform his duties, he was culled. That this was not Ruarc's fault, that he could not plead his own case, that his companions would willingly go on looking after him even if there was no improvement—none of this would make a bit of difference. Anyone who challenged the decision was likely to find himself paying the price at the Gathering.

I read on Toleg's face how much he hated this, how hard it was for a healer of many years' standing to let such a thing happen. I wondered, not for the first time, why he had not seized some opportunity to walk away from this place and from his duty to the king. Surely he'd been tempted, on one of his solitary trips into the forest, to turn his back on Summerfort and head off into the hills, never to return. One day, I told myself, when all this was over, when the battle was won, I would ask him. He was a man of conscience. That was clear in everything he did, even at the times of ill temper. Perhaps he stayed because, in this place of fear and cruelty, his work gave him a rare chance to do some good.

When someone knocked on the infirmary door, my heart jolted. All of us turned our heads; none of us spoke.

"Open the door, Ellida," Toleg said.

I expected Brydian. But the man who stood there was Galany of Bull Troop, Ruarc's leader. Someone was going to have to tell him about the queen's visit.

"Shut the door," Galany said. "Toleg, something to ask you." His voice was hushed, urgent.

"Go on, then." Toleg glanced at me, at Ruarc and his two comrades. "Unless this is private?"

332

"You'll all need to know. It's about him, Ruarc. You know Owen Swift-Sword? He's agreed to try mind-mending, if we can arrange it. Might help, might not, but worth trying. Not an enthrallment, you understand, but the other thing, the old way. Owen's the only one who can do it. Will you consider it?"

Toleg opened his mouth and closed it again at the look on Galany's face, all naked hope.

"Galany," I made myself say, "even if the king would agree to that, we've just had Queen Varda in here, and she expressed dissatisfaction with the situation." I wasn't going to talk about culling in front of Ruarc, though I was fairly sure he was beyond understanding. "She is sending Brydian to . . . to make an assessment."

"When?"

"I don't know. Soon, perhaps."

"Then we need to do this now." Galany squared his massive shoulders. "Get him down there, give him the draft—"

"You're not thinking," Toleg said. "Owen Swift-Sword?"

"Galany," said one of the Bull Troop men, "do this without the king's approval and you'll find yourself in the cell next to Owen."

"Say I go out that door and come in again," said Galany, "and we forget we've had this conversation. All I'll do is ask my troopers here to bring their wounded comrade out of the infirmary; all I'll tell you is that you're to pass him over into my custody. We'll convey him elsewhere, and when Brydian comes, you'll say it was taken out of your hands."

Black Crow save us. The man was writing his own death sentence.

"And risk losing all four of you, instead of just the one?"

Toleg's tone was mild. I guessed he admired Galany's courage as much as I did. "You're not thinking, friend."

Footsteps outside; another knock at the door. My hand was shaking as I opened it. Not Brydian; one of the household servants, a youngish man in gray.

"You are Ellida, the assistant healer?"

"I am." What was this?

"King Keldec has sent for you. You're to come with me immediately."

The king was in a council chamber, alone. The servingman announced me, then retreated, closing the door. Keldec had his back to me; he was standing by one of the long windows, looking out over the silver-gray expanse of Deepwater. From this vantage point, it might be possible to pretend for a little that the unhappy household, the chaotic army of fey and human folk, the visiting chieftains and their followers did not exist, and that all was peace and beauty.

I stood with my hands behind my back, waiting in silence. This could be anything. Someone—Brenn, Ean, Whisper, even Flint—might have cracked under pressure and revealed who and what I was. Or I might have revealed my gift in some way without realizing it. I tried to remember everything I had said to Esten when he'd begged me for help; had I shown too much understanding? But that had been some time ago. Why had the king only summoned me now? Perhaps he had an ailment that needed tending in private. But he'd surely consult Toleg for that, not me. I breathed slowly, making my mind calm, as the Hag had taught me. *Be strong, Neryn.* The silence drew out.

Eventually, Keldec turned, as casually as if I had only just entered the chamber. "Ellida," he said with a smile.

I was struck, again, by how ordinary he looked. If I had not known who he was, I would have thought that smile quite pleasant. His manner was open and friendly.

"Yes, my lord king." I performed the curtsy, eyes down.

"Come closer. Sit down, here." The king motioned to a bench. I sat, and so did he, on a rather grand oak chair carved with little creatures. There was no table between us. Whatever this was, it was not a formal hearing. I wondered if I was to be tidied away like Ruarc, made to disappear because I was inconvenient. "Don't look so worried," he said. "I won't eat you."

I failed to force a smile. "No, my lord king."

"I wanted to thank you, Ellida. I understand you did my son a service today."

Oh gods, was this all? I released a long breath. "I did tend to Ochi earlier, my lord king. He was more frightened than hurt. His guard, Maelan, helped me very capably; Ochi seems to trust him."

"Maelan, yes," Keldec said, "a good man. My son is fond of him." He scrutinized me. All I'd had time to do was take off my apron; I was in my working clothes, with my hair caught back under a kerchief so it would not get in my way. That was just as well, since it was some while since I'd had a chance to reapply the dye. Not that the king would recognize me from last year's Gathering; I had not been close enough to him.

"You must be proud of your little boy, my lord," I ventured. I wanted to add that I suspected Scia's children were not responsible for the bead incident, but I held back.

335

"He's a fine boy, yes. I think, sometimes, it is more curse than blessing to be born a future king, Ellida. On occasion I find myself wishing my son had a choice in the matter; that he could follow his own path. What do you say to that?"

His candor startled me. How could I possibly answer such a question? Most certainly, I could not point out that under the law Ochi had no claim to the throne. This was a man who could—and would—change the law as it suited him. "Morven and I have no children as yet, my lord king." I chose my words with care. "If we are blessed with them some-day, I would wish for our sons and daughters that they lead good, wise, and happy lives, no matter where their paths take them."

He got up and went back to the window, resuming his contemplation of the loch. "You would not wish them riches? Power? Status?"

"When my husband is fully trained, he will be one of your Enforcers, my lord king. I have my own work as a healer, sat-isfying work. I would not wish more than that kind of life for our children."

"No?" He did not turn. "Then I must not insult you by offering silver, or a promotion for that husband of yours. But it would please me to reward you for your services to my son today. You speak well; what you said makes it difficult for me to determine what I should give you. Perhaps you should de-cide that, Ellida. What would please you most?"

Black Crow save me. My mind filled with all manner of impossible requests: *Send Esten home, set your fey captives free, pardon Owen Swift-Sword. Stop listening to your wife. Become a just ruler.* "Your thanks is sufficient reward, my lord king." I waited to be dismissed.

336

"You have Ruarc of Bull Troop in the infirmary just now," Keldec remarked.

Let this not be a confirmation that Ruarc was to be culled. I willed my heart to slow. "Yes, my lord king. He's gravely ill. We're doing our best for him."

"A fine warrior. One of my bravest and best. I have been much saddened by the news of his injury. Is it true what they tell me, that there is no cure for this?"

Far from slowing, my heart now threatened to leap out of my chest; my palms were clammy. The king's manner suggested he was genuinely concerned; his expression was one of sorrow. And here I was, with an opportunity to make a difference for Ruarc, if only I were brave enough to risk it.

"Toleg does believe we're close to exhausting the possibilities, my lord king. But . . . some of the men were talking today, and I heard them say there might be a way to help Ruarc. They were talking about an ancient practice called mind-mending. It's been suggested that if someone with the right skill tried that, the damage might perhaps be reversed."

A lengthy pause, then, "Go on."

I had hoped I might not need to say more. I held my hands together behind my back to conceal the shaking. "I heard there's a man here who can perform mind-mending, my lord king. One of your Enforcers."

"Owen Swift-Sword?" The king's tone was not encouraging. "The man's locked up and awaiting punishment for a grave offense. I imagine that news has reached the infirmary by now."

"Yes, my lord king." I should curtsy again, thank him for his kindness, and make a retreat for the sake of the greater cause. But the memory of Ruarc's cries was strong, along with the look in the eyes of his comrades earlier today. I could not walk away from this. "But could not Owen Swift-Sword still be asked to help Ruarc?"

"You know Owen Swift-Sword, Ellida?" There was something new in his voice now, something like pain.

"I met him on the day Morven and I arrived here, my lord king, but I have not seen him since."

"Once my most loyal man. Once my trusted friend. He turned against me."

I held my silence. How long would it be before someone came in and my chance was gone? Perhaps even now Brydian was in the infirmary determining that Ruarc was too much of a burden to be kept alive.

"Why would I allow Owen to do this? He might work his magic against me; use some trickery to turn this man into another like himself, wayward and disloyal."

It seemed to me Keldec was not talking to me now, but thinking aloud.

"The men were suggesting the mind-mending could be done in the place of incarceration, my lord king, with guards present." This was dancing on eggshells. "Might not this be an opportunity for Owen Swift-Sword to make amends?"

"Owen deserves no further opportunities." Keldec did not look angry, only deeply sad.

I forced the words out. "No, my lord king. But Ruarc surely does."

He paced for a little then, arms folded, brow furrowed. I had risen to my feet when he did, and I waited, not daring to hope for anything except that I might get out of the chamber unharmed, and that he would then forget about me. He halted, turned, looked me in the eye. I could not read his expression.

"Very well," he said. "Tell Toleg he has my approval to try this. Owen Swift-Sword is not to leave the place of incarceration, and the full complement of guards is to be present at all times while this process is taking place."

"Thank you, my lord king." My belly was tight. I could not walk out of here without telling him about the queen and Brydian, even if that meant he changed his mind. "My lord, Master Brydian was due to make an assessment of the injured man, perhaps today. For purposes of . . . of deciding whether it was appropriate to keep him in the infirmary any longer." My heart was hammering.

"I see." Keldec strode over to the door and called, "Guard!"

Breathe slowly, Neryn.

The door opened. A guard in Stag Troop uniform stood there. "My lord king."

"Fetch your troop leader. He's to accompany Ellida here back to the infirmary. She will explain to him what my orders are."

"Yes, my lord king." The man moved off down the hallway; a guard who had been stationed farther away came to take his place by the door.

"This decision won't be popular in every quarter, Ellida," the king said. "That makes it all the more important that the treatment be successful. Much hangs in the balance here. You should hope Owen Swift-Sword does not fail."

A threat. So I had indeed taken a dangerous step. I swept into my curtsy once more. "I understand, my lord king."

"I believe you do," Keldec said, and as Rohan Death-Blade appeared at the end of the hallway, the king went back into his council chamber.

While Rohan and I made our way to the infirmary, I discovered he already knew about Galany's mind-mending idea. I told him about Brydian's assessment and what the king had said. Rohan asked a question I had not expected.

"Will you be alone in the infirmary at some point later?"

"I think Toleg will want to supervise getting Ruarc to the cells. He may wish to be present during the mind-mending. Scia is ill; she won't be at work today. So I'll be the one who makes up the draft to send Ruarc to sleep."

"Oblivion."

"I imagine that's what will be needed. One dose for tonight, and if further treatment is required, a fresh brew each time. Oblivion doesn't keep its potency for long."

We were nearing the infirmary, and there were guards in the passageway. "I'll come and speak to you later," Rohan said in an undertone, "after we've installed Ruarc down there. Try to make sure you're on your own."

No time to reply to this, for we were at the infirmary door, and the voices of Brydian and Toleg could be heard from inside, arguing, along with the sound of Ruarc weeping.

"Make this work," murmured Rohan, "and every Enforcer in Summerfort will be your friend."

"It won't be me making it work, it will be Owen Swift-Sword."

He glanced at me sideways. "Then they'll be friends to both of you," he said, and opened the door.

*　　*　　*

Rohan's authority as acting troop leader, along with the fact that we had brought a direct order from the king, silenced the dispute that had been raging when we arrived. Brydian departed, looking displeased at the waste of his time. With little fuss and much speed, Rohan and Galany organized a team of men to convey Ruarc down to the cells. I bundled up bedding and other supplies to go with him. Toleg went too; he would stay as long as he was needed.

When everyone was gone, I sat for a little while staring across the empty chamber. I had seldom felt so exhausted. The place was eerily quiet. But this did not feel like peace; it felt like the calm before the storm.

I made myself get up. Work to be done, a man's life to be saved. In the back of my mind, as I fetched what I needed from Toleg's locked cupboard, was my dream of Flint behind the bars, his hand close to mine, his voice drained of hope. Would that be today? And if he had indeed become that shadow of himself, half blind, how could he be called upon to practice his demanding craft?

Much hangs in the balance here, the king had said. If Flint proved incapable of curing Ruarc, might my impulsive request spell death not only for the sick man but for the rebellion as well? What if Keldec had me culled, not for my canny skill, but simply for poor judgment? Tali would think this was a mistake. Whether Ruarc lived or died had nothing to do with the cause.

But this felt right. Just as the White Lady had shown me the one-in-all, Ruarc's plight was showing me the all-in-one.

I had seen how patiently the Bull Troop men tended to their damaged comrade. Yes, they were the same Enforcers who rode from Summerfort every autumn to carry out the Cull; they were the same men who hammered down doors and torched buildings and put folk to the sword. Ruarc too must have done that. Perhaps some of them enjoyed the power, the excitement, the status their work for the king provided. Some doubtless performed those duties without question, simply because that was their job. But they were not evil men. I had seen their courage, their forbearance, their generosity of spirit. Whatever lay in their past, at heart each was the man the old song spoke of: *I am the warrior, sword in hand.* Yes, even poor, damaged Ruarc. Saving him was the same as saving Alban.

I set out the components for Oblivion on the workbench. The formula was not complex, but it was important to make no errors in the measurement. Before he left, Toleg had made me promise to check everything twice, no matter how busy I might be. I was fortunate; nobody disturbed me until I had the mixture ready in a corked jar and the bench clean and tidy. When the knock on the door did come, it was Rohan Death-Blade. He entered and slid the bolt shut.

"The draft is ready," I said. I was tense again, not knowing if this was a time for the revelation of perilous secrets. "Will you take it down to him?"

Rohan did not answer. He came to sit by me on a bench, elbows on knees, hands clasped, looking at the flagstone floor.

"Rohan," I said, "was there something you wanted to ask me?"

He looked up. Like Flint, he was good at masking his

expression. Rohan's face had a naturally guileless air, and it was not hard to imagine him in a different kind of life, as a craftsman, a trader, a farmer, with a loving family and honest work for his hands. He was not a man who fit the trappings of an Enforcer.

"A simple request." His voice was held quiet, though there was a locked door between us and the nearest guard. "Owen has had a look at Ruarc and spoken to Toleg about him. He's fairly sure the healing can't be completed in one night's work. So he'll be needing you to make up the draft three days in a row. Possibly longer."

I waited, sensing there was more to come.

"Can you make a double dose each time? Without anyone else knowing, I mean?"

I stared at him. "You do know how dangerous Oblivion can be if not administered correctly."

"I've assisted Owen more than once in an enthrallment. Yes, I know."

What in the name of the gods was this? A trap, designed to see me lose my position as Toleg's assistant and perhaps my place at court? Or something quite different? "Can you explain why?"

"Best if you don't know that."

"Then how can I do it, when I know a double dose could kill a man?"

"Does it help if I say nobody's getting a double dose?"

So he planned to drug not only Ruarc, but someone else as well. Why would that need to be secret?

"When you say nobody else should know, does that include Toleg? Scia?"

343

"It does." My doubt must have been plain on my face, for he added, "I'm acting on Owen Swift-Sword's instructions."

Black Crow save us. This was perilous indeed. Could their target be Esten? But no. With Ruarc needing one dose a day, Rohan's request would not provide them with sufficient Oblivion to do more than put one more man to sleep for a night. The draft did not keep for long enough to be used in any other way. Besides, he'd said nobody would get a double dose.

"Very well, I'll do as you ask. You'll need to fetch it yourself. You realize how much trouble this could cause for me if it became known."

"High stakes," Rohan said. "For all of us."

"You'll be wanting to take the fresh draft for Ruarc; it's here."

"Ah. Owen's asked that you bring it down yourself; he thinks both you and Toleg need to be present. We'll leave two men on duty here; one of them can come and fetch you if there's a patient needing urgent attention. It's nearly suppertime. Shouldn't be too much call for your services now."

Flint had asked for me. For a moment that was all I could think of. Somewhere inside me, I felt the flickering of a tiny flame, hope in the darkness; my heart grew warmer.

"One more thing."

"Yes?"

"A simple poultice for the eyes; Toleg said you'd know how to make it. Something that'll soothe inflammation quickly. Wants you to prepare it and bring it with you now. I'll organize the guards while you're doing that, then I'll escort you down there."

"For—" I stopped myself just in time.

"For Owen. Sustained some damage when they put him in there. Seems to think he can still do the job, but Toleg says he needs this first. Maybe each night. You'll be busy, Ellida."

"I'm always busy." I managed a smile, though my voice was shaking. "If I prepare a poultice now, it'll have cooled too much by the time I can apply it. Is there a brazier down there?"

A grim smile. "There is."

"Then I'll get the components ready and make the poultice when we get there."

Lacking a ready supply of fresh leaves, I powdered dry ones and mixed them to a paste with a little hot water. I found clean bandages and rolled them; packed everything in a basket. Curse the need to do this in such haste! If there'd been time to go up into the woods, I'd have been able to gather several herbs whose juices were effective in eye drops. I could have made a tincture of rue, with honey to keep it fresh. I could have . . . Never mind. The best I could do right now was make this basic cure with as much love as I had in me, and hope Flint's eyes were not as badly hurt as my dream had suggested.

By the time Rohan came back, I was ready: a picture of calm efficiency, with a fresh apron over my gown, my hair tidily covered by a clean kerchief, and my basket on my arm. Underneath, a whirl of emotions, a stomach tight with anxiety, a heart yearning to see my man again, yet dreading what I would find.

*   *   *

We went into a part of the keep I had not visited before, along past the men's quarters, through an unobtrusive doorway, and down a set of stone steps to a level that must be underground. Then along a narrow passageway illuminated by oil lamps hung high on the stone walls. It was a place to conjure nightmares even in a man whose mind was healthy and whole. The air was heavy with fumes from the lamps, and shadows clung to the corners.

The passageway came to an end before a formidable door with enough iron reinforcements to keep a giant in. There was a small square window set into the door at a man's eye level, and Rohan stepped up to it. "Brocc! Rohan Death-Blade. I've brought Toleg's assistant."

A big Enforcer came to let us in. My heart was hammering now. I failed to summon any of the techniques I had been taught for staying calm. Inside the door was a guard post with a heavy wooden table, a couple of benches, a shelf bed with folded blankets. A tray with the remnants of a meal; a jug and several cups. A brazier in the corner, well shielded—in a place set so deep, a fire out of control would be truly disastrous. A tiny barred window up near the roof. Outside, the light was fading.

Rohan introduced us. "Brocc of Wolf Troop, who's the head guard here. Ellida, the other healer. Ellida needs to make up a poultice for Owen's eyes. The brazier, some water—anything else you need?"

"A kettle, if you have one. But I should look at his eyes first. Where is Toleg?"

"Down the end with the others," Brocc said. "Follow me." There were four cells on either side of the central walkway, each with its own barred door. The place was cold. Nobody in the first pair of cells, the second, the third. My heart beat faster as I wondered when the dream would come true and I would see Flint on the other side of the bars, looking like death.

It did not happen. We reached the last pair of cells, and the doors of both were wide open. In the cell on the left, Ruarc was lying on a pallet, covered by a blanket. He had his eyes open, but was mercifully quiet. One of his comrades was on a stool beside him, and the other stood nearby. In the cell on the right, a group of men stood in consultation: Toleg, Galany of Bull Troop, and a Stag Troop man I knew as Tallis. And, seated on the edge of another pallet, Flint. Flint not in Enforcer black, but in an assortment of ill-fitting garments that might have belonged to a scullion or groom. Flint with bruising to the face and neck, and great dark shadows around his reddened eyes.

Calm, Neryn. A moment, that was all I had before they saw me; a moment to remind myself that to Toleg and Galany, to Brocc, perhaps even to Rohan, I was no more than a healer's assistant who happened to have seized a chance for Ruarc. That Owen Swift-Sword and I were almost strangers to each other.

"Here," said Brocc, and headed back to the guard post.

Flint looked up. I clamped a tight control on the part of me that wanted to rush forward and embrace him; to erase the lost look from his face in any way I could.

I summoned a polite smile. "I've brought the draft you asked for, Master Toleg. And the makings of the poultice. I'll put it together at the guard post. Perhaps I could have a look at Owen's eyes before I go ahead with that. An opportunity to learn." Toleg would have checked thoroughly before he requested the poultice, and compared with him I was a beginner.

"Bring the lamp closer, Galany," Toleg said. "Put it on the bench there. Yes, that's right. And you fellows can move out to give Ellida and me room. Owen, lie down again."

I sat on the stool beside the pallet, hoping I was doing a little better at shielding my expression than Flint was—he looked at me as if I were an impossible dream, something longed for that could never be obtained. As a man dying of thirst imagines freshwater; as a lost child imagines home and family. I laid my hand on his arm, felt how tightly wound he was, and wondered how he could possibly help Ruarc when he so badly needed help himself.

"I can't see you very well," he said in a whisper. "Didn't I meet you once? The day Rohan came here . . ."

"I'm Ellida, wife of Morven, one of your trainee Enforcers," I said, keeping my voice steady. "Tell me what you can see. Is everything blurred? Dark? Is one eye worse than the other?" Toleg would already have asked all these questions and more. I was wasting time. But to be so close, to be able to touch him, to hear his voice . . . I would hold on to this gift while I could. This might be the last time we saw each other.

I touched my fingers to his wrist, feeling for the beating of the blood. I bent closer, looking into his eyes. The steadfast, clear gray was surrounded by angry red. He wore a strange mask of bruises.

"Hazy," Flint said. "At even a short distance I cannot tell one man from another."

"How long ago did this injury occur?"

He managed a smile, and I wanted to weep. "In this place, a man loses the sense of time passing. Not so very long."

I looked up at Toleg. The other men had gone down to the guard post; I could hear them talking. "The poultice will relieve the swelling," I said. "But . . . this man needs time to heal. He needs rest and ongoing care. How can he be expected to tend to Ruarc tonight?"

"I gave my word that I would do it." Flint wrapped his hand around mine, holding fast. "I don't need my eyes for mind-mending. Apply the poultice by all means. But no delays. Today we have the king's permission to try this. Tomorrow that could change."

If Toleg noticed we were holding hands, he chose not to comment on it. "You'll need to eat and drink too, Owen. Not prison fare, something nourishing. We'll send one of the guards up to fetch rations for all of us. This may be a long night." After a little, he added, "You'd best go back up, Ellida. I can finish off the poultice. This is no place for a young woman."

Flint's hand tightened on mine. He did not say a word. In my mind was the night I had watched from a hiding place as an Enthraller worked his magic on my grandmother; the night the charm was botched, and instead of becoming loyal to the king, she lost her mind. I remembered the fake enthrallment Flint had carried out on Tali at the last Gathering, and how, for a while, I had believed her ruined in the same way. I loathed the art of enthrallment; its practice was a blight on the land of Alban. It had taken me a long time to accept Flint's gift, and to believe that once, in the time before

Keldec, that same art had been used to heal, not to bend and break. I never wanted to see an enthrallment again. And mind-mending, though it was different in its purpose, would probably look exactly the same.

I drew a deep breath. "If you permit, I would like to stay. To be present when Owen does his work. I could learn from that." I need not learn to forgive Flint; I had done that long ago. But if I stayed, he would know I still believed in him.

"You surprise me." Toleg did not sound at all surprised. "Very well. If I understand anything, it's that time is short. I'll go and make up the poultice. I have some drops for the pain as well, in my basket. Ellida, you stay here for now. Owen, you know the rules. The cell doors have been opened only for the purpose of helping Ruarc. Try anything else and this is over."

Then, for a short and blessed time, Flint and I were alone together—still in view of Ruarc and his comrades in the cell opposite, but they were absorbed in their own conversation and not interested in us. We did not embrace; we did not say much at all. Flint raised our clasped hands to his face and touched his lips to my fingers. I brushed away a tear.

"Toleg's right," Flint whispered. "This is no place for you."

"You asked for me," I whispered back.

"Wanted to see you. Couldn't help myself. Are you all right?"

"Mm. What will happen to you? What will they do?"

"Shh. Just sit there. Just hold my hand."

My heart ached. The tears built behind my eyes. I moved my thumb gently against his palm.

"You don't need to be here," Flint said. "When I do it. I would spare you that."

"I want to be here."

He closed his eyes. I thought he would not say more, but after a little he spoke again. "They said you went to the king. Got his permission for me to do this." A pause. "How did he seem?"

"Sad. He offered me a reward for tending to his son; that was how I obtained the permission. But . . . he spoke of Ochi, his boy, quite fondly. Of the lack of choices for the future. For a short while he seemed like a different man." I would not mention the threat; best if Flint went into this not knowing that my safety, and that of all involved in arranging this for Ruarc, might be jeopardized if the treatment failed.

Flint said nothing for a bit, then he opened his eyes once more and whispered, "Neryn? Put your face close."

I leaned over, wishing I could press my cheek to his, holding back.

"I love you. I have faith in you. Stay safe, dear one. When the day comes, you'll stand strong and win this, I know it."

My heart full to bursting, I had time only to whisper, "I love you," before Rohan came striding along the walkway and appeared at the cell door. Flint let go of my hand; I straightened up, swallowing my tears.

"How soon for the draft?" Rohan asked. "He's quiet now; could be a good opportunity to get it down him without a struggle."

"Let Toleg apply the poultice first," I said, though he was not talking to me. "You'll give Ruarc his best chance if Owen has his eyes tended to before he starts work." I could not quite believe, really, that Flint intended to do this; he was surely in no fit state to do anything but rest.

"You can dose him now," Flint said, putting his arm up over his eyes. "The poultice doesn't matter."

"Nonsense," I said firmly, knowing I must not shed more tears tonight. "You should have the poultice applied and you should try to eat and drink before you start this. But perhaps Ruarc could be dosed now anyway; Oblivion will keep a man asleep all night, provided you choose to let him wake naturally."

A trace of a smile passed over Flint's lips. "I won't argue with that," he said.

From the moment Galany had asked him if he would attempt it, he had wondered if he still had the strength, if he still had the will. He had wondered if the dark acts he'd performed in the king's name, over the years since he'd left the isles and the wise guidance of his mentor, would render him unfit to heal, incapable of plying the ancient craft Ossan had taught him. No mind-mender, but a mind-breaker. No healer, but a killer.

The knowledge of a comrade in trouble had compelled him to say yes. And that itself was laughable, when he remembered the warriors of Boar Troop, whom he'd led into Regan's ambush in the valley below Shadowfell. That day he had been no comrade. He had been a betrayer. He had acted for the cause; the cause must come before anything. And it had been a victory for the rebels, no doubt of that. A whole troop gone; the king's forces significantly weakened. But it had not felt like a triumph. It had felt like another ugly stain on his spirit, another diminishing of the good man Ossan had sent out into the world with his blessing.

Now here he was, sitting at the head of Ruarc's pallet with

his hands on either side of the injured man's face, in an iron-barred cell. His eyes made even familiar friends into shadows. Rohan, who had been so stalwart in his defense; Toleg the healer, a shorter figure, standing close in case he might be needed; Galany, looming at the back, with Tallis beside him. Ruarc's two comrades from Bull Troop, and by the door, Brocc. Brocc, whose allegiance must be to the king. If Neryn had not obtained Keldec's permission for this, Ruarc would have been culled. The cure must succeed, or Ruarc would die. As simple as that.

The change in his comrades was startling; it gave him hope even in this dark place. Not only Rohan and Tallis, but those others—Galany, who, according to Rohan, would have arranged this without the king's permission if necessary, and Ruarc's friends, and the men of Stag and Wolf Troops, who had supported his unconventional approach with the Good Folk knowing Brydian disapproved. There was an undeniable will for change among the men. Perhaps it had begun even before the king made Buan kill Duvach last midsummer; before Buan's lonely death at his own hand. How it would play out at the Gathering was anyone's guess.

As for what Rohan had whispered to him, the secret plan, he could not think of that until tonight was over and he knew if this had worked. The plan was audacious. Perilous. The thought of it made his heart career on a wild course of its own. It was something he had long wondered about. Could it be possible? Could he begin to make good his betrayal of his craft? He could not explain to Rohan that he did not want to escape. He needed to be here. He had to be at Summerfort for the Gathering. To lift his voice. To speak the truth at last, if he died doing it. Neryn was over there beside Tallis. He did not need his eyes to see her; she was in his heart every moment of every day. She had chosen to stay. Despite everything, she would be here with him tonight, watching. What must that be costing her? *I love you,* he told her silently. *I honor you for being here.*

"I'll begin now," he said. "This may take a long time. Go in and out if you wish, but stay quiet and leave me to get on with it. Brocc, there needs to be a man at the main door."

"It's done, Owen. I've a pair of guards outside. There won't be any interruptions."

"Thank you." He drew a long breath. Heard Neryn's silent voice: *You can do this. I believe in you.* "Thank you all for your presence. If Ruarc could be healed by goodwill alone, he would be restored to himself even now."

It was long. Longer, perhaps, than it might have been if he had carried out the procedure in the time when he was full of hope and energy and goodness. When he had not yet set foot on the path that had led him here, to this keep, to this cell, to this particular time of darkness. He made his way step by slow step into Ruarc's mind. Like a fine embroiderer unpicking a ruined tapestry and remaking it thread by broken thread, he moved through the shards of Ruarc's hopes, the shattered remnants of his dreams, the hot path of his furious frustration, the baffled hopelessness, the fighting spirit now turned back on himself and those he trusted. He found the child from long ago, a sturdy boy who loved nothing more than helping his father on the boat; he found the lad of ten or twelve who watched warriors ride by and dreamed of becoming one of them. He found the proud new Enforcer, polishing his silver troop badge, grooming his long-legged mount, laughing with his comrades over a jug of ale. Other memories too he found, images that were less wholesome, but still essential parts of the man Ruarc was.

Ossan had trained him to tread softly, to go carefully. The pieces must be put together with a gentleness of touch, as if one were tending to an orphaned lamb or a newborn babe. Rush this, and there was a risk of losing control and doing more harm than good. He coaxed out the good things, the fine memories, the pride and love and contentment. He wove new dreams, using what would make Ruarc stronger: hope, comradeship, courage, brotherhood, his father, the village, the boat, the sea. He wrapped Ruarc's mind in a fine net of all the man loved, all he valued, all that made him what he was; and he breathed into his patient's dreams strength for the future, no matter what came. A hope that would stay with him even if his injury meant he would never fight again, never ride his horse, never serve with the king's men. *Your comrades love you, or they would not be doing this. Your family loves you. You can be a son, a father, a brother. There is a life for you, my friend. And as long as you need us, we will stand by you.*

When dawn came, beyond the tiny high windows, he rose to his feet, shaky as a new-hatched chick, and felt pain lance through his body, crippling in its intensity.

"Careful, lad." Someone caught him before he fell, someone eased him over to a bench. Gods, the light was blinding. "Easy, now." Toleg's voice; Toleg's hand around his arm, reassuring him. "You've been sitting still a long time. Go slowly. Ellida, some water."

Ellida . . . Who was Ellida? His eyes burned.

Now someone was holding a cup to his lips, someone was murmuring, "It's all right, Owen. One sip at a time."

"Neryn?"

The moment the name left his lips, he knew what he had done. But it was too late to take it back; all of them had heard it.

"It's Ellida," came a firm female voice. "Toleg's assistant. Don't try to talk, you're exhausted. You've been sitting there all night." The same voice went on, "He's too tired to think straight."

"I should be here when he wakes." His voice was as weak as a child's.

"You'll lie down on your own pallet and rest." Toleg again, taking charge. "We'll wake you as soon as he stirs. That's a promise. Come, lad, let's get you over there."

Someone—Galany?—half carried him across to the other cell, put him on the pallet, covered him with a blanket. Darkness spread over him, and he slept.

Toleg made me go back upstairs in time for breakfast in the hall—Tallis went with me—and told me not to return to the cells. Someone had to be on duty in the infirmary, and he wanted to stay with Ruarc until the result of the mind-mending was known. As for sleep, we'd have to snatch it when we could.

I'd hoped Scia might be well enough to return to work today, but she was not at breakfast. Tallis went to sit with Stag Troop, to tell them the news, such as it was. I took my usual place beside Devan. I ate my bowl of porridge, then a sizable hunk of bread and cheese. I noticed Brand was looking uncharacteristically somber; he had dark shadows under his eyes.

"Do you know if Scia is still sick?" I asked Devan. "We had a difficult patient last night, and Toleg and I are both short of sleep."

"You haven't heard?" Devan's voice was hushed, though it was unlikely anyone else would hear her over the general din. "I thought you'd be the first to know, since you were the one who tended to the prince when it happened."

"Heard what?"

"The queen ordered Brand to whip his son for what he did to Ochi. She told him that if he wouldn't, she'd get someone else to do it. So Brand had no choice. Ten lashes, that was what she ordered, with Brydian present to make sure they were hard enough."

My heart was cold. Little Dai was only five, and the apple of his father's eye. "Is he all right?" I murmured.

"I don't know. But Scia's a healer; she'll know how to tend to him." Devan turned an assessing gaze on me. "You do look tired, Ellida. I don't think Scia will be there to help you today."

"I'll manage." By all the gods, I would manage every day and every night until midsummer, so I could see the queen removed from her position of power. There she was at the high table with the king, laughing and gesturing. Brydian was on her other side, and beyond him Esten. *On midsummer day every one of you will be gone. We will sweep through this place of wrongness like a cleansing tide, like a great tempest, like a purifying fire. We will show you a strength as deep as Alban's bones. That I promise.*

"Are you all right?" Devan was frowning. "You look quite odd."

"Fine," I said grimly. "But I'd best get back to the infirmary, if I'm to cope on my own today."

I was busy all day and fighting to stay awake, but I managed reasonably well. A man from Stag Troop brought me food and drink, and with it the news that Ruarc had awoken and had seemed a little confused, but not distressed. He had taken a light meal, spoken with his keepers, then fallen into a natural slumber. Toleg would be back soon.

I made up the double dose of Oblivion that Rohan had asked for. Each dose was only half a cup; it was possible to use the same corked jar as I would for a single dose. I tidied everything away. When Toleg came, Rohan was with him, and it was an easy matter to hand the jar over with no questions asked. Ruarc was doing well. Owen was tending to him. Perhaps a fresh poultice later. Toleg would take it down. There had been a discussion, the details of which they did not give me, but it seemed a decision had been reached that I should not go back to the cells. However, Owen had asked that I be the one to brew the Oblivion he needed for the next three nights, as he wanted the draft to be exactly the same each time. I did not tell Rohan this was nonsense, and nor did Toleg, though each of us knew we would brew it the same way, with meticulous measurement of all the ingredients. I did not allow myself to be hurt by the decision, though it kept me from seeing Flint again. Ruarc was mending; Flint was, if not well, at least strong enough to consider repeating the mind-mending if he had to. It was as much as I could hope for.

In the days that followed, a greater than usual number of Enforcers visited the infirmary, not because they needed the services of a healer, but to thank me for helping their comrade. We were not yet sure Ruarc was fully healed, but he was making steady improvement. The men knew I was the one who had obtained the king's permission for the mind-mending; they knew I had stayed up all night while Owen carried it out. They seemed to think I had worked a miracle. Men brought me posies of wildflowers from the woods beyond the fortress wall. They brought me sweetmeats from the kitchens. One gave me an embroidered kerchief I was sure must have been intended for a sweetheart. I thanked them all and prayed that Ruarc would fully recover. And I prayed for Flint. If a miracle had been performed, it was his miracle, not mine. And while I might win praise, gifts, even affection from these men, Flint won nothing. He was still a prisoner; he still awaited the king's punishment. For him, this was a road of no return.

CHAPTER THIRTEEN

WHEN RUARC WAS WELL ENOUGH, HIS COMRADES moved him quietly to the annex where Wolf and Bull Troops had been housed since they'd taken over the job of training Keldec's so-called special forces. It was a part of Summerfort seldom visited by Brydian or the queen, and there, Brenn told me, Ruarc could be accommodated in a private area and supported by his friends until it was clear whether he would ever be fit to resume his duties as an Enforcer. If he was not, Galany would find a way to get him out of Summerfort and back to his home village. But not until after the Gathering.

Now that I'd acquired a large number of friends among the Enforcers, I heard all the news. The Good Folk had been moved to a hastily constructed shelter alongside the annex. It was well screened so visitors to Summerfort could not see them. The Good Folk were restless there; their human minders were using iron to keep them under control. But it was necessary if Keldec's uncanny army was to be unveiled only at the Gathering.

It was drawing close to midsummer; the days were rushing past. One by one the chieftains rode in. They and their families were accommodated in the keep; their retainers slept in the area by the river. The encampment where, under Owen Swift-Sword's rules, the Good Folk had sat by their little fires was expanded to cater to the large crowd.

The king's table filled up with richly dressed folk, and the meals became more elaborate. I learned to put names to faces. Erevan of Scourie was a tall, spare man with watchful eyes. Gormal of Glenfalloch, whose support had made possible Brenn's and my safe passage to court, was a solidly built man, more given to smiles than frowns. I could not look at the tow-haired, youngish Keenan of Wedderburn without a shudder, for this was the chieftain in whose stronghold Regan, beloved founder of the rebellion, had been done to death. Sconlan of Glenbuie and Ness of Corriedale were yet to arrive, as was the powerful northern leader, Lannan Long-Arm.

The infirmary remained busy, and there was no further opportunity to leave the keep. With so many folk about, I wondered when the endless combat drills would cease. As more folk came to Summerfort, it would surely become impossible for those drills to continue without everyone guessing what Keldec planned for the Gathering. Even without the combat practice, it would be hard to go between outer and inner gates without knowing there was someone, or some-*thing,* housed in that concealed part of the yard. Uncanny voices could often be heard, wailing in distress.

Esten was still appearing at supper, with Brydian a constant presence close by. The king's Caller looked old beyond his years. He looked like a man pursued by nightmares. With the day of reckoning so close, I knew I must take some practical steps. I'd already got Toleg's permission to go out and watch my husband in action on the first morning of the Gathering. Once down among the crowd, I'd need to head for a good vantage point, somewhere I could not only get a clear view but also stay safe until the battle was won. I should try to get to the area where ordinary folk stood, the place I'd been in last year, since that was where Tali and the rebels would be stationed among the crowd. The secret lookout, with its wide view and relative safety, I had dismissed as too far away from the practice area. My instincts told me I would need to be close to Esten if I wanted to counteract his call with one of my own. I had seen the devastating power of his gift on the day when Flint surrendered his authority as troop leader. Before midsummer day, I wanted to watch Esten at work again.

Osgar was busy with training now, along with the rest of Wolf Troop. And the Stag Troop men were on guard duty in the keep, though I had heard that some of the Wolves had the job of guarding the king's special prisoner. So much for the remarkable work Flint had done in drawing Ruarc back from the nightmare of his head injury. That miracle had won him no favors from the king, and I wondered if I had imagined that look in Keldec's eye when he'd spoken to me, a look that suggested a deep and genuine affection for his once-trusted friend.

On a day when the infirmary was reasonably quiet, I got Toleg's approval to take my midday meal with Brenn, who along with the rest of Stag Troop was now part of the household guard. Instead of heading down to the hall, we made our way to the secret lookout.

"I'll open the trapdoor for you, then I'll stand guard down here," Brenn said at the foot of the steps. "Don't stay up there too long. If one of those men in the yard happened to look in the right direction, he'd see you, and it could be difficult to find a credible explanation. It's hardly the spot for a tryst with your husband."

"I'll keep it as brief as I can."

We climbed; he opened the trapdoor; I clambered through it and out onto the narrow ledge, making myself breathe slowly. It was so high. The wind caught at my garments, doing its best to unbalance me. Not unlike the cliffs of Far Isle, I told myself, and felt steadier.

"All right?"

"Fine. You go back down."

"If I see anyone coming, I'll whistle."

Nobody in the practice yard save a couple of men sweeping with heavy brooms. I guessed they were leveling the ground after the disturbance of combat training. Both inner and outer gates were closed; the place was not in public view. I practiced the patterns of breathing the Hag had taught me, trying to imagine how it would be down there on the first day of the Gathering. By nightfall on midsummer day, if everything went to plan, Keldec's rule would be over. In future years the Gathering could be restored to what it had once been, a celebration, a coming together of the clans, an opportunity for bonds to be strengthened and difficulties solved amicably. That future Alban was hard to picture.

My careful breathing failed to quiet the churning feelings

in my heart. So much hung on my call; what if I got it wrong on the day? Beneath that terror, I was full of sadness for the evils of the past, and for the losses we'd endure in the winning of this battle. For our rebels would fall in their blood down there, both humankind and Good Folk. Nothing was surer than that. Even if my call was the very best I could manage, even if I used absolutely everything I had learned, I could not prevent that: the Guardians had made it quite clear. And Flint, still immured in the cells . . . what dire punishment did Keldec plan for him? Would I have to stand by in silence, waiting for the right time to call, while he was humiliated, tormented, and killed out there? Would I have the strength to hold back? I could not use my gift until Tali stood up and declared herself. That was the plan we'd agreed on, and I must follow it. No matter what.

Tears filled my eyes and spilled hot down my cheeks. I'd been told often enough why Regan's Rebels had a rule against letting love develop between comrades, and I'd seen the wisdom of that rule even though Flint and I had broken it. But I had not really understood what it meant until now. "The cause," I muttered to myself. "The cause comes first. Alban. Peace. Justice." In only a few days, we could change our country's future. We could begin to right the wrongs and heal the wounds of sixteen years of tyranny. We could achieve the dream that had sustained Regan and his comrades through their long struggle; we might see humankind and Good Folk share the realm of Alban in a new spirit of amity and goodwill. *I'll be strong enough,* I told myself. *Even if . . . I will be, I have to be.*

Something was happening down there. The annex had

been opened up, and so had the screened area. And now out onto the practice yard came two teams of combatants. As in the bout I'd seen the first time I came up here, one team wore tokens of green, the other blue. The teams were made up of both fey and human folk, the human fighters being the young men from the south. As the two teams moved to take up positions opposite each other, Enforcers armed with swords or spears moved to encircle the entire area. The human combatants had weapons: thrusting spears too pale to be of iron, one or two clubs, something that looked like a whip. The Good Folk were unarmed. As the opposing teams arranged themselves in rough formations, I glimpsed two men moving up into the area of raised seating from which the king's party had watched last year's Gathering. Brydian and Esten. They seated themselves side by side in the front row. Now I felt cold inside. This was what I had climbed up here to see. But I would have given much not to have to watch it.

At a shout from one of the Enforcers—Gill, the Wolf Troop leader, I thought—the teams rushed forward to engage each other. For a short while it looked orderly, or as orderly as any fight can be, with small groups of combatants engaging one another and exchanging blows that seemed almost rehearsed. But then, suddenly, it became chaotic and bloody, no practice combat but a real one. Gill and his assistants began yelling instructions, but nobody seemed to be listening.

A call welled up in me. I should stop this. I should bid the Good Folk hold back. Then surely Gill would order the human fighters to do the same, and this would end before more damage was inflicted. But I could not call. If I did, chances were that at least some of those folk would look up toward me, acknowledge me. It was only one step from there to finding myself immured in the cells alongside Flint, robbed of the chance to make any difference at midsummer.

A surge forward by the blue team, screams of challenge. Several men fell, and the tide rushed over them. The green team retaliated, pushing the assailants back. Esten raised his arm, and the big creature I had seen earlier, the one with rocklike features, sprayed out a plume of smoke or steam, moving his head as he did to catch three young men from the opposing team right in their faces. They fell to their knees, screaming. Gill gestured toward Esten, and the king's Caller cried out, "Stop!"

The Good Folk stood still as if turned to stone. The young men lowered their weapons; I could hear someone moaning in pain. Then Gill yelled something at Brydian, and Brydian responded, and suddenly everyone was shouting. The rock-headed being waved a monstrous fist. A chorus of fey voices rang out in fury. They had complied with Esten's call because they had no choice. He had forced their instant obedience. But despite that, they were making their anger known. Despite the Caller, despite the iron, they were making their voices heard. If Esten could stop the battle so abruptly, surely he could also calm the angry crowd. I considered what I would do if I were in his shoes right now; imagined a call drawn from the depths of earth, quiet and still, solid and unchanging. A strong, steady call. I felt it deep within me, and made myself hold it back.

Wolf Troop men ran to bring stretchers from the annex; with the aid of the young men who had survived the bout, they laid the remains of the fallen on these and bore them away. Others stumbled off the field, propped up by their friends. There was Ean, helping an injured man to safety; it was a relief to see him apparently fit and well. I could not see Whisper. Had my friend already fallen victim to one of these ill-conceived performances?

The Good Folk were making their fury plain, and not only by shouting. Flames licked the wooden benches, and a cloud of gray-green vapor began to drift up toward Esten and Brydian. The voice of Gill came to me clearly now, above the racket. "Keep on like this and we'll have no men left!"

Brydian turned to Esten and said something. Esten lifted both arms.

No question of what was coming. The urge to call was like a flame burning inside me. Oh, how I longed to bid these folk rise up against their captors, to run or fly or travel by magic away from the stone walls of Summerfort and back to their homes in forest or lake or mountain, where they need never be subject to such evil again. I wrapped my arms around myself, stifling the burning will to act. Perhaps I did have the power to set this captive army free, even when cold iron hemmed them in. But there was another army to command, Tali's fey army, our allies at the Gathering. Without me, they would not fight alongside Tali and her rebels, because that was simply the way the Good Folk were made. I could hear Tali's voice in my mind, strong and clear. *You are our secret weapon, Neryn. Hold back until it's time.*

So I looked on as Esten used his destructive call again, and the fey folk down there fell to their knees, wailing. Quelled, powerless, hurting. The young men who remained out on the field simply stood there, as if beyond feeling anything. I had no words for this; all I could think was how sad, how horrified, how disappointed Flint would be if he could see it.

"Not a pretty sight."

I started violently, losing my footing, and teetered on the brink. A strong hand came out and grabbed my arm, steadying me. "Careful, now. We wouldn't be wanting you to fall. Not so close to midsummer day."

The Master of Shadows. He was right beside me, today no old man but a prince in his prime, his features hawklike, his midnight hair long and flowing, his eyes a flickering blend of black and red. He wore a swirling dark cloak over a deep red robe. No sign of the dog. Perhaps it didn't like heights.

"My lord," I said in shaking tones. "This is . . . unexpected."

"Surprises keep life interesting. What do you think?" He waved an elegant hand toward the practice area, where the Enforcers were now herding the Good Folk back toward their temporary quarters.

I must choose my words with care. He might disappear at any moment. He might decide to push me over the edge simply to amuse himself. I must make sure I asked the right questions. "You speak of surprises," I said. "There is one surprising thing here, and it is that you apparently trained that man, the one we just saw using what you taught him to harm your own folk. When we last met, you tested me and recognized me as a Caller. You seemed to understand what it was I intended to do. Why would you train a second Caller and allow him to be brought here?"

He gave a slow smile. "What, you don't have the ability to override that fellow's call?"

368

"I'm only asking why."

"And if I said it was for my own amusement, would you accept that answer?"

He had once told me he loved playing games. He'd said that before we met again, I would need to get better at it. I did not understand this game at all. "You are a Guardian," I said. "I suppose you can do as you please. But I thought the Guardians were . . . wise in ancient ways. I thought they were forces for good."

That smile again, knowing and mischievous. He turned his gaze back to the practice yard, where Gill was still in dispute with Brydian as the last of the Good Folk were moved out of our view. Esten was slumped on a seat in the raised area, his head in his hands. "Your king is a human king," the Master said. "Your queen is a human queen. Their Caller is an ordinary man. I did not summon those folk into captivity; I did not herd them like cattle or subject them to pain and terror. It was your kind that did those things."

"But you trained him," I said. "He spoke of you, an old man with a little dog, a man carrying a bundle of sticks. Just the same as when I first met you."

"You're wasting time," he said. "He is here, and you are here, and midsummer is only days away. Choose your questions more wisely."

"Very well." I drew a deep breath. "How can I protect my fey allies against cold iron?"

He threw back his head and laughed, a wholehearted sound of genuine amusement. I waited for Brenn to come rushing up the steps, but he did not. Perhaps only I could hear it. "That is quite a question, Neryn."

"Now you are wasting time," I said. "I sought the answer with three Guardians, and in the end I was told that if anyone knew, it would be you. There will be a battle at midsummer; there's no avoiding that. I cannot call our allies in unless they can resist iron. Otherwise, they will suffer a worse fate than those poor folk that Esten dominates with his call."

"What answer are you expecting? If it were a matter of hanging a charm around the neck, or putting a clove of garlic in the pouch, or saying a spell before a body went into battle, what could you do about it now? You cannot pass the word to your allies out beyond the walls before midsummer."

And when I said nothing, feeling the weight of bitter disappointment, he said, "The answer's right before your eyes, lassie. Fleeting as a shadow, maybe, but you're quick enough. That's if you're still the woman you were last autumn."

Fleeting as a shadow . . . Could it be as simple as that? The first time we'd met, I had captured his profile on the wall with a piece of charcoal when the fire had thrown it there in shadow. The old lore said that if a person did such a thing, the one whose true image was caught had to grant a favor. I had told him then that I would not claim my reward straightaway, but would wait until a time of need.

"Quick now," he said. "I've my wee dog waiting."

"You owe me a reward," I said.

"Aye, I do."

"Then protect all the fey folk against cold iron, at the Gathering."

"A big reward, that. Almost too big."

I said nothing. If he could play games, so could I.

"All the Good Folk? Even those ranged against your rebel forces?"

"If my call is strong enough, they will all fight for us. Even those who have been imprisoned here; even those so hurt and damaged that they have good reason never to trust human folk again."

"You're sure that's the favor you want? Quite sure?"

"I'm sure." I knew enough from the old tales to understand the peril of magical gifts. Ask too much—for instance, that the Master of Shadows should ensure my call was stronger than Esten's on the day, or that we would win with no losses, or that somehow peace could be restored without the need for any fight at all—and what seemed a boon would turn out to be a bane. There would be a trick in it designed to teach the wisher not to overreach herself.

"Done, then," he said. "For the length of the battle, and for as long as it takes your survivors to limp home, I will shield them."

"Thank you." I felt a great weight leave my shoulders.

"I would wish you luck." He looked quite serious now, his strange eyes fixed on my face as if they would read what was in the deepest part of my mind. "But this is not a matter of luck. It's courage, strength, resolve. And knowing the right moment to bring it to an end. Don't forget that, Caller."

"I won't."

"You wonder why I offered that fellow training," the Master said. "I did not seek him out. He came to me asking to be taught. I obliged, up to a point. Such a gift is best guided well, nurtured and shaped as, say, a fine apple tree might be. In some, such as yourself, the gift is strong, the mind is keen, and the heart is sound. In others, flaws become quickly apparent; flaws that can never be remedied. Thus it was with this young man. I withdrew my support."

"And now he's here at Summerfort with a powerful gift that he doesn't know how to use wisely."

"That is for you to deal with," said the Master of Shadows.

"Ellida?" Brenn's voice came from below the trapdoor. "Who are you talking to?"

"Nobody," I said, glancing down. And when I looked back toward the place where the Master of Shadows had been standing, it was true. From one moment to the next, he had vanished.

Two days until midsummer, and the last of the chieftains arrived: Sconlan of Glenbuie, Ness of Corriedale, and the formidable northern leader, Lannan Long-Arm, a towering figure with a mane of red hair and a look of harnessed power that put me in mind of an eagle. Such a substantial force had come with Lannan that the level ground beyond the fortress walls was full from one side to the other with horses, men and women, and all the paraphernalia required to sustain them. The keep was bursting at the seams.

There were two guards stationed outside the infirmary door all the time now—someone had put this arrangement in place straight after my night down in the cells. So close to the Gathering, I was especially glad of their presence. The small gifts and kindnesses continued; if Brenn had really been my husband, he might have had cause for jealousy. This all seemed somewhat odd, but I had no time to ponder it. Midsummer was looming, and I faced the test of my life.

The special forces ceased training. Instead of dealing with combat injuries, we were tending to folk with cuts and bruises, pains in the belly, chronic complaints of one kind or another. Our job was made easier by the presence of two other healers, one from the household of Sconlan of Glenbuie, a chieftain whose allegiance I did not know, the other from that of Erevan of Scourie, who had been behind that raid on the home of the wise women. They'd set up a makeshift infirmary out in the encampment and were looking after the folk housed there.

I had little news of Flint. The men were still saying the king planned to make an example of him at the Gathering. They talked about it often, and it seemed to me the anger among them was like a bed of coals that might flare high at any time. I felt a change spreading through the whole household. The punishment of Dai, the small son of Brand and Scia, had upset many people. Scia would not talk about it. Pale, red-eyed, composed, she went about her work in a tight silence as effective as any shield. Dai had recovered from the whipping; that much I knew. But I saw something new on Brand's face as he stood in the great hall, watching the king and queen. The place felt like a spring wound close to snapping point.

At suppertime, Devan and I stood up in our places with everyone else as the chieftains of Alban and their wives made their way to the high table: Erevan of Scourie, Gormal of Glenfalloch, Keenan of Wedderburn. Sconlan of Glenbuie and Ness of Corriedale. At the end walked Lannan Long-Arm, proud and tall in his princely robes. If the battle was won, he would play a key part in Alban's future, most likely as coregent. I watched him as I picked at my supper, wondering if he would be a better leader than Keldec, or whether power might turn him too into a tyrant. I wondered what would happen to Tali and the other rebels if we won. What would their place be in that future Alban?

Brenn was coming over to our table. Now that Stag Troop had been relieved of training duty, he and his comrades ate in the hall with the rest of us. He had another man with him, a sturdily built fellow in the green of Gormal's household.

"Ellida, you remember Macc, don't you? Gormal's master-at-arms?"

I rose to my feet. "Macc, it's good to see you."

"And you, Ellida," said Macc, who had never met me before in his life. "Lord Gormal sent me to deliver an invitation, seeing as Morven here will be participating in some of the activities of the Gathering. You're not a tall girl, and there's always such a press of folk out there on the day, you'll be lucky to see anything. Lord Gormal says you're welcome to sit with us. Some of the men have their wives with them; you'll have plenty of company. We'll be well positioned in that raised area—you know the spot?"

"That would be wonderful, Macc. Please pass on my thanks to Lord Gormal." Elation and terror fought within me. Yes, it would be an ideal place; I would have a clear view across the open area. It would also be close to the king and queen, and to Esten.

"Back row, most likely," Macc said in apologetic tones. "Among the men-at-arms. But you'll get a good view."

"I'm grateful. I mustn't miss the chance to admire Morven in action." Someone had arranged this perfectly for what I must do. I did not ask questions, simply accepted the gift it was.

Brenn bent and kissed me on the cheek. "I hope to do you proud," he said.

Devan looked at me a little oddly as the two men made their way back to their own table. "I suppose it's different when your man's an Enforcer," she said quietly.

"Different?"

"Just . . . Well, I've heard some talk about what the Gathering's like, and I think if I had the chance to spend the day in the infirmary, I'd be glad of it."

"Shh!" The woman on her other side hissed a warning. "Don't speak like that, someone might hear you."

Devan applied her concentration to her plate.

"I don't imagine I'll be out there long," I said lightly. "Toleg will be needing me."

One day before the Gathering, and the place was strung still tighter. Toleg had gone grim and silent, and Scia kept dropping things. When Rohan Death-Blade took a turn on guard duty, I left my work and went out into the hallway to speak with him.

"May I have a word privately, Rohan?"

He nodded and we retreated out of earshot of the other guard.

"What is it? All well?"

"I was wondering . . ." I shouldn't ask. But . . .

"Wondering what?"

"Rohan, what will they do to Owen? Is there no way he can be saved? He . . . he seems a good man." For that speech alone, to the wrong ears, I could find myself on the list for the king's punishment.

"I can't answer that, Ellida."

Of course he could not; we both knew the king intended Owen Swift-Sword to die, one way or another, before the

Gathering was over. "I don't suppose . . . ," I began, then stopped myself.

"He told me nobody's to go down there today." Rohan had guessed what it was I could not bring myself to put into words. "Brocc and Ardon are both on guard."

Enthralled men, the two of them. The king was taking no chances, not with this prisoner to be paraded before the loyal people of Alban tomorrow.

"What about you?" I asked, blinking back tears. It had been a slim chance anyway; I could not think of a plausible reason to go down to the cells. For four nights after the mind-mending, I had brewed a double supply of Oblivion, and Rohan had collected it from me in the infirmary; for several days Toleg had gone down regularly to check on Ruarc's progress and to treat Flint's eyes. But Ruarc was no longer in the cells. And if Flint had said nobody was to go down there, it meant he did not want to see me. Not even to say farewell. Not even to say goodbye forever.

"I'll be there tonight," Rohan said, lowering his voice still further. "I may be acting troop leader, but Owen's my leader—always. I'll stay with him until we have to march out in the morning. He won't be on his own."

I nodded, unable to find words.

"Want me to relay a message?"

I swallowed. "Only that I wish him well. That I wish him courage for tomorrow."

"I'll tell him. You'd best go back in."

"Thank you, Rohan. I think you are a good friend."

"Thank me when tomorrow's over," he said.

* * *

At suppertime I couldn't eat a single bite. Chances were that by tomorrow's end all of us would be dead: me and Brenn, Ean and those young men, the captive Good Folk, Tali and her rebel band and everyone who stood up beside them. And Flint; if the king acted as everyone expected, he might be the first to go. Unless Tali declared herself before Keldec enacted whatever punishment he had in mind for the man who had once been his friend. I sipped at my ale in silence, my head full of dark thoughts.

"Are you unwell, Ellida?" Devan asked.

"A little nervous about tomorrow. It is my first Gathering. But excited too, for Morven's sake." Oh, the lies.

Devan made no further comment. Despite the crowd, the mood in the dining hall was subdued—no buzz of anticipatory chatter, no making of wagers on likely events. Instead, a brooding quiet in which folk glanced at each other and looked away. Up at the high table, Keldec was in conversation with Lannan Long-Arm, who was seated beside him. Queen Varda had Esten next to her, with Brydian on his other side. If I succeeded tomorrow, if my call did prove stronger than Esten's, what would become of him?

I would have left the table early, but the rules of the royal household meant I must stay until Keldec and Varda got up. When at last they did so, Rohan Death-Blade made his way over to me.

"I'm heading up to have a word with Toleg. I'll walk with you."

Halfway there, he drew me into a little alcove at one side of the hallway, first checking to make sure nobody was close. "I hadn't planned to be in the hall for supper, but I have something for you. Keep it hidden." He reached into

377

his pouch and brought out a small item wrapped in a handkerchief. He laid it on my palm. Without unfolding the covering, I closed my hand around it and knew what it was. A terrible grief clutched at me; a sob threatened to burst out.

"There was no message," Rohan added. He was watching me closely. Surely, after all this, I was not now being trapped into revealing the truth. "To me, he said, 'Best if you forget me.' But he seems calm. Strangely calm, considering all."

"Thank you for bringing this," I managed, slipping the handkerchief bundle into my own pouch. "I should get back now."

He walked with me to the infirmary, where Toleg was eating his own supper from a tray. Rohan settled on the bench to talk to him. I went through to the stillroom and shut the door behind me. Seated on the edge of my pallet, with my throat tight and my heart breaking, I took out the bundle, unfolded the handkerchief, and revealed the talisman Flint wore always around his neck, the dream vial his mentor had given him when he'd completed the long training as a mindmender. A shard from a particular cave in the isles; an ancient, precious symbol. Within its depths, something stirred and shifted, as nebulous as a dream. The crystal was set in a clawed silver fitting, and around the top was twisted a lock of my hair. In this small artifact, Flint had carried the memory of the two people he loved most in the world.

I touched the talisman to my lips, then stowed it away again. Tomorrow I would carry it with me to the Gathering. I lay down on my bed and wept.

Chapter Fourteen

Now that the day had come, I felt oddly calm. I rose, washed, and dressed, thinking of all I had learned on the long journey to this point. When I was ready, I performed a ritual, based on those Silva had taught me. I paced in a small circle. With Toleg moving about just beyond the stillroom door, I spoke my words of salutation in a whisper. "Hail to you, Hag of the Isles, and to the flowing, changing power of water! Hail to you, Lord of the North, and to the deep, enduring power of earth! Hail to you, White Lady, and to the quickening power of light! Hail to you, Master of Shadows, and to the purifying power of fire! I seek your wisdom and guidance. May the powers of Alban work through me today. May I make choices for good, not ill. May this be a day of freedom, not of loss."

In the center of the circle, I laid my offerings: the white feather I had found by Brightwater, still stained with blood; the dried head of a thistle; the drum I had brought with me from the south; and a piece of charcoal from the brazier.

Flint's dream vial had been against my breast as I slept, strung on a ribbon. Now I slipped it over my head and laid it down with the other things. "I won't ask you to keep him safe," I whispered, "though I want that more than almost anything. But I know he would say the cause comes first, and today we make the cause reality. I won't ask you to protect my friends." There would be so many there: Tali and the rebels, the Good Folk who had given us their trust and support, the new friends I had made, against all expectations, here at the heart of Keldec's court. "All I ask is that I be given the wisdom and courage to get this right."

I stood in silence a few moments, until I heard one of the guards come into the infirmary with Toleg's breakfast. Then I unmade my circle and tidied the offerings away. I slipped the ribbon back over my head and tucked the dream vial down inside my dress, out of sight. *Beloved. I will carry you with me right to the end.*

Toleg made me share his food. There was a question in his eyes, but he did not ask it. He was an astute man; very likely he had put together enough clues to tell him today's Gathering would not conform with people's expectations.

"Eat, Ellida. What you see out there this morning may be enough to turn your stomach, but that doesn't mean you can skip breakfast when there's a day's work ahead of you. Here, there's plenty for two." A pause. "I'll stay inside, I think. Give me an opportunity to scrub the shelves, if nothing else."

I managed a few mouthfuls. "You've been good to me," I said. "Taught me a lot. And you've been so patient. Thank you."

He chuckled. "Patient? First time anyone's called me

that. You've got a good heart, Ellida. And capable hands for healing. Whether you and that man of yours stay here or go your own way, I wish you well."

I nodded. Breathed. Held on to the calm feeling I'd woken with, the certainty that I could meet this challenge armed with courage and wisdom. I was buoyed by the Guardians' support, strengthened by the comradeship of Shadowfell, warmed by Flint's love.

Soon enough came a knock at the door. Gormal's men-at-arms, resplendent in the green tunics of their chieftain's clan, had come for me.

"Be safe," Toleg said.

"I'll see you soon." Hope. It was all about hope.

We assembled in the great hall, ready for the formal procession out to the viewing point. Each chieftain, with his family, would be followed by his household retainers; once through the inner gate, each would be joined by his men-at-arms.

I walked with the women of Gormal's household. Out the keep doors, across the courtyard, through the open gates, and into the practice area.

The crowd was immense. I'd thought the place packed last summer, but now it was full to bursting. In some spots the barriers that held the onlookers back, keeping them out of the packed-earth circle where the games and combats took place, had been shifted forward to accommodate the press of people. There seemed to be more coming in through the outer gates even now. In such a crush I'd have little chance of spotting Tali and the others.

We reached the raised seating and climbed a set of steps

to one side; the seats were built against a natural rise, and were in tiers. Gormal and his immediate household sat at the front of our allocated area, leaving the first two rows empty for the royal party and their entourage. The rest of us went behind. Suddenly my two guards were with me again, edging me away from the other women and ushering me up to the back row. Someone had put a great deal of thought into this. In this line of armed men, I was the only woman. The next row down held only men-at-arms. But directly in front of me they had left a space. Even if they all stood up, I would have a clear view of the open area. Folk would no doubt think this an odd arrangement, if they cared at all about such things, but nobody was looking at me.

The other chieftains took their seats; their households settled behind them. Each chieftain had a certain number of men-at-arms close at hand, but this seating could not accommodate all the men, so blocks of warriors in clan colors also massed in the general viewing area to either side. Gormal's folk, a sea of green. Lannan's retainers in gray. Sconlan's supporters in russet, and Erevan's in dark brown and yellow. Keenan's men in blue, and Ness's in light brown with a cream stripe across the chest. No chieftain from the isles, since Keldec had ordered the deaths of both Regan's father and the other western leader and had not replaced them. So there were six chieftains here, and if their word was to be trusted, at least three of them would stand up beside us today. *Breathe, Neryn.*

A blare of trumpets, and the king and queen came out from the keep, followed by their councillors, their Caller, and a small group of folk from their inner circle. Keldec was in black to match his Enforcers; the queen was in red. Once they reached their seats, I could see only the backs of their heads, and perhaps that was a good thing. Directly below the king, Stag Troop formed a double rank of black-clad, armored strength, facing the crowd. How many of them would still be standing when this was over? How many of my new-found friends would fall this morning, to rise no more? *Be strong, Neryn.*

A familiar voice rang out, that of the same court official who had announced each event at the last Gathering. "People of Alban! Welcome your king!"

Roars of acclaim. Folk knew what was expected for the three days of the Gathering, and they understood what might happen if anyone was observed to be showing less than adequate enthusiasm. All around the circle Enforcers were posted, watching the crowd.

The noise died down. The king spoke.

"People of Alban! Welcome to our sixteenth midsummer Gathering! This is a time of celebration, an opportunity to renew pledges of loyalty and to admire displays of strength and prowess. I welcome my chieftains and their people. Some of you have traveled far to be with us today." Keldec spread his arms wide, as if to embrace them all. "You are accustomed to seeing games and contests on the first day of the Gathering; that has long been our practice. But this year we have something special for you: a display such as no man in Alban has ever seen before. You have observed my Enforcers in action; you know what peerless warriors they are. Today you will see a different kind of army. My people, today we harness the uncanny creatures of Alban to fight for us."

A sound of astonishment from the crowd; the Gathering was known for surprises, most of them unpleasant ones, but despite the odd sounds they must have heard from within the screened area, none of them would have expected this. For the ordinary populace of Alban, even to mention the Good Folk was perilous. To see and hear them at close quarters was unthinkable.

"Yes, it is true," Keldec went on. "They are reclusive folk; most of you would hardly know they existed outside the ancient tales. But thanks to the very special talents of this young man"—he motioned toward Esten—"I have been able not only to bring them here, but to train them into a fighting force, working in perfect cooperation with a body of young men from the south. Esten is a Caller. He is Alban's new treasure. He will help me build an army whose likeness no king in all the world has dreamed of. Today we will give you just a taste of what is possible." He paused; there was not a sound from the crowd now. "But first"—the king's tone had become heavy with sadness—"there is another duty to be faced. At the last Gathering, my people, you saw me carry out punishment against those whose conduct had offended me during the year. That included several of my own Enforcers, one of whom I had trusted for years. That man stood up at last midsummer's Gathering and was given another chance. But he has failed me again, and he has run out of chances."

My heart was cold. This was my worst fear realized. Flint would endure his punishment before Tali stood up to identify herself. She'd made it quite clear that I must wait for her to do this before I called. He was going to die in front of my eyes, and I could not act to stop it. I laid my hand against my breast, where the dream vial hung.

"The man I refer to is Owen Swift-Sword, who was a troop leader and my trusted friend. This man was given the all-important task of preparing my new fighting force. The training was difficult. Taxing. Unlike anything my Enforcers had previously attempted. But achievable, thanks to my Caller's remarkable abilities. Owen Swift-Sword bungled the job. When challenged on that point, he defied my authority openly. That a man to whom I had granted my personal friendship would do so pains me deeply. Before we enjoy the spectacle I have planned for you, he will face his punishment." He squared his shoulders. "Bring out Owen Swift-Sword!"

Breathe. Perhaps this will be quick. Perhaps whichever comrade has the terrible task of culling him will be merciful. My eyes stung with tears; my jaw was clenched so tight my whole head ached.

They came out from the annex, two Enforcers with Flint between them. Neither of the guards was wearing the mask that was part of their uniform, and I knew them both: Brocc and Ardon, the enthralled men who had guarded Flint in the cells. Their prisoner had his wrists and ankles shackled with iron, and they were half dragging him along, as if he'd had another beating and was too weak to walk straight. His eyes were bandaged again. *Breathe, Neryn.*

They halted in the open area, looking up over the ranks of Stag Troop to the king. Brocc and Ardon held Flint upright between them.

"Owen Swift-Sword." Keldec's tone made me shiver; there was no doubt this was a pronouncement of execution. "I have given much thought to what punishment is appropriate for your offenses. Many times during your years as my valued battle leader and most talented Enthraller, your conduct has been called into question. Every time, you have explained yourself and I have forgiven you. Until now. You spoke out against my Caller. You challenged my senior councillor. You questioned the wisdom of my grand new venture. What can you possibly have to say in your defense?"

With a visible effort, Flint straightened. Were his eyes still damaged, or was it only that after his long confinement in the cells, the sunlight was too bright for him to bear? His guards released their grip on his arms, and he managed to stay standing. A profound hush fell over the crowd.

"Only this, my lord king." Flint's tone was ragged, but he had tapped a well of strength deep within him, and his voice carried clearly. "I denounce your rule of tyranny and repression. I denounce—"

"*What?*" Keldec cried out, and the councillors Brydian and Gethan leapt to their feet, shouting. There was a rumble of shocked response from the crowd. Two chieftains also rose, protesting: Keenan of Wedderburn and Erevan of Scourie.

Flint's voice carried over it all. Brocc and Ardon made no move to silence him, simply held their pose on either side. "Your reign has been one of cruelty and injustice from the first. Under your authority, the people of Alban have lived in fear. You have turned neighbor against neighbor, friend against friend, brother against brother. If I must die today, let me die speaking the truth! Your meddling with the Good Folk of Alban offends the very heart of this great country! It goes against all that our mothers and fathers, and their mothers and fathers for countless generations, taught us to believe in."

"Guards, silence that man!" commanded Brydian.

I trembled, caught between terror and an immense, heart-stopping pride in the man I loved. But Brocc and Ardon did not move. Both seemed suddenly deaf.

"It makes a mockery of all that is good and wise!" Flint went on. "Your choice to involve a group of untrained young men as part of your ill-conceived experiment is not only cruel, it is foolish."

"My lord king!" cried Brydian. "This outrage cannot be allowed to continue!" He turned to Esten. "We must call forth the fey army! Let them make an end of this disobedient fool!"

"What better way to rid ourselves of this canker in our midst?" It was not Keldec who spoke, but Queen Varda, her tone as smooth as silk, yet carrying clearly. "If the king agrees, of course."

For a long moment, Keldec did not answer. Could it be that even now, deep down, the king wanted to pardon the man who had been a rare friend in a sea of enemies? My heart threatened to leap out of my breast.

"This man once served me well," the king said. His voice was shaking. "Let him die in fair combat, as a warrior. Esten, call forth the two we spoke of; for now, only them."

I could guess which two he meant. Fair combat? In his current state Flint would be lucky to last to the count of ten. *Come on, Tali,* I willed her as Enforcers moved to open the shelter that housed the captive Good Folk. *Speak out now— quickly!* Yes, she'd said I must wait for her sign, trust her choice of the perfect moment. But if now was not that moment, I could not imagine what might be. Why was she waiting?

Esten rose to his feet. He stretched out his arms. "Come forth!" he shouted. The words were for the crowd; I knew he could call the Good Folk silently, just as I could.

And it was too late. They surged from their shelter, the big warrior with rocklike features in the lead, and behind him a red-crested creature with human arms and clawed bird-legs. The place was alive with magic, tingling, vibrating, shimmering all about. In the crowd people screamed, shouted, crouched down, shielding their faces.

"This man betrayed your trust!" Esten yelled. "Take your vengeance now!"

I wanted to cover my eyes, to shrink down into a ball. I made myself stand strong. And something odd happened: instead of ripping Flint apart straightaway, the two large beings halted three strides from the captive.

"Ye gave us a promise and ye didna keep it!" roared the rocklike one. "Ye didna hold your nerve, and ye lost the chance tae mak' guid your vow!"

"Oor friend died because ye couldna keep control o' your ain men!" snarled the red-crested one. "Scorch gave ye his trust. Ye repaid it by lettin' ane o' yours rip his guts oot. Why shouldna we dae the same tae ye reet noo?"

"I won't fight you," Flint said. "We are on the same side in this battle, you and I. We are on the side of justice, of peace, of hope for the future."

"Kill him!" Esten's command rang out loud and clear. "Make an end of him!"

Everything in me strained to countermand him. I fought the rising tide of the call. Why didn't Tali declare herself?

The uncanny warriors moved in. And suddenly Brocc was

in front of his prisoner, drawing his sword. Ardon reached down and did something to Flint's shackles; the chains fell to the ground, and he was free. Then Ardon too moved forward and drew his weapon. Not restraining their captive; defending him. Enthralled men, the two of them. The crowd gasped.

A roar of annoyance from Rock-face, a shrieking cry from the other. Bird-claws struck the sword from Brocc's hands, and Rock-face seized it. I had asked for all the Good Folk to be protected against iron, and they would use that to their advantage. *Now, Tali! Now!* Bird-claws slashed at Ardon's legs with his talons, and Ardon fell. Flint had reached up and slipped the bandage off. He narrowed his eyes against the sunlight. Rock-face was grappling with Brocc, stopping him from reaching his knife. Ardon struggled to get up, his leg bloody. The crowd shouted as Brocc went down. Still Flint did not move. Rock-face set a great hand around Flint's neck, thrusting his face close. Bird-claws moved in behind. What was Tali waiting for? Why didn't she speak?

Bird-claws hit Flint over the ear, hard. He swayed but kept his footing. Rock-face released a burst of steam from an aperture in his neck, missing Flint's face by a hairbreadth. They were playing with him as a cat toys with its prey before the final strike. Bird-claws lifted his foot and ran a talon across Flint's back, slitting his tunic. Flint staggered, then steadied. He was sheet white, with his lips pressed tight together. The two of them circled him. Rock-face slammed a fist into his other ear. The talon made another slicing move, and Flint could no longer hold his silence. A gasping cry of pain came from him, but he stood strong, his eyes on the king. Rock-face released a second jet of steam; Flint struggled to stay on his feet. A claw across his face, once, twice; blood streamed down, a red flow. I started to get up, I had to call, I could not let this go on—

"Sit down." A familiar voice came from beside me, where one of Gormal's men had been sitting a moment ago. The Master of Shadows. Nobody was looking at us; all eyes were on the spectacle. Besides, most likely only I could see him. "No grand gesture required, only a trick. But hurry."

As Rock-face lifted Flint off the ground and shook him, a rabbit in the wolf's grip, I used what the White Lady had taught me. A call for one individual only; a call strong enough to overwhelm Esten's, but carefully shaped so it would neither expose me nor spark a mass attack before Tali was ready. I pictured Whisper, waiting in that screened area with the rest of the fey army. His soft white feathers, his big strange eyes, his feet in their little felt boots.

Whisper, I called, and in my call was the strength of stone, the bite of the cold, barren north from which Whisper had come, and in it was the living flame that was part of Alban too, both destructive and life-giving, flame that could scourge and scar and ruin, flame that could warm and comfort and sustain. I laid my hand over the dream vial again. *Whisper, heed my call. Be deaf to the other. Save Flint.* And I pictured what I hoped he might do.

"Aye," murmured the Master of Shadows. "Aye. Let's see what the king's Caller makes of that."

Rock-face threw Flint bodily into Bird-claws' arms, then gathered himself, becoming taller, broader, more formidable. He sucked in a mighty breath. The crowd seemed to draw breath with him. The king, the queen, Esten, and Brydian were all standing now, leaning forward to watch the climax to this uneven combat. Rock-face released a huge burst of steam; Bird-claws stepped forward with Flint in his grip, lifting him toward the scalding flow. *Whisper, now!*

From the screened area flew a white form, winging its way toward them, diving right through the hot jet still issuing from the rock being's body. Screams from the crowd. And where there had been steam, now there was ice, splintering over Bird-claws and Flint, then crashing in shards to the ground. Bird-claws dropped his burden. Flint lay motionless on the ground; I could not see if he had been burned.

Bird-claws was enraged, but the ice had slowed him. Rock-face roared in fury. He plunged a great hand into his own body, near the heart, and pulled out a stone the size of a man's head. With a speed belying his ponderous build, the being hurled the missile straight at Whisper. My friend fell to the ground in a burst of white and crimson, his small form broken, his last flight over. My cry of anguish was drowned by the roar from the crowd.

Now Bird-claws raised one great foot above the prone form of Flint. "No," I breathed. "Oh no, please."

A new defender stepped forward. Where she had come from, there was no telling; I had not called her, but suddenly there she stood between Flint and his giant attacker, a wee woman with a mop of gray-green curls, her staff in her hands, the weapon pointed at the two fey fighters. Her voice came to me with perfect clarity, despite the sounds of amazement from the onlookers. "Dinna meddle wi' me, big lumpies! Touch this laddie again and I'll make an end of you, I swear it! Hold back and hear me. Or do Southies lack the wits to tell friend from foe?"

The rock being stared at her. "What ye sayin'?"

"I'm saying wait, you fool. This man's a good man. Stand back before you do something that will haunt you the rest of your foolish life." Sage brandished her staff at him, and white light flashed from its tip. The two creatures took a step back. Was this the same staff Sage had used to rescue me, long ago in the attack at Brollachan Brig? That day it had been broken in two, and she'd said the only person who could mend it was the Hag of the Isles.

"Esten!" The king's voice rang out. "Call out my fey army! Let us make an end to this ridiculous performance!"

Esten raised his arms again, and I rose to my feet. That was the man I loved out there in peril, and beside him my precious, brave little friend. That was Whisper lying by them, my stalwart guide and companion, killed by a single ill-considered blow because he'd answered my call. Never mind that Tali had not yet given the word. If the fey army was coming out, it would not come out under Esten's guidance, but under mine.

Only a moment to do it, only an instant before Esten called. I conjured an image of Alban as it was in the old song, a wild, lovely place, a free, good place. Crags and islands, lochs and ocean, the sun and the wind and the wilds. Without a word, I reached out to every fey being at hand. *Come forth. Come forth to my call, in the name of Alban and of all that is good. Be strong as earth, fluid as water, powerful as fire, free as air. The strength of the Guardians is in you. From this moment on your minds are closed to this man's evil call. Your bodies are armored against it, armored with ancient wisdom. When we fight today, we will fight for a free Alban.*

Esten was calling; I saw it in every part of his body. The fey army marched out of their enclosure, big folk, small folk, folk of many and wondrous kinds. They moved to the area before the king and stood there waiting, still and quiet. They were not looking at the king's Caller. All had their eyes on me. I could no longer see Flint or Sage, but Rock-face elbowed his way to the front of the assembled throng and looked up at Esten.

"We willna heed ye mair," the big creature said bluntly. "There's a new voice tae follow, a voice o' hope and goodness. That pleases us better than the voice o' power and cruelty, I can tell ye."

"Oh, well done," murmured the Master of Shadows.

"Forget about that wee show your kingie there wanted for the crowd," put in Bird-claws, coming up beside his comrade. "We willna be cooperatin' wi' that foolishness. But if it's a fight ye want, we'll gie ye a battle ye'll no' soon forget. Think ye've seen the best we can dae? Think again, *Caller*."

"What in the name of the gods is this?" Keldec's tone was harsh with fury. Around him, the chieftains of Alban and their supporters were talking in excited undertones; the crowd was riveted by the spectacle. "Esten, take control of these folk immediately!"

Esten was wordless; he looked unsteady on his feet. Beside him, Varda gesticulated, trying to explain something, while Brydian, quickest of the king's party to understand, had begun to look about, clearly seeking the source of the dissent. And now others too were following the Good Folk's

393

gaze to where I stood among the tall men of Gormal's household, exposed to view by the gap that had been left in front of me so I could do my work.

"It's her!" shouted Esten. "That woman from the infirmary, she's doing it, she's blocking my call! I knew she was up to no good!"

Gormal's men-at-arms were quick. They closed up around me, a wall of warriors with weapons drawn. No arrow could reach me; no spear could touch me. I glanced at the Master of Shadows; he wore a wide grin. "As tricks go," he murmured, "that one wasn't at all bad."

I could see very little, but there was a lot of shouting, and in it I heard the king's voice, roaring in outrage: "Gormal of Glenfalloch! Have your men taken leave of their senses? Order them to lay down their weapons at once! Deliver that woman to my custody!" And, a moment later, "Stag Troop leader, get your men up here to restore order! Wolf Troop, draw your weapons and form a barrier around those uncanny folk!"

A new voice spoke, a deep, resonant voice I recognized as that of Lannan Long-Arm. "Hold, all of you! Before this so-called celebration descends into outright slaughter, let us pause for thought. Keldec, we heard a voice of protest today, the powerful and honest voice of a man who, I gather, was formerly one of your strongest supporters and a personal friend. Before we proceed, let us hear a still more powerful voice: the voice of your people. The true voice of Alban."

"Let us hear Alban's voice!" another man shouted, and all the warriors around me raised their right arms with fists clenched, yelling, "Alban's voice!" Gormal's retainers had been prepared for this.

The king could not dismiss Lannan as he might a lesser person, for Lannan was here with an army big enough to do serious damage even when pitted against the might of the Enforcers. Gormal too had brought a sizable force of men-at-arms.

"Be seated, people of Alban!" Lannan called. "Draw breath. Men, sheathe your blades."

The men around me did no such thing, but those in front did step aside sufficiently to let me see again. One of Gormal's men-at-arms had an arrow in his shoulder; comrades were tending to him. The chieftains were arguing, but all were in their seats. Lannan had spoken with the voice of authority. Out in the open area, the Good Folk stood quiet—they were waiting for my next call. As for the Wolves, they had moved out behind the captive army as ordered, but not one of them had drawn his weapon.

"People of Alban!" A clear female voice; a voice like a high, strong trumpet. She stood at the far side of the circle near the outer gates, a straight-backed figure in her plain trousers and tunic, cropped hair raven-dark over her sharp, pale features, her sleeves rolled up to show the clan tattoos with their spirals and flying birds. Fingal was on her left, Andra on her right, and behind her were Brasal, Gort, and Big Don. In clear view, because all around them the crowd had shrunk away. The reason was plain: behind the rebels loomed a monstrous figure, huge, dark, shadowy, a being with fists as big as platters and a grinning mouth with rather a lot of teeth. Hollow. Hollow had left his bridge and come to stand up with us today. My heart began a wild, exultant dance.

"I am Tali, of the ancient line of Ravensburn!" Tali called out. I thought I could hear the distant skirl of ghostly pipes, the beating of ancient drums; my flesh went into goose bumps. "My brother and I are descended from Ultan, the last true chieftain of that great holding." Fingal too had his clan markings on proud display. "I speak for the rebels of Shadow-fell!"

A murmuring rippled through the crowd as she spoke this name. While Shadowfell was a place often thought to be mythical rather than real, everyone knew what the word signified.

"It is time to strike for freedom," Tali went on, "to stand up against oppression, to win back our fair land, and to make it once more a place of justice and peace! For some time a movement for change has been growing in Alban. We have seen how King Keldec rules by fear and intimidation. We have seen the cruel punishments he inflicts on all who disobey his laws."

"I won't listen to this!" the king yelled. "It's preposterous! Seize those miscreants!"

"Silence that woman!" screamed the queen.

Enforcers moved in on the rebels, elbowing a way through the crowd, climbing over the barrier, all steady purpose. Hollow roared a challenge, and they halted.

"Troopers, hold back!" called Lannan, his voice iron-strong. "Keldec, you will listen to your people's voice! Is not this the true purpose of the Gathering, to allow grievances to be heard and dealt with under the ancient laws of Alban? Open your ears to the truth!"

They'd planned this, I realized. Tali and Lannan Long-Arm. They must have done. It explained why she had not declared herself until now. Because Lannan, a respected chieftain, had challenged the king in the protected setting of a Gathering, whose traditional purpose was to bring disputes into the open and settle them, Keldec and his supporters were obliged to listen, for now at least. So Tali had her opportunity to be heard before the king could call his Enforcers in to destroy her and her supporters. But Keldec would not give her long. He must realize now that the tide was turning.

"Keldec must go!" cried Tali. "We have allowed him to silence us! We have allowed fear to stifle our knowledge of what is right! This is no king! This is a tyrant, a bully, a travesty. He must be deposed!"

"The king must go!" shouted the rebels standing around her.

Alban's folk had long ago learned the perils of speaking their minds under Keldec's rule. But now a murmuring arose, and then one or two people called out support, and then the chant began, at first soft, but gradually building to a full-throated cry: "The king must go! The king must go!"

Tali raised a hand and the crowd fell silent again. Out in the open area, the Good Folk and the men of Wolf Troop stood quiet, watching her. One of the men close to me murmured to his companion, "That's the woman who was enthralled last midsummer. Has to be the same one, look at those tattoos."

"Wasn't she turned into a half-wit?"

"Seems not."

"We have come here with an army of our own," Tali went on. "And if we must fight to remove this monster, we will fight until every last one of us is cut down. We have made sacrifices aplenty; all Alban has endured losses. It is time to make an end of that. It is time to say enough, no more, and to set our dear country to rights again. There is no man of the royal line who could become king now, only a lad of nine summers, the son of Liana of Scourie. But we have able chieftains. A strong regency could be established until the heir is a man and ready to lead. There are proper processes for that, but under this king's rule, those processes have been set aside. Keldec has been a law unto himself." She looked directly across the open area to the royal party. "If the king would step down," she said, "this could be achieved without more bloodshed. If he would cede his authority to the chieftains, we might restore Alban without further loss of life. Keldec, there are those of your chieftains who support our cause. Will you take the honorable path and stand aside for the sake of your people?"

"This is outrageous!" the king shouted. "Who do you think you are? Eagle Troop, apprehend this woman immediately! Horse Troop, Hound Troop, clear these folk from the area!"

"Stay calm," said the Master of Shadows. "Keep your focus. And remember what I told you."

"Free Alban! The thistle!" screamed Tali, lifting her sword above her head as three troops of Enforcers advanced grimly on the area where she stood.

I closed my mind to doubt. I thought of fire, searing, burning, scorching. I thought of a flame of truth, a light in the darkness. The comforting glow of a hearth fire. The raging terror of a wildfire. I thought of the upheavals Alban had endured. I thought of a little candle, guttering, flickering, struggling to stay alight.

"Good Folk of Alban!" I called aloud, and sent the flame

of my call out to kindle the heart of every fey being here, not only those hidden among the crowd as part of Tali's rebel army, but those who still stood before the king, with the men of Wolf Troop behind them. "Fight for freedom and justice! Fight for the future! The thistle!" And I sent my call far beyond Summerfort, over the mountains to the hall of the Lord of the North, for it seemed to me those uncanny warriors would travel here by their own paths. "Scar! Stack! We need your help! Bring us your army!"

All around the circle, people had thrown off concealing cloaks to reveal weapons of wood, of bone, of the pale shining substance I had seen in the north. Everywhere, men, women, and Good Folk hurled themselves against the might of the king's men. Beings flew down from the sky, appeared from the earth, shimmered into substance from thin air. Tali's rebels, both human and fey, could now be seen to be wearing white tokens: scarves, ribbons, belts, headbands. I guessed Tali had ordered this so her army had some chance of telling friend from foe in the chaos.

The noise was like a wild creature: the area rang with the battle cries of the combatants and the screams of the onlookers, for not everyone in the crowd was a fighter. Folk scrambled to get out of the way as battle spilled beyond the open area into the space intended for people to sit on the grass and watch the Gathering. Keldec was shouting orders; the queen was screaming at Esten. The Caller was shouting too. Dimly I heard it as he stood with arms outstretched, something about obedience, compliance, a dire punishment if they did not obey. But in the power of my call, Esten's was lost.

"Fight for Alban!" yelled Rock-face.

"Doon wi' the king!" screamed Bird-claws, and Keldec's uncanny army was off, charging toward the melee. Wolf Troop moved with them. Not to hold them back, but to help them; to protect them. The Wolves were fighting on our side. The men of Stag Troop did not move from their position in front of the royal party.

"Have faith," said the Master of Shadows, gazing with interest as Enforcer clashed with Enforcer, and men began to fall. "But do not flag." For I was feeling queasy now, as if I might be sick or collapse in a dead faint. Where was Flint? I could not see him anywhere. Where was Sage?

"Stay strong," the Master said. "Your work is not yet done. Remember what I told you."

"Forward, the north!" yelled Lannan Long-Arm, and from all around him men in his gray colors vaulted the barrier and ran to join the battle. "To arms, Glenfalloch!" shouted Gormal, and men in green poured down to add their support to Lannan's fighters. There were white tokens on the clothing of both households, revealed only now. But no tokens for the men of Wolf Troop, in their Enforcer black. They'd surely be attacked by rebel and king's man alike. To my untutored eye, it looked as if the Wolves were not the only troop to change allegiance—on many parts of the field, Enforcer now fought Enforcer. Had Seal Troop too switched to the rebel side? This was indeed a day of change.

"All troops, forward!" cried Keldec. "Rid me of this rabble! Stag Troop, to me! Seize these disobedient chieftains!"

The seating was now empty of warriors, save for six of Gormal's men-at-arms who held their positions around me and the Master of Shadows—he did, in fact, seem to be invisible to them. The confrontation down there dwarfed the battle I had witnessed last autumn when Regan's Rebels had accounted for the whole of Boar Troop. Indeed, so much was happening that people seemed to have forgotten that I was playing a part in it. The chieftains of Alban were all on their feet.

As the battle raged, Stag Troop obeyed Keldec's order, splitting into two groups. One team stayed in place down below the seating, using their weapons to defend themselves if any of the combatants came too close, but not moving out into the fight. The other team climbed the steps in a grim, black-clad line, with Rohan Swift-Sword in the lead. When they reached the king's level, they moved to encircle the royal party and the chieftains in a formidable human shield.

But no; this was not a shield, it was a cage. These troopers weren't protecting Keldec and Varda, their councillors, their Caller, and their loyal chieftains, but making sure they didn't get away. My jaw dropped as I saw Rohan let first Lannan, then Gormal, then Ness of Corriedale, and lastly Sconlan of Glenbuie leave the guarded area. The four chieftains ran onto the field of battle, drawing their swords and rallying their clans.

"Four," observed the Master of Shadows. "Remarkable."

The men of Corriedale and Glenbuie charged forward at their chieftains' call and joined the fight. I struggled to keep my concentration; to remember what I had been taught; and to be ready to call again. It was a confusion of screams and shouts, the thump of blows, the shriek of metal on metal. It was blood and death. My stomach churned; spots danced before my eyes.

"Do not weaken," said the Master of Shadows, "or the other may try to seize control from you. Apply what you have learned."

What I had learned was threatening to slip from my mind altogether to be replaced by a fog of panic. I made myself breathe as the Hag had taught me. I sharpened my focus, seeing with the clarity of air. I made myself open to change, fluid as water, seeking a way into the mind of every fey being who fought in that hideous spectacle before me. *I am too small, too weak, too lacking in wisdom,* part of me protested. And the answer came clearly: *It is not your own strength you use for this task. It is the strength of Alban itself, deep as the roots of a great oak, fresh and good as a tumbling mountain stream, strong as the west wind, bright as summer sun. It is as old as story. Nothing can stand against it. Nothing.*

And I remembered what the Master of Shadows had said earlier. *Know when it is time to end it.* The battle was raging without my needing to direct it; Good Folk and humankind stood shoulder to shoulder. In the turmoil I caught glimpses of many familiar friends: there were Tali and Fingal, back to back like twin warriors from some ancient tale, wielding their swords against a well-disciplined group of Enforcers; there was Andra, skewering an attacker with her spear. Hollow appeared to be enjoying himself mightily, picking up king's men as if they were dolls, wringing their necks and tossing them away over his shoulders. A chorus of screams followed him around the field. And I saw that the army from the north had come to my call. Over there by the wall were the stalwart, golden-haired warriors who were personal guards to the Lord of the North, the brothers on whom I had bestowed the names Constant and Trusty. Close by them were the fighters Tali had befriended during our stay in the Lord's hall: Scar, Steep, Stack, Grim, Fleabane, and many of their kind, wielding their weapons with savage efficiency.

How long could this go on? The men of the north, of Corriedale, of Glenfalloch and Glenbuie, were fighting strongly, assisted by Wolf Troop and, I was certain now, most of Seal Troop; the Good Folk were wreaking havoc wherever they went. But most of the king's men had stayed loyal to him, and they were expert fighters, trained with the utmost rigor. Their code would see them battle to the end. They would go on, if necessary, until every Enforcer on the field was dead. And the rebel side, kindled into action both by Tali's stirring speech and by my call, would not give way now that freedom was in sight. This had been a long time coming. The people of Alban could taste a new age, and if it must be paid for in bloody losses, they would pay gladly. Already, the field was strewn with the dead or dying. As they fought, folk stumbled on the bodies of comrade and enemy alike.

There was Tali, struggling with three Eagle Troop men for possession of a spear; she fought like a wild thing, but they were slowly pushing her back against the barrier, trying to get her off balance. And now here came Andra, sword in hand, slashing with casual expertise as she moved in. Tali wriggled free only to see Andra struck down by a heavy blow to the head; six men in black now surrounded the two rebel fighters. Andra lay limp; one side of her head was all blood. The White Lady had taught me to hear one voice among many, and Tali's shriek of rage and grief came to me over the great, hideous noise of battle. She charged like a mad bull, throwing herself bodily into one attacker. Before the others could seize her, Constant and Trusty strode up. Each of the fey brothers known as the Twa dwarfed the biggest of the king's men, and with a flick here and a twist there, the six Enforcers were accounted for. Tali went down on her knees beside her second-in-command; the Twa stood guard. Even from so far away, I could see that Andra was dead. My stomach felt hollow. Who would be next, Fingal, Big Don, Tali herself? Would I see all these good people, all my brave friends, struck down one by one? And where was Flint in that maelstrom of violence? He'd looked barely strong enough to stay on his feet. "The thistle!" yelled Lannan Long-Arm, leading a group of his men against a tight formation of Enforcers. "The North!" A slash of the sword, and a man's head bounced and rolled on the hard earth. Around the field, sudden fires were breaking out, causing panic. Someone was coaxing flames to burn by magic. A king's man brandished an iron bar; one of the Good Folk laid hands on the weapon and used it to batter his opponent over the head. Great winged creatures flew over the field of battle, diving from time to time to pluck a man from the fight, lift him high, then drop him back down into the chaos below.

"Stag Troop!" Keldec shouted. "To arms!"

The men of Stag Troop stood unmoving, maintaining their guard around the king's party. Whatever orders they were obeying, they were not Keldec's. Now the king called out, "Galany of Bull Troop! Get your men out here!"

The men of Bull Troop had stayed on guard outside the annex. Now they forced their way through the sea of combatants to the front of the seating, where they formed up, facing the ranks of Stag Troop. Galany looked up at Rohan

Death-Blade, who was standing right behind Keldec, and gave a little nod.

"The men of Bull Troop no longer serve you, Keldec." Galany's voice was strong and sure. "Our loyalty is to the kingdom of Alban, and to our comrades-in-arms. Good men have died on your watch; men whom you have broken for the slightest word out of turn, men you have forced to perform acts that will weigh on them their whole lives. We have seen friend after friend fall; we have laid down comrade after comrade, and remained obedient because those were our orders. Because we had no faith that it could change. Today is the day of change. Today we are no longer king's men but men of Alban."

What Keldec might have said in reply, I never knew. No sooner had Galany finished his speech than a look of mild surprise appeared on his face, and a moment later he toppled forward, the shaft of an arrow protruding from his back. Two Enforcers with bows had climbed the wall and were taking shots from a vantage point half concealed by a section of the annex roof. A second Bull Troop man fell.

Rohan Death-Blade moved as quick as an eel. Now his knife was at the king's throat. "Call off your forces, Keldec," he said. "Or you die now. Do not doubt me."

"Esten," screamed the queen, "do something!"

I saw him stretch out his arms, heard him draw a gasping breath, sensed him preparing himself for the call of his life, the call that would restore him to the king's favor and bring him the recognition he so desperately craved. And I knew he was no longer a threat. I felt the utter certainty that my call could prevail; that the ancient magic of Alban was the strongest weapon of all. Earth, air, fire, water. Endurance, vision, purpose, courage. This time my call had no words, except perhaps *Help* or *It is time*. People told me later they saw a white light, or felt a tingling in the air, or heard a sound like a thunderclap. I knew that suddenly, from a clear sky, rain began to fall. But after I felt those first drops, I fainted, to come to myself with Gormal's guards bending over me and with my head, much to my shock, pillowed on the Master's bony knee. Now he was not the splendid lord I had seen before, but the frail old man of our first meeting.

"All right, Ellida?" one of the guards said.

"I will be."

"Fellow says he's your grandfather. Came from nowhere."

"Oh. Yes, that's right." I looked up at the Master of Shadows; he was grinning.

"Sit up, then," he said. "Slowly does it. You took a risk with that call. Seems it may have paid off."

I had always thought that for a Caller to summon a Guardian was wrong, that they were too ancient and powerful to be brought forth in such a way. That such a call should be used only in the last extreme. I had not argued the case with myself today; I had simply done it. And there they were: the Master of Shadows here with me, come of his own accord, and not far away the Lord of the North in his white fur cloak, his noble features somber as he gazed out over a field now littered with the terrible aftermath of the battle. Beside him stood a strange creature, in shape a lovely woman in a flowing gown, but not of solid flesh, for she was made up of many tiny beings, shifting and glimmering, their small bodies somehow joining together to create her form. The White Lady, made whole again. Close by stood the Hag of the Isles, tall and strong in her cloak of fronded weed, with her hair spilling moon silver over her shoulders. As I sat up, then stood, leaning on the Master's arm, she made a pass through the air before her, and the sprinkling of rain became a torrential downpour—not over those of us in this raised area, but precisely on the combatants still hacking and slicing and killing out there on the open ground. So heavy was the fall that it became impossible for them to go on fighting. The ground turned to a quagmire; folk struggled to hold on to their weapons; quite plainly, foe could not see foe through the sheets of rain. The sound drowned out even the cries of the dying.

As abruptly as it had begun, the rain ceased. A voice rang out: that of the Lord of the North, who stood by the Hag. "Let no more blood be shed here!" he called. "Let the killing cease. Lay down your weapons, humankind and Good Folk alike, and let the work of mending begin."

"May light conquer dark," came the voice of the White Lady. "May kindness take the place o' cruelty. May wisdom banish ignorance and fear." Many eyes were on her now. Perhaps, in the heat of the battle, folk had not realized the wondrous thing that had taken place here; had not recognized the powerful magic that now enveloped them. But they were starting to see, and now, one after another, folk dropped their swords, their knives, their spears and clubs to the sodden ground. Rebels, Good Folk, Enforcers.

The battle was not quite won; the losses were not quite at an end. In a spot near the outer gates a band of king's men still held out despite the losses, despite the presence of the Guardians, despite everything.

"Men of Hound Troop, stand fast!" Brydian's shout was hoarse and ragged, a last burst of hopeless defiance. "Defend your king! Down with these traitors!" As for the king himself, Rohan Death-Blade still held him with a knife at the throat, and he could not say a word.

"If you heed that advice, you're nothing but fools, and you deserve the rule of a tyrant!" roared out the Master of Shadows, startling me so much I nearly fell. "Would you fight until every last one of you lies dead on the field? If any chieftain here is still loyal to the king, let him declare his surrender now! See to your fallen! Save your loyalty and your sacrifice for a leader who merits it." He reached a fist above his head, then opened it. A towering jet of flame shot out, casting a red-gold glow over the sodden ground, the weary fighters, the shocked onlookers.

"How dare you challenge the king—" began the queen, then fell silent. The Lord of the North had motioned toward his people, and the giant guards Constant and Trusty marched up the steps to relieve Rohan of his charge. Scar apprehended a spluttering Brydian, and the warrior named Fleabane had the councillor Gethan in his grip. And here was Sage, apparently quite unharmed, come from nowhere to stand with staff in hand beside Esten, who was slumped motionless in his seat, eyes closed.

Erevan of Scourie, who had been seated near Keldec, rose to his feet. "Scourie surrenders!" he called to his men on the field. "The king no longer has our allegiance. Men, lay down your weapons!"

A warrior stepped out from the throng down there, his tunic barely recognizable as green under the crimson stains. He faced the Guardians and bowed his head. "Wedderburn surrenders," he said, his exhaustion plain in his voice. "Our chieftain, Keenan, fell in this battle. We go forward under the thistle."

The fey combatants had backed off as soon as the Hag spoke; a few of them were helping the wounded, but most had gathered in groups, Northies, Southies, Westies, their eyes fixed in wonder on the Guardians. Over by the outer gates, Lannan Long-Arm was rapping out orders, and there was Abhan of Horse Troop beside him, and to my immense relief the last group of Enforcers laid aside their arms. Some of the Shadowfell rebels were shepherding ordinary folk out through the gates; men and women carried children across ground stained red, shielding the little ones' eyes as they passed. Over by the barrier, Tali had risen to her feet; Hollow cleared a way so she could walk forward. As she passed, a somber figure in her stained clothing, the whole place fell quiet.

"Come," said my self-styled grandfather. He led me down the steps, and along to a spot between the White Lady and the Hag. By the time we reached them, the Master had changed again, and was in his lordly form.

I searched the mass of people on the field for Flint. Where was he? Somewhere out there lying under a heap of bodies? In a corner, in the shadows, kicked aside because he was in the way? Tali had come to the front of the crowd, alongside the loyal chieftains, and there was Fingal, supporting a wounded Brasal, and there was no missing the imposing form of Hollow, but I could not see my man anywhere. Perhaps he had fallen at the first charge, trampled underfoot. He'd had no weapons. He had never intended to fight. Most likely he had thought he deserved to die.

All over the field now, comrade stooped to tend to wounded comrade, friend closed the staring eyes of fallen friend. But most of the fighters simply stood in place, shocked into silence by the immensity of what had happened: the rebellion, the battle, the losses, the Good Folk, the sudden, overwhelming appearance of the Guardians. Many people here would never have seen one of the Good Folk before; many might have hardly believed they existed outside the old tales. And now the king was overthrown, and everything was turned upside down. The yard of Summerfort was littered with the dead and dying. And magic was everywhere.

The Lord of the North stood tall and solemn, gazing over the scene of carnage. "Remember this day, people of Alban," he said. "Let the wisdom of the old ways never again be forgotten. Let the power of ancient peoples never again be dismissed. There have been many losses, many sorrows. May this be a day of healing for humankind and Good Folk alike. May we work to mend this broken realm."

"The light shine upon ye all, and bring ye tae paths o' truth." The White Lady's form might be that of a beauteous goddess, but her voice was exactly as it had been before. "This realm o' oors, 'tis full o' the strange and wondrous, ye ken? Full o' mystery and power. Heed what the Lord here tellit ye. Dinna forget the auld banes o' Alban, the tales and songs, the rites and the prayers. Those things, they hold a body up when times are hard. They give a body strength when sorrow comes. They lift a body oot o' the mire o' despond. Lose them, and ye rip oot Alban's very hairt. Heed them, and Alban's hairt beats inside ye, keepin' ye strong and true." She turned toward me, and her movement was a shimmer, a

410

dance, a celebration. As she spoke, one tiny form detached itself from her and flew around my head in exuberant loops before returning to its place. Piper, without a doubt. I found myself smiling through tears. "This lassie, Neryn, she's done a grand job today, though some o' ye may no' ken that," the Lady went on. "Wi'oot her, there could be nae working together, nae cooperation between humankind and Good Folk. There's some will reach oot the hand o' friendship wi'oot the need for a Caller, aye." She looked at Sage, at Hollow. "There's some hae an understanding o' this, deep doon. But make nae mistake. This battle's been won by the work o' this lassie, and by brave folk that werena prepared tae lie doon and let this fellow here"—she cast a glance Keldec's way—"ruin and spoil the land o' Alban."

"Who are you?" spluttered the king. "What are you, that you assume so much? I am the rightful ruler of Alban! I have done only what was necessary to keep my kingdom safe! How dare—" He fell silent as Constant's large hand came casually around his neck.

"If ye dinna ken wha we are," said the Hag, "ye dinna deserve tae be king, that's the truth." She turned to me. "Would ye speak tae these folk, Neryn?"

I was so tired. All I wanted to do was lie down somewhere quiet, shed my tears, then sleep. But I had to do this. "Come, lassie," said the White Lady. "Ye can dae it. I'm thinking ye can dae anything ye put your mind tae."

I straightened my back, lifted my chin. Breathed as I had been taught, slow and steady. "My name is Neryn." I did not use the ringing, powerful voice of the call, but spoke as I might to trusted friends. "I come from a village called

Corbie's Wood, which was sacked and burned during the Cull four years ago. And I am a Caller. My canny gift allows me to bring humankind and Good Folk together to work for a common cause. My family died under Keldec's rule. I have lost many friends along the way. But I have also found new friends, among the Good Folk and among the wonderful people of Shadowfell, so staunch and true, so steadfast in the cause of freedom." I looked down at Tali, and she looked back at me, her face blazing with pride. "Regan, who formed the rebel movement and who died in its service. Tali, who led the uprising today and who has given so much of herself to ensuring this day came. The man most of you know as Owen Swift-Sword, who gave himself to the rebellion mind, body, and spirit; who trod a difficult path during his long years as Shadowfell's spy at court."

"I knew it!" cried Queen Varda. "I told you! I told you that man was rotten to the core, a traitor from the moment he came here! If you'd taken heed, if you hadn't been so—"

The crowd shouted her down, but she turned on me a look of fury so venomous that it was like a blow. Keldec too was gazing at me. His earlier anger was gone; in Constant's grip he looked, quite simply, bereft. He had understood, more quickly than his wife had, that all they had built was gone; that their world would never be the same.

"The rebels welcomed me despite their reservations," I went on, struggling to keep my voice steady, "and made me one of them. These wise presences, the Guardians of ancient lore, watchers over our fair land, shared their wisdom with me and taught me to use my gift well. Good Folk great and small offered me their trust, their friendship, their guidance and protection, and many died for their commitment to our cause.

"I am not the only one who has suffered losses. All of us grieve for family, friends, comrades fallen on the long path to freedom. Some of you may struggle to accept the change that has come about today. Remember that we are all brothers and sisters under Alban's wide sky. The fire of Alban's truth burns in our hearts. The light of Alban's courage shines in our spirits. Each day we breathe the clear air of Alban's hope. And the river of Alban's story, flowing from time before time, brings a wisdom we must never again set aside. Remember this day. Tell the tale to your children and your grandchildren. Let those we have lost on this field of battle, and all those fallen over the years of Keldec's reign, never be forgotten." My knees felt suddenly weak; I sat down. The crowd was roaring approval.

"People of Alban," said the Master of Shadows, drawing himself up to his full, more-than-human height. "You've a lot of mending to do. Make sure you do it well. This was a wrong brought about by humankind, and it's for humankind to set it to rights. You have good leaders; let them guide you forward. We will depart, taking our own folk with us, and leave you to begin the long work that lies ahead. But there's a question to be answered first: what's to become of this so-called king of yours?"

Shouts from the crowd then. "Death!" "String him up!" "Kill the tyrant!"

The strong voice of Lannan Long-Arm came over the baying for blood. "Even for the most base of tyrants, there should be due process."

The shouting grew louder, an insistent chorus. "Death to the tyrant! Death to Keldec!" I saw indecision on Tali's face, and on those of several chieftains. The king was silent. "Death! Death! Death!" I remembered my brother breathing his last at fourteen years of age, with an Enforcer's spear through his chest. I remembered the flaming boat in which my father had died, and Sorrel screaming with an iron chain wrapped around him, and my grandmother after the enthrallment, a pathetic shell of her old self. Regan's head strung up on the walls of Wedderburn fortress. Garven crushed and broken. Little Don, Ban, Killen, all slain for the cause. Every village sacked during the Cull, every life lost, every family destroyed. All those who lay now on this field in their blood. Did the man who had done all that deserve mercy?

"My lords. My ladies. People of Alban."

My heart gave a great leap. The voice was Flint's. People made way as he came to the front of the crowd, supported by a Wolf Troop man on one side, and on the other, the rocky being who not so long ago had tried to kill him. His eyes were masked with swollen red, his face was marked by the rents of that great claw, his clothing hung in tatters. But he was alive. I put a hand in front of my mouth to stifle a wrenching sob of relief.

"I understand your need to see punishment meted out against this man who has so wronged you, and who has so wronged Alban," Flint said, his voice growing stronger. "It would be easy to do as you ask and string him up right now, so you could watch him die and reassure yourselves that he was truly gone forever. It is not for me to decide what becomes of him. But I would ask that you consider this: if we satisfy our

414

need for quick and bloody resolution of our grievance, are we not showing ourselves to be no better than he is?" His eyes were on Keldec, and the look in them was not of hatred or resentment, but of compassion. "This should be given time," he went on. "Time for all of us to come to terms with the great change that has occurred today. Time for us to think on loyalty and on the reasons why we sometimes obey orders when we know in our hearts that they are wrong. Lannan is wise in asking for due process. The king and queen and their advisers should be held in secure custody until the regency is established, then tried in an open hearing. If the verdict of that hearing is death, so be it." A pause; nobody spoke. "Each one of us has in him the capacity to do good or ill," he said. "Each of us bears some spark of greater things." He looked up at the Guardians. "Not all of us manage to find that spark. Not all of us keep it alive. But even he, even this tyrant, has the ability to change. At least give him time to contemplate what he has wrought here."

I glanced at Keldec and saw to my astonishment that tears were rolling down his face. Varda was quivering with rage; a red flush stained her pale cheeks. Brydian sat with his head in his hands.

"What place of incarceration would be strong enough to hold such a man?" asked Gormal. "And which of us would want to keep him?"

"Entrust your king to me." It was the Lord of the North who spoke. "In my hall there are many chambers, and all of them are guarded by magic. I will keep him safe until you are ready."

"And the queen?" asked Lannan.

"Oh, leave her to me," said the Master of Shadows. "My folk will have a fine appreciation of the task."

"I'll house the councillors and the Caller," offered Ness of Corriedale.

"This fellow's deid." Sage spoke flatly from where she stood beside Esten's limp figure.

Had Esten's last attempt to call stretched his body and mind beyond endurance? Or had someone from Stag Troop helped matters along with a pair of thumbs to the neck, choosing a moment when people's attention was elsewhere? Had Brydian removed the protective shield once it became clear the king's Caller was no longer useful? I tried to feel sorrow for a man who had been more misguided than bad, but my head was swirling and everything had started to turn in circles around me. The White Lady was saying something, but her voice kept fading, and then everything else was slipping away, and I thought, *Maybe I am dying too. Maybe that's what happens when Callers overreach themselves....*

CHAPTER FIFTEEN

My eyes struggled open. Dim light. Quiet. Somewhere familiar, indoors. I was bone-tired, my aching body already tugging me back toward sleep. But I could not sleep; something had happened, something important. . . . I sat up with a start, and everything spun around me.

"Slowly, Ellida. Or should that be Neryn?"

Toleg was sitting on the side of the pallet, reaching out to steady me with a hand on my shoulder. I breathed, blinked, came piece by piece back to myself. I was in the infirmary, on one of the beds reserved for the sick.

"I was getting concerned," Toleg said with a smile. "You've taken a long time to come back to us." He peered into my eyes, then got up and fetched a waterskin. "Drink. It will help the headache."

The headache was a dull throbbing, not unbearable, but enough to make me crave the oblivion of sleep.

"Best if you stay awake now," Toleg said. "Drink more water, eat a little. There are rather a lot of folk waiting to talk to you. But I've only let one of them in."

I turned my head, and there was Flint sitting on the next pallet, a ghost in borrowed clothing—Gormal's green—with the claw marks livid across his face. The wounds had been cleaned and salved. Within the mask of bruising, his gray eyes gazed at me steadily. There was no need for him to say a word.

"It's true, then." My voice came out as weak as a kitten's mew. "We've really done it. The rebellion's over."

"I'm still finding it hard to believe." Flint rose and came over to take Toleg's place beside me. "But yes, it is true. A new Alban. The place of justice and peace we longed for. Really here. Not a hopeless dream but . . . tomorrow and the next day and all the days after. I thought you would never wake up."

Through the fog of weariness I felt warmth stealing over me. Tomorrow. The time after. Perhaps, until now, I had not truly believed there would be a future for the two of us beyond today.

"I'd best go." Toleg picked up a laden basket. "We're tending to the wounded in the annex, since there are so many. Scia's down there with the other healers; they'll be needing me. Send a guard if you want me; there are men on the door."

"How many were injured?" How could I hold so much happiness and so much sorrow at the same time? "I should come and help—"

Toleg halted in the doorway. "You'll stay here, the two of you, and that's an order. Eat, drink, talk about something inconsequential or don't talk at all. And don't let too many folk in at once. You're worn out."

He left, shutting the door behind him. I sat up, and Flint's arms came around me. He held me gently, as if he feared I might break or disappear. I knew how he felt. I could not help wondering if it was all a dream, and I would wake up in the women's quarters to find midsummer was still to come. For a while I let myself drift in the warmth of his embrace, hardly able to believe we were free to touch at last, free to speak without watching every word. Then I made myself say what must be said. "Toleg didn't answer my question. How many were killed?"

"Toleg said you should eat first, and that was sensible advice, dear one. Let me fetch the tray."

A flask of mead, a platter of delicate little cakes, some bread and sliced mutton, fruit in honey syrup. A feast for an invalid. With so many out there hurt and broken, it did not seem right to eat it.

"A bite or two, Neryn. It's good for you."

I nibbled obediently. "Don't try to soften the truth for me," I said. "If friends have been killed, I want to know. I saw Whisper die. I saw Andra cut down on the field. Who else?"

"Both Brocc and Ardon. Those deaths lie heaviest on me, since I brought the two of them back from enthrallment only to see them cut down trying to protect me."

"You *what*?"

"I had wondered for a long time if the enthrallment charm could be reversed. It was not something my mentor ever taught me or spoke about—it was not relevant to the true practice of mind-mending. Rohan convinced me to try it, thinking my guards might be prepared to set me free if I could break their loyalty to the king." He looked down at his hands, avoiding my eye. "There was no certainty that it would work at all, or that if it did, they would not go straight-away to report me to Keldec. In their situation, I believe my strongest feeling would be anger at those who enthralled me in the first place. But Brocc and Ardon kept their anger for the king. They chose to stand alongside us at the end. For that, they paid with their lives."

"You didn't try to escape once you'd reversed the enthrall-ment?"

"That was what Rohan intended. But I couldn't do it. I needed to be there. I wanted Keldec to hear those words from my lips, even if he killed me for it."

"So that was why Rohan wanted a double dose of Obliv-ion. In fact, enough for four more men."

"Our two enthralled men from Stag Troop were also treated. They too chose forgiveness over anger. Both sur-vived the battle." He sounded weary to death. Weighed down by sorrow.

"Who else has been killed?"

He told me. The Shadowfell rebels had lost not only Andra, but nine others, including Dervla and Gort. And Galany had not been the only friend I had among the Enforc-ers who had fallen today; many had lost their lives. It made no difference which side of the battle they had been on. Only that they had fought bravely, and that they were gone.

"I thought Andra was invincible," I said, wiping away tears.

"There's more, Neryn. Take a sip of the mead, that's it."

I waited.

"I'm afraid Morven is dead," he said. "He was among those found on the field afterward. I'm sorry."

"His real name was Brenn." A brave man. A sweet, good, funny man. A stalwart friend and a courageous rebel. If he had not volunteered to come with me, he would still be alive.

"What of your comrades in Stag Troop?"

"Stag Troop avoided the worst of it. Rohan planned their role; he wanted to make quite sure the king did not escape justice. Not that all of them knew what was coming. But they trust me, and they trust him. The Wolves were the same. Becoming sickened by the loss of good men over the years, growing weary of the mad decisions the king foisted on us. Other troops also had their dissenters—the Seals, the Bulls. Obedience goes only so far. Galany was a great loss. He and I clashed often over the years, but at the end he was a strong voice for truth." He fell silent for a little, then said, "The men have been talking to me about you. Asking me whether a Caller can influence human folk as well as Good Folk. They've been saying things changed here from the day you first arrived, even when they hardly knew you existed. You became their friend, and men who not so long ago were obedient to the king's orders, misguided as those orders might be, became open to thoughts of freedom and justice, even though you never spoke a word of those things."

"I don't think that can be right. It's not in the old tales about Callers."

Flint gave the sweetest of smiles. "Nonetheless," he said, "it seems you've made many friends here. One man said you were like a candle burning in the dark; another that you were a bright flower growing in a place of shadows. Not the kind of words one expects from Enforcers."

We ate a little more, drank a little more. Held each other's hands, gazed into each other's eyes. I began to feel stronger. "Are you ready for visitors?" Flint asked.

"Is Tali here?"

Flint opened the door and there she was, leaning against the wall and not quite managing to look nonchalant. Beside her was Rohan Death-Blade. Flint let them both in. Tali had changed her bloodstained clothing; she wore a neat tunic and trousers in Gormal's colors. Her face was white, and the lines and shadows on it spoke of the long, weary preparation for this day, and the terrible losses endured along the way. But she was composed, as always; a true leader.

"Neryn," she said, and reached up a hand to wipe her eyes. Seeing my strong friend shed tears was the last straw; my own tears spilled, and then Tali was taking Flint's place on the pallet and hugging me. "You were wonderful today. What a stirring speech! And the way you brought those fey folk in . . ."

"You too," I managed. And I wanted to tell her I could not have borne it if she had been killed, but I held back the words, knowing how close she and Andra had been. And before that she had lost Regan, the love of her life, the heart of the rebellion. Peerless warrior my friend might be, but she was vulnerable, and she needed time to deal with this, just as we did.

Rohan Death-Blade had busied himself putting a kettle on the brazier, as if to leave us to our private conversation. "Did you know, Rohan?" I asked him. "Were you one of us all along?"

"It crept up on me." He did not sit down, but stood a little awkwardly, his fair cheeks flushed. "Owen and I had a wary understanding; as the time passed, we talked more openly about the possibility of change, but it was not until last night that he told me the full truth. We've learned to guard our words under Keldec. It will take time to unlearn that." A pause. "What you did," he said, "it was . . . astounding. I thought calling was an evil practice, designed to quell and dominate. That's what we saw with Esten. But you . . ."

"It's all in the training. And this wasn't just me, it was everyone together. In the end, the Guardians themselves."

"Speaking of fey folk," Rohan said, "there's a wee green-haired woman out there with some news to give you. Waiting to have a word."

"Sage? Here in the keep?" I remembered the Master's shield against cold iron, which he had promised would remain until all the Good Folk had made their way safely home. "Could you bring her in?"

Then we had three visitors at once, breaking Toleg's order. Sage stepped over to the pallet, stood on tiptoes to kiss me on the cheek. She took the jug of mead and refilled my cup.

"Drink up, lassie," she said. "You look like the urisk, all big eyes."

"I don't know how to thank you, Sage. What you've done is too big to put into words." She had supported me from the first, when I hardly knew what my gift meant; she had stayed strong through grief and loss; her belief in me had never wavered. And today she had saved Flint's life. If anything had been apparent out there on the field, it was that her small form contained not only a mighty courage but a powerful magic. She had stopped the two big warriors in their tracks, even when they had been under Esten's orders. One day, I would ask her about that.

"No need for thanks, lassie," she said. "We all played our part, at the end."

Tali had dried her tears. "You know Andra's gone," she said. "But for her, I wouldn't be here now."

"It's a great loss. Tali, she'd be nothing but proud of what you've done. I know she's looking down on you and saying, *If I had to go, at least I died a warrior's death.*"

Tali put her hands on my shoulders, examining me. "You look terrible," she said bluntly. "Here, eat some of this food; it looks a lot better than what they gave us. Mind you, I don't suppose the household is at its best right now; everyone's in a state of confusion. Just as well there's a good steward to give the orders."

"Tali, what happens now?"

"The king and queen are gone—the Guardians whisked them away promptly—and most of the Good Folk have left as well. Lannan's called a council of the chieftains for tomorrow. He invited me and any representatives I want to bring. I appreciate that; I'd wondered if we'd be forgotten once it was over. The chieftains who supported the king are changing their tune fast now they see a new age coming." Her voice was grim. "It's going to be hard to put the past behind us. But we have to work together. Just what my role will be, or even if I'll have one after tomorrow, remains to be seen. Lannan's likely to want Flint's services in establishing something in place of the Enforcers. Yours too," she added, nodding at Rohan. "And those of any fighting men open to change."

Flint said nothing.

"Most of the fellows will welcome that," Rohan said. "But there will be some who will want to go back to their home villages and start a different kind of life. It'll be good if they're given that choice."

"What happened to those young men from the south?" I had seen nothing at all of them today.

"Not deployed," said Rohan. "As things fell out, there was no need. Gill ordered them to stay in the annex until he called them, and he never did. We'll send them home, those who survived the training." A pause. "One of the young fellows is out there now, among the crowd waiting to have a word with you. Says he knows you."

So Ean was still alive. After Andra, after Brenn, after all the others, each survivor was doubly precious.

"Neryn's exhausted," Flint said. "She can't talk to everyone. This can wait, surely."

"If anyone's exhausted, it's you, friend," said Rohan.

"With this council tomorrow, you'd both better get as much rest as you can," said Tali. "You'll have tales to tell, no doubt, but those can wait."

Flint looked at me; I looked at him. But it was Sage who spoke.

"As to the council, I dinna think either of them will be in attendance, important though it may be to the future of Alban," she said firmly.

Tali's dark brows creased into a frown. "Lannan's expecting both of them."

"Use your eyes, lassie," Sage said. "They need time away, time to grieve, time to rest."

"Time away?" queried Tali. "Away where?"

"Ah. Let's just say there's a boatie waiting down on the loch, and friends to sail it home. You and your chieftains, you'll do well enough without these two for a while."

"How long is a while?" Tali's tone told me she had recognized a force too strong to be argued with.

"As long as it takes. There'll be a part to play for the Caller, and for her man, in the mending of Alban—how could it not be so? But not before they're ready. You're a leader, lassie. You're wise enough not to push folk too hard."

Tali narrowed her eyes at Sage. "This boatie. It wouldn't happen to be one I've traveled in myself, would it?"

Sage grinned. "It might."

They must mean the magical craft in which the Hag of the Isles had ferried Tali and me out to a lonely skerry last summer. I felt my heart lift.

"I'll come back for you at dusk," said Sage, glancing from me to Flint. "See you safely away, aye?"

"Thank you," Flint said, and I heard in his voice the same profound relief I was feeling. "Neryn, shall we tell all those folk out there to go away?"

"No, I need to see them. Time enough for rest tomorrow." Before Sage left, I had to ask her something. "Sage, how bad were the losses among the Good Folk?"

"You'll have seen Whisper fall. He died bravely."

"He died answering a call from me, to intervene and save Flint. I knew my work today would lead to deaths; I'd been warned to prepare myself. But . . . that was cruel."

"You did what you had to do, lassie."

"Hollow?" I made myself ask.

"Gone back to guard the bridge," said Sage, managing

426

a smile. "Sent his regards and said you'd understand why he couldn't stay to greet you in person. Asked me to tell you his door's open to you anytime you fancy a bit of conversation and a roast dinner."

"What about the Folk Below? And your own people?"

"The Northies came through it; they're hard folk to kill, especially when someone's decided to take the magic out of cold iron. That was quite a surprise. How did you do it, in the end?"

"I asked the Master of Shadows for a favor. But it's only until you all get home."

Sage stared at me, her bright eyes astonished, her mouth curled in amusement. "Oh, aye? Can it be you have power enough to charm even a Guardian?"

"Power, no. It was a trick. Something he understood. Tell me about your own people, Sage. Did any fall in the battle?" *Let it not be Red Cap*, I prayed. *Or Gentle, or Daw, or Blackthorn.*

"We're not a clan of fighters. They'll have been watching on from up in the woods. You called well, Neryn; I think you dinna ken just how well. Brought the ones you needed; spared those who would have been cut down before they could make a difference. Ended the battle before the losses were so grievous folk could never forgive."

"The last part happened almost despite me," I said. "As for fighters, you are one, surely. You showed that today."

"Ah, well." For a moment she seemed lost for words. "I'll be off, then, and let you chat with your visitors. Pack a wee bag before dusk; you too, laddie."

She left, but Rohan and Tali stayed. Rohan let people in one by one; Tali kept our mead cups full and made sure nobody stayed too long. There were indeed many who wanted to see me, and more than a few who wanted a word with Owen Swift-Sword. Osgar, who had shown me the secret lookout; Tallis of Stag Troop, with a bandage around his head. Gill of Wolf Troop. Devan the spinner, eyes round with wonder, hugging me and babbling about how she'd be able to go home now, her daughter was almost one year old and she hadn't seen her since soon after she was born, and how she'd owe me a debt forever. And Ean, Silva's brother.

"You did it!" he said, not bothering with preliminaries. "I can hardly believe it!" And after a pause, "I'm sorry about Brenn. He was a good man. Neryn, he told me Silva's safe down at Callan Stanes."

"When I left her, she was settling in there," I told him. "What happened today, the appearance of the White Lady, means Silva has done something extraordinary, Ean. When you get home, you must tell her exactly what you saw. She'll know what it means. Will you head back there straightaway?"

"I'd best do that." He looked at Rohan, at Flint. "I wanted to fight today. I should have been part of it."

"You, perhaps, might have made a difference out there," Rohan said gravely. "If Galany had sent the others in, they'd have been mowed down like ripe barley before the scythe. Be glad he had the wisdom to hold you back. If you're still minded to be a warrior after you've been home to see your people, I think there will be work for you here. Everything's changing, but there's always a need for fighting men. Seek me out if you do choose to return."

"Time's up," said Tali. "Neryn's tired."

"Give Silva my love, and say thank you."

"I will." Ean hesitated, then added a little diffidently, "And thank you, Neryn. I'm starting to understand what a debt we all owe you."

I spoke to a long string of folk: men-at-arms, others whom I had tended to in the infirmary. Then Fingal came with a group of Shadowfell rebels, and Tali let them in all at once. They brought ale and more food, and despite the losses of the day, their mood was buoyant. We spoke of hope and of the future. I wondered where they would go now, and what they would do. Would they find work in the fighting forces of the new regency or with the chieftains, or would they return to their home settlements, the rebel fellowship broken, their lives once more quite ordinary? That would not be easy, for Shadowfell had forged powerful bonds.

At a certain point, Tali said, "Everybody out now. Neryn has to rest. And then she and Flint are going away." Some protested at this, but she hushed them. "Only for a while. People don't do what they did today without a cost. Come on, all of you. We need to talk about this council, prepare what we have to say."

I bid them farewell, one by one; I wondered how many of them I would see again. Last, I embraced Tali. "I've never had a sister," I said. "Until now."

"Odd pair of sisters: raven and lark. But I feel just the same." She gave me a squeeze, then stepped back. "Not quite goodbye yet anyway. Dusk, wasn't it? I'll be down there to see you off. Though how she's going to get the boat from Deepwater to the isles, I can't imagine."

"The same way she got us off that cliff top and into the

boat, I should think." I remembered the powerful magic that had picked us up and whirled us down into the vessel.

"Sooner you than me," said Tali.

The boat was moored at the Summerfort jetty, or not moored exactly, since this particular craft held its position without the need for ropes or knots. At midsummer, dusk came late, and the sky was a shimmer of blue and pink, gold and gray. Birds flew overhead, crying farewells to the day, winging their way into the darkening woods on the hillside above. In the encampment outside the fortress walls, people were sitting around little fires, preparing food, tending to horses, as if this had been an ordinary day.

We walked down to the shore. Rohan carried Flint's bag, and Tali mine. Flint and I had only a staff apiece. Sage led the way, her small, cloaked figure moving on steady feet. Her own staff, which had blazed with light as she stepped out to defend Flint, seemed now no more than an ordinary length of oak.

The Hag's boat was long and sleek, finely made in every particular, with an elegant high prow and a single mast from which hung a sail that shimmered even in the uncertain light of dusk. Beside the fishing boats tied up at the jetty, it stood out like a lovely swan among humble ducks. That it was a thing of magic, nobody could have doubted. And there was the Hag, waiting on the jetty.

Don't tell me I can't bring Flint this time, I willed her. *Because if you do, I'm not coming.*

"Ready?" she asked.

"We're ready." I made sure I looked her straight in the eye.

"Bid your friends farewell, then, and step aboard."

I hugged Tali; Flint and Rohan exchanged a manly embrace. I heard Flint say, "You've been a friend in a time when friends were rare. You took a great risk."

"None took more risk than you, Owen. Safe journey, comrade."

"Farewell, Sage," I said, crouching down to kiss her. "Please tell your people I'll be forever grateful for their help. And bid them farewell from me, for now."

"No need for that," she said. "Look yonder."

They were there, all of them, standing on the shore ready to wave goodbye. Delicate Silver; Blackthorn, gnarled leader of the clan; Gentle the healer; Daw the bird-man in his garment of night-black feathers. Others behind them. And with them also Good Folk from Shadowfell: Bearberry, Hawkbit, and the wise woman Woodrush. And there was Red Cap, with his little one out of the sling, holding his hand and standing on its feet. But the sling was not empty; an even tinier pair of ears poked up over the top. I waved, tears half blinding me, and Red Cap waved back.

Flint took the two bags and climbed aboard. He helped me in. I did not see the Hag embark; between one breath and the next, she had left the jetty and was seated in the prow, the pale strands of her hair lifting in the light breeze.

"We'll be on our way, then," she said. And without her moving a finger, the sail filled with air, the boat turned, and we moved away westward along the loch. Tali raised a hand in farewell; by her, Rohan stood strong. The Good Folk waved wildly. But soon enough we picked up speed, and they were lost in shadow.

"Hold tight," said the Hag. And we were taken up and whirled about, water and trees and sky a dizzying confusion around us, until the boat steadied and settled, and we found ourselves not on the peaceful inland loch of Deepwater, but sailing westward through ocean swell in the summer half dark, with the isles rising in mysterious hummocks around us like great sea creatures resting.

Flint put his arm around me. I laid my head against his shoulder. The boat sailed on, finding its own true path. Gulls flew out of the night to land on the rim rail, a guard of honor to welcome us home. And in the dark water beside us, something was swimming, sleek and graceful as it surfaced and dived, surfaced and dived.

"Himself is glad to see you," the Hag observed. "And he won't be the only one." Then, after a silence, "I'm proud of you, lassie. You did fine."

But I found, suddenly, that I was bone-tired again, too weary to manage even the words for a thank-you.

We were in the little cottage where we had stayed once before, on Far Isle. In a secret cave on this island, last spring, the Hag had taught me the magic of water. In this modest but cozy dwelling, Tali and I had stayed while I underwent that rigorous training. In this chamber, Flint and I had once spent a night in each other's arms, with no certainty that we would ever do so again. We had exercised great restraint that night; to conceive a child would have been to give the king a powerful weapon against us. Now here we were once more. The cottage was ours for as long as we wanted it. The local folk knew about us and would provide supplies. If we needed

432

to see the Hag, all I had to do was go along the cliff path to the designated spot and call Himself.

I had thought myself too tired to be surprised by anything. But what the Hag had said as we stepped onto the jetty on Far Isle had startled me.

"You'll be wanting a handfasting, aye? Be at the usual spot tomorrow early, and we'll be ready."

Now, as Flint made a fire on the hearth and I found cups and herbs for a brew, those words were in the silence between us. It was only when we were seated before the fire and the kettle was starting to steam that Flint said, "You remember the day we said farewell at Shadowfell, when I went back down the mountain? You told me I was a good man despite everything, and I found myself believing you. I had hope for the future that day. I saw it bright and clear: the two of us together, in a place something like this, with our children around us and good work for our hands. Husband and wife together in an Alban reborn. But . . . I wonder now if I can ever be that man. I think I am too broken. I think I am too stained by the evil I have done, unfit to be husband or father."

I was fighting back tears. I moved to lift the kettle from the fire, to fill the cups, to put one in his hands. "Hush," I said. "Sit quiet and drink your tea. Listen to the stillness."

And not long after that, I took the cup from him again, for he was shaking with sobs. He bowed his head, hands over his face. I sat by him, my hand lightly against his back, careful of his wounds. My own tears fell in silence while he released his grief. At length the weeping died down, and he wiped a hand across his face.

"What has it all been for," I said, "if not for this? There

was the grand purpose, yes. To dethrone the tyrant; to restore Alban. But also to let people like us live our lives in peace. To let us raise children without fearing for them every moment of every day. To let us work and love and do the ordinary things. To set us free."

He said nothing.

"It will get better," I said. "I promise you. We'll work on it together. We'll help each other to mend."

"I've done such terrible things. Worse than you can imagine. Far worse. How could I ever explain that to a child? But I would owe my son or daughter the truth."

"There's a right time for every story to be told. When that time came, you would tell them how it was. And they would understand, because by then they would know what a good, kind, courageous man their father always was, even when he needed to pretend to be a different sort of man." When he looked unconvinced, I added, "Besides, you have started to undo those acts you talked about. What about those four men whose enthrallments you reversed? You could do the same for others, couldn't you? And think what good you could do as a mind-mender, if you chose to return to that."

"I look at myself, and what I see is not a mind-mender. It is not the good, kind, courageous man you speak of. What I see is a killer. A breaker. A liar."

"You were a spy. You acted your part well. Now that is over, and you can be yourself again. If it takes time for you to do that, perhaps a long time, you might look on that as the penance you must pay for those misdeeds. But, Flint . . ."

"Don't cry, Neryn. Please."

"Don't punish me for what you see as your own failings.

434

I want to be with you more than anything in the world. I've dreamed of this since that day you spoke of, the day you called me 'my heart' and surprised me with a kiss. Never mind the handfasting, if you don't want that. But please don't push me away. I know you love me. I love you with all my heart. Please give this time."

He put his arms around me, holding me close. He murmured something against my hair, perhaps "I'm sorry."

"We should sleep," I said. "Everything may seem clearer with the dawn."

So we slept, wrapped in each other's arms just like last time, but even more chastely, for both of us were so tired we fell asleep almost as soon as we lay down. We woke before dawn, and as rosy light crept in through the windows of the little house, we touched and kissed and came together with gentleness and restraint, with tenderness and passion, and at the end with a sweet inevitability that seemed to wipe away his doubts, at least for now. When it was over, we lay quiet, hands clasped, as the day brightened and birds began a cheerful chorus beyond the windows. And when we judged it to be time, we rose and dressed, and went out to the place where the selkie used to meet me every day to take me to the secret cave for training.

There he was, a great bulky creature with the form of a man and the face of a seal, his clothing an intricate drapery of weed, his mouth stretched in a welcoming smile. We followed him down the cliff path to the cave, and there was the Hag, with a fronded circlet of seaweed on her silver hair, and there was an old man with twinkling blue eyes in the wisest, calmest face I had ever seen.

"Ossan," breathed Flint. The old man held out his arms, and Flint walked into them. Ossan, his mentor, the master mind-mender whom he had once been ordered to assassinate in the king's name; Ossan, whom he had saved, at great cost to himself. This would be a powerful tool for healing.

With Ossan and Himself as witnesses, the Hag performed the ritual of handfasting, binding us together by earth and fire, by water and air, until death and beyond. She wished us the blessing of each other's love, the joy of children, the satisfaction of work for our hands, and the bright light of inspiration. When it was done, we made our farewells—Ossan would come to the cottage later to share a meal—and walked back along the cliff path. The sun was climbing; the sea glittered with light. Out there, creatures dived and leapt in a mysterious dance. Above us, gulls passed and passed, calling their harsh messages. Closer at hand, folk were hanging out washing, herding geese, gathering herbs in walled gardens. In time, all Alban might return to this. There was a great work of mending ahead, not only for the leaders but for ordinary people too. It would not be easy and it would not be quick. That we would play a part in it, I had no doubt at all. But not yet. Not just yet.

We stood on the doorstep.

"I have something for you," I said, and took from my pouch the dream vial on its ribbon. "Will you wear it?"

He bent so I could slip the ribbon over his head. "I must earn it all over again," he said.

"You will," I told him, touching my lips to his cheek and feeling my body stir to his. After this morning, everything felt different. "Have faith." We were husband and wife, and the sun was shining, and despite everything, I found myself full of hope.

Flint scraped his boots against the step; I slipped off my shawl. He opened the door and the two of us went in. For now, we were home.

ABOUT THE AUTHOR

Juliet Marillier is the author of *Shadowfell* and *Raven Flight,* the first two books about the enchanted land of Alban, as well as the popular young adult books *Wildwood Dancing,* which *School Library Journal* called "riveting" in a starred review, and *Cybele's Secret,* which *Kirkus Reviews* declared "bewitching." She is also the author of several highly popular fantasy novels for adults, including the Sevenwaters Trilogy and the Bridei Chronicles. She hails from New Zealand and now lives in Western Australia. Learn more about Juliet and her books at JulietMarillier.com.